The Master of Deception
By George C. Baker

This is book one of a six part **Mastermind** international thriller series introducing a new breed of radicalized terrorist leadership developing new unprecedented multiple level attacks threatening the stability of the world.

I0561404

*The **Master of Deception** is dedicated to my mother, wife, sons, and four grandchildren for their love, unending support and incredible patience.*

Image Credits- Licenses

Dreamstime _Dubai - Image 27136570.jpg

Dreamstime _Cruise Missile_ Image 68580117.jpg

Dreamstime Atomic Power Plant Stock Photo - Image: jpeg 42339401

Prologue: Rage Has No Limits
Friday, August 31, 6:00 a.m. GST (UTC/GMT+4)
Prince Tower, Dubai, UAR, Conference Room Foyer

An imposing male figure rapidly entered the foyer from the private elevator with a serious limp in his using cautious steps. He seized a prized Cezanne painting off the wall, pausing for a moment, then violently smashed it against the marble floor. He was flushed with rage as tears ran down his cheeks. He ripped an adjacent Jackson Pollock painting shattering the frame against the wall and hurling the remaining piece of frame across the large elaborately decorated foyer. The action set off the silent security alarm protecting the priceless art, while three security guards watched on their monitor.

The guards remained motionless, not moving a millimeter as they watched the man rip a Roy Lichtenstein painting shattering the frame, stomping on the painting and dropping it on the floor. Intrigued they watched as the destruction continued with several pieces by Monet, Matisse, Van Gogh, Degas, Dali, Basquiat, Ernst, Mondrian, Johns, Calder, Hockney, Warhol and Picasso in the same manner in less than twelve minutes. The unheeded art security alarms were flashing and buzzing for each art piece creating a bizarre scene in the security office. The guards recognized the vandal as the building owner and famous art collector. The guards knew that any act on their part interfering with Yassar Kaffi would bring rage greater than the wrath of Allah on their lives. Forty minutes later the huddle mass of destroyed frames, ceramics and canvases were in the middle of the foyer floor when the figure lit a lighter and set the oil paintings on fire.

The guards watched the total destruction of 8.8 billion United Arab Emirates Dirhams of art ($2.5 billion U.S dollars). The art collection became ashes. The fire alarm issued its unbearable deafening warning and the sprinkler system squirted for eight seconds, sputtered, and stopped. The faulty sprinkler spray failed to extinguish the fire, as Yassar wept falling on his knees head in hands. Tears drenched his clothing as he watched the remaining art turn to ashes. "I need to make them pay!" He shouted repeatedly.

The deafening fire alarm was blocked out of Yassar's consciousness, continued as background while the foyer fire peaked, diminished, and stopped on it's own when the art collection became a mere pile of ashes on the polished marble floor. Only after the art disappeared did the figure appear to move out of his trance like state and breath a huge sigh of relief. The figure was unaware and could care less about the utter chaos his actions had in the building security office and fire brigade below.

One guard turned to another and said, "Well, that proves that our world class architect was wrong. The systems water pressure is not sufficient to control a fire on the upper levels of the Prince."

Yassar Kaffi was an impressive figure of a modern Arab business mogul, despite his 54 years. He had the physical presence of a youthful 30-year-old, confident and full of an air of authority gained through his amazing international business success. Yassar's stellar rise to power came from financing the development of Dubai and his prominent position within diverse Arab societies.

Yassar was tall, reaching two meters (6'6") before he had reached 20, which suited his muscular athletic frame of 95 kg. The effect was that he appeared very trim and fit, a physically impressive presence. He was clean-shaven with clear olive complexion. His full head of medium length flawlessly styled black hair accented his best feature, his piercing blue eyes. He was well educated with a degree in Computer Science from Pennsylvania University and an advanced degree in International Finance from the Sorbonne. He was accustomed to modern business attire buying custom tailored suits in London, Paris and Hong Kong; rarely donning *thawbs*, the traditional Arab robes unless a special occasion dictated. His financial ventures had made him extremely wealthy rivaling the oil rich sheiks of Kuwait, United Arab Emirates, and Saudi Arabia. Yassar looked like a 35 year old Ralph Lauren model enhanced by his sophisticated manners, openly gregarious and generous persona. He was amused at the number of women that gave off subtle messages of their availability when in his presence. The good life was what he was accustomed to as a player on the international financial scene throughout the Arab world, Europe, Asia and the Americas. He was extremely polished, poised and accomplished in building relationships with people around the world, which allowed him to be the primary financier that developed Dubai into the biggest accomplishment of the modern Arab world.

As a young boy Yassar had engaged his father and anyone around him in the game of chess every chance he got. His father gave him several books documenting every move in the greatest chess matches in history. Yassar relished the unique opportunity to study the chess masters and dissect their thinking in matches. He became extremely proficient at the game, learning to think in strategic terms anticipating opponent's moves and counter moves.

Yassar developed the skill of thinking in terms of five to seven moves ahead of his opponent and understanding the varied options of each move. Skills he learned and honed in playing chess and dealing with global leaders, corporations and governments.

People gravitated to him as a world figure with celebrity like status. His warm persona and panache made others around him very comfortable. He was an astute talented student of languages, cultures and people. Yassar could read the slightest nuances in people's eyes and body language like an open book, giving him the ability to blend into any setting with ease. He was a masterful negotiator and visionary selling the local sheiks on making Dubai an up and coming world class city. After earning his first hundred billion UAE *dirhams*, he felt more comfortable in the casinos of Monaco than the crowded mosques of Mecca.

Yassar was not the typical Muslim. He was much more comfortable in sponsoring charity events like the Dubai International ATP and WTA Tennis Tournament, PGA Golf Tournament, and Formula 1 events. He personally attracted the Mission Impossible movie producers and cast to Dubai with tax incentives and free use of *Buri Khalifa* facilities. His idea of being charitable was throwing galas for international celebrities for a variety of causes or parties to engage Hollywood production crews filming in Dubai. Yassar was never concerned about world poverty, religious zealots, environmental issues, social justice or the general public's interests. He intentionally remained above the fray, being apolitical, and only Muslim by name rather than in daily practice. Yassar did participate in the call to prayer when it was expedient to do so.

Yassar's life had been amazing for this talented international billionaire. He lived in the utter lap of luxury travelling the world for business and pleasure. A full entourage anticipated and catered to his every need. He loved having others bow to his power and influence, especially the sheiks. However, life had changed dramatically over the past 48 hours.

Two days earlier he and his family were attending his second wife *Abia*, sister's wedding in Yemen. It was a joyous occasion with incredible food, music and dancing shared with over a hundred and fifty relatives and friends. The wine and alcohol flowed freely, despite the Muslim religious ban, as the wedding party took on much of the appearances of a western style wedding, which was very popular among the rising Arab business class.

A massive explosion rocked the huge enclave destroying everything in its path. It was an incredible massacre with body parts and debris everywhere. Fireballs and smoke filled the air, replacing the sweet aroma of flowers and the desert with the stench of burnt human flesh. Mentally unable to focus, heavily bruised, and bleeding from numerous lacerations and abrasions, and pieces of metal caused severe bleeding in his right leg, Yassar began attempting to push away the debris with his bare hands and using a scrap piece of wood attempting to dig, hoping to free himself. His ears continued to ring from the explosion. As reality struck, he became aware that the high impact explosion put everyone including his parents, in-laws, family and wedding entourage in harms way.

Everything Yassar held as important in his life was lost in a horrendous nightmarish blood soaked mess. His efforts over what seemed like hours seemed in vain, if it weren't for the only other survivor, *Amid Fafar*. Amid, the chauffer for one of the other guests suddenly appeared in a blinding flash of sunlight working to extricate Yassar from the debris. Once he was extricated Yassar took a short respite to gather his senses and began searching through the debris. Rage filled him as he only found bodies and body parts of identifiable individual family and friend's remains. He was hoping beyond hope to find family survivors. His personal anguish reached a peak when he unearthed the two small bodies of his only grandsons under pillars and beams. The boys had been his pride and joy. His physical injuries and mental anguish brought tears with the acute awareness of how the explosion impacted his life.

Unknowingly an American GBU-39/B bunker buster cruise missile had shattered his very existence. Yassar made the assumption that given the magnitude of the explosion that it was caused by the United States in their unending search for terrorist leaders had wreaked death and destruction on a mostly civilian wedding party. The U.S. reaction to 9/11 burnt alive deep within in the American psyche. It caused strategic errors in decisions to pursue terrorist that would ultimately cause massive civilian deaths. Collateral damage errors were quickly turned as propaganda against the U.S by jihadist.

Incredible despair can cause a man noted for his calm demeanor, extraordinary control and rationality to become irrational. Yassar interpreted his incredible escape from death in Yemen as a message from Allah that he needed to change his ways and take up his own personal *jihad* against the Americans.

Later he viewed the ruins of his art collection in the Prince Tower foyer as the start of a path for a man bent on going beyond grief to focusing his anger into revenge against the west.

Friday, August 31, 1:00 p.m. ADT (UTC/GMT+3)
Al Zagaheer Television Studio 1, Doha, Qatar
"This is Nuru Monaga reporting from our *Al Zagaheer* studios in Doha, Qatar. We have an official United States Pentagon news release of the successful U.S. cruise missile attack on a residential compound 12 km southwest of Sana'a, Yemen. The attack killed *Ali Abdullah Saleh* and *Sameera Dejahir*, two critically important *al- Qaeda* leadership targets. Both leaders were high priority targets in the US most wanted terrorists deck of cards.
The official Pentagon report added that such attacks are utilized only when there is certainty of a minimal civilian presence, unfortunately there may have been some collateral damage during this recent successful attack in Yemen. Our correspondent in Sana'a filed the follow-up report on the devastation caused reportedly by the cruise missile fired from the USS Lake Erie, a Ticonderoga-class guided missile cruiser stationed in the Gulf of Aden." The screen cut away to a brief video footage showed a U.S. guided missile cruiser firing a missile.

Nuru continued, "The Pentagon reported that a U.S. cruise missile slammed into the large compound killing the two alleged *al-Qaeda* targets. Local authorities reported that the attack also killed 137 innocent civilians including 18 children. The compound was the private home of *Kaseen Al Kindi*, a prominent Yemeni international banker. The attack took place during the celebration following Kaseen's daughter, *Lamya's* wedding. The blast from the missile could be felt as far away as the capital center of Sana'a, sixteen kilometers away. The huge crater destroyed the entire compound.

—

8

There is no evidence that any guest or members of the wedding party survived the attack. Pentagon sources refused any further comment other than that extreme precautions are taken to protect civilian lives prior to launching any attack against high priority terrorist targets. Yemeni officials have filed an official protest for the attack within the United Nations General Assembly. The U.S. and several other members blocked it before it entered the Security Council. This is Al Zaga the number one news source in the Middle East."

The newscast was followed by a commercial for a university that showed students studying in the library.

CNN and the major U.S. news networks reported the Pentagon's official statement of the deaths of the two al-Qaeda leaders without mentioning the confirmed collateral damage to the non-combatant civilian population or details of the missile attack on the wedding party.

Seven years later………

Chapter 1: Meeting of the Shura
Saturday, May 1, 7:15 p.m. GST (UTC/GMT+4)
Prince Tower, 2nd tallest building in Dubai, UAR,
Conference Room

The destroyed western art collection had been replaced by an impressive museum quality collection of Arabesque, Moresque and Islamic paintings, calligraphy, metal work, carpets and ceramic tiles. The new collection included works by Sadequain, Sugha Rababi, Tyeb Mehta, M.F. Husain, Ismail Gulgee, and Abdur Rahman Chughtai. The paintings were enhanced by the rich colors of the setting sun through the building's slightly tinted windows. The climate-controlled foyer was a constant 22 degrees Celsius (72 degrees Fahrenheit) and relative humidity of 45% to protect this highly valued collection.

The exterior views from the tower were enough to take your breath away looking out at the manmade *Palm Deira* archipelago and the islands dotting Dubai's Persian Gulf coast below. Slightly to the south was the architectural wonder of Buri Khalifa; the silver bullet pinnacle spire pointed skyward 828 meters (2716 ft.), making it the tallest building in the world. The Prince Tower dynamic view gave one the sensation of floating in the air at two thousand feet. That was until you recognized that the *Buri Khalifa* had an additional 61 floors dwarfing the structure. If all went well Yassar planned on building and owning another skyscraper that would top the 255 floors.

———

"Please see to getting the elevator cooling system repaired properly," Yassar said entering the foyer from a private secured glass elevator. His entourage, seeing to his every need, followed him closely a mere four meters behind. "And have maintenance conduct another water pressure check for all fire suppression stations above the 90th floor." He ordered to no particular person within the entourage. "The last failure of the sprinkler system test was absolutely unacceptable." For the last seven years, Yassar had been mourning the loss of family members and friends killed in the cruise missile attack. The official American administration line to Yemeni officials blamed poor intelligence for the huge toll of over 137 civilians by the deadly *GBU-39/B cruise missile*. Yassar often pondered the politics involved in the U.S. Administration and Pentagon's posture of downplaying the civilian deaths in the tragic event and wondered about civilian populations in other such reported attacks. The U.S. spin-masters and media had buried the real story adding insult to injury.

He believed the American news reports and diplomatic channels had failed miserably to make any attempt at apologies or reparations for the civilian deaths, and failed to fully understand the Omani cultural requirement of "awb isaba" that required individuals to act in revenge for immense personal injury.

The history of Oman is traced back to Arabian Nubian roots over 100,000 years ago. The relatively conservative *Ibadism* tribes along the Persian Gulf had numerous long-standing nomadic tribal traditions that predated the adoption of Islam in the 7th century. Among the Oma-Muscat traditions was the strong emphasis on انتقام or awb isaba revenge against those that harm, dishonor or disgrace your family.

Yassar as a western thinking progressive businessman was awe struck when he felt his loss compelling him to uphold the traditional formal duty of *awb isaba* for his family. The missile incident termed by the American administration as "minor collateral damage" changed this incredibly successful Omani, peace loving, international financier, billionaire and altered his life forever. Prior to the attack Yassar enjoyed a life of privilege and luxury with his family, friends and business associates. Yassar struggled within himself, but the past few years of grief had transformed him into the newest highbred form of terrorist leader. He was motivated by the responsibility of *awb isaba* to use his capabilities wielding an arsenal of economic, financial, cyber, and terrorist attacks for revenge well beyond the normal mode of terrorism.

In that single event, Yassar lost both of his parents, three siblings, wife, four children, all of his seven grandchildren and numerous friends. The incredible loss of loved ones, including his beloved twin grandsons, his legacy broke his heart. The one saving grace was that his daughter *Amal*, who had been away studying for comprehensive exams at Cambridge University, missed the wedding. Yassar was severely wounded in the attack, but elected to have one piece of the missile shrapnel remain as an ever-present physical reminder of that horrendous night. The wound left him with a barely perceivable limp, but the pain from the metal lodged in his leg was a merely a token of physical pain compared to the heavy melancholy that blanketed his life with grief. His will to live centered on avenging the deaths of his family became far more global as he became more radicalized and clouded in his thinking in believing that the Americans and their allies were responsible for death and destruction throughout the Muslim world.

Yassar was thankful to *Amid Fafar* for saving his life by pulling him from the burning debris. Amid, a devoted friend became Yassar's personal driver.

He displayed extreme loyalty due to their shared experience escaping death. Yassar was certain that Amid would sacrifice everything including his own life in his service.

Over the past few years, Yassar began plotting a complicated strategic plan of revenge as his sole reason for living, creating and leading a new organization of sophisticated Muslims in a sacred *jihad* against the imperialist Americans and their allies. Since the cruise missile attack, *Yassar viewed the United States as a deadly enemy oppressing and striking other nations at will motivated primarily by economic greed and the need to maintain world domination of resources and people. His previous shallow religious convictions, occasional practice and views fell along the wayside as he became fanatical in a new radical religious awakening.*

Yassar thought hard about the geopolitical circumstances in the modern world and came to the conclusion that despite the contrary rhetoric, the US did not respect the borders of other sovereign nations, nor did they value innocent lives in foreign lands. They were an economically and militarily powerful enemy that needed to be put in its place. This enemy had a long history of using deadly force without conscience against enemies and civilian populations, supporting oppressive dictators, and providing the world with munitions causing havoc and instability in huge parts of the world. Yassar thought, *I am more than justified in my duty to awb isaba in my revised enlightened view of the world.*

Yassar had discreetly filled the leadership vacuum caused by the assassinations of *Osama bin Laden* in 2011 at the hands of elite Navy Seals Team 6 and *Ayman al-Zawahiri* in a US drone attack in Afghanistan. Their deaths had stalled the larger *al-Qaeda* movement and created an opportunity for splinter groups to form.

ISIL (Islamic State of Iraq and Levant) led by *Abu Bakr al-Baghdadi* is an extremist Sunni terrorist splinter group indiscriminately killing Christians and Muslims in both Syria and Iraq, and destroying world-class Assyrian archeological treasures in Nineveh and Palmyra. The brutal brand of ISIS terrorism used terrorism to force Syrian President Bashar al-Assad from power to create a caliphate in northern Iraq and Syria. ISIS tactics were viewed by the west as barbaric. Their attacks destroying the Russian flight from the Sinai and multiple staged attacks in Paris and Belgium brought new light to their abilities and international threats.

Al-Shabaab led by *Mohamed Mohamud* perpetrated attacks in six African countries including the blatant attack on Christians at Garissa University in Kenya, has associated itself with both al-Qaeda and ISIL.

AQAP (al-Qaeda in the Arabian Peninsula) led by *Nasir al-Wahishi* was materially support by Iran to overthrew the Yemeni government and expel international diplomats. These splinter groups employed the same violent tactics including mass murder, genocide, suicide bombers, slavery, and kidnaping for ransoms.

Yassar called his new secret splinter group the *Mumt Uf'uwan (Avengers)*. He used revenge as the primary focus for taking on a larger global form of retaliation for years of war waged on Muslims by the Americans and other western powers.

Yassar's lifelong passion for chess had provided him with useful skills in acquiring and developing important relationships, finding resources, and detecting the slightest weaknesses in his competitors. His brilliant mind and ability to engage others with words and imagery made him a natural charismatic leader.

He had nurtured numerous friends, partners and colleagues in his homes in Dubai, Riyadh, Paris, Tokyo, Beijing, Jakarta, Zurich, London and Istanbul. Such partnerships secured him limitless additional funds to supplement his personal fortune to develop his personal secret brand of terror directed at America and it's close allies.

U.S. drone and missile attacks and NSA communications monitoring had paralyzed *al-Qaeda, Taliban, ISIL* and other splinter movements. Thinking strategically, Yassar chose to remain under the NSA radar making preparations within his own secret financial network. He was aware of appearances and worked hard to maintain his corporate image, development projects and continued to be seen within the elite echelon of Middle Eastern business world. The complex nature of resurgent international terrorism required a new signature of leadership well under the NSA radar to distinguish itself from the continued but diminished leadership of *al-Qaeda,* world reaction to ISIL, as well as from other terrorist offshoots and sporadic rogue individuals. Thus the *Avengers* splinter group was founded led by an "Inner Circle" of advisors called the *Shura*. He carefully hand picked this powerful council of trusted leaders dedicated to maintaining the solitary goals of Osama bin Laden's original network, but with the personal call for *awb isaba*. A significant requirement for the group was the importance of maintaining absolute secrecy in recruiting, training, acquiring resources, and preparing to stage their attacks. Today the *Shura* would hold a two-day meeting on the symbolic anniversary of the cruise missile attack to finalize the final stages of a new strategic plan of operations and initiating attacks.

The *Shura's* meeting location was in the Prince Tower's conference room, beneath Yassar's penthouse. Yassar lived and worked from his trendy pinnacle apartment on the 95 through 99 floors. Over the years Yassar had created a megacorporation composed of multinational corporations headquarters in his tower. His complex networks of corporations were specialized in finance, development, banking, insurance, transportation, mining, agriculture, manufacturing, and high tech technologies. He had numerous international corporate offices around the world and nearly half located in the lower floors of the Prince Tower.

In Yassar's mind his impulsive destruction of his western art collection purified the foyer area for his new Islamic collection of art. Over the past few years Yassar became determined not to act out of emotion and to repurpose his energy to a strategic plan of attacks against the west. The *Shura* was operating under the very nose of five known CIA and four SIS agents that used Dubai as their haunts. Yassar's complex corporations and international holding had created the perfect egress for dignitaries and corporate representatives from UAR, Saudi Arabia, Bahrain, Kuwait, Qatar and the Sultanate of Oman without raising the slightest Mossad, NSA, CIA or SIS suspicions.

Yassar and *Shura* members had enjoyed incredible mobility due to his complex global business interests requiring a fleet of helicopters, yachts and Learjets. The *Shura's* secret terrorist training operations and launch site was located in the Al Hajar Mountains in western Oman. The operational center was hidden in a sophisticated complex of caves within Yassar's international mining operation. The Shura had spent millions in creating the high tech support, training and operations complex behind the monazite and limestone mines obtained in a corporate buyout six years ago.

The high quality limestone ore was used in global steel production and offered the perfect cover for moving men and materials worldwide. The mining complex and caves were within sight of the United Arab Emirates border and a mere 190 kilometers from Yassar's Dubai global financial and corporate headquarters. The mining operation secretly supported the *Shura's* terrorist operations center and coordinated all aspects of their missions.

Yassar understood the value of taking time to prepare his operations. He had planned and worked patiently for the seven years following the loss of his family. During this time he grew his credibility with the Arab sheiks by assisting plans for the development of desert land; desalinization plants; quality K-12 schools, colleges and the New York University Dubai campus; industrial and commercial complexes; a world class airport; conversion of oil fields to high tech production enterprises; and numerous highly profile projects. His access to industrial and military materials worldwide made him attractive to Arab and Muslim leaders as well as being very discreetly on the fringe with global terrorist leaders. Yassar had used his financial assets and influence to manipulate aspects of the American recession in 2008 without being detected as one of the prime factors. The simple act of calling in a significant number of bundled mortgage loans caused a panic among Chinese and Indian investors invested in mortgages and set in motion the 2005 toxic mortgage aspect of the US recession. He used clandestine warlords as a front for supporting nearly forty small terrorist groups from Chechnya to Brunei.

As the oldest in the *Shura* leadership, Yassar acted like as CEO and a benevolent father, a position he cherished in both his commercial interests and as mastermind commander of the *Avengers*. He had ambitions that went beyond being one of the wealthiest men in the world, rising above the level of local sheiks and kings. His motivation of vengeance would become clear to the world in due time. This clever very patient financier and developer were viewed as more than capable of making and breaking royal families, and affecting the geopolitical dynamic of the world. He was ready to sacrifice his life and fortune to settle the score with the America and its close allies.

As Yassar formulated the complex stages of his terrorist strategy he evaluated the tactics and factors effecting recent international terrorist attacks. He felt that they demonstrated more individual passion than the planning and patience he felt would be necessary to successfully deal a greater blow intended to cripple the enemy, and bring greater understanding of American aggression. The obvious exception was the unique gains of ISIL in domination and controlling areas of northern Iraq and Syria. ISIL provided a focal point for world powers giving the Shura the ability to operate unnoticed by counter-terrorism and intelligence organizations. The attacks on the New York City World Trade Towers and the Pentagon in 2001 raised the world consciousness to the real threat of terrorism. A few passionate Muslims inflicted serious damage to the very psyche of the American public on their soil. Yassar likened himself to a world class chess master set to attack his opponent with a series of ploys and deceptions aimed at the mighty industrial, financial and military heart of America and its close allies. His opponent would be limited to easily predictable responses as the master toyed with his prey using tactical movements to distract him before unleashing a series of devastating attacks.

Yassar understood that the long term American troop presence in Mecca and Medina, Saudi Arabia had been a tipping point for radicalizing *Osama Bin Laden* as he interpreted the Prophet Muhammad as "banning the permanent presence of infidels in Arabia." As Osama claimed the infidels had occupied the holiest of Muslim lands plundering its oil riches, dictating to its rulers and establishing spearhead bases through which to fight Muslim peoples in the Middle East. In fact, recent *Al Zagaheer* broadcasts sponsored by the *Shura* had focused public attention on the historical close relationship of Saudi King Fahad with a long line of former US Presidents beginning with George H. Bush up to and including the present U.S. President. The televised revelations and implications of corrupt leaders supporting the Americans against Muslims worldwide were unprecedented and intended to shake the foundations of rulers in Jordan, Syria, Egypt, Saudi Arabia, Libya, Algeria, Yemen and Indonesia. These newly well-defined relationships with the U.S. continued to unsettle much of the Arab world as the masses saw it as manipulation by American puppet masters and reacted with the "Arab Spring" to unseat puppet rulers. This list of televised U.S. sins paled to the personal vengeance that Yassar held as his sole focus for living. He felt that his life had ben spared by Allah so that he could act as an avenger for all Muslims.

Yassar and his disciples of the *Shura* had not been selling typical terrorist rhetoric propaganda in every market and bazaar, mosque, meeting place, and online sites frequented by Muslims, or counter intelligence agencies worldwide for the past seven years. Instead, they had been planning in utter secrecy under the corporate veil of secrecy, carefully recruiting, training, and placing resources for what would be events changing the course of modern history.

Yassar's mind was filled with the details of his strategic planning against the U.S. *My multi-pronged plot is so deceptive that it will be admired by chess master Gary Kasparov and military strategist*, Yassar thought. Yassar, the ultimate chess master loved toying with his opponent. He was set to attack his opponent with a number of complex ploys, feints and deceptions. *I am not playing against Fritz the computer like Kasparov or even IBMs Watson, but the best minds of the CIA and NSA can muster and their super computers.* Yassar thought to himself.

Mousaffa Al-Moubati, second in command greeted Yassar as the group entered the cool secure conference room. Mousaffa was Yassar's lifelong childhood friend. He was Syrian, but grew up with Yassar in Oman. Yassar had played thousands of games of chess for over 19 years with his dearest friend. He had developed the ability to read his body language, nuances of his eyes and successfully used patterns to predict his thoughts and actions. Yassar's used this highly developed skill to predict behavior in others in both business and his personal life. Their gaming was interrupted years earlier when Mousaffa went off to attend King Saud University in Riyadh, Saudi Arabia, and started his career with Interpol for three years. When he returned to Dubai, Yassar recruited his friend to join his enterprise as his Chief of Staff, and to head his *Shura* operations.

Within minutes Yassar and Mousaffa joined the group in the large comfortable conference room, the center for their strategic planning and communications. Meeting daily for two solid years had made the group extremely cohesive and singular in their mission as *Avengers*. Sitting at the table were seven other *Shura* members dressed in traditional *thawbs*. Yassar had noticed the acute excitement in each of their faces when he sat down.

They all nodded their respects as he acknowledged each of them with his eyes. The group's excitement center a round their anticipation that the years of hard work and extensive planning was finalized and ready to go operational.

In Yassar's mind the *"Arab Spring"* has barely started and would only continue to an end with new leadership controlling numerous Muslim countries. There was no doubt that the Shura's completed plan would add and additional dimension to the Arab world and be praised as righteous revenge for the wrongs against Muslims. As Yassar formulated his complex plan, he decided to use names taken from the titles of his grandson's favorite Arabic children's books as irony to identify the various operational cells that would press a series of coordinated terrorists attacks. The online titles of the Arab children's books on separate Pinterest boards would be used as a simple means of communicating with his strategic cell and leaders in the field. The obscure Pinterest site was well outside the normal realm of NSA and other intelligence agency monitoring. Pinterest operated as a simple application using boards on a wide range of separate subjects. Each board had visual images as pins and individual comments as a means of communicating about the piece of children's literature. There were thousands of boards and pins that could be commented on from around the world.

The elite members of the *Shura* each had both a history of service in various aspects of Yassar's business enterprises, and unique skills necessary for supporting Shura's strategic and tactical operations against the U.S. and her allies. Above all they had Yassar's respect and trust after suffering their own personal loss of loved ones in actions involving the United States. The Shura was composed of individuals of unquestionable loyalty, secrecy and commitment to *awb isaba.*

Kenji Habbi, a 49-year-old Head of Communications, is responsible for the daily communications with his nearly 620 different business and financial ventures worldwide. A Kenyan, trained at Georgia Tech, Kenji had worked in the Atlanta Center providing communications worldwide for CNN correspondent. His technical knowledge and skills was key to both business and Shura operations. Kenji's oldest brother, Mohammed, an engineering student was killed by U.S. Special Forces in an operation to clear elite Iraqi Republican Guard troops within the campus of Nahrain University in Baghdad.

Angri Kafti, was Yassar's 37-year-old Omani cousin on his father's side, served as Chief of Financial Operations. Angri was a brilliant summa cum laude graduate with a MBA from Harvard's Business School. He was hired away from Goldman Sachs to manage Yassar's personal and global business finances and coordinate *Shura* operational funds. Angri's amazing business sense and astute analytical abilities went well beyond his role in the *Shura*. His personal pain rivaled Yassars' at losing part of his family in the same missile attack in Yemen. It made Angri a firm advocate for revenge. Yassar felt very comfortable with Angri, as a family member handling the complex depths of his global financial operations.

Mohammed bin Ahmed, is a 26-year-old Iraqi, serving as the Chief of Security. The Americans in Iraq had trained him and provided him with a deep understanding of the military and intelligence protocols and techniques used against terrorist. His training put him in contact with CIA operations and gave him access to lower level CIA communications. Mohammed had loss his sister and mother to rapist killers in the Iraqi Army while under the supervision of the U.S. Army 86 Airborne Division outside Ramadi. Persistent rumors within the local community placed U.S. troops with in the room as the rape took place. He was fully committed to the Shura.

Amin al-Haqm, a 52-year-old Omani cousin of Yassar, serves as video editor for the Shura direct feed to Al Zagaheer, a rising Arabic news network. Amin used his eight years of experience as a BBC intern and journalist to ensure that the correct spin was created on various new and historical events. Amin had lost his son Habi in 2003 during the US cleanup operation that killed Udav and Qusay Hussein, Saddam Hussein's sons in Mosul. He was already planning for when the time came for Al Zagaheer to reveal the *Shura's* complex operations and plans so the world will understand the rationale for the sequenced acts of revenge.

Khalid al- Habib, is the 43-year-old Yemeni, Chief of Training and Global Strategic Commercial Operations. He came directly from the procurement department of Royal Shell Oil in Saudi Arabia and was accustomed to acquiring sites and equipment for Yasser's multinational industries. Khalid had lost two sons from a Yemen chopper attack by clandestine CIA operatives. His own *awb isaba* was not yet finished.

The last member of the *Shura* was *Saleh al-Somali* the 47-year-old Afghani Chief of the Military Operations. Saleh had been trained by U.S. Marines in Camp Lejeune and used his unique tribal language skills to serve as an advisor to varied military units in Afghanistan. He had witnessed the American actions causing "collateral damage" on numerous occasions in both Afghanistan and Pakistan. Pay back was his personal mantra.

Today was a momentous occasion for the *Shura* as the time for implementation of the masterful attack plans were about to be put into action. Truly a moment to be savored as each detail of the multifaceted plan was reviewed with the intent to wreak tremendous havoc upon America and its close allies.

Playing with the minds of his enemies as he anticipated their reactions was all Yassar needed to inspire the members of the *Shura*.

"Praise Allah" Yassar said, opening the meeting as he laid both hands flat on the massive marble table. This religious invocation was a huge part indicating the significant change in the new Yassar. In his former westernized life he had used Islam to only further his own financial and personal interests. It had only played a surface role in his life. But after surviving the missile attack, he became fully committed to the religion of his youth. As part of that change Yassar now invoked the support of Allah at each and every meeting.

"Mousaffa, are all our cells in place?"

"Yes, Yassar," Mousaffa answered. "Saleh has all cells ready and awaiting your command. The cells are set up to act totally and independently in the sequence we discussed in our meeting Thursday. They do not know about the missions of other cells."

Khalid added, "I have supplied the cells with the necessary equipment, vehicles, arms, and defined in detail escape plans. They are in place and ready to go on your command."

Mousaffa quickly stated, "Each cell will learn of the depth of the other elements of our plan as it hits the media worldwide." Mousaffa was recognized by the other members of the *Shura* as the next logical leader of the "Avenger" group in the event that anything should happen to Yassar. Mousaffa was semi-anointed by the *Shura* to be the next ruler of Syria if the freedom fighters brought down ISIL and the al-Assad regime.

Yassar loved him like a brother. He had in fact taken Mousaffa's youngest sister, *Abia*, as his second wife. She was killed in the Yemen cruise missile attack with her son and daughter. This cemented a tremendous bond between them and ensured that *awb isaba* was a focal point in the *Shura's* plans.

Yassar fully understood the vast power of marriage in firming up important relationships and was planning for his daughter, *Amal* to be used in an arranged marriage with Sheik *Mohammed bin Al Rashid Makto* son Sheikh, *Hamdan bin Mohammed bin Al Rashid Makt.* The marriage to the Crown Prince of Dubai was to solidify Yassar's power in the region. *Amal*, as a dutiful younger surviving daughter, had consented to this marriage and steps had been taken to begin the formal courtship process. Yassar knew that the marriage would put him into the royal lineage of Dubai, but first he needed to deal with his American opponent.

"Kenji," Yassar asked, "is the plan for communicating with the cells in place?"

"Yes, Yassar," Kenji said clearly. "Your orders will be sent by encrypted satellite message to appear in TV ads on the *Al Zagaheer* network and on our selected Pinterest boards online.

Kenji had served well as a teenager in both bombing attacks against the Unites States Embassies in Nairobi, Kenya and Der el Salaam, Tanzania in 1998 as well as the initial successful attack on the London Tube and bus system in 2005. Kenji and his unit had easily escaped and were not connected to either of the coordinated bombings. They had easily dispersed into the masses of Africans living in Britain.

His communications training at M.I.T., command of the English language, ability to recruit African Moslems, and overall field experience makes him an extremely valuable asset for Yassar. He was the most recent addition to the *Shura*. Kenji's numerous negative MIT experiences in Cambridge brought a firsthand voice about racism, ethnic repression and poverty for blacks in America. Kenji though that racism was just another of the opponent's sins that could be exploited across the Muslim world.

Kenji had developed the concept of using Yassar's grandsons' favorite Arabian children book titles for each individual cell right under the noses of the Homeland Security, NSA, CIA, and FBI agencies. He had researched and determined that the untraceable Pinterest chat boards for each child's book provided an easy access forum for communications. This contemporary website designed for sharing pictures and comments would serve the *Shura* well.

Amin piped in, "I have worked with Mousaffa, and we have already crafted a series of new cell phone text and voice messages on the pending attacks against a London bridge that will originate from 22 different countries and then spread worldwide. I will also edit a brief video that we can post online of our cells preparing for their attacks. There is nothing like footage of terrorists in preparation for an attack to raise the enemy's level of anxiety."

"*Al Zagaheer* has served us well over the years," Yassar responded. "Please thank *Nuru Monaga* for her dedication to our cause. We will have her team be the first to break the news of each cell's phased attacks from target one to our final *Avenger* detonations."

The group took a moment of reflect on how their efforts would ultimately redefine the meaning of global terrorism. Nuru had been in a short-term romantic relationship with Kenji since they worked together at CNN. Their relationship ended on friendly terms when Kenji became engaged to Aluna Makouri. Nuru pledged to help the secretive splinter group as the lead reporter on the new *Al Zagaheer* Arabic television and online news network. Yassar had invested heavily in the founding of the network and planned to utilize Nuru to ensure that his personal spins are presented to the Muslim world.

Yassar continued, "Angri, we need to further extend our commitment to *Al Zagaheer*. Let's up our untraceable contribution by 55 million dirhams ($15 million US). There is no doubt that *Al Zagaheer* has been important in furthering the message of our cause. It will be money well spent and pay huge dividends in the long run."

"Yes, Yassar," Angri said, "I will tell Nuru and thank her for her efforts personally." Angri had recently entered into a romantic relationship with the news reporter. In his role he has actively involved in secretly funding *Al Zagaheer*, requiring several highly discreet meetings in his Four Season's Hotel room in Doha. Nuru became enchanted by Angri's personal style, financial position and obvious power. "I would suggest," Amin added, sipping his mint tea, "upgrading the equipment for Nuru's camera crews to ensure we have the best HD video and audio quality."

Yassar nodded. "There is no doubt that *Al Zagaheer* will be important for our cause as we go operational. Let's invest an additional 18 million *dirhams* ($5 million US), and require it to be only used for HD equipment for Nura's news teams."

"As you wish, Yassar," Angri acknowledged. "I'll have the money transferred from our Swiss account in the morning. Consider it done." Angri looked momentarily distracted as the door opened and Nassar Bin Hassan entered the conference room. Nassar was a young man dressed casually in his usual western jeans, tee shirt and sandals. He had a pair of Maui Jim sunglasses hanging from a lanyard around his neck. He had shoulder length black hair pulled back in a ponytail that appeared when he took off his blue New York Yankees baseball cap after entering the room.

Nassar had married Yassar's oldest daughter while they attending their MBA graduate programs at the United Emirates University. They had provided Yassar with the short-lived legacy of two wonderful grandsons. Nassar's lost his family in the missile attack. Due to an aircraft delay, he was extremely late to the Yemeni wedding compound. He arrived two hours after the deadly attack. Nassar shared Yassar's deep grief and was more than ready to avenge the loss of his beloved wife, sons and family. It took weeks of Yassar assuring him that a hasty response would be foolish, but he would witness a series of attacks. Revenge would be his reward for patience. Nassar had been summoned to the meeting to lead the most important cell in the plan. It would be the most dangerous of all the missions, but one that Yassar knew he could rely on Nassar to complete without fail. Nassar was after all the most reliable and trustworthy on the fringe of the *Shura*. His hatred of the Americans was unparalleled.

Standing before the *Shura*, Nassar bowed briefly and nervously took a seat against the wall at the far end of the table showing his immense deference to the importance of the *Shura* leaders. He was unaccustomed to being in the presence of their entire leadership in one room. His only hope was that he could live up to whatever mission he was expected to perform.

Nassar had suffered a tremendous loss and felt the veil of depression would be lifted when he avenged the loss of his family. His fear was of potentially embarrass Yassar and thus dishonor the deaths of his family in pursuing his own personal revenge, but he also saw it as an opportunity to advance into the *Shura's esteem.*

The door opened again as a well-known figure entered the room distracting the Shura. The imposing tall, dark eyed, ball-headed man dressed in his usual white linen hooded Salwar Kameez and sandals. Akmed Momani's height of 1.9 meters (6'3") and muscular 125 kg (250 lbs.) had the same effect whenever he entered a room. The occupants of the room would generally attempt to look away. Yassar had introduced Akmed to the Shura five years earlier as a key operative responsible for recruiting, deep vetting, and training cell members. He was to be known simply as *Akaman.* This man had become a legendary figure as an assassin sought by Interpol and law enforcement throughout the world for high profile political and corporate murders. He was also nicknamed *Houdini* due to his extremely high intelligence, linguistic abilities, use of sophisticated weapons, poisons and explosive devices, and uncanny ability to change his appearance moving freely from country to country and seemingly disappearing into thin air. Despite modern technology Interpol never had *Akaman*'s picture, description, DNA, voice or fingerprints and were unable to assess his nationality or background. In fact this Jordanian by birth had worked for clandestine operations for Mexican Sinaloa drug cartels, Chinese Triad's Dragon Master, Japanese Yamaguchi Gumi, Russian Solntsevskaya Bratya, Italian American Camorra, and Italian Ndrangheta.

He regularly eliminated internal competition within crime organizations and effectively disposed of external law enforcement and justice figure for a huge fee. Yassar had successful recruited *Akaman* by giving him an identity and real life in Muscat, Oman as well as the resources necessary to be the key in preparing the Shura operations.

"Welcome," Yassar smiled as Akaman seated himself at the single remaining seat at the conference table. "I have requested that Akaman attend the end of our meeting today to give us an update on the readiness details of our varied cells."

"Thank you, Yassar," Akaman's deep voice. "All the phase #1 cells are trained and either currently in place or in transit to their assigned mission. They have undergone extensive scrutiny and training over the past few years. I can assure you that their success will give notice to the world that there is no safety within their borders. The required confusion and chaos of the attacks will have intelligence agencies under extraordinary pressure as each coordinated attack demonstrates their inability to secure their own borders."

Yassar tapped lightly on the table with his fingers before spreading them flat on the cool marble. "Thank you, Akaman. Today is a momentous occasion," he said, glancing at everyone. "The uprisings in Egypt, Tunisia, Libya, Syria, Yemen and Iraq, along with the continuation of the Arab Spring and varied successes of ISIL, and terrorists attackers in Europe and the United States have distracted the West. Now is the perfect time for the implementation of our carefully sequenced attacks."

The group took a moment to reflect on how their efforts would ultimately redefine the meaning of terrorism and impact the psyche of their enemy.

—

"My friends," Yassar continued, grinning, "our planning stage is over. Now the chess game begins. It is time to engage our enemies." Everyone in the room perked up in their seats, nodding their approval and in unison repeating, "May Allah bless our efforts launching our long term strategic attacks."

"Amin", Yassar said sternly, "significantly increase our cellular phone traffic with calls specifically to the United Kingdom and the United States, so the intelligence directors of our opponents know we are about to initiate a threat against London. NSA has ears on all Arabic communication, so let's give them a lot to listen to and analyze. Mousaffa, let's see what we can pick-up from MI6, CIA, and NSA transmissions to embassies, consulates and military bases. We wouldn't want the infidels to think they didn't have an opportunity to respond? Would we?" Yassar loved to ask rhetorical questions to an anticipated response from the entire *Shura*. The *Shura* leaders did as Yassar expected as they nodded their approval in unison. Akaman glowed in his knowledge of the operational details and quality of the preparations.

Chapter 2: London Goes on Alert
Sunday, May 2, 4:05 a.m. BST (UTC/GMT)
10 Downing Street, London, UK

Spencer Wendell, Director of Counter Terrorism for the British Secret Intelligence Service (SIS/MI6), hated getting roused up after less than two hours sleep, even if it was to report terrorist activity directly to the Prime Minister. NSA had reconfirmed the terrorist threat intercepted by the SIS during monitoring overnight communications from areas frequented by terrorist. The threat was urgent enough to work all intelligence agencies into a frenzy of activity. Spencer at age 67 was well past the normal retirement age at SIS. He had been asked eight months ago to stay on to assist with the transition of the new SIS Director of Intelligence, Admiral Harold Johnson. Spencer felt honored to be working on the transition team and more importantly monitoring the terrorist threats facing the UK and most of its allies. It had become a very different world since terrorism took center stage.

Spencer had dressed in his best British tailor-made, but well-worn Charles Tyrwhitt suit for the special Prime Minister briefing and even shaved again before leaving his Mayfair flat and catching a black hackney carriage. There were no car parks near 10 Downing Street, so it was pointless for him to drive in his favorite means of transport, a vintage black 1965 Austin-Healey 3000 Mk III roadster.

Rushing to his meeting, Spencer could not help but notice the extreme security precautions in place to protect the PM's official residence, the Parliament building and the Westminster area. Heavily armed military guards standing behind armor vehicles stopped Spencer's black hackney twice.

Each checkpoint verified both the cab driver and Spencer's identification as bomb-sniffing dog circled the vehicle while a Lance Corporal scoped a mirror on a pole to view the hackney's undercarriage. The PM's office was contacted to verify his appointment with the PM.

London had always been a target for terrorist attacks since1605. More recently the number of bombings connected to various Islamic jihadist had increased with three in London since 2005. The current higher level of security was a result of his section at SIS intercepting cell calls. Spencer watched the hackney driver masterfully maneuver his fare past the last cement blockade, tastefully disguised as huge understated flower basins. They finally approached the wrought iron fence fronting Downing Street. Visiting the PM's residence was taking a step into British history as PMs had occupied the home since 1735.

Spencer paid his fare, took his receipt, and opened the cab door. The PM's security staff had been forewarned and had watched the hackney's progress on the security video system over the past two blocks. The video oversight of London, government buildings and the entire country had increased dramatically after 2005 attacks in the tube stations and in preparations for the 2012 London Olympics. Chatham White and Charles Fitzroy greeted Spencer at the door. The 87-year-old Chatham served as the official porter for PMs over the past sixty-one years. He was a constant recognized fixture at 10 Downing Street despite the changes in PMs over the years. Chatham's continued service was a wish of HRM Queen Elizabeth, herself. He greeted Spencer with a hearty, "Good morning, Mr. Wendell," and led Spencer into the famed black and white checkered tiled reception hall.

Charles, the Head of the PM's Security detail, immediately hurried Spencer toward a full-blown sophisticated body scanner that that displayed silver tooth fillings and any unconventional weapon that normally slip past other metal detectors. The scanner was a vast improvement over the commonly used Rapiscan used at most airports. It was developed at Hitecs Laboratories outside London using an imaging that rivaled the best of the CT scanners used in the medical field. During testing the scanner detect the image of the newest plastic firearms and other non-metal explosive and poisonous materials with its additional special odor detection feature.

Charles noted, "Prime Minister Graham is awaiting your arrival in the study. Admiral Harold Johnson is on his way and will be joining you in about five minutes."

Chatham escorted Spencer up the magnificent white marble Grand Staircase lined with the paintings of former PMs. On the third floor he knocked on the foyers' solid oak French doors decorated with hand carved wooden figurines of two rampant lions. Pausing a moment to catch his breath Chatham opened the door to the PM's study.

Thomas Graham, the dashing fifty-one year old bachelor and Labour Party Prime Minister rose from his brown leather Chesterfield chair adjacent to the fireplace and offered his hand to Spencer. The PM's hand was calloused and showed his familiarity with hard manual labor as a stevedore, unlike his many predecessors rising out of the privilege and entitled British upper crust. Graham came from a long family line of dockworkers from Eirth, Borough of Bexley, in Southeast London, who lived in utter poverty and were fully committed to the unions.

The PM had a reputation for working his way up from the docks through the union, until a lawsuit claim involving a back injury won him the funds to attend college at the age of 29, much older than his fellow students. He was as much a product of the school of hard knocks as the genteel class of the usual gentlemen from Oxford. The gates of Exeter College at Oxford University had opened a prestigious apprenticeship as an aide to a well-known barrister. He pursued his law degree at Cambridge, graduated magna cum laude, ranking first in his class. Graham's don and professors considered him as among the brightest law students to grace Cambridge.

Graham had forgone his personal life as he toiled on legal cases to protect the less fortunate. He was a rising young star in the United Kingdom politics and on the world political stage, known for his straightforward approach and unheard of brutal honesty. Graham was a natural leader who was able to build compromises with Conservative, Unionist, Green, and Labour parties. He shined in the eyes of the public during the daily television broadcast of Parliament. He was slightly over 1.9 meters, 175 lbs. on a muscular frame. Graham had a handsome, yet boyish appearance that betrayed his Scottish heritage. His full head of neatly trimmed auburn hair, clean-shaven pale skin showed the lack of exposure to natural sunlight. He had crystal clear blue eyes that could penetrate and make one feel intimidated; yet softened with emotion when the circumstances warranted. His good looks, poise, sense of humor and charm were apparent despite his working class background.

The daily tabloids had listed Graham as the most eligible bachelor in London until recently when they confirmed his relationship and pending engagement to Helena Hassler, Curator of the Tate Modern Museum. The speculation within the Front Street sheets was on par with the daily items following of the Royals. London bookies carried odds on the dates of Graham's engagement and nuptials.

"Good Morning Spencer," Graham greeted using his first name.

The use of first name familiarity was something that was special that Graham reserved to those few that attended Exeter College at Oxford and studied under the same don. Spencer relished being called by this first name.

"Good morning sir,"

Chatham reappeared with a full silver tea service with a wide variety of cut fruits and warm lemon scones fresh from the PM's staff baker. It was well known in London circles, from the Daily Telegraph and other daily news-sheets, that despite Thomas Graham's working class background and modern approach to leadership, he was very fond of the household staff and acquired a taste for the traditional English tea and warm scones at all hours.

"I hope your anti-terrorism section are holding up well. Sorry that this is such an ungodly hour." Graham asked of Spencer.

"My section is doing well, sir. Thank you for asking. No worries about the hour. "

"The Admiral will be along shortly. Please take a cup of tea and scone."

Spencer turned and helped himself to a cup of organic Chamomile tea and warm lemon scone with a pad of real butter.

Just then there was a knock at the door, Admiral Johnson appeared at the door accompanied by Chatham. The Admiral was amazingly fit for sixty-two. The PM shook hands with the Admiral in a manner that confirmed his profound respect. Johnson was a retired Royal Navy Admiral, and the new Director of Secret Intelligence Service. He had headed several Anti-Terrorist positions within Scotland Yard's cyber offices and moved up the ladder rapidly as his sector foiled some minor terrorist plots. The Admiral's frugal SIS budgetary policies were a hit with conservatives in Parliament. But for some within SIS he was seen as a mere pencil-pushing bureaucrat with tremendous political connections in both the military and Parliament. Johnson was not as well versed in the levels of intelligence operations and global interagency cooperation processes as most of his processors. The Admiral was still somewhat unproven to hold such a key position in the intelligence world. Without invitation, Johnson moved quickly to the silver tray, poured his own tea, seemed to ponder on his choice of scone before selecting the largest, and seated himself in a comfortable Chesterfield leather chair. He was accustomed to the PM's study for small meetings. He loved the opportunity to be seated in Winston Churchill's favorite chair. The rich scent of history in the chair gave him an even greater sense of his own self-importance.

"May we get on with it," Johnson said looking at Spencer. "I have a feeling this is going to be a busy day for all of us."

The Admiral was noted for his no games approach to everything. Many opponents had found his highly competitive nature overwhelming on the golf course, cricket grounds or tennis courts. His no nonsense approach had SIS snapping to a new level of competence with total confidence of being well supported by the highest levels in UK politics.

What Johnson did not understand in the intelligence game was rapidly compensated for through his efficiency, political savvy, and administrative style. He was a pretentious political player with friends in high places in government and society.

Spencer opened his favorite Oxford leather bound portfolio. He had been in the Oxford's Balliol College, and St Stephen's House years earlier than the PM, but shared a pride in their shared educational background despite their family origins. He removed three copies of the communication intercept summary report.

Quickly distributing the reports, Spencer began. "Please, let me skip directly to the end of the report. All of our joint expert analyst agree that the intercepts point to an extremely credible threat against one or more of London's bridges crossing the Thames. Quite frankly, we have anticipated an attack similar to the terrorists attack on London's Tube and bus system in 2005. Our assumption is that the railway bridges and perhaps the symbolic Tower Bridge, as an iconic symbolic target are the most viable targets. *Al Zagaheer* has already reported in a broadcast that reliable sources within the undisclosed terrorist leadership have verified that London bridges are marked targets. Those unnamed sources have also reported "the bridges will remain targeted until the United Kingdom abandons its support for the United States tyranny in the Middle East." After pausing briefly, Spencer continued, "If I may, I would like to go into the data supporting our conclusions."

An hour and twenty minutes later Spencer had concluded the details. The grim briefing was interrupted by the arrival of General Maxwell Hatch, Commandant of the Royal Army, Chief Superintendent retired General Geoffrey Nash of the New Scotland Yard and Assistant Commissioner of the Information Directorate, Riggs Turnhill.

Spencer grimaced, as he knew he would have to hold separate briefings with the new arrivals at the conclusion of the meeting. His stomach rumbled loudly as the scone failed to fill the void. Bangers, baked beans and scrambled eggs with English muffin and marmalade would have to hold off until afternoon. Spencer thought about his typical physiological response when he was thinking of food and feeling the pangs of hunger, this was not the time for becoming unfocused or bringing attention to his service well beyond the usual age for retirement.

The briefing ended with a flurry of questions and the unanimous decision to respond on several levels by increasing visible security by the military on all London bridges, and enhancing the high tech surveillance camera system on every bridge near the Thames. Turnhill role was to work with BBC, CNN, and all the daily tabloids on Fleet Street to ensure that they provided a positive spin on the extensive coverage so the terrorists knew that the plot was uncovered and the UK security response made the plot difficult if not impossible. The internal security level increased surveillance of suspected terrorist, monitoring of all Arabic communications, made contact with informers within all thirty-two UK mosques, tightened immigration security at all UK airports, the Chunnel train, ferries and seaport harbors. The task of securing the thirty-four bridges within the city boundaries would be completed within the hour. SIS secretly monitored phone calls and e-mail contacts with *Al Zagaheer* personnel in hopes that they may be able to trace their sources and reveal the terrorist leaders.

Each of the participants felt thankful for the intercepted warnings, but recognized the potential panic situation for Londoners who still bore the angst from previous Tube bombing. The amazing increased security effort made during the Olympics had lessened some of the public's fears, but the new threat would shatter that tenuous sense of security.

Spencer wished for the old World War II undeniable spirit created by Churchill in Londoners facing the Nazi air attacks. He read extensively about the Churchill era and the prevalent unique public spirit. Londoners today seemed to lack the same spirit in facing unspecified terrorist threats. The fact remained that masses of Londoners had given up on the "Tube" as the ridership had declined to less than two million per day from 5.2 million before slowly showing signs of an increase during the Olympics.

Johnson commented, "I am afraid that word of a credible threat of an attack against our bridges would put the city into hysteria much greater than segments of the population that left London during the Nazi U2 rocket bombings during World War II."

The PM was reserved, but gracious in thanking Spencer and his staff for the briefing. The Admiral added his commendation for Spencer and his anti-terrorism communications team. After all, the section was under his direct supervision and only confirmed his own competence in his new role at SIS. The PM sent the group off to do their urgent task. As the group took their leave, Graham opened a wooden cabinet behind his desk and turned on the hidden flat screen television to the BBC One Breakfast to see what Londoners were waking up to this morning, as was his norm after scanning the papers.

Spencer left 10 Downing Street on his way to SIS Headquarters at Vauxhall Pleasure Garden just as the city was coming to life. He had arranged to have a follow-up meet with Hatch, Nash, and Turnhill in an hour after checking with his five counter terrorism teams. By now the threat would be top news on the BBC Home News and the daily tabloids. The terrorist had once again altered the day-to-day sense of security by adding the cloud of fear to the slight wisp of morning London fog.

Spencer mouthed a short prayer for the threat to disappear just as the morning mist began burning off.

Spencer had a moment to pause just as his silver and black hackney passed Parliament to cross the Westminster Bridge over the Thames. His thoughts of potential or eminent danger crossing a bridge would become a common thought for millions of Londoners over the next few weeks. The responsibility for their safety was beginning to wear heavily. In the back of his mind, he wished the world had returned to a time of relative innocence like the eras of the 1950s and 1960s prior to the Cold War. The unending threat of terrorism had cast a huge shadow and placed a greater importance on his anti-terrorism section's efforts. He urged the hackney driver to pick up the pace recognizing the urgency to get to the office to launch his teams into following up on this latest terrorist plot. Minutes later, he paused for a moment gazing out his office window with a direct view of the Vauxhall Bridge. The world had changed in ways that made him feel uneasy, but at the same time gave importance and urgency to the role he and his section played in preempting and countering terrorism.

His office would be a key in monitoring and coordinating the counter terrorism response. It did not look like the section would be getting much time off for sleep over the next few weeks or longer unless the threat was neutralized. Thoughts of breakfast were lost again in trying to organize the section's task and setting immediate priorities. They were about to increase the pressure on all terrorist suspects in the UK in the hope that the precautions forced abandonment of the plan to target London bridges. Spencer made a personal call to Hub Nolan at NSA. Hub was and old friend willing to give the American take on the threats and hopefully share if they had any additional intelligence.

As a young lad, Spencer had joined his family in traditional annual foxhunts years well before Tony Blair sign off on the law banning the hunts as being inhuman in 2004. The hunts had been a huge part of his family's sporting life for over 200 years on their Yorkshire estate. There was something amazing about riding across the countryside in chase of a fox being hounded by a pack of trained beagles. One of the distinct socio-economic differences he had with the PM. He knew the thrill of the hunt and how to run down the prey. The fox was loose and it was up to SIS to unleash the hounds, follow the scent and run the prey to the ground ending the threat. Walking out of his office Spencer thought. *The game was afoot!*

The London Attack Preparations
Sunday, May 2, 10:00 p.m. BST (UTC/GMT)
A flat on Sloane Square, London, United Kingdom
Hamid Kouri paced the floor of his small flat. He had been in London's South Kensington district since mid-December and that was much too long in his opinion. But indeed this was not his decision. Each day made him and his cell more edgy especially during the suddenly increased high security alert. At any moment New Scotland Yard or SIS security forces might round up all suspected Muslim sympathizers and endanger his cell by some unforeseen small detail.

Hamid at the age of thirty-four, was a connoisseur of Middle Eastern foods. Despite the availability and variety of good Middle Eastern restaurants in Baywater and Mayfair, he preferred the short stroll to the *Al Bustan* on Old Brompton Road in South Kensington. It was the only establishment that came close to satisfying his need for an authentic Saudi meal. Hamid was looking forward to returning to his mother's home cooked *muttabag* in Saudi Arabia.

Nothing compared to it if followed by *shisheea*. Hamid was certain that he would have gone insane with sheer boredom if he had not invested so much time searching for authentic food. His physique was showing the, additional 9 kilos he was carrying in his abdomen and love handles due to the lack of exercise. Sitting around flats waiting for orders to go operational placed a strain on every member of his cell.

Hamid's day job was as a representative of an Omani mining company providing essential limestone for steel mills in the United Kingdom. The company maintained a suite of offices in the Herron Tower. The tower was the third tallest building in London. He spent his days in his plush office on the 87th floor with a view north overlooking Liverpool Station. He was certain that he was not given leadership of *Al Salwa* cell because of his knowledge of limestone mining. It was far more likely his leadership was because of his critical role in the attacks on the United States Embassy in Kenya and Tanzania. He had planted an explosive device in a London tube station in 2005 and escaped to Saudi Arabia. His dear friend Kenji had rose to being a member of the elite *Shura*, indeed an honor to be within the inner circle of the Avengers. Kenji had encouraged Hamid to select his favorite children's book as a name for his cell. *Al Salwa* was a famous series of illustrated children's books that taught children to read and learn about different languages. It was his childhood favorite. Now it was the key component in maintaining communications with the Shura. The concept was simple. An online site for sharing pictures and comments call Pinterest had a special board for *Al Salwa* where encrypted messages could be passed without counter-terrorism detection.

The men of *Al Salwa* were very patient with Hamid's incessant talk about Middle Eastern food delicacies.

He and his cell had discussed that other attacks would be prior to their mission and how their observation of the security on the bridges would increase and lapse significantly in the near future. They were also patiently waiting to hear the *Al Zagaheer* broadcast of the attacks of other cells. *Al Salwa* was composed of ten members all having resided in the UK for six or more years. Except for Hamid, each of the others originated from areas in North Africa and adept at blending into their varied local Muslim communities. The team members were kept apart, except for their occasional meetings. They never revealed their real names, jobs, or residential area, using only aliases for communicating. Hamid only informed them of the detailed steps in their planned attack, but never shared anything of the splinter group organization, communication system or leadership structure. For security reasons he did not disclose their escape plans to prevent the capture of one member eliminating the successful route for the rest of the cell.

Several of the *Al Salwa* members were very uncomfortable living in the very different British culture. The presence of Christian churches, public parks and museums with statues and paintings of nude women, lyrics of western music, immodest public dress and immoral attitudes of the young girls, bland foods, fixation on football and cricket, and assortment of shops. They found the commercial emphasis on consumer goods as an ugly aspect of British pseudo-capitalism, yet admired the strange socialist twist in providing free high quality medical care. Akaman had recruited the cell because of their outspoken hatred for the western world and personal loss of a loved one. Many cell members attempted to maintain their balance by attending prayer services, despite Hamid's warning that SIS was probably monitoring the mosques for potential terrorist.

SIS was known to infiltrate mosques by having their informer's join, monitor, and attempt to become friends with mosque members. Their participation in mosque activities endangered the cells mission.

Hamid monitored the *Al Salwa* messages on the Pinterest board for the unit's marching orders. Each evening *Al Zagaheer* broadcasted reports on aspects of the Arab Spring and bringing joy to Hamid's cell as they understood that following the completion of their mission they may return home to a radical changed Muslim world.

Hamid, "Praise Allah for he will show us the way to complete our mission successfully. We were destined for greatness in this sacred *jihad* in dealing the British a serious blow for participating in the Iraq invasion and supporting the Americans in their "war on terrorism."

Chapter 3: Exploring an Innovative Nuclear Redundancy System
Monday, May 3, 4:45 p.m. PST (UTC/GMT-9)
California Institute of Technology Campus, Watson Lab Office, Pasadena CA

Dr. Sean McMurray had just finished reviewing the data on a super-computer simulator system test and saved it on his department's secure network. It had been a long day working in his office on the top floor of the Thomas J. Watson Sr. Laboratories of Applied Physics, on the campus of Cal-Tech. Taking a moment, Sean gazed out the window at Beckman Auditorium, the center of campus; he relished the thought of finalizing his refined post-doctoral dissertation on a nuclear redundancy system that has taken over eight years to finally verify the design. If all went well and he could find the funding, the design could be installed and tested on most nuclear facilities in the United States within fifteen years, and perhaps the world within twenty-five years. The thought of securing nuclear facilities with his redundancy system was part of a boyhood dream.

Sean and his team of gifted graduate students were going to celebrate their simulation results, end of the semester, and progress on their redundancy system with a camping and climbing trip to Yosemite. Weather permitting the team planned to climb Nutcracker's, the challenging 5.8-route just a quarter mile east of El Capitan in the Yosemite Valley. Rock climbing at the level of difficulty necessary to climb the five pitches on the 650' granite face gave an adrenaline surge through the climber's body that was hard to imagine unless you were an extreme sports fanatic. Sean admitted to himself that for a self-described nerd, he loved living on the edge and experiencing the climbing rush. In his early teens, he had passing thoughts of being a Marine or Navy Seal to experience the same rush, but succumbed to the offer of a full academic scholarship as having greater opportunities for his future.

In fact, Sean was in superb physical shape. He had amazing strength in his arms and legs from climbing and running with his team of graduate students. "Not bad for a 29 year old" Sean mused "Thanks to working out on the walls of the ARC Climbing Facility and hundreds of hours on granite rock faces."

As a young boy, Sean had been fascinated by the extraordinary wartime and peacetime power of both nuclear fission and fusion. That interest was fueled when his father gave him a book entitled Nuclear Power and the Environment (1996) by Sir Brian Flowers. Sean's dad was a chemist working for DuPont Chemical. He encouraged the development of Sean's keen interest in science, but especially nuclear research following World War II. At ten, he had a sophisticated insight into the enormous economic benefits of generating safe electrical nuclear power and lessening the world's dependency on depleting fossil fuel supplies. By the time he was twelve, he had read every article and book on the subject of nuclear physics written since 1940. If ever there was an example of early childhood academic specialization, Sean met all the classic criteria. Some childhood prodigies specialized in dinosaurs and becoming expert paleontologist, a few taught themselves to play the piano at concert levels before entering elementary school, while others interested in the dynamics of the stock market becoming financial wizards and millionaires before becoming young adults. As other boys played sports or mastered video games, Sean's growing passion and focus was on studying and creating models of nuclear reactors. Sean wrote letters to his favorite nuclear physicists Ishfaq Ahmad, Paul-Henri Rebut and Gerald Goerttzel asking about their research, and cherishing their responses like most boys value their favorite baseball cards or athlete autographs. He did not have your typical teen's interests or passions to say the least.

At the age of fourteen he had completed high school, won several national science fair awards, raising the attention of noted scientists for his sophisticated knowledge and passion. Sean scored the maximum on the PSAT and maximum score of 1200 on the SAT. He frequently attended scientific lectures and was given scholarships to special science camps, where he continued his dialogue with nuclear physicists. At fifteen, he accepted a full four-year scholarship to Cal-Tech to explore his specialized interest in nuclear physics. California Institute of Technology was the smallest of colleges offering scholarships, but by far the most prestigious in the area of applied sciences, mathematics and engineering. At nineteen he had completed his masters and started his doctoral degree. A short two years later he completed and defended his dissertation and totally impressed his committee during his oral comprehension examination to the point that Cal-Tech offered him a tenure track teaching position. After two years as a faculty member at Cal-Tech he had established himself as being in the top five nuclear scientists in the United States and leader within a distinctive group of globally renowned nuclear scientists.

At the end of year departmental meetings, he had opportunities to expand his research with additional selected graduate students. A faculty investigator had initiated various levels of inquiries after three faculty members had opened his tenure sponsorship. Several of the older established faculty members were clearly jealous of Sean's mercurial rise to scientific stardom at the young age of twenty-nine. On the other hand Cal-Tech did not want to take a chance of losing Sean to other more rewarding university positions. It was rumored that Sean was being considered for a prestigious extremely well funded Physics Chair at MIT, and Emeritus Professorship position at Princeton were in the forefront of campus gossip.

The Cal-Tech Provost and faculty did not fully understand Sean's passion for climbing granite in California held an emotional and physical hold that made it difficult to shake to accept a different academic position. His early childhood in East winters had severely discounted any consideration of positions in cold climates.

Sean viewed teaching as a way of making a difference in his world, giving back to society and furthering the opportunity to assist in significant advancements in nuclear physics. Luckily his stellar reputation attracted only the brightest and best graduate students as research and teaching assistants. His life really centered on his passions for designing reactor systems and rock climbing. Sean loved every aspect of his life. When he was not spending fifteen hours a day working on supercomputer stimulation data and design variations of nuclear reactors on campus, he was climbing at Arcadia Rock Climbers or the granite faces of the San Gabriel Mountains overlooking the Los Angeles basin with his graduate assistants. The air within the basin had improved, but remained being among the worst in the United States due to numerous forest fires. It was hard to do local climbing when the ozone levels reached the highest levels in the United States for 137 days in a year. Sean's draw to California went well beyond the San Gabriel's in Los Angeles County, as California had over seven hundred world class climbs, with Yosemite and Pinnacles within an easy five hour drive.

Graduate students climbing with Sean always felt it to be a highly intellectual experience as most of the conversation centered on aspects of the nuclear reactors and his redundancy system they were working on in the lab rather than the normal chatter of climbers. Sean loved to challenge his students mentally as they faced the technical and physical challenges of a rock face. The group's rock climbing skills developed while their in depth knowledge of nuclear reactor systems expanded exponentially.

Sean knew that the experience of climbing created a personal bond that went well beyond their academic working relationship. The time spent harnessed on a granite pitch, or holding the rope belaying another climber, holding the life of each other in their hands, brought this bright talented group into a relationship of utter reliance and trust that would be hard to duplicate in any other setting. Sean's team of grad students was a new breed of climbers, enriched by experience and committed to Sean's redundancy project.

The spring semester ended, faculty meetings were finished, grades submitted; graduations celebrated; Sean had just finished a review of computer stimulation data and was about to head out of his third floor office. He had barely shut down his computer, enjoying the view of the very center of Cal-Tech out his office window, when there was a solid knock on the door. Sean had second doubts about dealing with a student or faculty issue so late in the afternoon, especially with thoughts of a brief vacation front and center in his thinking. Reluctantly he opened the door to a very distinguished looking man, fine groomed, clean-shaven, salt and pepper haired, non-academic type, dressed in a refined dark suit and red tie. He identified himself as Dr. George Bennett, the Deputy Director for the United States Department of Energy, Nuclear National Security Division.

"Dr. McMurray, I'd recognize you anywhere from your many pictures, scientific researcher profile and NRC credentials. I work directly for the Under Secretary of National Nuclear Security." He flashed his official looking government identification for the National Nuclear Security and the Department of Energy. Both picture identifications were displayed in a stylish black, Pierotucci hand tooled soft Italian leather wallet of the finest quality, consistent and befitting his immaculate attire and government stature.

Sean wondered about the visit by the impeccably dressed government bureaucrat. Dr. Bennett was so unlike the underpaid pencil pushing bureaucrats he had met in the past as he applied for government grants for his Redundancy System research.

"It's a pleasure to meet you Dr. Bennett," he said. "Please call me Sean."

Bennett intervened, "I much prefer to call you Dr. McMurray. It will help keep business in perspective and define our professional relationship parameters."

Sean was somewhat rebuffed by the comment, "Very well Dr. Bennett, you will have to excuse me at this hour. I'm in sort of a rush. I was just heading off for a weeklong vacation to do some rock climbing in Yosemite with some of my research assistants; weather permitting as a storm front is moving in tonight. Please take a seat."

Sean moved back away from the door to reveal a well-worn oak chair that faced his desk. The chair's wooden armrests had the Cal-Tech Beaver mascot carved into them. It was a gift from a former class of students.

Taking a minute to deal with Dr. Bennett, Sean asked, "I'm a little confused. What brings you on our campus and my office in particular? Is there a problem with my grant application?"

Taking the offered seat, Bennett seemed to be paying extraordinary attention to not wrinkle the creases in his pants as he watched Sean seat himself at his well-organized desk in an otherwise cluttered office space.

"Dr. McMurray, I'm sorry to delay your departure for your vacation, so I'll attempt to make this as brief as possible. I am here to see you on an important government matter. Before we precede any further, I would like to have you call this number to verify my credentials. It will quell any questions you may have about the veracity of my mission." Bennett handed Sean his business card with another number written on the back.

Hesitant but curious, Sean picked up the office phone. He called and asked the Director of Campus Security to place the long distance call to verify the number he had been given on the back of the card. All the while wondering whether this was some sort of background check for a colleague involved in the Cal-Tech venture with NASA's Jet Propulsion Lab in La Canada or had something to do with his work or tenure investigation. He then requested that campus security trace the exact location of the number.

While waiting for the verification, Sean asked, "Dr. Bennett, how long is your visit to the Los Angeles area?"

"I will be departing LAX on a red eye this evening. I have several scheduled meetings tomorrow morning with Dr. Gibson and a special task force she has put together."

"Flying east on a red eye can be exhausting as you will lose three hours. I hope your meeting isn't too early."

Within two minutes the security officer called back with verification that the number was to the Director of Research and Development, Department of Homeland Security, Office of National Nuclear Security in Washington, DC. Having confirmed the phone location, Sean asked to have place the call. Almost immediately a woman answered the call.

"Hello this is the National Nuclear Security office. How call I assist you?"

"This is Dr. Sean McMurray at Cal-Tech."

"Dr. McMurray", I'm the Executive Assistant to Dr. Grace Gibson, Director of NNS. She has been expecting your call and desires to speak with you directly. Please hold as I forward your call."

"Dr. McMurray, this is Dr. Gibson from NNS. As you may know my office's responsibilities include securing all the national laboratories using nuclear materials, nuclear energy facilities, disposal of nuclear waste, and to support further research and development that directly impacts both our national nuclear energy production and security. Recently there have been several incidents where terrorists have been photographing and recording information about nuclear plant personnel in Belgium, France and Germany. NSA assumes that similar terrorist surveillance is ongoing here in the U.S. We have a new Congressional mandate with significant appropriations to secure our nuclear plants. Dr. George Bennett is on a special assignment to visit you because of our firm belief that your extensive research into designing a nuclear power plant redundancy system is vital to securing our nuclear facilities. I'm hoping that you will be interested in our NNS proposal. For security reasons I'll let Dr. Bennett give you the specific details regarding our interest in your design. Do you have any questions?"

"Not at this time, but I may have after hearing more details of the proposal from Dr. Bennett. I'll call you for clarification if necessary. Thank you, Dr. Gibson."

"I'm sure you will have questions. Please feel free to call me with any questions or concerns. This call was to verify Dr. Bennett as part of the NNS team and to confirm our specific interest in supporting your redundancy project proposal." Sean was a bit shocked and yet pleased that NNS was interested in his system.

Within seconds he sensed that Dr. Gibson seemed intent on ending the call as quickly as possible, as she continued, "Dr. McMurray, I sincerely hope you are willing to see your redundancy system design through to completion. I'm sure we will have an opportunity to meet at a future date. I look forward to meeting you soon. Goodbye, Dr. McMurray."

Sean felt that the lack of niceties and social protocols within the call indicated that these government officials were all business further underlined the importance of Dr. Bennett's mission. Thinking about what just transpired, Sean decided that it wasn't just bureaucrats, perhaps it was the late hour in Washington DC.

"Well Dr. Bennett," Sean said, "it looks like I may be calling my grad students to cancel or delay our climbing plans for Yosemite. So lets discuss the details Dr. Gibson mentioned proposal for my project."

He gave Dr. Bennett a small knowing grin, as he had expected a visit, but not at this stage of his design system design research. It seemed a little premature, but what scientist argues with the government and their financial support. Somehow he had expected the government to initiate their interest by a formal invitation to visit Washington, rather than an awkward visit by a bureaucrat and a confirmation call to DC.

"I'm hoping your vacation plans can wait, Dr. McMurray, I imagine that a unique opportunity to develop your project into a full operational mode, is a dream come true." Dr. Bennett returned a slight smile. "I'm not a physicist, but I know that the top nuclear scientists have been following your design work very carefully since you initiated grant eight years ago as part of your post doc follow up on your dissertation. They have also been following your beta test using the Cal-Tech supercomputer. You may know Dr. Theodore Powers, leader of the NNS Task Force. Members of the special task force have been charged with the responsible for making our nuclear facilities more secure. The task force conclusion was that your project showed tremendous merit. In their preliminary report they concluded that the project needed to be funded, expedited on a Beta trial basis. If the on site testing verifies the viability of the project, it should be implemented as soon as possible to secure our nuclear facilities. The Secretary of Homeland Security, and Secretary of Energy concur and immediately allocated funds for the project should you accept our offer. I have been tasked with offering you and a team of your choosing a sizeable grant to install and test your redundancy system in a nuclear power generating facility. If the design works as expected, we would negotiate a financial arrangement for each additional nuclear installation. Such government contracts and negotiations fall into my field of financial expertise. The entire task force assumed you would be interested in this extraordinary opportunity to implement your design."

"I do know Ted Powers. He is a well-respected colleague. I was unaware that the NNS had established a task force. I certainly appreciate the government's confidence in my redundancy system design. Sure, I have been waiting for the Nuclear Regulatory Commission or some other government agency to recognize the value of my design in securing our nuclear facilities. Frankly, Cal-Tech has done a great job in funding my initial research, but does not have the financial resources to complete a fully functioning design without building a nuclear facility here on campus. So where do we go from here?"

"Dr. McMurray, I do need to confirm your commitment to work on the redundancy project with Dr. Gibson and the NNS task force."

"Dr. Bennett, I'd be more than happy to commit to work with the NNS on my project pending we reach an agreement on the terms." Sean offered his hand to Bennett with a small smile.

"Dr. Gibson and the members of the Task Force will be pleased that you are on board," shaking Sean's extended hand. "I'm flying back to DC this evening and plan to meet with the task force Tuesday morning. We'd like to have you consider the composition of your team and what resources you will need for implementing the project. We'd like to have you meet Dr. Gibson and the task force as soon as possible. Urgency requires that we get your project launched with a nuclear site system testing within the next six months. Dr. Gibson and the task force want a timeframe that works for you." How soon could you put together your team?

"I am certain that six months is more than adequate for implementing the system and doing beta testing. We can easily put the team together with the talent here at Cal-Tech. We have access to the research resources. However we need to acquire the necessary special equipment, develop some specialized circuit boards for the NNS and Homeland Security satellite interface system, build communication networks, and install the equipment on the Beta test site. I'm sure we could begin work within three weeks if not sooner."

"Excellent, please call me at the number on my business card any time on Tuesday afternoon or Wednesday morning at the latest."

"I will give you a specifics on my arrival in Washington on Tuesday. If I'm reading you and Dr. Gibson correctly, the urgency is apparent on your part, so I will initiate the project as soon as possible. I am curious as to why, but will hold pursuing my questions until we meet face to face with Dr. Gibson and the task force. Just to clarify the timeframe, we should have the first test facility fully operational before the end of November."

"That is correct. Now do you have any idea on which facility you'd like to select and use as a Beta test site?" Dr. Bennett inquired.

"If I had my way we'd start with the Palo Verde facility in Arizona, unless the task force thinks otherwise. The three reactors in one location and thus presents the greatest test for my redundancy system." Sean was already thinking of the immense tasks and the extremely tight timeframe, yet confident that he and his team was ready for the challenge.

"Excellent choice, but not a surprise as the task force expected that you would want to start with Palo Verde due to it's size and relative proximity. Why not secure the largest nuclear facility in the nation first? You haven 't disappointed them in the least. If the design works there it should work in all our other nuclear facilities. I will ask Dr. Gibson to initiate discussions with the Palo Verde Facility Director. "

"How should we handle the expenses?"

"I have a cashiers check written in your name for $350,000 to get you started and with a direct credit line for $3 million. That was the task force estimate on the initial installation and testing. We can discuss additional funding, if there are overriding expenses. Do those sums seem adequate?"

"Given my prior estimates, the sum should be more than adequate to fund the project."

"You will just have to sign this receipt for the check." Bennett passed Sean a Mont Blanc pen engraved Dr. George Bennett and a formal document indicating the receipt of the check and Bank of America line of credit for his university account.

Sean half laughing and a bit nervous at the task lying ahead of him and his team, "Well, there goes the rock climbing trip!"

After Sean provided the signature, Bennett carefully placed the receipt in his briefcase, shook Sean's hand, "We are very excited to have you join our NNS task force. I hope all goes well with the installation and testing of the redundancy project. I look forward to meeting again later this week. I expect we will also need to work together during the negotiations phase for subsequent nuclear facilities."

"I'll be sending you a packet of documents via special government courier for your review giving details on access to the line of credit, expenditure accountability, and security requirements. You can work out some of the complicated technical details with the task force during your visit. Please let me know if you have any questions or concerns. If I cannot answer your questions, I can put you in touch with our staff members that can. You have my card and phone number."

"I'm extremely excited at this great opportunity to see my project fully developed. It's been great Dr. Bennett. Please thank Dr. Gibson and the task force for their recognition of my work and offering the opportunity to make my system design a reality. I'll call on Tuesday afternoon."

"Goodbye Dr. McMurray. I look forward to working with you on this project."

Sean was already mentally handpicking the graduate students for his team. Each of the selected team members had specific unique talents to bring to the project. He knew the students would be ecstatic with the opportunity to see his design work put in place in a real nuclear generating facility. He planned to offer each student twenty thousand dollars as a stipend for working on the project.

He picked up the office phone to leave a voice mail message canceling the rock-climbing trip. As a follow-up he text messaged the group of rock climbers. Over the next two hours Sean initiated calls to his Dean and the graduate students he selected for his team. The students were extremely excited to hear the news. The sudden change setting aside their vacation climbing plans and initiating the organization of the team would require a whirlwind of meetings. Sean began serious planning for the meeting and formulating a list for acquiring necessary equipment.

———

Chapter 4: London Goes On Full Alert
Tuesday, May 4, 7:30 p.m. BST (UTC/GMT)
10 Downing Street, London

Admiral Johnson was finishing a lengthy security briefing with Thomas Graham and the Cabinet Ministers. He had coordinated the past 24 hours intelligence report with Field Marshall Andrew Perkins and General Nash of New Scotland Yard's technologies. Johnson had been assured that preparations were complete securing all of London's thirty-four bridges. The Royal Army had attached special armor units on both ends of the high profile bridges including the Tower, London, Cannon Street, Southwark, Blackfriars and Westminster. Each of the priority bridges held a piece of iconic history and critical locations in the city center. But without knowledge of specific plans of the threatened attack, the precautions stretched their somewhat limited security resources. Admiral Johnson was convinced that the entire threat was a ruse to divert attention away from other more likely targets including the financial center around Paternoster Square. The area was rated as the most important financial center in the world. He seriously doubted that the terrorist would target the RAF Spadeadam missile sites, High Wycombe Army Headquarters at Andover, Faslane nuclear submarine base on Gare Loch, or weapons depot on Long Loch. He also ruled out any attack against the Admiralty building in Whitehall as it was already under unprecedented tight military security. The London bridges presented highly visible targets, thus the mere threat would have the effect of rising anxiety, and have a major impact on normal life for Londoners.

The Cabinet and the SIS analysts readily agreed with the Admiral. Graham felt at a loss, he just could not permit an attack to happen in London nor could he ignore providing protection to the financial center and other more likely targets.

The threat on London was now ever present and a big part of his subconscious. He found it difficult to focus on other international matters as protecting the UK was his responsibility, regardless of the increased security precautions, public safety fell clearly upon his shoulders.

As the last of Cabinet Members departed the room, Graham reached for the phone and asked his personal assistant, Margaret, to connect him with United States President Mark Reynolds.

"Margaret, please place a call to President Reynolds. I will be in the study when he is available."

Margaret quickly responded, "Yes Mr. Graham, as usual his Chief of Staff will inquire into the general topic or issue of the call. What should I inform Mr. O'Toole of the conversation topic?"

Pausing slightly Graham stated, "The topic will be the terrorist threat on London bridges." Then as an after thought, "Margaret, before I take the call, please ask the kitchen staff to prepare dinner for two at 9:30 p.m. in my quarters."

Within seconds the phone in the study rang. Graham reached for the encrypted secure phone.

"Good Afternoon, Thomas Graham here." Thomas always relied upon his ability to compute different time zones within conversations when calling internationally.

"Good evening Mr. Prime Minister, this is Jerry O'Toole, President Reynolds's Chief of Staff. President Reynolds will be on shortly." A few seconds later the silence on the line was broken by Mark Reynolds distinguished deep voice.

—

"Good evening Thomas, I hope I have not kept you long. My meetings do drag on."

"No Mark, it has been just seconds. How are you doing?"

Reynolds paused for a second before responding, "Busy as always fighting the political battle with a split Congress, budgetary challenges, and a FEMA disaster situation. All in a days work. How are you fairing?"

"Frankly this threat to attack a London bridge has taken my full attention and affecting my sleep. I would hate to have any attack take place during my watch as PM. The safety of a nation is a huge responsibility. Then again I am preaching to the choir."

"The security issue seems to dominate my thoughts too and I don't have the buggers knocking on my front door at the moment. I hate when we have to increase our Homeland Security Advisory alert, but we cannot ignore these threats."

"It is nice knowing that you face the same pressure due to damn terrorists. The higher alert with the security precautions we have in place have Londoners going crackers. Do your intelligence agencies have anything on the terrorists that might help us?" Graham looked briefly at his Rolex Daytona.

It looked like his dinner date with Helena that evening would have to be a quick bite later than usual.

"I just had a security briefing led by Gayle Swartz, Secretary of Homeland Security (SHS) with Dexter Ford, NSA Director, (DNS) and Gary Dessile Director of CIA (DCI) in attendance. They are convinced that the international cell chatter will result in an attack. I had Ford break down NSA analysis of the chatter and related information. A majority of the information gathered independently by all twenty-three U.S. intelligence agencies and collated at Homeland Security, points to a credible threat to London. Unfortunately, there was nothing in the briefings that helps pin down a specific bridge or area on the Thames River, type of attack, nor more importantly a timeframe. CIA postulated that given past attacks in other countries, the attack would probably be a vehicle loaded with explosives and lone wolf suicide driver. "

Thomas had hoped that the Americans would have something that would help the SIS and security forces in place on the bridges. He quickly acknowledged the assistance, "I appreciate that our intelligence teams have reached the same conclusion. Please let us know if your intelligence teams come up with anything more substantial. Thank you, Mark, for taking the time out of your busy schedule. Please pass on our appreciation to your intelligence teams. I would love to host a Presidential visit to out Parliament, if your schedule permits and Susan would like to explore shopping or sightseeing in London. Perhaps she would like to visit Harold's with Helena."

"You are more than welcome. I will ensure that our NSA counter terrorism team share directly with your SIS folks. I would love to take you up on a visit. I will have Jerry check on our upcoming European state visits and G8 conferences schedules to see what works. That might take some time, but I will put it on a list for my travels. I do have an appointment and have to run. I hope that this threat is only that! Goodbye Thomas"

The Americans only reconfirmed what SIS had already confirmed on their own. The fact remained that little new or hard information about any London bridge plot had been uncovered over the past week. Constant surveillance of the bridges wore on the patience of the security forces as their presence was continually noted on the BBC broadcast. Londoners were nervous and anxious about the potential threat, and served as the current key focus in the British media.

Graham thought, *it's interesting that the cell threat in itself ties up our resources. The buggered al-Qaeda doesn't even need to act. Perhaps the Admiral is correct, this is a ruse. If the cell chatter were a ruse, it had successfully tried British patience and forced them to commit military resources. Graham wished he had more time to develop a more personal relationship with Reynolds. He was unable to attend President Reynolds's Inauguration ceremony in January. Perhaps extending the formal invitation to Mark and his wife, Susan would make times like this much easier. The President certainly understood the enormous cloud of angst and anxiety connected to the terrorist threat looming over London. He thought of starting the process by having Jeffrey Crane, Home Minister, and Margaret Dillon, U.S. Secretary of State begin working out details of a formal state visit. Given both of the world leaders complex schedules it might take months before Air Force 1 actually touches down at Heathrow.*

One thing Graham appreciated about Reynolds was that his political philosophy and agenda was much more simpatico than that of former presidents. Thus Graham's political persona was not receiving the huge negative media attention or sharp criticism that his predecessors had been subjected to as a result of their alignment with the Americans on the Iraqi and Afghanistan Wars.

The 2000-2008 era certainly was a low point in Anglo-American relations in the eyes of a significant part of the UK public.

Graham picked up his secure mobile phone and selected the speed dial #1. On the second ring he heard Helena pick-up. She obviously was working late at the Tate as the sound of Debussy played in the background.

"Hi Helena, how are things at the Tate today?" Graham had one of his executive assistants constantly monitor the media for items both positive and negative about the museum housed in the refurbished old Bankside Power Station. His relationship with Helena had evolved from their political views and mutual love of art. The fact was that Helena played a unique role in getting the relatively conservative London art scene to accept new directions of art through her vision and leadership as the Director of the Tate Modern Museum. Graham knew that the three articles in the Evening Standard, Sun, and Telegraph on the new exhibit at Tate Modern had been positive. He hoped in his heart that her day was as positive. Helena's professional world played an important part in Graham's personal life.

"Thomas, the word is out that my Soutine and Cezanne exhibit is getting high praise internationally, but as usual I'm knee deep in finalizing the arrangements for our Kandinsky exhibit in November. I've been on the phone with art collectors and curators in eight different time zones all day. If this comes together as I'd like, it will be a major coup for the Tate. Can we stay in for dinner tonight? I'd like nothing more than a cozy dinner in your quarters. Will you have James make one of his wonderful Thai chicken salads?"

Graham knew that such a verbal onslaught was symptomatic of times when Helena was pressed for time and was under considerable pressure.

He quickly responded, "Of course, I was just going to suggest the same thing given the bloody terrorist issue and the state of my desk. I'll order James to prepare dinner and add a chocolate mousse dessert. Does nine-thirty work for you?"

"Perfect, see you then, love. Goodbye"

Before Graham said goodbye, the mobile phone indicated that it had lost its connection. He wondered if the constant pressure of their high profile positions, duties, responsibilities and presence in the public eye ever offered the opportunity to decompress.

Graham immediately placed a personal call to James, Chief of the Kitchen staff, and ordered Thai chicken salad, dinner rolls, chocolate mousse, and two chilled bottles of California Mirassou Russian River Pinot Grigio for two to be served in his personal quarters at 9:30 pm. He returned to the pile of dispatches, messages and phone calls he had been neglecting all day.

I'll be lucky if I'm finished by ten, he thought, *luckily there is nothing in the dinner menu that will get cold.*" The sound of his secure phone line shifted his focus.

"Good evening Mister Prime Minister, Spencer here."

Graham responded, "Good Evening, Spencer, I hope you have some good news."

"I am afraid not, sir. I just wanted to confirm that the terrorist cell chatter has dramatically increased in volume, and originating countries with active terrorist communication intercepts worldwide. There has been a 40% increase in the mention of London bridges. I've sent you an e-mail news video clip from *Al Zagaheer* outlining their assessment that a London bridge is the primary target despite our increased security precautions. SIS has not been able to uncover any direct contacts between the terrorist leaders and *Al Zagaheer.*"

Graham, "I'll take a moment to watch the clip, Spencer. Is there anything else from SIS, NSA, or our other allies?"

"No, sir. My sector is monitoring all intelligence resources, including the Israel's Mossad. I have also updated the entire security advisory team. We have informants actively working undercover attempting to gather intelligence from within the 46 Muslim communities. They have not uncovered any plot at thus time, but understand the urgency given the attacks in Paris, Brussels and Istanbul. We have significantly increased our scrutiny and vetting of refugees from Syria and Iraq, and all points of entry into the UK. The UKBA (UK Border Agency) has doubled it's staffing. On a side note, Admiral Johnson is concerned about the increased financial pressure the extra security is placing on our SIS and military budgets."

"It sounds as if your sector are doing everything possible. I certainly do not want a devastating attack on London during my tenure. Please put the Admiral at ease, Spencer. Given the credible threat, we have no other option but to increase your SIS and our military budgets from other sources."

—

"Will do, sir. I will keep you updated on any further developments. Have a good evening, Mister Prime Minister."

"Thank you, and please thank your sector and teams for their extraordinary efforts. They are of such a vital importance for all of us. We just need to keep calm and carry on. Goodnight Spencer."

"Goodnight, sir."

Graham took a sip of Twinings Prince of Wales Tea. He pushed the cup aside discarding it as it was cool, slightly bitter, and lost its' rich flavor. He went to his desktop computer and opened the video clip. Graham thought about *the significant change in the world since well before the U.S. September 11th attack. The developments following the invasion of Iraq including the failure to find weapons of mass destruction ultimately changed the dynamic of the Middle East. The steady rise of al-Qaeda feeding religious jihadist added to the dynamic. Now the world was dealing with the Arab Spring and ISIL movement like a potent genie in a bottle. Once out of the bottle this evil genie was going to be very difficult if not impossible to contain.* Graham looked at the pile of diplomatic dispatches, budget projects, and Parliament initiatives sitting on his desk. He wanted to put a significant dent in it before Helena arrived. He picked up the house phone and ordered Chatham to have a staff member bring a fresh pot of Prince of Wales tea.

Chapter 5: Organization of the Cal-Tech Team
Tuesday, May 4, 8:15 a.m. PST (UTC/GMT-9)
California Institute of Technology Campus, Pasadena CA

Sean's urgent phone calls, e-mails, text messages, and voice messages stirred tremendous excitement among the eleven contacted members of the Cal-Tech team comprised of graduate students and a faculty member. As he had anticipated, they all expressed a desire to participate in the NNS project.

Sean had worked extensively with each of the ten graduate students and easily pulled the best of the best students based on their specialized talent. Harry Youngman is an incredible statistician capable of simply analyzing huge amounts of data, creating logarithms, and finding anomies. Sarah Hughes is a computer genius capable of setting up extensive networks, interfacing with other systems, hacking when needed, and a brilliantly talented nuclear physicist. Jake Murphy is a gifted physicist, extremely creative and capable of trouble shooting and fixing anything mechanical. Krishna Karbayan had a double major in electrical engineering and nuclear energy with a real talent in designing and modifying electrical designs and circuitry. DeJesus Trujillo is the most gifted team member having taken the concept and creating the nuclear control room override system, and integrated the video system with interface capabilities with NNS and NSA.

Willie Goldman, at 28 is the oldest having completed eight years working on highly secure satellite surveillance in the Air Force, an expert on creating links to classified military, intelligence and commercial systems, and talented computer hacker. Craig Stevens is a phenomenal electrical engineer with tremendous expertise in communication systems. Sam Ridder is the computer expert experienced in linking remote data into the super computer, trouble shooting issues and retrieving relevant trends. Harold Fong, an exchange student from Taipei, is an incredible physicist that assisted Sean in modifying the redundancy system to interface with the traditional reactor controls. Elsa Dean is the team's link to reality working on logistical procurement of highly technical equipment, time schedules, and maintaining the financial budget for the project.

The only faculty member was Ned Toppin, a highly regarded Cal-Tech inorganic chemistry professor. Ned is a tenured professor, creative genius with over forty chemical patents and developer of numerous new products. He is a talented problem-solver capable of modifying any issues as if he were the initial designer. His help would move a critical part of the project forward. *My redundancy system design stands on it's own.* Sean thought, *Ned is a key to getting this important security aspect completed if he can manage our specialized chemical needs.*

Each member had a very deep personal relationship with Sean, which would make project security a non-issue. Each of the team except Ned had a detailed working knowledge of the redundancy system, and assisted with the numerous theoretical models designed and tested on Cal-Tech's supercomputer.

Within fourteen hours, eight team members were sitting in the lab located across the hall from Sean's cramped office anxiously waiting to hear details of the project that lay ahead. This was no small task given the end of the semester as students and faculty dispersed to the far ends of the earth. Two of the team members were bleary-eyed from flying red-eye international flights to return in time for the meeting.

Sean had been busy creating lists of resources they needed to obtain, creating a Managing By Objectives (MBO) flow chart, initiating a timeline of sequenced specialized tasks for each member, and organizing preliminary numbers for the budget. There was no way for him to sleep given the incredible opportunity to build his dream system.

The air hung in the lab as the coolness of the morning wore off. Sean quickly used his key to turn on the air conditioning to ensure that everyone was comfortable. The day promised to be hot and stifling for the entire Los Angeles San Gabriel basin. The six million plus moving vehicles in LA County and a smoke alert from two local forest fires resulted in the sixty-ninth Health Alert day, forcing children, elderly and most athletes indoors.

Sean initiated the meeting by apologizing for the lab's AC not being activated sooner. Then stated, "A physics student was hit in the head by a brick falling from a four story building. He lost consciousness. When he awoke he immediately started smiling." Sean paused, "The onlookers were worried, so they asked him why the smile. The student replied, 'I just realized how lucky I am because the kinetic energy is only half mass times velocity squared.'"

The team broke out in laughter. That simple joke set an immediate relaxed tone for the team. This was going to be a serious project, but as usual fun would be had at the expense of Sean and team members along the way. The joke was a signal that their relationship was not changed despite the pressure to prove the effectiveness of Sean's redundancy system design to the Feds in Washington and the world. He would be mentoring and treating them as always and not be overbearing. It was so like him to relieve the onset of stress with his natural sense of humor.

"Hey Doc", Jake called, "I've got one about the absent minded physics professor. Do you want to hear it?"

"No thanks, Sean responded, "We don't have to go there, I'm a living example."

All his graduate assistants chuckled at the levity and good humor, knowing Sean brings it into any setting or situation if possible and appropriate. He would have to help Ned, as he too would ultimately be the target of some good-humored ribbing. Ned was going to get some heat as part of an unspoken initiation into the team.

The team loved this opportunity to work with Sean especially on a project that held huge professional career opportunities. Sean was a rare character among his serious academic colleagues, because he was typically younger than those who had difficulty showing their human side and the slightest bit of humor especially with students. The team appreciated that the importance of the project had not changed the team's dynamic.

"If we can see straight for a few minutes", Sean told the team, "I'd like to get us focused on the opportunity the government has presented in funding the redundancy system to making what was a mere series of linked computer models and tests into a reality. The Feds want us to build a prototype system, link it via satellites, and test it within six months. If all goes well, and we know it will, we may well be in for the long haul installing and modifying redundancy systems in nuclear facilities from here to Timbuktu." Sean's facial expression mirrored the excitement he felt in having the NNS support in funding his system.

There was a roar of approval and applause. The entire team immediately realized that they suddenly had the possibility of long-term professional employment and more importantly doing significant work within their specialized professional areas.

"For this project," Sean Continued, "I would like to form a corporation called *NukeSafe*. Each of you would get an initial salary of $20,000 for your work this summer and 2% of the shares in the privately held corporation, that in itself will be worth significant amounts as the contracts for future installations mount." With a grin on his face, Sean asked, "What do you think?"

There was unanimous cheering that rippled through the room as the reality of the work and the financial reward hit home. Over the past five years the team recognized the project's potential, as simulation after simulation yielded data confirming that the redundancy system worked as the supercomputers analyzed the data and multiple contingency factors.

"You mean, I won't have to bus tables this summer and during school semesters," Harry joked. "I'm not sure I can handle all that free time. Using my brain on something aligned with my studies is both a blessing and a curse. It will be definitely better than my mindless restaurant job. But when I'm into a project it becomes all consuming."

"What do you mean free time?" Sean quipped. "This project will take considerably more time than any part-time job you will ever have."

"This means getting an apartment with my own private bathroom." chimed in Sarah. "I won't have to put up with three roommates trying to get ready for classes at the same time and their god awful grungy messes. This works for me."

"Sarah, somehow I anticipated that you'd be excited about having your own bathroom." Jake smiled. "I'm going for new wheels and lay my 1999 Chevy truck to rest. I can't imagine life without having my truck breaking down every other week and calling you guys for help. If you play your cards right Sarah, I might even give you a chance to ride in my new forest green Subaru Forrester. I won't have to rely on Sarah picking me up in her black beast Honda any more." Jake laughed at his own comment as others nodded their heads.

"Sean, how much time will you need from me?" Ned asked, "I've got two summer grants that have demands on my time. I'm trying to balance things, so Josie and I can swing the down payment to purchase a larger house in Arcadia while interest rates are still low."

"Ned you can do most of your work in your lab developing a gas source, storage systems, and a rapid application deployment mechanism. But you will need to be available by cell to problem solve when necessary and make site visits from time to time as we install the system equipment. Can you work that into the time necessary for your summer grants?"

"Sure, that will only be about three weeks work. I'm in!"

Sean paused and added, "Best of all you won't have to take any of the barbs of abuse from this motley crew if you are in your own lab."

A twinkle in Ned's eyes said that the project was going to be the capstone on financing his new home in the sleepy suburb of Arcadia. Homes in that area were at the high end for a professor, running from $850,000 for a fixer up to $2.5 million.

"Great, I need to bring you up to speed on the entire design for the redundancy system and the specs on the necessary gas. Can you stay for about an hour after we end this meeting with the team?"

DeJesus quickly quipped, "I hope the gas is nitrous oxide, I could use a good laugh without going to the dentist. Can you do that for us Doc Toppin?" A chuckle rippled thru the group.

Ned said, "Sure, no problem, DeJesus, but your body won't be able to function while laughing." Ned had a sense of how to handle the team, adding as he turned to Sean, "But I do need to pick-up my daughter from soccer practice. It can wait for an hour. If I head home now my summer honey-do list will be waiting."

Talking to the entire team, "If we are ready to commit, I'll need to have your word that you will not discuss the project with significant others, family or friends. I'll head off to Washington early Wednesday while you get started on your assigned tasks. Now for your basic work assignments and areas of responsibility. Check over your task sheets and revise so that your area is completely covered. We will do a review and make revisions as a group in our next meeting." Sean reached into a binder and pulled out and distributed task sheets for each team member.

Krishna said, "I know you want me to line up our supercomputer access, interface it with our new computers, and duplicate the redundancy software. How much time do we get on the supercomputer? How soon can I begin working with Willie on the necessary NSA satellite link-ups?"

Sean said, "You've jumped the gun, but you got your assignment right."

The team fell into silence studying the work assignment. Three of the team, Elsa, Craig and Willie had not arrived in time for the meeting, so Jake said he planned on meeting with them to bring them up to speed while Sean was in Washington.

"I'd like to meet with each of you separately next Saturday afternoon to go over your revised assignments and progress. We will meet as a group to see if we can suggest further revisions. So let's get on it. This redundancy system isn't going to build itself." Sean smiled at the intensity that the team displayed in getting their task.
In a matter of five minutes the team had dispersed to begin their specific tasks. Ned and Sean left to cross the hall into his office. Sean reached into his compact refrigerator and pulled out two bottles of ice-cold water, offering one to Ned.

The next sixty minutes was a technical review of the complexities of the redundancy system. Finally Sean turned his focus on Ned's role.

"Ned, I need you to develop an effective gas concentrate that can fill specific sized room volume to render those in the space unconscious or totally incapacitated for about one hour. It must be clear, odorless and not do any permanent damage to the occupants or sensitive equipment. Is that something you know of or can develop this summer?"

Ned nodded his head as he responded, "Sean, the Russians have a gas made from an opiate compound called haldrane-fendanyol. It does everything you just specified. I'll need to develop the manufacturing process, work on the storage and quick release dispersion system, and find out how to create concentrated amounts to meet the spatial requirements. Do you have the specs for the rooms or areas we need to apply the gas into?" Ned smiled at the windfall this project presented and added, "This is going to be even easier than I thought."

"I can get you the specs and data for each of the rooms. How long does haldrane-fendanyol render the individual unconscious?" Sean asked.

"They really were not unconscious just totally incapacitated, aware of what is happening around them, but unable to move or speak. The National Security Police introduced the gas through the heat vent system, against armed bank robbers during their attempt to rob the Central Bank of Russia, in downtown Moscow. The robbers, employees, and clients were in a stupor and unable to move, but aware of everything around them. They fully recovered in about 90 minutes.

The time period of incapacitation is generally 40 to 90 minutes depending on the concentration, room ventilation, number of occupants, and amount inhaled by individuals. Why?"

Sean simply stated, "I need the individuals out for a minimum of one hour. More is fine, but it cannot be a minute less. If necessary can we extend the period with a higher concentration or do we give them a second dose of gas after they begin to revive?"

"Let me handle that. You have plenty to worry about in getting all the components for the redundancy system together." Ned looking at his watch, "I need to get going Sean. My daughter's soccer practice ends in fifteen minutes. I'll call you on Thursday with an update. Looks like our new house is going to become a reality. "

Sean smiled, "Chao, Ned I'm glad you're onboard. I was impressed with your retort to DeJesus."

With Ned's departure, Sean grabbed his laptop and began working on his Washington, DC flight and hotel reservations online. After 30 minutes he turned to tweak his PowerPoint presentation of his Redundancy System knowing full well that the NNS Task Force needed greater background information on the system and attempted to anticipate their questions. After completing the presentation, Sean checked in on his team working in the lab. Everything was moving full speed ahead.

Chapter 6: Washington Encounter
Wednesday, May 5, 6:15 p.m. EST (UTC/GMT-6)
Washington Mall, Washington, DC.

Sean suffered from a fairly severe mixed case of fatigue and jet lag. He had worked past midnight on the project, gotten up at 2:30 am to provide the two-hour cushion necessary for travel time to Los Angeles Airport (LAX) and to get through security to take a 6:00 a.m. direct flight to Dulles Airport (IAD). Like most Americans living in the post September 11th era, he really resented the Homeland Security precautions. Sean saw the terrorist winning a small victory over everyone facing the nuisance of long airport security lines, taking off their shoes, belts, jewelry and having their carry-on x-rayed, searched, and scanned for explosive residue. Being patted down by a TSA officer was the most intrusive security procedure. The new airport full body scanners were a new concern. As a nuclear scientists Sean wondered about the long-term effects and potential dangers of radiation used in the scanners, despite the TSA's significant assurances that it was a safe procedure. It wouldn't be the first time a government agency's assurances missed the mark.

The 40-mile trip from Dulles Airport to downtown was significant without considering traffic to get to his hotel near the National Nuclear Security Administration office on Independence Avenue. There were a series of scheduled meetings on Thursday with the possibility of meetings on Friday. Due to the traffic backed up on Interstate 66, Sean had an hour and 20-minute cab ride before registering at the DC Downtown JW Marriott on Pennsylvania Avenue. Sean had requested a non-smoking room with a view on the fourth floor. His perfect room was one with an unobstructed view at a height high enough to muffle street noises, away from elevators noise, and capable of being reached by fire apparatus.

He was pleased to find that the Marriott had met all of his requirements. Sean was thankful there wasn't a meeting scheduled upon his arrival. He decided to force himself into his Brooks Ghost 8-shoes, non-descript tee shirt and jogging shorts, to take his routine three-mile run around the Tidal Basin. Sean's plan was to run off the fatigue, shower, order in something light for dinner from room service and enjoy a goodnight sleep despite the considerable street noise below.

It had been nearly twenty-three years since Sean had been in the nation's capital. His grandfather, Aidan, a career Master Sergeant in the U. S. Army and a veteran of the Korean War, and two tours in Vietnam, brought Sean to see the city in 1988. It had been part of his grandfather's personal pilgrimage to honor colleagues in arms that had given their lives. Sean remembered walking the slight declined pavement down into the area of the Vietnam Memorial Wall. He had been struck by the sheer number of names etched into the ebony wall and the tears that rolled down the cheeks of his grandfather, a man not known for showing emotion. That trip had been a very special time with his grandfather. Patriotism had been highly valued in the McMurray family. The trip was during the economic boom and optimism of the Clinton Era. Aidan McMurray died two years later after giving up a long fight with cancer and his exposure to Agent Orange during his second tour in Vietnam. The Veterans Administration's poor treatment of his grandfather and other Vietnam era veterans soured Sean personally on the war mongering militarism associated with the U.S. intrusions into Iraq and Afghanistan.

Sean felt the same boyhood thrill run through his body as he recognized the various famous Washington landmarks from his trip with his grandfather. Washington was still a vibrant and exciting city.

One could easily sense the powerful presence of the nations leaders past and present as he took his run down the National Mall, pass the Smithsonian, under the towering Washington Monument, across the new World War II Memorial, and along the Reflection Pool to the Lincoln Memorial. The twilight hours brought out hordes of military types in their close-cut hair, running in small packs in locked step. The heat of the day was wearing off but the humidity gave Sean the opportunity to work-up a good sweat. He held his usual pace of five & half-minute miles despite the distraction of the memories and the amazing sites he passed.

Sean sprinted up the steps of the memorial and stopped under the seated marble statue of Abraham Lincoln gazing over the Reflective Pool. From this vantage point, to his right was the Potomac River, before him the Washington Monument and Mall were an amazing sight giving one an absolute sense of awe. There was so much history presented in the nation's capitol. He had seen the video of Martin Luther King Jr. giving his "*I Have A Dream*" speech from this very spot on numerous occasions. Sean turned to his right looking over the Potomac River with the Arlington National Cemetery beyond. He recognized that so many had sacrificed so much for the freedom, liberty and rights that most Americans just took for granted in their day-to-day lives. It had been a long time since Sean remembered having these feelings. As an adult, he had a slow but steady change of heart, becoming more and more cynical about the faulty decision-making and leadership during the Bush Era failing to find the weapons of mass destruction (WMD) in Iraq, and both President Obama's and President Reynolds' military missions in Afghanistan, Pakistan, and Yemen. The simplistic idealism of Sean's youth came rushing back as he sat for a moment on the marble steps. To his left he saw the dim dark image of the black marble Vietnam Memorial through the trees. He wondered if he had the courage to visit it again without facing a flood of memories of his grandfather's suffering.

——

An attractive brunette broke the mood stating, "I get choked up too standing here and looking back at the Mall and Capitol in the distance. It makes me feel a debt of gratitude." Sean turned to see the source of the intrusion. A slim young woman dressed in running attire, hair pulled back in a tight ponytail, was standing a few feet away. Her words were as if reading Sean's mind. Sean smiled.

"I hope you don't mind my intrusion, but I have been running behind you at the same pace him for the last two miles. It is hard to find a non-military runner that sets a good pace. I just could not help myself as I saw the emotion in your expression."

Sean detected the faint aroma of vanilla. Her huge dark curls were matted to her forehead and around her ears. Her well fitting gray Georgetown Hoya tee shirt covered her slight form and somehow made her even more attractive. She had colorful Asics Excite-3 gel running shoes with a touch of gray matching her tee shirt and her runner's shorts. Sean thought *she is a serious runner that pays attention to her appearance even when jogging.* His focus shifted up to her cautious smile and crystal blue eyes.

"Not at all, I just haven't had that feeling in such a long time," he told her. "My political leanings have not been aligned with them since the conservative militarism of George W, Cheney, and Rumsfeld crews. I have been much more aligned with Obama administration and Reynolds's policies. I'd thought that any of my boyhood feelings of patriotism were lost forever, and then they bubbled up to the surface."

"Oh, my," she mused, "I've run across an intellectual liberal pacifist here in D.C. I guess Homeland Security neglected to screen you out at the airport.

But maybe President Reynolds imported you in a vain attempt to return the capital to some form of rational balance."

"Well, I heard the D.C. borders were open again, so I popped in for a few days!"

"Well stranger, do I detect a western mentality? Welcome to these parts and the Mecca of our political dysfunctional establishments." She offered her hand after a quick wipe on her shorts, "I'm Kathryn, a rare local subversive progressive."

Sean was surprised by the strength and firmness of her petite hand. He looked into her deep blue eyes and smiled again.

"I'm Sean," he said, "It's a pleasure to meet my first real Washingtonian. I'm an easterner by birth, but living and working on our far left coast. It is far more aligned with my current political thinking."

Inside his head, Sean was wondering just who was talking to this attractive woman. He had always been somewhat shy and bashful around attractive women. More often than not he felt awkward with dealings with the opposite sex, other than in his purely professional relationships. He wasn't into the bar scenes, coffee shops, or fix-up's by friends or colleagues, so he was semi-resigned to being a nerd bachelor for the foreseeable future. His work was his passion and feared that a woman would find this difficult to manage within a relationship. This flirting dialogue was so out of character for him, but seemed to be coming easier and easier without much thought on his part. He thought *I've got to just relax and enjoy the moment, otherwise you will blow it..*

"Oh don't get me wrong, Sean, I'm not a Washingtonian. I was born and raised in Georgetown, a small liberal enclave just west of here. We live in the District of Columbia, but shun the Washingtonian label. I'm also a doctoral student in International Affairs at Georgetown University, which is under the auspices of the good old liberal Jesuits."

"Kathryn, are you responsible for greeting all joggers that seem in awe of DC's sights or just those you suspect to have liberal leanings?"

Kathryn begins stretching on three steps, "No, I'm very selective. I've had so many negative experiences with the jughead marines and military types from the Pentagon, that just seeing someone with longer hair, an athletic stride, and a warm smile made me want to do my civic duty and welcome you to the northern bank of the Potomac."

"So you have been stalking me. Should I be calling the Park Police?"

"I do like a man that has a sense of humor. I don't think you need the police just yet. I'm basically harmless, unless you take a political position opposite of my own, then watch out. I did follow you at a distance trying to determine whether you were jogging alone."

The fatigue and jet lag had evaporated immediately as Sean quickly responded, "Perhaps we should determine if our politics are really compatible or a ruse. After all, there are all different flavors of liberals and self-proclaimed progressives. I am from California the land of political fruits and plenty of nuts. Besides I have been warned that DC has nine single females for every eligible male.

Are there eight more single women out here running the Mall to meet me? Our meeting could be just a pretense to find liberals and turn them in to the National Republican Party." Again the voice deep within him *questioned just who was this guy making small talk with this woman. He felt a new sense of confidence as he watched himself in what almost seemed like an out of body experience.*

"I do like and respect a man who is direct," Kathryn said. "I just think that if the chemistry is right, one should pursue one's initial impressions. You know the whole concept of going with your gut being usually right. You seem like an intelligent guy, a rare thing compared to the military GED types in these parts or the pencil pushing bureaucrats trying to escape from their government cubicles and hooking up with local women while their wives are home with the kids in Virginia."

"Looks can be deceiving,' Sean said raising his eyebrows. "You assume our politics might be simpatico, but I could be a criminal or a pervert for all you know." Sean *almost kicked himself for that off-the-wall comment, wishing he could somehow retract or better yet delete it. Where is Groundhog Day when you need it?*

"I don't think you're a criminal or pervert, but I will be cautious." Kathryn smirked. "I've always felt that nothing ventured, nothing gained! I like to live on the edge. Would you like to meet later for coffee or a drink?" Kathryn looked Sean up and down. "Besides following Schwarzenegger's commitment to three strikes policy and his ability to build and fill twice as many prisons as his predecessors, your liberal Governor Jerry Brown has set all the druggies, muggers, and criminal element in California free due to overcrowding and early release programs.

The criminal element won't think of leaving California because once arrested, you would be set free in weeks. So you must be okay."

"Jerry has been cleaning up the state and basically restoring civil rights as he is doing it. But that's another discussion. I'm at the Marriott Hotel on 12th Street near the corner of H Street. When and where should we meet for that drink?" Sean was pleased that she took the initiative. He looked at his new FitBit Surge sports watch, a present to himself that had a load of scientific functions. "It's 7:15 right now."

"How about a little Russian Bistro called Maxim's in Foggy Bottom at 8:45. It's located at "1725 East F Street, not far from your hotel. Technically it is in Georgetown, so we should be safe talking trash about the Conservatives and the Tea Party." Kathryn smiled and tilted her head slightly asking, " I didn't catch your last name? "

"It's McMurray, and yours?" Sean smiled.

"McCarthy. See you at Maxim's at 8:45."

"Sounds good, see you then unless you are just playing me." Sean watched as she ran off towards the famous Watergate complex and Georgetown beyond.

Kathryn turned with a smile, "Oh you would know if I was playing you."

Sean smiled to himself not sure how the previous exchange happened, but comfortable with the interesting development. He turned to run along the Reflective Pool, but at the last second turned left and ran past the Vietnam Memorial. Thinking to himself, "This is for you grandpa. I'll always remember you and your service in Vietnam."

Sean finished his run with a nice cooling breeze hit him as he passed the Jefferson Memorial, circled the Tidal Basin and headed to his hotel. He would need to hurry it was 7:45 already.

The short run back to the hotel and hot shower completely revived Sean. In fact he was feeling great physically and a bit strange emotionally. He still was in shock over the way he had flirted with Kathryn. A new confidence was coursing through his veins, and that feeling in itself was a new experience. Sean felt competent and confident in so many areas of his life, but this was new and unexplored territory.

It took Sean barely twenty minutes to walk to Maxim's in Foggy Bottom. He broke a small sweat and was unsure if it was from the brisk walk in 85% humidity or his nerves on the impending meeting with Kathryn. He arrived early and found a small cocktail table adjacent to the bar area where he had an unobstructed view of the rather dated and well-worn entrance. Mazim's must have been a popular watering hole for the DC bureaucrats much further than a few years back. It certainly needed to be updated.

At 8:45 p.m. on the dot, Kathryn walked through the door. He had been initially attracted to her intellect and witty sense of humor, but as they talked he became acutely aware of how her physical appearance played a growing part in his attraction. He had not been overwhelmed, tongue tied or simply evasive, as was his norm in these type situations. Functioning exceptionally well in the classroom, with colleagues, and in giving presentations, Sean felt, awkward and all thumbs in dealing socially with women on a social level.

Kathryn's ponytail and tee shirt had been replaced by shoulder length hair with a slight curl at the tips, and a short blue dress that clung to her upper body and swung along her thighs as she walked. She was taller in her four-inch heels. Kathryn wore light make-up and that amazing scent of vanilla. Kathryn was a vision of loveliness. Sean got choked up just thinking about how he was going to pull off the continuation of his conversation with this beautiful woman walking towards him.

"This meeting maybe doomed to failure." He fretted.

Kathryn smiled as she approached the table, "Well at least you didn't stand me up like some of the bonehead marines." Kathryn paused as she took her seat, "It is amazing how an articulate woman with half a brain and opinions that conflicts with the typical military mentality can put a 220 pound muscle bound macho man into a tailspin." Picking up her menu, "Most of the non-military males in Washington are married and live in the burbs of Maryland or Virginia, not that most of them don't try to impress the local single girls. The fact is that women outnumber men almost fifteen to one. I was somewhat surprised that you didn't have a pack of single women running after you."

Sean was not able to take his eyes off her as she gracefully seated herself. Thinking to himself, *Dam I should have held the chair for her.* Sean blurred out, "I cannot see how any guy in his right mind would ever pass up the opportunity to have a drink with an intelligent liberal Georgetown grad student. On second thought perhaps I should run on the mall again tomorrow and see if I can attract a pack of ladies. There may be more fish along the banks of the Potomac." Sean again questioned himself silently, *Where in hell did that line come from? Fish...really.*

"I will give you a pass on the fish comment. So you like liberals. I guess we will just have to see how liberal you really are. My aunt always warned me to watch out for closet libertarians and conservatives in liberal clothing. Male wolves will say anything to impress a woman to get them in bed. Why are some men such jerks?"

"That's a tough question. Before I try to answer it defending my gender, and we get started on the liberal test, I think we need to order our drinks."

"Sure," Kathryn said looking at the wine list, "I would like the 1996 Beringer Merlot. I usually prefer the Beringer to other Merlots; it's my absolute favorite. What do you usually drink?"

"I usually prefer a Merlot like a 2001 Adobe Creek. The winery is a small relatively unknown vineyard in Sonoma County that has produced some world-class wines. They have the Beringer 1996, but not the Adobe Creek on their list. I will try the Beringer."

Sean got the waitress's attention and ordered drinks.

"Preferring wine over a domestic beer or microbrew. Nice taste Sean. Now let's get some of the basic background out of the way before the big test. Why don't you start first?"

Sean wasn't sure how much he should disclose about himself. Immediately he decided to downplay his intellectual prowess and academics. He thought *this was a potentially dangerous discussion. Being too egotistical might be a real turn-off for her. Be careful, Sean, you could blow this real easily. Tread lightly.*

"Let me begin I was born in western New York. My parents were killed in a car accident when I was ten." Kathryn's eyes widened at the revelation. "My first generation Irish-Scottish American grandparents raised me to be a good Catholic. Aidan, my grandfather was career military and a huge influence on my life. I'm in good health with a healthy life-style, don't smoke or use drugs, and I hate to go to the dentist. I have been a vegetarian for five years, but I fall off the wagon every once and awhile and have fish. I'm allergic to MSG, love spinach, and currently distrust GMOs. I'm well educated, financially secure, employed the past six years as a faculty member at Cal-Tech in Pasadena. I'm hoping for tenure this year. I love my work and living in Southern California. When I'm not working my favorite pastimes are serious rock climbing and running. I drive a silver 2009 Chrysler PT Cruiser convertible. I guess that it is bound to become a classic now that they no longer make them. The Cruiser barely holds all my climbing gear. I love classical and turn-of-the-century art deco architecture and subscribe to Architectural Digest. I shop and dress myself as you can see. I am single and not in a relationship. I live alone in a condo in South Pasadena. What you see is the real me. Now it's your turn."

Kathryn had been listening intently "Very interesting," she said, "we certainly have more than a few things in common as you will see." A slight smile crept across her face as she gazed into Sean's deep brown eyes.

The waitress appeared with their wine and menus. "Can I get you something, or do you need a minute to review the menu."

"Please give us a minute, I would like a light appetizer," Kathryn said

"Yes," Sean nodded, "something light will hit the spot."

"I'll give you a moment to review our menu. I could give you the entree specials if you like."

Sean answered looking at Kathryn to see if she had any interest in hearing the specials. "No thanks. Just give us a minute." The waitress retreated across the room to the bar.

"Where to start," Kathryn said.

"Say whatever comes to mind," Sean suggested.

"Alright, I'm twenty-six, born here in George Washington University Hospital. My mother died during childbirth. My father was a colonel in the Air Force. He was a computer instructor at the Air Force Academy for eight years. My dad was posted around the world with tours in Japan, Florida, Germany, England, Vietnam, and the Pentagon. He spent most of his free-time teaching me about computers and various uses of electronics and technology. He died in a small Cirrus T-53 trainer aircraft crash. I was fourteen. My single aunt took care of me when it was impossible to join my dad during some of dad's deployments. She raised me like a mother and adopted me legally after my dad passed. For high school, I was lucky enough to attend Foxcroft, a boarding school in Middleburg, Virginia. I ran cross-country and hanged out with the school nerds. Then I attended Princeton for a BA in Political Science with a minor in Computer Science. I got my MBA in International Finance from Bryn Mawr. Now I'm in my third year at Georgetown working on my doctoral in International Relations. I am a teaching assistant with three 201 level Political Science classes in the Walsh School of Foreign Service.

If all goes well, I may finish my dissertation and defend my thesis in November. My hero is one of my professors, Madeline Albright. I'm single, been in only one real long-term relationship. He split, unable to make a real commitment. I have tried vegan, but found my cravings for meat protein too overwhelming. I play coed volleyball in a league two nights a week, and just started climbing in an indoor gym. I've always wanted to attempt some granite climbs in New Hampshire, but do not have enough experience under my belt. I love to travel mostly to South America, Asia and Africa. Living with my dad in foreign postings and ravel always fed my interest in international relations and politics. I hope to serve in the diplomatic corps or find a position in a NGO to help refugees in disaster stricken countries. I love sushi. I drive a refurbished 1974 white VW bug convertible. VW collectors consider my model VW bug a classic. I drive it as little as possible due to the impossible parking situation in Georgetown. My bike is my lifeline between school and my aunt's brownstone. I still live with my aunt and love working in her garden. I read mysteries and biographies. I have no allergies. I guess that's it..... Oh I forgot, I'm a major geek. I love computer hacking. One of the many passions I inherited from my father. Sorry, Sean, I've given you way too much information for our first real meeting."

Sean said, "Amazing that we both are orphans that rose to the challenge from an early age and ended up in academia. Important family members with a career military background." He found himself genuinely fascinated and amazed.

The waitress saw the break in the conversation and approached with a small basket of warm rolls and butter, "Are you ready to order or do you need more time?"

"I'll have the small prawn salad with Thousand Island dressing. Thank you." Kathryn had not looked at the menu, so she obviously had eaten here before.

Sean looked at the waitress's nametag, "Joyce," he said, " I'll have the coconut shrimp with a mixed green salad, honey mustard dressing on the side, please."

"We still have not resolved the male jerk phenomena." Kathryn smiled as she broke off half of a homemade dinner roll and applied a small pad of real butter. "Then again I guess there really isn't a solution. Is there?" At this point Kathryn wasn't sure that they should continue this topic. She'd look for a way to change the topic.

"You're right," Sean said, "Some men give the rest of the gender a bad reputation. They play games, lie and cheat and make unethical promises they have no intention to fulfill. They can be real jerks, but women can be just as deceptive, manipulative and unethical too."

There was a bit of tension in the air as Kathryn responded, "Granted, but in my view a vast majority of the players are males."

Sean took a sip of the Merlot and decided to change the topic if Kathryn permitted. "How about moving on to your liberal test?" With a somewhat uneasy smile, hoping she'd accept the new change of direction.

"Of course you are right. I know men don't want to talk about such matters. If you are ready here comes my test! What is your position on abortion; capital punishment; euthanasia; welfare and entitlements; three strikes laws; immigration; maternity and paternity leave; gay rights and marriages; cost of prescription drugs in the USA; access to medical care; the Supreme Court's ruling on undisclosed campaign contributions and Citizens United; NRA position on 2nd Amendment gun rights; and justice and penal system reforms?" Kathryn took a slow sip of wine waiting for Sean to respond and watching him as he processed the plethora of topics.

Sean was ready to comment but was interrupted by the waitress delivering their light meals. "Can I get you anything else?" she asked.

Saved by the waitress, Sean bought some time by responding, "No, I think we are all set for now. Thank you"

"Bon Appetite" The waitress retreated to take the drink order of a nearby table of distinguished well-dressed men in suits discussing the phenomenal success of Steven Strasburg, the Washington Nationals pitcher.

"You've given me a very serious test here." Sean said, "What do I have to do to pass?"

"I think 80% or better qualifies you as a real liberal," Kathryn replied. "So get busy. I'm going to dive into the prawn salad while you answer. Good luck."

Sean looked into Kathryn's intense blue eyes and knew that she was serious, but in a kidding manner. *I just hope my honesty shows through and I don't blow this.* "Here I go."

Sean cleared his throat and began the test. "I agree that a woman has the right to choose what happens with her own body, but would state that unless it threatens the life of the mother an abortion should be performed before the last trimester. I oppose capital punishment and feel we need to build better education systems rather than more prisons. I believe that humans should be able to make a decision about the end of their life after counseling much like in the Netherlands. Everyone should have easy access to good quality medical care. I feel that welfare has numerous problems, but again the solution is a good education and jobs for everyone not just those able to afford private schools or live in good public school areas. I'm opposed to any three strikes laws. I believe in maternity and paternity leave for 6-8 months as in Sweden. I believe in the right of gays to marry and to have the same rights and benefits as a legal spouse. I believe in the American dream and the right of all immigrants to pursue it. I believe that drug companies are making billions off the poor, elderly, and government. They rank just under insurance companies as having the worse scams in our economy. I think that campaign contributions should be fully disclosed to avoid having contributors exert influence on elected officials leading to corruption. I support term limits of not more than 12 years. I think that we have a right to life trumps the right to own automatic weapons. We rely on cheap immigrant labor, but have not shown them a pathway to citizenship." Sean took a deep breath. "So, how did I do?"

"Take a bite of your coconut shrimp before it gets too cold," Kathryn advised. "My preliminary assessment is that you are either the real thing or an expert at reading what I my expectations of how a true liberal would respond. Are you a psychology professor?" Kathryn smiled.

"Actually I'm a nuclear physicist," Sean answered, enjoying his shrimp. "Everything I told you is my real opinion in assessing the issues facing the political landscape. How do I stack up with your liberalistic test and personal positions?"

"Lets say that you went way past the 80% mark," Kathryn smiled again, "and while under considerable pressure." Kathryn's body language showed her interest. Sean's eyes drifted down to her breast. He could see the outline of her nipples through the light material of her dress. The AC made it apparent that Kathryn was not wearing a bra under her frock.

"I see you don't mind my liberalism in my attire." Kathryn said, noticing Sean's focus well beneath her eyes. She blushed slightly. "You have been more than patient indulging me. Lets enjoy our evening together. By the way, just how long are you in town?" Kathryn gave a warm smile, then focused on her salad.

"I have a late flight on Friday night, but will anticipate being back several times over the next eight months or more."

"I had assumed that you were here for business. I bet it is government related given the location of your hotel. What do you do as a nuclear physicist?"

"I'm working on an innovative nuclear power plant design project that is just starting. There isn't much more I can tell you without violating the code of secrecy and being shot or whisked away to a secret location by the CIA and FBI."

Kathryn laughed and focused on eating her meal. "Seems like every guy in this city uses the same line about a code of secrecy, and here I thought you were real."

"I didn't think of that, but mine isn't a pick-up line," Sean said in a serious tone. "My project is part of a unique monitoring design that makes nuclear power plant safer on numerous levels."

"Relax Sean, I was just pushing your buttons. I like to keep my dates on their toes." Kathryn reached across the table and held Sean's hand before going back to eating her salad.

The touch was electrifying as a warm feeling coursed through Sean's body. His internal introspection continued as he thought, *you almost blew it with the most beautiful intelligent woman you have ever met. I think her touching my hand is a good sign. Try not to sweat. Don't you dare mess this up, Sean*! Sean put down his fork and took Kathryn's hand with both of his hands for a second. "Seems like us liberals need to hang together and provide mutual support in this bastion of conservatism."

Sean finished his shrimp in a flash after enjoying the house salad. He later had no recollection of how it tasted. He felt energized, and the fact that he was enjoying an evening out with a beautiful woman. She was intriguing, intelligent, with a keen sense of humor. The moment lapsed as Kathryn slowly pulled her hand away and resumed eating her prawn salad and sipping her wine, as her eyes studied Sean's face.

After finishing Sean reached across the small table and took Kathryn's hand again. He hadn't thought about the gesture, it just felt so natural. Both were engrossed in their conversation and didn't acknowledge this small act of intimacy on his part.

———

Several hours later the evening ended with Sean walking hand in hand with Kathryn to her aunt's brownstone home in Georgetown. They talked the entire way and laughed at the Republican politicians from the past thirty years. The recurring cast of Ronald Reagan, George Bush, Dick Cheney, Donald Rumsfeld, John Boehner, Mitch McConnell, John McCain, Ted Cruz, Marco Rubio, Donald Trump, Paul Ryan, Donald Trump and the Tea Party seemed easy prey.

As they parted Sean asked if Kathryn was free on Thursday night. Kathryn was enthusiastic and gave Sean her cell number. She suggested that they run together at 5 p.m. and then load-up with carbs at a little Italian restaurant around the corner from Sean's hotel. Then in a flash she kissed him on the cheek and disappeared behind a beautiful natural oak door with an inserted stained glass window, amazing brass knocker and doorknob. If it were not for trying to process this last moment with Kathryn's kiss, Sean was sure he'd have been studying the architectural accouterment of the fantastic spider web Georgian window, a special aspect of brownstones. He had only seen pictures of the features in architecture books and magazines. Pasadena certainly did not have anything like this authentic late 18th century structure.

Kathryn was not like any other woman Sean had ever met. He was so comfortable with her. Their conversation was easy and seamless. In his heart, he wished the evening had never ended. Then reality popped into the picture. Sean caught a cab on Wisconsin Avenue after realizing that it was 1:15 a.m. and he had a meeting at 9 a.m.

Chapter 7: London's Increased Security
Thursday, May 6, 8:00 a.m. ADT (UTC/GMT +3)
Al Zagaheer Television Studio 1, Doha, Qatar

As the Nuru prepared her notes, she got the usual signal alerting that you are about to go on air, as the Production Director pointed at her. "This is Nuru Monaga reporting from our *Al Zagaheer* studios in Doha, Qatar. Anonymous governmental sources reported that counter terrorism and intelligence agencies around the world have significantly heightened levels of security as a result of an extraordinary increase in cell phone chatter related to threats against London bridges. The obvious problem is how does the United Kingdom keep London's 13.5 million residets safe by protecting all thirty-two bridges across the Thames without impacting daily life."

Nuru cuts away as UK Correspondent Arthur Dennis, appears live on the screen with a London Tower Bridge in view in the background.

Dennis began his segment immediately, "As you can see military troops on duty securing the iconic Tower Bridge behind me." The camera shot switched to showing troops and armor vehicles on the south access to the bridge. "London has increased the armed security on all thirty-two London bridges and the waterways of the Thames. The security has had a major impact on Londoners traveling by tube and rail across a London bridge as each train is stopped and quickly searched by troops and teams of specially trained sniffer dogs. Needless to say, the presence of the security forces has also increased public anxiety in the United Kingdom about the potential for a terrorist attack. An estimated 1800 British Army troops are on 24 hours a day security duty on the bridges and an additional 18 patrol boats are highly visible on the waterways."

The video cut from the bridge to a patrol boat with mounted machine guns swiftly moving towards the camera. "London seems well prepared for any terrorist attack, but Londoners appear more than anxious about the threat. This is Arthur Dennis reporting from London for Al Zaga, the number one news source in the Middle East."

Following the report from London, there was a *Great Books* commercial featuring young Muslim children and a grandparent reading an Arabian fairy tale. Parents and grandparents were encouraged to order the series immediately at a special 30% savings.

Chapter 8: National Nuclear Security Meeting
Thursday, May 6, 7:15 a.m. EST (UTC/GMT-6)
Marriott Hotel and Offices of National Nuclear Security, Washington, DC.

Sean slept like a baby. The hotel phone rang at exactly 7:15 a.m., Sean picked up the phone and was confronted by an overzealous real voice on the other end, "Good morning Dr. McMurray. This is your 7:15 a.m. wakeup call. Have a nice day." The phone went silent almost as abruptly as the initial ring. A second later, Sean's iPad alarm rang. It was his contingency in the event he missed his wakeup call. It was one of Sean's traits to always provide for a backup in the event that the primary system failed.

During a slow hot shower Sean reflected again on his meeting and evening with Kathryn. *What a lucky set of circumstances*, he thought. *We were so simpatico on so many different levels. Meeting her was by far one of my best personal non-professional encounters since before high school..*

Sean walked the short distance to the Department of Energy, cleared their medium security area, and was directed to the National Nuclear Security Office on the fourth floor. Where there was a metal detector and another security check before entering the offices. After checking in with the receptionist, Sean took a seat in the large foyer decorated with large photos of several nuclear plant facilities and the interior of a nuclear plant control room. Sean recognized three of the four facilities.

Five minutes later, Dr. Bennett appeared from a large French door to the left of the reception desk. He approached Sean offering his hand. "Dr. McMurray, welcome to our NNS office. It is a pleasure to see you again. I hope you had a pleasant flight?"

Shaking hands, Sean replied, "Thanks. The flight from LAX was okay," Sean thought more deeply about the trip and replied. "It was on time and without any weather issues. I did have a baby in the seat directly behind me that cried during both take off and landing. Other than that, it was fine."

"Good to hear, as long flights can be quite uncomfortable." Dr. Bennett stated. "Here," as he handed Sean a laminated bar coded NNS identification badge with Sean's picture. "You will need this badge for each of our meetings. Please follow me. The task force is assembled in our executive conference room."

Sean clipped the badge to his suit coat pocket. He immediately recognized his picture as being the one he submitted with his grant proposal to the Nuclear Regulatory Commission in 2014.

Dr. Bennett led Sean to a private elevator. He swiped his security card to activate the elevator for the short trip up to the seventh floor. They exited and took the corridor to the left, and entered the large oak paneled executive conference room. The room was well equipped with multiple eight-foot screens for video conferencing and presentations. The biggest feature of the room was an amazing view of the White House, the Eclipse, and the Washington Monument in the distance.

A very well dressed woman with radiant red hair pulled neatly in a tight bun moved forward and offered her hand. Sean recognized her immediately. After their extremely brief phone conversation, he had carefully researched Dr. Grace Gibson online.

She was a noted "wunderkind" at M.I.T. Before turning 21, she earned her BS, MS and PhD in Applied Physics. She then completed another doctorate in Electrical Engineering while teaching Physics at M.I.T. At the young age of 30, she was recruited to join the faculty at Princeton to fill a newly created endowed Physics chair. She was nominated for a Nobel Prize in Physics for innovative theory on cold fusion, and also served as a member and later Chair for the National Endowment for the Sciences. Anything she pursued brought her accolades and honors. President Reynolds was very fortunate to have been able to attract this uniquely talented scientist into government service after she declined multimillion-dollar commercial offers in the nuclear energy industry. At 58, she was an accomplished talented woman with style and panache making her appear to be a lot younger than her age. She had lost her husband to lung cancer a few years back and had not remarried. Her physical attributes and stylish outfit gave her the distinguished appearance of the professional class, accustomed to power and success. Her trim figure, graceful movement, reddish hair and bright blue-eyed smile gave her the complete and perfect look.

"Welcome, Dr. McMurray, it is nice to finally meet you. I'm Dr. Grace Gibson, I'm Director of the Office of National Nuclear Security, but please call me Grace. May I address you as, Sean?" Not waiting, Grace continued, "Let me introduce you to several of your nuclear colleagues Dr. Theodore Powers, Dr. Randolph Ford and Dr. James Leary. They have served the NNS over the past three years on a special Task Force to make our nuclear facilities safer."

Sean shook hands with each of the Task Force members. He had met Randy and James most recently at a forum held at M.I.T. last year. Ted Powers had been a nuclear guru who had written several books that Sean had read over the years. They had been corresponding by mail since he was 12. Sean met him face to face for the first time three years earlier at a NRC conference.

Ted extended his hand with a big smile, "Sean, it is a real pleasure having you aboard. I hope your postdoc work can change the paradigm for NNS."

"It is good to see you again Ted," Sean shook his extended hand. "I am honored to have this amazing opportunity."

Grace continued her introduction. "The Task Force group of nuclear experts has taken on the challenge of making our nuclear facilities significantly more secure. As my father always said; "Never start a challenge on an empty stomach," so, let's take a few minutes to get further acquainted over coffee and a light breakfast. Please help your selves. Grace revealed a long table set at the end of the room that had enough food to feed a group four times their size.

"It is a pleasure to meet you again, Sean." Randy stated. "I'm so pleased that we were able to convince NNS to pursue your Redundancy System Design. It is a huge step towards making our facilities more secure." Randy stated as he filled his coffee cup with decaf. "Would you care for decaf? At my age I just cannot handle the pure jolt of caffeine any longer."

"No thanks, I appreciate that caffeine jolt in the morning."

"Here is the high octane. Help yourself. I'm looking forward to working with you through the completion of the project. James will be the onsite coordinator with NSA for your satellite links. I think you will really enjoy working with James. He is an excellent resource and sounding board for any issues that may arise."

Before he could respond, James approached Sean. "These fruit tarts are amazing. I'll have to get the name of the patisserie and take a box home to my wife, please try one!" James took a seat next to Sean.

"I'm trying to be good and avoid all the high caloric items," Sean replied. Especially the ones laced with sugar. This bran muffin will do me just fine. Randy has been telling me about your NSA role in supporting my project. How are you doing James?"

"Excellent, I am enjoying life as my youngest son just graduated from Amherst. I established a policy that our kids pay for their own graduate school experiences, so Alice and I are tuition free for the first time in twenty-five years. With that off my mind, I cannot wait to get this project rolling and completed."

"I'm impressed. How many kids do you have?" Sean asked.

"Four sons and three daughters. Alice came from a large family and we decided early on in our marriage that a full house was the way to go. Probably the most expensive decision I've ever made, but I'd do it again in a flash.

I appreciate Randy filling you in on my role of coordinator with NSA satellite links. The decision to have me be the coordinator really was a no brainer. I worked for NSA on satellite surveillance of foreign nuclear sites and have numerous friends in their satellite division. Seeing how your design has critical points with NSA, I am sure I can facilitate whatever you need."

Grace approached, holding a bowl of fruit topped with bright kiwi slices. At that moment Sean became aware of the scent of Grace's perfume, she asked, "Sean, how are you finding the East coast?" she asked.

"Just fine, I have not been in Washington for a number of years, actually since I was a boy. DC is an incredible historic and cultural city. I wish I had more time on this trip. Perhaps I will get an opportunity in the near future. How long have you lived here?" Sean inquired.

"My husband bought a beautiful brownstone house over twenty years ago, I moved into it four years ago. I'm still learning my way around and trying to see everything. By the way, this mixed fruit salad is really delicious. Have you tried it?"

"I have not, but I will. I love a wide variety of fruit. I'll usually quadruple the recommended daily portion of fruit. Thanks for the suggestion."

"Yes, I'm guilty as well. I've become a vegan recently, although I still have a mild craving for protein from time to time. Beans and tofu can be a challenge. I hope you enjoy your stay. I am sure our future meetings will give you a chance to really explore the city."

"I'm pleased to be here," said Sean. Grace moved on to speak with Randy.

Ted forked two fresh rings of pineapple from Maui and added them to his already piled high plate of melons, strawberries and kiwis. He spoke as Sean served himself the fruit salad. "It is nice to see you again after all these years." Ted smiled as he spread cream cheese on a warm cinnamon raison bagel. "The guys at the Nuclear Regulatory Agency would die if they saw this spread. They just don't have the budget allocations that Grace gets here due to Homeland Security funding."

"I am pleased to be here and see you again. This continental breakfast buffet is better than the Marriott sans the omelet chef."

"Excuse me, Sean," Grace interrupted. "We are a little pressed for time. I understand that you have selected your Cal-Tech team and are prepared to make a presentation. Jamie, my assistant here, will help with whatever you need."

Sean took the final bite of fruit with a sip of his coffee. He arose quickly, set up his MacBook Air adjacent to the projection system, and asked for the Wi-Fi code and logged in. "I'm all set whenever you would like to begin."

"Excellent, lets get started," Grace announced. "I would like to finish up with the initial presentation by lunch. Jamie will distribute a menu from a local deli. If you write your name at the top and circle your selection, she will have everything ready for a working lunch around 1 p.m. We need to end the meeting before 4 p.m. so Dr. Leary and Dr. Ford can catch their flights."

Task Force members made their lunch selection quickly as Jamie picked up their orders and disappeared into the adjacent office area.

Sean spent the next three hours presenting the fundamentals of the Redundancy System, the backgrounds of his Cal-Tech Team, their areas of expertise, and their roles in the project. Then he followed up with the current design elements of the Redundancy System, as well as the enormous simulation testing that had been conducted on the system and the data collected. The task force members seemed impressed, as the newer system was far more developed from the original model they were familiar with. Sean finished up by focusing on the time line for the beta test installation in Arizona. The presentation was interrupted from time to time with technical clarification questions and specifics about the video interface with the NSA satellite system and NNS. A major point during the morning sessions was the Task Force approval of the Palo Verde facility for testing the redundancy system.

Lunch was a blur for Sean, after finishing his presentation he was having difficulty trying to focus without thinking about his date with Kathryn.

Following lunch, Dr. Bennett joined the Task Force. He had prearranged for a video conference call with Dr. Lawrence Grant, Director of the Palo Verde Nuclear Facility; and Daniel Hoppe, Plant Security Director. After twenty minutes, the secretive arrangements were confirmed for the Cal-Tech team's installation of the system. Dr. Grant was very excited to have Palo Verde be the first nuclear facility with the new security system. Hoppe assured the Task Force that just a minimum of key security personnel would be aware of the team's presence within the facility and the installation project. He would facilitate and interface with the Cal-Tech team during all phases of the project. Proper arrangements were made for direct contact with the facility and Cal-Tech team.

Grace thanked them for their willingness to be the beta test site for the system. Dr. Grant was more than gracious in underlining the importance of heightening the security of his facility and appreciating the opportunity to beta test the system. Grant was very aware of Sean's research and looked forward to seeing the project to completion.

After the conference call, Dr. Bennett pulled Sean aside to confirm that the packet of paperwork he had submitted had two areas that had to be resubmitted to meet the Government Accounting Office (GAO) requirements. "The documents need to be completed and submitted to my office at NNS as soon as possible." Dr. Bennett confirmed that the NNS line of credit was in place and the Cal-Tech team was able to draw on the account. He would be working with Sean on necessary accounting for the NNS project funds.

Sean had always disliked the bureaucratic red tape and paperwork involved in applying for grants and special projects. He was surprised that out of the 29 pages submitted only two did not meet with Bennett's or GAO approval. He smiled to himself perhaps the importance of the design project had some additional benefits.

At the end of the meeting Grace asked Sean to see her for a few minutes in her private office. As they entered, Sean noticed that it did not feel like a government office. It had a lot of personal touches, impressionist paintings, lilac color walls that set a subdued tone, indirect lighting, and bookshelves. Sean thought that *the fact that she was unmarried might indicate that she was not bound very tightly to her family.* There were no family pictures on her desk or displayed in the office. Clearly the time demands of her position would have made having a family difficult.

Perhaps the biggest surprise was that there was no computer on her desk, nor any impressive display of degrees that frequent the walls of the less secure bureaucrats. Her reputation made the usual display of academic degrees and honors unnecessary. Grace had taken this typical government office and created a unique work place that reflected her personality, taste, and professionalism.

"Care for a soft drink," Grace offered. "Water, tea, coffee or any other beverage?"

"No, thanks."

"Excuse me if I have some water." Grace poured a glass from an ice filled pitcher on the credenza. "Please, make yourself comfortable on the sofa."

"I appreciate the effort you and your staff have made to make us feel comfortable for the meeting," Sean said, sitting on the sofa. "You have been a very gracious host."

"Well thank you." Grace said joining Sean on the sofa. "I'm very impressed with both the quality of your design, but also your enthusiasm and organization of your Cal-Tech team. Had you ever thought about doing any government work before agreeing to join our task force?"

"No, I really had not entertained the thought of working in the public sector simply because I'm not very good with the endless red tape of bureaucracy. I think it takes a certain personality to deal with multiple layers of red tape, political infighting, media scrutiny, funding delays and uncertainty, and the political favors. I guess over the years I've become cynical about varied levels of government work."

"So was I," Grace said, "I had some of the same serious qualms prior to taking on this position. One topic we did not discuss in the meeting is that after the installation and testing of the system in Arizona, subsequent funding will depend on our increased Homeland Security appropriations. So bureaucracy does make a slight demand on your project. Much of our future plans hinge on the Senate Intelligence Committee chaired by Senator Rex Nunn. You may help our cause if you meet with Senator Nunn after you have successfully initiated installing the system and firmed up testing dates. We are confident that the results will sell themselves. Nunn has a passion for clean energy and fears about the safety of our nuclear facilities."

"Sure," Sean nodded, "I would love to meet with Senator Nunn. Please let me know when and where."

"Excellent, Sean. This will be a great benefit to our task force. Since you will be in Phoenix conducting your beta testing. We have the opportunity for you to meet with Senator Nunn. My understanding is that he is scheduled to be in Phoenix attending the Homeland Security and OEM State Emergency Response Directors meeting the last weekend of August at the Phoenician Resort. I'll have my assistant Jamie confirm and make an appointment for you following the conference. He will provide you with all the details as soon as Nunn's staff confirms the meeting. I really appreciate your willingness to do this. In the long run having your redundancy system up and running in all our nuclear facilities will go a long way in making our country far safer."

"Thanks. I look forward to getting the meeting details and garnering Senator Nunn's support."

"I'd like to have another meeting of the Task Force after you have completed a preliminary check of the system in Reactor #1 before Beta testing. When do you think that will be?"

"If all goes well with my project timeline we should be at that stage in middle to end of August. I'll keep you posted as we get closer to that milepost."

Grace put down her glass and stood up. Sean immediately joined her sensing that their private meeting was over. "Thank you, Sean, for all your time, effort, and your excellent decision in joining us. I look forward to our next meeting. May I show you out?"

"It has been a pleasure, Grace. I appreciate your confidence and support of my work. That's not necessary. I can make my way out very easily."

Sean shook hands with Grace and let himself out of her inner office. Jamie was waiting outside with a large manila envelope containing the two pages that needed to be submitted to Dr. Bennett. She also walked him through both security checkpoints and collected his NNS identification badge. "Your badge will be ready for all your subsequent NNS visits," she said. "I hope you have a good trip back to LA." Jamie shook Sean's hand, turned, and entered the foyer elevator.

Sean left NNS at 4:15 p.m. He was elated at how things had gone in the meeting. He had intentionally given himself an additional day in the event that things did not go as well or required more time. He hoped he to spend the next day with Kathryn.

Chapter 9: The Second Date
Thursday, May 6, 4:45 p.m. EST (UTC/GMT-6)
Marriott Hotel, Washington, DC.
After arriving back at his hotel, Sean quickly showered, shaved, and changed into his running clothes. He was certain that he had applied more deodorant than necessary. Thank goodness he had an extra shirt to run in. As it approached 5 p.m., he found himself anxiously pacing and wondering what the next chapter of the fledgling relationship might bring. The hotel phone rang interrupting Sean's thought process.

"Hi Sean, are you ready?" Kathryn was in the lobby using the house phone.

"Sure, I've been looking forward to a workout. You know how daylong meetings can be. I'll be down in a minute."

"Would you mind if I dropped off a change of clothes in your room? The Italian pasta place I mentioned is just three blocks away, and it will give us more time together."

"Yes, please do. I'm in room 514."

Sean was immediately trying to think through what the change of clothes really meant. Kathryn would have to shower in his room given the early evening humidity. It seemed a bit forward on her part, but then again he was not at all surprised. He did not want to read into it anything more than Kathryn intended. Sean thought *I guess I just have to play it by ear.*

Five minutes later, Kathryn knocked on his door.

114

"Open up," she commanded. "We heard there was an alleged liberal in this hotel room. I'm conducting a door to door search for the National Republican Committee."

Sean laughed as he opened the door.

Kathryn stood in the hallway grinning. "Sir, I'm afraid you are under arrest for consorting with one of our confirmed local Georgetown liberals. That's a pretty serious charge in this town. What do you have to say for yourself?"

"Guilty as charged."

"Wait a minute, sir, I'll will give you one more chance to prove your innocence. No conservative in his right mind would ever wear this tee shirt. If you put it on I'll have to arrest you as a liberal. If you don't wear it you will be set free."

Kathryn held up her D.C. souvenir tee shirt. On the front was a picture of an elephant and a donkey. The print read, "Let's be friends. I'll shake your GOP Elephant's trunk if you kiss my Democratic Ass."

Sean grinned mightily. He grabbed the tee shirt, removed his, and put the obnoxious tee shirt on. "I'm afraid you will have to take me off to jail."

"Well, you have passed my final liberal test with flair, Dr. McMurray." Kathryn entered his room and kissed Sean on the cheek. She put down her knapsack, quickly removing a skirt and blouse, and hung them in the closet.

"Let's escape before the real conservative Gestapo make their appearance."

Sean headed out the door with Kathryn.

"Don't you need your key?" she asked.

"No, the hotel has a new security system where they scan a palm print when you register. Then your room door scanner confirms your palm and opens it without a key or card. Cool isn't it? I can hardly wait to tell my grad students. Us geeks are impressed with all the newest techy stuff. I'm not sure, but I think this security device has not hit the hotels along the west coast yet. It really should have been in the Silicon Valley area first."

"You are a real techno-nerd aren't you?" Kathryn laughed.

"Guilty as charged. I even took pictures of the registration scan and door scanners."

"I'm a real geek too, perhaps even more than you. But that is yet to be determined. Let's make our run around the tidal basin out to the tip of East Potomac Park. That should be long enough to get us ready for some great pasta."

"Lead on my Georgetown liberal."

Kathryn gave him a grin and took off out the door towards the elevator.

It was an amazing early evening as they set a solid pace around the Washington Monument, to the World War II memorial, crossed over to the southern side of the Tidal Basin under the Japanese cherry trees towards the Jefferson Memorial. They stopped briefly at a water fountain near the park ranger's office adjacent to the Franklin Delano Roosevelt Memorial. Sean had never known this memorial even existed. It was totally outdoors constructed of huge granite red stone with elaborate waterfalls and shallow pools.

The complex was dedicated to FDR's life and his four terms as President. The words carved in granite moved Sean in a way he never expected. As he read aloud, "No Country, however rich, can afford the waste of its human resources. Demoralization caused by vast unemployment is our greatest extravagance. Morally, it is the greatest menace to our social order." Sean and Kathryn cooled off as they walked quietly through the vast seven-acre complex stopping to read the quotes. Mixed in the complex were numerous bronze statues of FDR in a wheel chair, Eleanor, and bread lines of unemployed men. Sean was struck by, "Among American citizens there should be no forgotten men and no forgotten races." Sean saw the amazing vision and commitment of government to social issues so lacking in recent administrations.

"Thank you Kathryn. Stopping at this memorial means so much to me. At times I had lost sight of how good government really can be for the impoverished and desperate. After seeing increased numbers of homeless, understanding our failure to educate children, the inaccessibility of universal health care, enslavement of immigrants, inability to control weapons on our streets, plight of those on drugs, huge issues of violent crimes in urban areas, and massive populations of minorities inhabiting our prisons, I had become increasingly cynical about the governments real commitment to people rather than supporting big business. I didn't know this memorial existed. I suspect that you knew that I needed to see this as a way forward. But do we have the countries commitment to all people now? I think FDR had a clearer vision and was able to garner the commitment with the opposition of the Republicans. It was a simpler time as we united behind efforts to take us out of the depression and to victory in World War II."

"Hmmm was I that obvious?" Kathryn smirked and broke into a laugh.

Sean took Kathryn's hand, drew her into his arms, and gave her a long tender kiss. It seemed so natural, but so unlike his nature.

Kathryn had read the emotion and idealism in Sean at the Lincoln Memorial, but nothing prepared her for this moment. He was a good man who obviously had lost faith in the power and workings of government. The cynicism was waning as the work of FDR brought to light the fact that governments can change. This memorial gave everyone hope that after awhile the pendulum swings back in the other direction and rectifies the wrongs done in previous times. She felt closer to him knowing they shared their common hope. This was her favorite place in Washington. Sean passed her test easily hitting the 99% mark.

Kathryn hugged Sean, drawing him close. "Thank you," she whispered, "but if we don't move on, I am sure the conservatives will be after us." She gave Sean a shove and set the pace towards East Potomac Park.

Sean passed her easily and taunted, "They'll only catch you if you're behind me."

They would have to hurry. It was not a place you would want to visit after dark despite the constant National Park Police patrols. Both understood that the nations capital was amazing during the day, but dusk brought out a subtle uneasy and awareness of typical urban problems for city dwellers.

Six miles and ninety minutes after leaving Sean's room, they returned to the same elevator. Sean felt a little awkward about Kathryn coming to his room. As they walked the hallway, he decided to be the perfect gentleman. "Kathryn, I'll wait down in the lobby for 20 minutes while you shower and change."

"Don't be silly," Kathryn grinned. "We're both adults. I think it is chivalrous that you offered, but after all, I'm the one who invited myself into your hotel room. Besides you need to use your palm print to open the door."

Why don't you turn on the TV and see what the local media is saying about nuances of our present administration's battles with a do nothing congress.

"You know," Sean said, hesitating to use the palm scanner on the door, "I'm not worried about me, but I'm worried about what you might do to me after getting a glimpse of my pheromone drenched body. You probably won't be able to control yourself."

"Oh, I'll try to fight off the impulse," Kathryn giggled. "It has been a long time since I've been in a man's hotel room. I think it was at the Model United Nations conference in New York during high school. A boy named Jerry asked me to his hotel room to work on a proposal to the Model UN Security Council regarding terrorism. It was in response to an attack by the Red Brigade and attacks by the IRA in Northern Ireland. We were very serious and never even kissed. In some ways I was disappointed, the nerd never even tried to kiss me."

"Thank goodness," Sean said, scanning his palm and opening the door.

Kathryn grabbed her knapsack and landed a sweet lingering kiss on Sean's cheek, and headed into the bathroom. "I'll only be a few minutes," she said, closing the door. "I'm really hungry."

Sean's mind was spinning as he took out a change of clothing for himself as Kathryn finished. He was enjoying every minute of their time together. She made things seem so easy and effortless. Something he had not experienced with any other women. But where was this all going?

The door opened, Kathryn emerged in tight jeans and a sleeveless peach blouse that left her midriff slightly exposed as she moved. The stronger fragrance of vanilla filled the room again. Sean had a quick flashback memory of their initial meeting on the Lincoln Memorial steps. He had second thoughts about his selected clothing and reached into his suitcase for his jeans. The dress pants he selected earlier just would not work with her casual dress.

Kathryn saw his quick decision to change and pulled him into her arms for a longer more demanding kiss. It left both of them breathless. They fell back onto the king sized bed. Kathryn was on top of Sean. His arms were around her slowly caressing her back beneath the blouse. He inhaled her vanilla fragrance and marveled at the softness he saw in her blue eyes. Sean was embarrassed as he felt himself becoming aroused as they shared a long deep passionate kiss. He turned and rolled to the right trying to alleviate his full weight and hide his hardness. Their tongues darted in and out for an instant then intertwined until Kathryn broke the kiss. She pushed herself upright and off the bed. Her cheeks were flushed as she straightened her blouse.

"I don't know what came over me. I guess the thought of your pheromones and manly body showering in the adjacent bathroom just got the best of me. You are a sweaty mess so off you go to take your shower." Kathryn was laughing and Sean joined in finally understanding her humor.

_____

120

"If we don't let up," she continued, "I'll need to take another really cold shower. Our reservation is at a very popular local Italian restaurant. If we don't get a move on we will lose our reservation."

Sean felt a bit frustrated as he grabbed his clothes and headed to the shower. If his mind had been spinning before, now his body was likewise. *Was Kathryn teasing him?*

Fifteen minutes later, Sean emerged refreshed and considerably calmer. Kathryn was sitting on the bed.

"I'm sorry, Sean, that was cruel. I just felt an impulse and couldn't help myself after your comment in the elevator. Will you forgive me and my weird sense of timing?"

"There is nothing to forgive," Sean said. "I brought the whole thing upon myself. I got a little carried away. Are you ready to head out for some pasta?"

"Are you sure? Come here." Kathryn slipped off the bed and gave Sean a quick peck on the cheek. "I'm really sorry. I want you to know that I really like you. I don't know where all this is going, but I do know that you are a great guy and I want the time we have together to be something special. I really didn't see that coming. I hope I didn't mess things up." A small tear formed in her eye and slowly ran down her cheeks.

Sean knew that she was sincere and was already thinking about his departure on Friday. His alter ego didn't know what to say or do, so he simply closed the distance between them and gently touched the tear with his fingertips as he took her in his arms for a hug.

"I feel the same way Kathryn," he whispered. "This is all very new to me. Now, no more tears. Let's get out of here and get that pasta."

Kathryn's tears subsided and were replaced with a smile. She rubbed her blue eyes, smearing her the slight application of mascara. "Goodness, I'm a mess," she said, looking into the large mirror on the wall adjacent to the door. "Give me a second to fix my face." She quickly reapplied her light pink lipstick and mascara. "I'm really famished.", Kathryn said. "A glass of wine and pasta dinner sounds great to me."

When she finished she grabbed her purse. Sean took her hand and escorted her out. A quick smile appeared on both of their faces.

Ten minutes later they were seated at a corner table at Tosca Ristorante on F Street. Sean ordered a bottle of their Castello Di Forterutolli Chianti Classico 2011. They shared orders of calamari and antipasto as their starters. Sean was famished and had the waitress bring second basket of garlic bread. They both decided on the fixed prix meal for two, two small pasta side dishes, roasted venison medallions with black winter truffles, and a risotto dish for two. The entree was named in honor of the Chef Gino Lanfranconi. Gino came out of the kitchen to serve them their entrée, taking the opportunity to give a wonderful explanation of how the recipe was developed by his great-great-grandmother in the Lombard district of Italy. His description was presented with a heavily Italian accent with such gusto that it drew applause from Sean, Kathryn and patrons at adjacent tables. Gino offered a sincere, "*Bono appetito*" before he departed from their table.

The conversation for the next two hours centered on aspects of how parts of their lives seemed so similar. They had lost their parents before becoming adolescents. The military and VA had treated their families unkindly after the death of a significant relative. They found great satisfaction in academia both in learning and teaching others. They had developed cynical positions on governmental policies affecting the poor, imprisoned, elderly and disenfranchised. As they talked, it became clearer that they had by accident happened upon a kindred spirit; a match beyond any they imagined. Both were feeling more and more comfortable as the minutes passed and they slowly broke down normal barriers and facades. Their side dishes and entrée were spectacular, but it was lost in the substance of their conversation. Two cappuccinos and a wonderful Lemon Amoretto cake brought the meal to a wonderful conclusion. Neither wanted the meal nor the evening to end.

Over dinner, they exchanged work numbers, and worked out a rough schedule to see each other on Friday after Kathryn taught her two classes and attended a meeting, but Sean's 8:00 p.m. flight out of Dulles did not leave them much time. Kathryn planned to drive Sean to the airport. Finally leaving the restaurant, it was a long walk back to Sean's hotel to pick-up Kathryn's knapsack. They rode the elevator together in a somewhat strange uncomfortable silence after the evening of flowing conversation. Each recognized that they were at an important, yet awkward place in their rapidly developing relationship. Sean demonstrated the palm scanner system with a grin.

"That's really amazing, Sean," Kathryn said, "I wonder if they have had any malfunctions due to greasy palms of all the DC lobbyist and government bureaucrats." They both laughed but felt there was a grain of truth in the comment.

"I'd wondered the same thing when I scanned my hand for the first time. We really are political techno-geeks." Both laughed again.

As the door opened the king size bed seemed immense, dominating the entire room. It stood as a real symbol of where their unspoken thoughts had been for the last ten minutes. Both reflected back on their flirtatious moment on the bed earlier. Despite being out of his element, Sean felt the pressure to initiate a conversation. "There is a great mini bar if you'd like a drink or snack. I hope you'll stay a little longer." He walked across to the window with an amazing view across Reserve Officers Park with the Washington Monument in the distance.

Kathryn was still staring mesmerized by the bed. Her body language betrayed her thoughts. Sean walked back to her, looking deep into her blue eyes as he took her hand and moved her into his arms. She was warm and responsive to his kiss as he stood just treasuring the sense of having her close. He slowly danced her backwards until he lowered her onto the bed. This time he was on top, eyes closed, and their lips locked in a passionate kiss. Their tongues intertwined. Sean could feel Kathryn's heart beating. The vanilla aroma tantalized his senses.

Sean felt compelled to move things on to a different level. Ignoring his subconscious voice telling him to *slow down.* Sean loved the feel of her lips on his when her lips parted and the tip of her tongue appeared. He slowly moved his hands tenderly caressed up her back.

After a minute or two he moved his hand forward over her breast and began to caress her nipples through the light material. Kathryn's nipples hardened to his soft touch as she moaned slightly. Sean had moved to settle himself between her splayed thighs, making an instinctive effort to press his growing hardness against her. He heard another moan escape from her lips as they kissed.

Kathryn was lost in the passion of the moment as she felt her own heightened arousal moisten between her legs. She still had confidence that she could stop this at anytime, but at this point that wasn't necessary, and she relished the moment. She decided to let him take things further after all this might be their only opportunity for physical intimacy for a while. Frankly, Kathryn loved the feelings Sean was producing deep within her. She could rationalize the situation if she wanted, but the fact was she couldn't help herself. She closed her eyes lost in the moment as Sean gently pushed her sleeveless blouse top up and over her head. She opened her eyes thinking he was so cute as he stared at her perky breasts and caressed her budding nipples.

Kathryn was a petite woman who took tremendous pride in what she considered to be her best physical features, her small natural breasts and tight abdominals. Sean's fingers covered her hard nipples as they sprang free from their cover. Sean delighted in the erotic feel he had as Kathryn's nipples hardened in response to his caressing fingers. He slowly planted a nibbling kiss on her neck below the ear, and continued lowering his head and took her right breast between his lips. The warmth of his lips and tongue was such a wonderful feeling, sending Kathryn's body into a series of small tremors accenting the sensations she was feeling. She really wanted him to take each of her nipples and suck them deep into his mouth using his coarse tongue and teeth to add to the sensual feeling.

She moaned and bucked against his aroused bulge as he began to aggressively suckle, biting her nipples lightly. Sean slowly rubbed his lower body into Kathryn as he unbuttoned and pushed her jeans lower and lower until they fell t the floor. He loved the way her tight runner's body responded to his touch. Sean's mind raced, thinking *she was a vision of loveliness that quickly gave way to how fantastic she felt in his arms.*

Kathryn tightened her grip pulling Sean's head to her as she arched her back slightly, allowing her tender nipples to swell and push deeper into his mouth. The little nibble bites excited her further. She looked down to watch as this wonderful intelligent man was making love to her swollen nipples, his saliva was coating her entire breast. She grinned with the intense pleasure, happy to be with a sexy man that intrigued her and stimulated her on numerous levels. She felt as if she was losing control, losing in her bid to control as her body as she surrendered to his lips.

Sean began to slowly rub his lower body into Kathryn. A primitive instinctive dance once started became harder and harder to control. Taking her face in his hands, he turned his attention to her lips and deeply kissed her. Their tongues met as they took their kiss to a new level. His right hand slide down caressing her flat belly and hips worked its way into her black silk panties. She whimpered slightly at the touch and gave a little moan as his hand traced its way back up to her wetness.

Kathryn moved his hand directly to her clitoris, teaching him the intimate caress her body needed. They reached a rhythmic movement as their tongues did the dance of lovers. Leaning back, Sean watched her eyes flutter as he brought her to her first and second orgasm. He reveled in her wetness as she had an intense orgasm.

Kathryn knew he wanted her, and she wanted him just as much. She knew she was lost as she felt him rise for a moment and undress. It was going to be up to her to stop then and there or make this time together special. Full undressed, she used the moment to excuse herself to use the restroom to retrieve a condom from her knapsack. A minute later she joined Sean on the king size bed in a passionate embrace. They both laughed as he had just opened another condom he purchased on the way back to the hotel from his NNS meeting. With some awkwardness he rolled it on.

A moment later, they reached for each other on the bed. Sean was lying on top of her slight frame. He rose ever so slightly, gazed into her blue eyes, the tip of his erection opening her clit, and slide slowly and gently inside her. They lay in each other's arms without moving, savoring the moment, until their rhythmic instinct took over. Slowly Sean pushed deeper and deeper as he gazed into Kathryn's eyes. Their passionate love making continued until Kathryn took a position seated upon him. Sean was thrusting upward racing to fill her until he felt the sweetness of her release squirting her orgasm signaling his own need to reach climax. His middle finger and thumb between them continued to rub her clitoris ensuring that she reached yet another orgasm. They continued the dance of lovers, until she reached yet a fourth orgasm. Sated they paused holding each other in a tender intimate embrace.

Kathryn wanted to etch every moment into her memory as they made love off and on for the next two hours. Sean was a complete lover using his tongue, lips and gentle fingers to keep her on the edge of orgasm after orgasm. He was gentle and rough at the same time. He surprised her with his incredible endurance and stamina. She felt as if she had been on a roller coaster reaching peak after peak of passion beyond any of her previous experiences and wildest erotic dreams.

Sean could not believe that he had just made love to the most attractive, exciting and passionate woman he had every met. His alter ego like his libido was on overdrive, and had been going on pure instinct, as all his previous experiences had been somewhat disastrous to say the least. His mind replayed highlights of their lovemaking as he wondered how this all came about. As he did so he felt himself become aroused again. He reached out and pulled Kathryn back into his arms.

"You are amazing," Kathryn smiled, leaning in for a kiss. Her lips were a bit sore as they began to make love anew. Her eyes widened as Sean penetrated her again, and then closed to savor the sweet moment of the sensation moving in unison towards her release.

It was 6:45 a.m. when she awoke again in Sean's arms. Twenty minutes later she was in a cab. She had to teach an 8:30 a.m. political science class at the Georgetown Intercultural Center. She planned to meet Sean at her home at 11 a.m. It was going to be hard to focus on teaching as she tried to keep an obvious smile off her face. It was going to be quite a challenge trying to maintain her focus while facing the early morning summer class.

The morning had passed with agonizing slowness for Sean as he waited to see Kathryn again. At exactly 11 a.m., he stood at her aunt's front door taking in the pure beauty of the brownstone. It was far more impressive in the shaded sunlight of the giant oak trees lining the street. He used the brass doorknocker twice without any response from within. Three minutes later the door opened.

"Sean, what are you doing here?" asked a somewhat startled and annoyed Grace Gibson.

Sean was at a complete loss for words, "Ah Dr. Gibson....", he said in a state of confusion.

"How did your get my home address?" Grace demanded.

Sean glanced at the house number to make sure he had the right address. "Well, I'm here to pick-up Kathryn McCarthy. This is the address she gave me. I had no idea you lived here. Are you her aunt?"

"Yes, I'm her aunt," Grace sighed and her body language seemed to become more at ease. "You shocked me. I didn't expect to see you again until after the project had progressed. I immediately thought someone at NNS gave you my address for some urgent reason for this unexpected visit. It was very disconcerting thinking a member of my staff gave you my home address. I do everything to possible to protect my private life."

"I'm a little confused too," Sean grinned. "We have a date at 11. I was supposed to meet Kathryn after her class. I assure you that your staff had nothing to do with my visit. No one betrayed your privacy."

Grace crossed her arms with a much more relaxed attitude, "I'm sorry," she beamed, "I just cannot get over your being Kat's friend. She has never mentioned you. Then again I have been putting in long hours and we have not had time over the past month to chat."

"Well, we just met Wednesday while jogging. Despite our long talks, she never mentioned you by name or position."

"Well that explains it," Grace smirked. "You know this could be a bit awkward if we let it."

Sean was reflecting on how his blossoming relationship might become a professional problem if it should fall apart. "It is what it is," he muttered. He felt a bit awkward that Kathryn had never given him the name of her aunt. He began to question *whether Kathryn had made the possible connection of her aunt at NNS and his nuclear project, then again there were numerous government agencies and committees dealing with nuclear energy issues.* Sean was brought back to focus on Grace.

"This is my home I've shared it with Kat for the past five years. We have lived together off and on for over fourteen years. She has always been more than welcome to bring friends home, but because we are working together I just don't want to have this complicate our budding professional relationship."

"It won't," Sean assured her. "I respect you both too much. To let that happen." He decided to change the subject. "You must be very proud of this incredible house. It has so many classical 18th century Georgian architectural elements." Sean said, stepping back to view the facade of the house. "I love the classical white pilasters, jack arch, fanlight transom and water tables. It is the best example I've seen in my limited time in Georgetown and in architectural magazines. We don't have anything like it from this period in California that isn't faux."

Grace smiled for the first time. "You seem to know much more than just nuclear physics, Sean. This house was built in 1815, after the British destroyed the city in the war of 1812. The original plans were drawn in 1725. It still has most of the original elements.

The house is a personal treasure belonging to my former husbands family since its original construction. Unfortunately Nathan died before the interior refurbishing could be completed and he never had the opportunity to live in it. I love every aspect of this old house. At some point I would love to show you the interior, but I have to run to a meeting."

Just then Kathryn appeared on her blue Novara Carema bicycle. She rushed up the small walkway to the house. She was carrying a tote bag and appeared to be in a hurry. "I'm glad to see you've met my aunt Grace," she said catching her breath. "I'm sorry I'm late."

"Hi Kathryn." Sean stated watching her every step. Trying not to give Grace any clue of the intimacy shared last night.

"Hi Kat," Grace interrupted. "I actually already met Sean earlier this week. We are doing a project together. He's been waiting for you while admiring our home's architectural features. I'm afraid I have to run, there is my driver." Grace's gaze was up the oak tree lined street.

A sleek black Town car pulled up to the curb. "Please excuse me. I need to get to the office for an appointment."

A black government town car with dark tinted windows stopped at the curb. Within seconds Grace opened the front door and reached inside for her briefcase on a table in the foyer. She walked down the steps to Kathryn. "We'll talk later, Kat," Grace said, kissing Kathryn on the cheek. She turned to Sean. "I'm expecting amazing results from your project, Dr. McMurray," she said sternly with a facial expression betraying that she was pushing his buttons.

"Yes, Dr. Gibson."

Grace hesitated for a moment and added, "Kat, I will be in late tonight, I have one of those obligatory charity events at the Corcoran Museum. Will I be seeing you and Sean this evening?"

Kathryn looked at Sean and responded, "Probably not as I am taking Sean to the airport this evening."

"Sean, I hope you enjoy a nice day together and have a pleasant flight home this evening." Grace nodded goodbye, walked to her car, got in, and disappeared behind the car's tinted glass. In a flash the driver pulled the Town car out and down the quiet street.

Kathryn looked shocked. "Out of all the hundreds of runners on the National mall," she said, turning to Sean, "I picked the one working on a NNS project with my aunt. I never put the two of you together. Do you think that could be a real problem?"

"Kathryn, I had a brief chat with her about that very thing. I promised her that I would not let our relationship affect my professional relationship with her nor my project. Your Aunt Grace and I will maintain our professional relationship."

Kathryn smiled, sensing Sean's honesty. She had never met a man like this before. "Come in the house. Can I get you something to drink while I freshen up? By the way my aunt isn't the slightest bit liberal. She is a die hard conservative Republican."

"No, thanks, I'm fine," replied Sean as he entered the foyer. He was struck by the incredible beauty of the classic home's interior. "I suspected as much in her role at NNS."

Kathryn watched as Sean soaked in the home's beauty. Kathryn gave him a warm hug and a peck on the cheek. "I would love to show you the interior of the house on your next visit. I think you would be interested in Grace's use of detailed period craftsmanship and use of authentic materials in the restoration. The original plans are amazing." She ran up the elaborate circling stairs calling back, "I'll be just a second."

Sean and Kathryn had an incredible afternoon exploring a sun soaked Annapolis and eating Chesapeake Bay blue crabs. It was the peak of the season for this amazing Maryland delicacy. Their time together ended all to soon. Kathryn drove Sean to Dulles in her refurbished blue 1970 VW bug and they spent the last half hour trying to figure out their complicated schedules for when they could see each other again. Their last passionate kiss before he entered through TSA security was enough to make his arousal noticeable. Kathryn kidded Sean about having a concealed weapon and having to go through TSA security. A broad beamed smile captured his state of mind as he walked to gate B14, turned and blew a kiss to Kathryn before disappearing into the massive series of gates. Within minutes his flight was called and he entered the massive plane mate transporter that took passengers from the terminal to the aircraft on the tarmac.

Chapter 10: London Reacts
Friday, May 7, 9:00 p.m. BST (UTC/GMT)
10 Downing Street, London, UK

General Geoffrey Nash, Chief Superintendent of Scotland Yard, was the last to arrive at the Prime Minister's residence. The usually obsessively precise and prompt Nash complained about the heightened security, doubling his normal travel time. The PM's porter Chatham White, and Security Chief Charles Fitzroy were already aware of Nash's approach when his driver stopped at the Birdcage Walk and Whitehall security checkpoints.

"Prime Minister Graham is aware of your arrival, sir," Chatham said. "Please give me your wet umbrella, rain coat, and hat." Chatham assisted Nash with the removal of his coat. "Miserable weather out there, sir?"

"Yes indeed, weather unfit for any beast," replied Nash.

"As an increased security precaution," Charles interrupted, standing in front of Nash, "I need you to step through the security scanner when you are ready. Then Mr. White will accompany you to the Cabinet Room."

The usually composed Nash seemed a bit flustered, as he was unaccustomed to being late for anything, but especially for a meeting scheduled by PM Graham. "Please give me a minute to dry off and pull myself together." Nash spent the next few minutes straightening his tie, and brushing his hair with a black comb before entering the scanner. "Am I the last to arrive?" He asked stepping out of the sophisticated full body scanner chamber.

Charles momentarily viewed the Chief Superintendent's scanned image and nodded his approval. "You are cleared, sir," he announced. "The other attendees arrived more than fifteen minutes earlier."

"Damn," Nash uttered under his breath.

"Please follow Mr. White, sir."

Nash followed Chatham up the ornate wrought iron Grand Staircase, past the hallway of traditional English countryside scenes, and through the beautifully carved oak doors of the Cabinet Room. The PM's group was comfortably seated around the Cabinet's massive conference table. Reginald Smyth, Lord Mayor of London; Jeffrey Crane, Home Minister; General Maxwell Hatch, Commandant of the Royal Army; Admiral Harold Johnson, Director of SIS; Field Marshal Andrew Perkins, the General Chief of Staff; Geoffrey Thime, Lord Chancellor; Gareth Fraser, Chancellor of the Exchequer; Charles Davis, Chief Secretary of the Treasury; Clarence Lloyd, Secretary of State for Defense, and Spencer Wendell, Director of SIS Anti-Terrorism Section were all engaged in light conversation with PM Graham while enjoying tea, with warm cinnamon scones and raspberry jam.

"Good evening, Nash." Graham nodded acknowledging Nash. "Please help yourself before we get started."

Nash smiled at Graham, thinking to himself, *He could always put one at ease.* He took a breath and helped himself to a cup of tea and a scone.

"I hate pulling everyone away from their families at this late hour," Graham said to the entire group, "but as you know we are under borrowed time. I have asked Admiral Johnson to give us a complete intelligence briefing before we assess the current security precautions, expenditures, and review public reactions. Admiral Johnson?"

"Thank you, Prime Minister. Our latest SIS threat assessment and the technical analysis of the credibility of sources will be reported by Mr. Wendell, whose sector has been working closely with nine different international counter-terrorism agencies. Mr. Wendell?"

"Thank you, Admiral. If I may draw your attention to the screen," all heads turned to face the large screen in the back of the room. Spencer used a remote to dim the lights. "Over the past nine days, the level of intercepted cell phone chatter has spread across the seventeen different countries as indicating." A world map appeared on the screen with individual countries identified and two numbers under each. Taking a minute for the group to study the map Spencer continued showing a graph. "The number in blue is the total calls and the red is the mention of London or bridges." On the adjacent screen was a bar graph listing countries in alphabetical order with a dual colored horizontal line. "The total volume of calls is represented in the bar graph. The red shorter area is the number of those calls that mentioned "London or the word bridge." As you can see the largest number of calls and the largest number mentioning London' or bridge is from Yemen, followed by Afghanistan, Iraq, Iran, and Pakistan. The fact that such a large number of calls that specifically mentioning London or bridge is extremely unsettling as it is absolutely unprecedented. There has never been this level of specific cell chatter forewarning of a terrorist attack or target in the past.

Most forewarning is just an increase of cell calls from known terrorist areas with little mention of potential targets. Our analysts are certain that there is a credible threat and that we are dealing with an evolved terrorist plot that we have never previously experienced. This threat is unlike the former *al-Qaeda* cell chatter due to the fact that they have been keeping a low profile following Bin Laden's death. Our colleagues in other counter-terrorism agencies have verified their data and reached the same conclusion. The SIS supports all precautionary efforts to secure and protect the bridges within London. At this point, we are monitoring all of our assets working undercover within varied Muslim groups in the UK, Europe, US and the Middle East, searching for any indication that the threat whether internal or external is turning operational. We suspect that the terrorist are more than likely already in position within the UK."

"Thank you Mr. Wendell," Admiral Johnson interrupted. "I also personally spoke with Dexter Ford of NSA at length. He and his team confirm the threat and have offered full access to the thousands of intercepted cell conversations from the countries shown on the graphic. There is no question that this terrorist threat is credible. SIS is certain that a terrorist attack is imminent and more than likely involving a London bridge or bridges."

Graham asked, "Are there any questions on the intelligence we have gathered?" After several questions and answers clarifying the facts, the group came to an agreement on the SIS threat assessment.

Graham turned to General Hatch and Field Marshal Perkins, "How are we responding to this threat? Seems we have come to an agreement about its credibility. Do we have concerns about our precautions and readiness to respond?

Can we assume that our military security efforts are sufficient and will deter or adequately respond to a terrorist attack?"

General Hatch opened the folder before him, "At this point," he read, "we have over 1,800 armed military personnel, including sixty four armour units providing security on the thirty-two bridges serving each of the three eight hour shifts. There are another sixteen armed small craft boats providing security along the foundations of the bridges; and another elite team of Special Forces with chopper air support ready to be dispatched to any bridge within minutes. Every lorry, bus and train crossing a bridge is stopped and inspected by bomb squads with sniffer canines on the entryways at each end of the bridges. The entire security force is under the command of General Thurgood Delany in coordination with Scotland Yard, London Police, and SIS. Our assessment is that our security response is more than sufficient to deter terrorist or defeat them if they attack. Are there any comments, issues or questions?"

"There is no doubt that our security is going to make any credible terrorist attack nearly impossible." Mayor Smyth interrupted. "However my concern does not lay in the actual size of the security force, but in the current procedures. Regardless of the real threat, the current procedures are seriously impeding the flow of commerce, cutting bus and rail ridership by 65%, overcrowding the tubes, and causing massive delays in our rail system. The procedures impact on the economy will be millions of Pounds and daily life of Londoners is significantly curtailed. The terrorists have already won a victory by chatting on their damn cell phones. We should alter the procedures now by making bomb inspections shorter or increasing the number of units inspecting public transport.

The average Londoner can adjust to the security precautions and delays for a time, but dragging this on for weeks and months seems absolutely untenable. The daily tabloid sheets are already analyzing the projected costs of the security forces and impact on the budget, general economy, as well as public opinions and that's not going to help anyone's upcoming elections."

Andrew Perkins, nodded his head and added, "Lord Chancellors' Thime, Fraser and I have discussed the issue and agree that the current precautions will deter any potential terrorist attack. Our concern is that it seems like overkill and the expense is unsustainable in the long run. There is no doubt that the impact on the city and the economy will ultimately be worse than the loss of a single bridge. I would like to know how the military arrived at the current level of security, inspection procedures and their estimated cost per day."

Graham, "So we are in agreement that the current threat is credible, and level of precautions are more than sufficient, but there are serious concerns about the level of precaution required to meet the threat, procedures, military assessment and the cost."

The Secretary of Defense, Clarence Lloyd turned to the Lord Mayor. "I can assure you that the military assessment was in the best interest of Londoners and the UK," he beamed. "Any successful terrorist event in a city causing loss of life or disruption of commerce will bring even greater changes in the next election. Your concern about elections is more than a little unsettling. We need to concentrate on public safety first. The bridges are secured and any terrorist group will be deterred by the presence of our troops. Hatch, Perkins and I are more concerned about preventing the attack than the temporary inconvenience or the bloody cost and any inconvenience to the public."

Spencer followed each of the comments carefully as the leaders voice their concerns and positions staking out little fiefdoms of their own power positions.

Graham looked perplexed, "Gentlemen, the facts speak for themselves. We are about to face a public disaster if we do not provide the necessary military precautions and there is an attack. The short-term impact on the economy is tough to judge accurately. It will take some doing, but we can circumvent rail that use most of the London bridges. I am sure we can revisit the expense issue in a weeks time."

Treasurer, Charles Davis cleared his throat slightly to take his turn. He had deferred to the other attendees, but felt compelled to address the daily cost issue. "The cost of our security troops on the bridges does not make a difference during the first seven days," he announced. "The troops are paid the same daily rate as if they were on their bases. The major difference is the fact that after the seventh day, the troops on the bridges will be paid an additional off-base duty bonus. The average soldier receives 15 Pounds and officers get 40 Pounds per day for off-base duty, combined with the cost of fuel and other material items runs the estimated cost to over 6,000,000 Pounds per day. For now the biggest impact is the huge disruption to the economy, which when combined with the military expense is calculated to be in excess of 45,000,000 Pounds per day. A figure that I feel is not sustainable for more than two weeks."

Mayor Smyth seemed to choke on those figures for a moment. "I certainly do not expect this to run more than a few days," he explained. "If we maintain the current levels of security, the cost overruns are unsustainable and they will also become a major election issue on our fiscal mismanagement.

I prefer that the city was safe at a lessor level of military presence with an easing of the bomb inspection precautions. I also do not want an attack during my tenure as mayor. It appears that we are in a veritable conundrum."

"I believe we have our answer," responded Home Minister Jeffrey Crane, "As I see it, for the short term we can handle the cost and the daily impact on London. If it is for the long term we will need to cut back the size of the force and reduce the impact on Londoners and the economy."

Graham slowly nodded, "Thank you, Home Minister. You are the voice of reason. We will set a tentative schedule for both the short term and the long term. I propose that we maintain the current security precautions for a week with the suggested increase in bomb inspectors thus shortening the searches on trains, and then set a marked reduction of troops for every four days until we feel confident that the threat has passed. I think that General Hatch should project my proposal and present the staged levels of reductions after conferring with his staff. Are we in agreement?"

"That is more than reasonable," General Nash intervened. "I will take up the issue of the timetable with my commanders and staff within eight hours and provide you with our findings."

There was a nodding of heads and voiced agreement with the PM's proposal. "Thank you, gentlemen," Graham said, glancing around the table. "Let's hope and pray that this threat is short lived or averted all together."

Graham dismissed the meeting and reached for his secure personal cell to call Helena. Helena did not answer her cell, so Graham left a voice message. Graham had been advised not to utilize text messages by his technical security staff.

Chapter 11: 11: Blossoming Relationship
Friday, May 7, 10:45 p.m. PST (UTC/GMT-9)
South Pasadena CA

Sean had an uneventful flight back to Los Angeles other than thinking about Kathryn more than he thought possible. He picked up his PT Cruiser and headed home. Given the late hour, traffic on the 405, 10 and 110 was relatively light compared to the norm where traffic jams tried the patience of most Angelinos. *Thank goodness I don't have to commute on these insane freeways*, Sean thought. His cell phone rang just as he was exiting off the 110 onto Fremont Avenue in South Pasadena.

"Hi, Sean", Kathryn's voice resonated. "Have you been missing me?"

"You have been occupying my thoughts since leaving Dulles. What are you doing up so late? It's nearly 2 am in Washington?"

"That would be late," Kathryn, giggled, "if I were in Washington. American Airline had an amazing last minute fare; so, I'm here in LA. I just got off the plane and I'm in a Super Shuttle on my way to South Pasadena."

"That's unbelievable," Sean grinned caught off guard by the news. "Are you always so impulsive?"

"Only when I know we may be apart for weeks. I missed you and felt that I wanted to be with you as long as I could this weekend."

"Well, at least this will be a temporary solution to my missing you. Are you really in LA, or is this a prank to get me excited?"

"You'll find out in 30 minutes, depending on the two other passengers in the shuttle."

"This is a phenomenal surprise, as I don't never have overnight visitors. Do you have my address? Sean said wondering, "I'd hate to see you driving around South Pasadena at this time of night trying to find my apartment."

"I had my ways of getting it, 2884 Grevalia St. Apartment 14A in South Pasadena. I read it in your folder on Grace's desk. I should be there before midnight." Kathryn added in a kidding tone, "Will you be waiting up for me or should I just camp out on your door stoop?" She could not help chuckling.

"You must be kidding," Sean began thinking about the state of his apartment. "I'll stop and get some wine and cheese. I'll see you shortly. This is going to cap off a great week."

Sean ran into Bristol Farms supermarket to pickup a few essential items. He couldn't waste much time because he wanted to straighten up his apartment before Kathryn's arrival. His apartment was frugally furnished and reflected his commitment to his work and rock climbing. It did not say much for his day-to-day living situation. Fifteen minutes later, he was dispensing with his dirty sheets after making the bed, when the doorbell rang.

"Who's there at this ungodly hour?" he called out in a kidding falsetto voice.

"It's a poor little doctoral student who has lost her way. She is seeking shelter for the night from numerous California conservatives. Please sir, do you have a room to spare?" Kathryn was laughing as her voice trailed off at the end of the sentence.

Sean opened the door. "I'm always willing to help out a poor lost grad student despite what my conservative neighbors might read into this scandalous situation."

Kathryn flew into his arms, "Thank you, kind sir. I won't be any trouble as long as you take advantage of me!"

"I'll do my best," Sean replied with a leer before carrying Kathryn into the bedroom and depositing her on the queen size bed.

"Oh kind sir, you have swept me off my feet. I'm not used to relying on the kindness of strangers. I'm sure you won't let me down."

"I'll do my best not to disappoint you."

They spent a wonderful night together. Sean awoke at 8:30 a.m. only to find Kathryn in the small kitchenette fixing breakfast. He hugged her from behind and kissed the nape of her neck. She was wearing his sun faded red sweatshirt and a pair of his running shorts.
"Good morning," he said. "How did you sleep?"

"Great," Kathryn said, facing Sean with a twinkle in her eye. " I woke up over an hour ago, showered, and went up the street to the market. Bristol Farms strikes me as a kind of organic health food haven for the local yuppies. It was way above pricey for my taste even considering a comparison to shops in Georgetown. Are all your food markets like that?"

"That's about as high end as you can get. Most locals go because they want to be seen there rather than the more reasonable Trader Joes or Albertsons. I don't shop there except in dire emergencies."

"I don't think I've seen so many Generation-X gathered in one place," Kathryn mused, "buying organic fruits and veggies while sipping their double decaf mocha lattes. Are they the same upper-middle class conservatives that voted Arnold the 'Terminator' into office a few years back? Goodness, I'd have to reassess your political views if it was your regular neighborhood market."

"Yes, I must confess." Sean said, crossing his arms, "some of the clientele are card carrying John Birch Society members of the moral Christian majority that have rolled the definition of ultra-conservative even further to the right of the Tea Party. Living on the far left coast of our fine nation seems to have given them the god given right to be more conservative than any other part of the country. Our conservatives are small in number but put Texas to shame. Last week they were outside the store property with signage to 'Get the U.S. out of the United Nations and NATO. They were an interesting group to chat with, but they're not your average Californians that elected Jerry Brown shop down the street at Trader Joe's. The LA area is a real mixed bag of politics, ethnicities, entertainment industry wannabes, immigrants, and freaks. If it wasn't for my great position at Cal-Tech and access to great rock climbing, I'd probably be living in Boston."

"It's an amazing morning anyways," Kathryn said, peering out the window, "other than for that miserable gray cloud of smog covering those mountains in the distance."

"This is your typical LA basin day," Sean quipped. "A morning rush hour filled with smog and Sig-traffic alerts, lacking real sunshine and fresh air. The smog can be cut with a knife. The San Gabriel mountains are closer than they appear due to the smog."

Kathryn laughed as she offered Sean a plate of scrambled eggs covered in melted cheese and mushrooms, with a side of fresh cut strawberries, pineapple and blueberries. The toaster sprang up a poppy seed bagel, which Kathryn quickly buttered and tossed to Sean. While he was catching the bagel, she bent over and gave him a lingering kiss on the lips.

Sean smiled, as he sat down at the small kitchen table. He was famished and hadn't thought much about food since last night. He drew Kathryn onto his lap and shared his meal. As they took turns eating, Sean was aware that he was becoming aroused, Kathryn nestling in his arms had that effect. She had a mixed sweet aroma of vanilla and his hair conditioner.

It was amazing how comfortable they felt together. They immediately adjusted to the rapidly developing romantic situation for both of them. Kathryn reached for her coffee mug. "Mmmm," she murmured with a sip, "this dark French Roast coffee is wonderful and rich. I think you may have better coffee on the West Coast. Then again you should at $26.50 a pound. Ouch, the thought of paying that much for coffee seems obscene and pretentious even for Generation-X."

        Kathryn laughed as she got off his lap, "What is left of your breakfast is getting cold!" She took another sip of her French Roast coffee. The morning conversation just flowed easily and somehow always with a humorous political edge to it.

        "Indeed," Sean said, sipping out of his Yosemite mug. "Californians pay through the nose for their morning Colombian caffeine fix, and then some pay even more for their afternoon snuffing of cocaine."

———

"So it is true," Kathryn mused, "that Californians are more into recreational drugs. Not that the folks on Capitol Hill don't dabble."

"Well you can believe it. Recreational drugs are California's largest cash crop and largest import crop. The drug cartels and growers in Humboldt County see to satisfying California's needs. Breakfast was amazing by the way. Thanks, I'm sorry I'm not much of a cook myself, but know some great restaurants."

Kathryn's next kiss had a slight taste of coffee and fruit. "I felt as if I needed to do something to repay you for taking me in last night. I'm sorry if I've disturbed your usual bachelor rituals or routines. I can't believe I'm sitting her in your man hut apartment."

"Sorry if it isn't much of an apartment. It has the basics that I need."

"What can I say? I am being much more impulsive than usual. It just isn't like me to be this way."

"I'm really pleased that you made the trip," Sean said, slowly rubbing Kathryn's shoulders. "What would you like to do while you are here?" Sean paused slightly, "I'll shave and take a shower before we head out."

Looking into Sean's eyes, "I'm happy just being here with you. I would join you but your mini shower won't accommodate two people." Kathryn pauses and added, "I've never been to LA. Why don't you surprise me?"

"Well, I'll need to run by campus first, but then we can hit some of the highlights of LA."

"That's great. After all the stereotypical hype about the Big Bang Theory cast put out about you Cal-tech guys, I'd love to see your office and lab where the real nuclear nerds hangout. Perhaps you can show me your comic book collection?"

Sean's cell phone rang, interrupting their conversation. Sean grabbed it off the counter.

"Hi Sean, Jake here. I was hoping to catch you before you headed to campus. How did your DC trip go with the big Fed honchos?"

"Hey, Jake. The meetings went better than anticipated. They are moving full speed ahead in supporting our redundancy system grant."

"That's great! It firms up my entire summer doing something stimulating other than bussing tables in my folks' diner."

"Actually, my new friend Kathryn from DC popped in unexpectedly for the weekend. She has expressed an interest in seeing the lab and campus. We'll try to head up to my office around 10:15. If we're late you can start without us, but I should be there until 1:30 catching up with the team. I'd love to have her meet the team and see the campus."

"Whoa you meet someone and she is here in Pasadena. That is incredible. Sounds good, Doc. DeJesus, Craig and Willie are already in the lab. They are writing code and downloading it into the system files. I'm picking up Sarah in a few minutes. I should be at your office about 10."

"Thanks."

Sean turned to Kathryn. She was smiling after overhearing his conversation.

"As your new friend from DC," Kathryn smirked, "I'd love to see your lab, but I don't want to interfere with your team's work. Are you sure you'll have enough time to show me the campus and lab?"

Sean kissed her. "I'm changing that to my smart and very hot close new friend from DC."

Kathryn grabbed Sean and pulled him close. "Talk that way and I may ask to get even closer," she laughed.

An hour later, they pulled into the faculty parking lot after using Sean's security swipe card.

"They need to get that palm identified security pass system," Kathryn joked. "You have such nice palms. You need to share the technology of the Marriott hotel palm scanner with your campus friends and colleagues."

"Oh, I will. I'm planning on sharing the pics I took of the devices. For now I have to check in on my team, and verify some of our vital equipment shipments. On second thought this campus needs the asshole identification security scanner system," Sean mused. "There are always more than a few visiting our campus."

"We'll be rich," Kathryn joined in. "We can sell the asshole scanner to Congress, screening lawyers, real estate agents, partner, or better yet start a dating service. The possibilities are endless."

The next half hour the couple toured the campus stopping at the bookstore to buy Kathryn a Cal-Tech hat, tee shirt, and coffee at the cafe. They ended the tour at Beckman Auditorium before entering the Watson building and climbing to the Sean's third floor office and lab just a little after 10 a.m..

Stopping just outside his office, Sean pulled out his swipe card and opened the door. "I just need to grab a few things before I show you the lab. I need to verify some equipment shipments for my team."

Once inside the office, Kathryn's attention was drawn to the diagram on the whiteboard. It appeared out of place for nuclear physics. "What's this?" she asked.

Sean looked up from a pile of delivery receipts. "Oh, that's a hypothetical game my team and I play," he said. "We try to anticipate a certain behavior based on motivation and known patterns before it happens using a series of logical progressions and logarithms. It is nothing more than a diagram of the intellectual nuances of our game. I am afraid we do not match up well with the "Big Bang Theory" crew. We real Cal-Tech nerds play more sophisticated games than Dungeons and Dragons!"

Kathryn seemed intrigued by the diagram on the whiteboard. "Interesting," she said. "So this diagram deals with the anticipated terrorist attack in London?"

"It is just the musing of my team as we brainstormed the pattern of terrorist behavior in the US, Spain, London, France, Belgium, Germany, Turkey, Iraq, Afghanistan, Pakistan, Israel and Egypt. The idea of terrorists announcing an attack against London bridges through cell chatter just doesn't make any sense to us given their prior patterns.

———

150

There were no such warnings in Belgium, Paris, Nice or other attacks. They have never forewarned any country with details of their targets before an attack. DeJesus, one of my team, thinks they are going to do something radically different from past patterns. Perhaps even attack New York bridges just to confuse the intelligence and anti-terrorism agencies. Nothing in profiling prior terrorists suggests that they do what their chatter indicates."

Kathryn was reviewing the elaborate diagramed mind map. "Fascinating, I always suspected a different target given the relative unpredictable nature of most terrorist attacks."

"We really do think alike," Sean grinned. He took Kathryn's hand and led her to the door. "I have to meet with my team. Later we can explore Hollywood, Disneyland, LA beaches, Rodeo Drive, or do a quick hike up into the San Gabriel Mountains."

Chapter 12: Cell Preparations
Sunday, May 9, 11:00 p.m. BST (UMT/GMT)
A flat in Southwark, London, UK

Hamid had called for half of *Al Salwa* to meet him at his flat to run through their minute-by-minute part in the planned London attack. The second half of *Al Salwa* was held in support to assist with the cell's escape using a freighter filled with limestone for the Essar Steel mills in the Midlands. Prior to his departure from Oman two years ago, Hamid was certain that he understood the precise role of each cell member in the *Al Salwa* plan. For over three months the unit had reviewed every aspect of the planned attack over and over. They had a high value target that was critical in the success of the attack, thus nothing was to be overlooked during the planning. It had gotten to the point that several of his men expressed sheer boredom at rehashing the same tactical details, while awaiting the order to go operational.

Maintaining a normal life in the midst of London while preparing to attack was not an easy task. Hamid was anxiously awaiting their Pinterest orders to go operational. It had been his leadership role to constantly demand that they remain focused and committed to destroying their target. They were avenging the numerous attacks on Muslims. He constantly used the *Al Zagaheer* reports on the war against terrorism and how it affected the lives of Muslims with his cell members. He used and reused the theme of revenge as the central focus permeating throughout the cell meetings to ensure the members recognized the importance of their efforts in fighting against the economic and military oppression of Muslims in their own countries. Hamid used the increased prejudice and discrimination against Muslims within London resulting from the Paris, Belgium and Nice attacks as additional motivation.

As Europeans reacted out of fear to each attack with prejudice and calls to eliminate Muslims or refugees, it fed the motivation of his cell. They were keeping a low profile while anxiously awaiting orders. One weekend per month members of his cell would spend time training on a remote estate located outside West Somerton.

Months later.......

Chapter 13: The Pawn's Opening
Monday, August 9, 10:30 a.m. MST (UTC/GMT-8)
Pacific Ocean off the Coast of Mexico

Akaman was a mixed Jordanian and Omani son of a close friend of Yassar's father. He was assigned to the integral role as primary recruiter, vetter and trainer of terrorist cells. He had the unique ability to identify an individual's potential, ascertain necessary motivation, and confirm the loyalty of each recruit. Each cell's mission relied heavily upon integral members and their personal motivation of revenge. *Akaman* used his well-honed skills to find, recruits willing to sacrifice their lives for the success of the cell's mission, and built on the hope that their action would help all Muslims.

Akaman personally selected each member of *Allim Tiflak* because of the importance of the cell's mission. *Allim Tiflak* was the cell assigned to kick off the initial Shura operational phase. The cell's members were highly motivated by their own personal *jihad* in response to the United States invasion of Iraq, Yemen, Afghanistan, and Osama Bin Laden assassination. Akaman had deliberately selected the *Allim Tiflak* cell to represent the Muslim lands being most negatively affected by the economic and military imperialism of the United States and the United Kingdom. The recruits had been carefully profiled physically and psychologically for their role and commitment to do harm to the United States. Their physical appearance, skin color, hair color, grooming and fashion were tailored to those common among their age group in the U.S. *Allim Tiflak* cell members were men and women willing to sacrifice their lives for Allah, their Muslim brothers and sisters, and to avenge their own personal losses. In reality they were small pawns in the opening of a much bigger game. In reviewing the cell's mission there seemed little or no little chance of getting caught before they completing their mission.

154

Allim Tiflak had trained for twenty-four months in Oman using the cover of his mining company operations. The cell was divided into three different teams: Alpha, Bravo and Charlie. The focus was learning American English colloquial and idiomatic phrases, culture, and dress as well as weapons training. The goal was to be seen and accepted as a typical young American. Each team had trained for specialized attacks within the larger cell mission. After their training, the three teams were transported in stages using ships to enter the ports of Los Angeles, Seattle, and Puerto Penasco (Rocky Point) Mexico.

The twelve-man Alpha Team's trip started with a clandestine meeting of their Greek ore freighter *MV Atlantikani* with a 112-foot yacht called *Dot Comer.* They rendezvoused at GPS coordinates 21.657428 and -113.774414 about 6000 km out on the Pacific Ocean. This locale was well away from the U.S. Coast Guard and DEA monitoring drug trafficking operations. The team was quickly transferred to the yacht, which delivered them to Puerto Penasco, Mexico. This was a small but growing seaside resort community known as a refueling port for groups of deep-sea fishermen and scuba divers. The *Dot Commer's* crew remained with the yacht in Rocky Point as Alpha Team disembarked. The yacht crew remained in easy encrypted radio contact with Alpha team leader using the lingo of typical all-terrain vehicle junkie dialogue.

"Hey dudes, hit the dunes hard today," called the Dot Commer captain. "Get some great airtime and watch your power slides. Let us know if you experience any problems. We expect to see you on the backside. Out."

"You got it dude. See you after our run," responded Jalal Hamundi, the 20-year Yemeni leader, and oldest Alpha Team member.

The Alpha Team was composed of carefully selected and trained Yemeni jihadists in their late teens that spoke Arabic Sanaani. A great deal of attention was paid to the team's appearance.as they resembled your typical American fun loving ATV fanatics. It was a perfect cover unlikely to draw attention because they did not meet the criteria for racial profiling used at the U.S. border crossing. The team felt very comfortable in the arid heat of the Sonora desert, having lived most of their lives in northern Yemen.

The team met Martha Chase, a 55-year-old motherly type in Rocky Point. She had transported drugs into the U.S. for the Sinaloa cartel for eight years, until she lost her son, Gene, when he was killed in a DEA drug raid outside Jalisco, Mexico. Her husband, Dave, lost both legs when his truck carrying drugs overturned during a U.S. Border Patrol interception near Lukeville, AZ. It was an emotional challenging ordeal with the loss of their son and seeing Dave confined in the Federal Correctional Institution in Tucson. Martha took up residence in Rocky Point, fostering a deep hatred for the U.S. that she verbalized throughout the relatively small city. Akaman easily recruited her for an important role in getting Alpha Team into the United States and securing the necessary weapons and equipment for the team's attacks. It did not take a huge cash incentive to get her to recognize that she could get revenge on the U.S. by assisting and supporting the subtle terrorist invasion.

Martha equipped alpha team with one Hummer and three large Coachman Pathfinder RV vehicles that each pulled a trailer hauling four sand covered ATVs. She provided each RV and ATV with distinctive Arizona license plates. She accumulated the equipment over the past eleven months.

Once Alpha team arrived, Martha worked separately with individual team members to verify their well-rehearsed American attitudes, accents and details of common knowledge about the Phoenix area for their crossing into the U.S. Ironically Alpha team intentionally now looked like every other group of ATV junkies out to have a good time on the Rocky Point beaches and Arizona-Mexican Sonoran desert sands. Martha spent two hours reviewing the typical Border Patrol questions with each individual team member and ensured that they were certain about their forged U.S. passport and the stamps indicating repeated trips to and from Rocky Point. After the extensive grilling trying to trick the individual cell member Martha felt that the chances of successfully crossing the border into the U.S. was still at 40-60. She was nervous about the possibility of getting tripped up and ending up in a U.S. federal prison.

U.S. Border Patrol Inspector Herb Miller stepped into the first RV driven by Jalal at the Lukeville, AZ border crossing. Jalal had five U.S. passports ready for inspection. Miller looked around the interior of the RV while another inspector used an extended mirror to examine the under belly of the vehicle.

Miller took his time examining one passport before calling out the name Scott. He stared at the face of the young man looking for any indication of nervousness or shifting eyes attempting to escape his gaze. "Where did you go to high school?"

"Shadow Mountain High School" came as an easy response from the youth.

"What was the school mascot?"

"We are the Matador's," came without hesitation.

"My son went to Shadow Mountain High School. I thought the school mascot was the "Firebirds.""

"No sir, we are the Matador's. I'm certain the Firebirds were Chaparral High School in Scottsdale were our close rivals."

Miller asked questions of each young man who nonchalantly read comic books or played a video game to add to their charade.

Miller examined the next passport and called out "Terry, where were you born?"

"St Joseph's hospital in Phoenix" came the immediate response.

"What high school do you attend?" scanning the youth for telltale signs or hesitation.

"I am a junior at Brophy College Prep."

"I heard that the good fathers of the Holy Cross were hard disciplinarians."

"I don't know. The only priest, I had at Brophy were Jesuits."

"Ah that's right, my error. Where did you go to middle school?"

"I went to Greenway. A real hell hole." Terry laughed slightly making fun of the school he never attended.

Miller continued constantly scanning each of the young men within the RV for any irregularity in their response, anything slightly unusual or signs of discomfort, while barely looking at their passports. Another inspector completed using a telescoping mirror on a pole checking the area beneath the RV vehicle and trailer for hidden drug compartments. Another Border Inspector quickly circled the RV with a drug sniffing Rottweiler. When the inspectors were satisfied they waved the first RV through the border checkpoint. It was nothing more than a routine border stop.

Martha was relieved as the first RV pulled away. She was driving the second RV. "Passports please," said Inspector Miller as he entered the vehicle. "How long have you been in Mexico?" he added.

"Just three days," Martha responded. "I hope the guys in our lead RV didn't give you a hard time. Teens these days can be pretty dam rude."

"They were fine." Miller quickly reviewing the passports, the inspector identified her son and spoke directly to Jake Chase. "How was your eighteenth birthday?"

"I had a great seventeenth birthday with my buds," Jake responded. "It couldn't have been better thanks to mom."

Turning to Martha, the inspector commented, "You really extended yourself taking this crew to Rocky Point. Most trips like this end up with a run in with the Federales for under age drinking or drunk and disorderly."

"I was just the chaperone trying to protect the team from tequila and women as they celebrated my sons 17th birthday. But they did manage to get a few Tecates while I was shopping for supplies Saturday night. Camping on the beach with the ATV's buzzing around drove me crazy. Frankly, I am glad we are heading home."

"You are lucky that nothing serious happened. What kind of team are they?"

"They are all baseball players on a Palomino Pony League team in Paradise Valley."

The inspector turned to one of the teens his passport identified as Gary and asked, "What position do you play?"

The immediate response was, "Second base and relief pitcher. Why"

"No reason. I use to play some ball. But it has been a while."

The response convinced the unsuspecting U.S. Boarder Inspector that Martha's sons, and baseball teammates were just returning from their ATV weekend birthday trip. The Hummer and last RV passed through the crossing without any trouble. Martha felt relieved as the caravan made it's way into Arizona.

The Alpha Team Mexican-U.S. crossing was insignificant other than to reinforce with the terrorists that the borders to the United States were still relatively porous despite post 9/11 efforts, if you knew where to cross and had adequate cover within the normal crossing traffic.

Martha knew that 99% of RV occupants did not have their passports scanned making the detection of the forged passports highly unlikely. Lukeville, AZ was a crossing where the Border Patrol efforts were concentrated on preventing drug traffic and detecting illegal aliens.

The team picked up arms, munitions and explosives stored by Martha Chase in a rented storage unit outside Ajo, AZ. She purchased the ordinance supplies over the last year in gun shows in Idaho, California, New Mexico and Nevada. Using cash she was able to purchase Akaman's entire list of weapons. It was simple tasks to have a local gunsmith in Idaho fully modify the weapons to automatic. The homemade TATP explosives were purchased from a black market survivalist dealer in Billings, Montana.

Five years earlier in the United Kingdom.....

Meerza Saliba had been reared in a well-educated upper class Saudi family from Jeddah, a suburb of Mecca on the shores the Red Sea. Hiss father was the President of the Islamic Development Bank and well established within the elite of Saudi society. He had always been a reverent and devout Muslim despite his parent's facade practicing a token form of the religion. He had developed a distinctive English accent during his eight years of boarding school at the British International School in Riyadh, Saudi Arabia. His two older brothers, who were active members of a terrorist group with direct ties to al-Qaeda (AQAP), heavily influenced his political awareness. At the age of nineteen he became acutely aware of social and political issues facing typical Muslims and the poor. He rejected his family's entitled lifestyle, refuted the tradition of Saudi Arabian absolute monarchy and it's feudal past, recognizing the huge class discrimination and economic inequalities within Saudi society.

Meerza's personal jihad was a result of losing his brothers. The Saudis executed both without trial, for their role in an attempt to assassinate three Saudi government officials. Local television revealed that the U.S. CIA uncovered the terrorists group's plot and informed the Ri'āsat Al-Istikhbārāt Al-'Āmah (**Arabic**: رئاسة الاستخبارات العامة), also known as the General Intelligence Directorate (GID) or the General Intelligence Presidency (GIP), the primary intelligence agency of the Kingdom of Saudi Arabia. Thus planting the seeds of a passionate hatred for the U.S. It was extremely easy for Akaman to recruit Meerza to follow in his brother's footsteps. He travelled to London taking a position as a clerk in a Soho bookstore. He spent weekends training with other terrorists in a large secluded estate located outside West Somerton. Prior to leaving the United Kingdom he was assigned as cell leader for *Allim Tiflak's*.

Earlier Meerza had stolen the identity of Samuel Kingston, a young man from Great Yarmouth, a coastal town on the North Sea 70 miles northeast of London. Kingston lived in the flat above Meerza. Kingston had applied to international law school programs at Rutgers and several other U.S. universities. It was simple for Meerza to intercept all the U.S. law program acceptance letters from Kingston's post box, and substituting basic rejection letters. The unsuspecting Kingston was accepted and ultimately enrolled at the University of Bath. Meerza used a forged UK passport that he obtained from a bribed British immigration official. He enters the U.S. taking on the new identity of Samuel Kingston. He enrolled at Rutgers University to attend their international law school program in New Brunswick, NJ on a foreign student "F-1" visa.

Meerza Saliba used the enhanced cover as Samuel Kingston, a British graduate student at Rutgers to take a role as a terrorist sleeper in the United States. Meerza was known as Sam, a gifted law student around the New Brunswick campus. He was extremely fit using his 6'4" inch 200-pound body to his advantage as the captain of the Rutgers's Rugby team. He enhanced his cover by dying his hair blonde, joining a fraternity, and frequenting the Olde Queens Tavern with teammates and frat brothers. No one suspected that he wasn't really Samuel Kingston, the student from Great Yarmouth, UK.

As time wore on Meerza's patience was wearing thin as he was about to graduate after completing the two-year law program. He yearned for the time he could officially enter into his operational service of Allah. While living in New Jersey, Meerza had witnessed the prejudice and humiliation of people within the local mosque by low life idiots for the deeds of both 9/11 and attacks in Europe. The message starting the cell's operation on the *Allim Tiflak's* Pinterest board was a welcome relief.

He made the easiest trip to Arizona riding in an air-conditioned Honda Odyssey Touring Elite mini van. Meerza met his cell outside Ajo, Arizona and supervised the loading of the duffle bags of explosives and weapons from the storage locker. Once the arsenal was inventoried, Meerza paid Martha her fee and a slight bonus in small denominations. Martha walked a short block to the Shifting Sands Motel for her Honda pick-up truck and headed east to visit her husband in Tucson. Martha planned to relocate back into the deep interior of Mexico outside Fresnillo, Zacatecas as soon as her husband was released from prison in a month.

The Alpha team caravan of vehicles travelled the 200-miles north to the Big River RV campgrounds outside Parker, AZ. It took five hours for the team to reach the designated desert campground. They had selected this facility because of its remote location and for being a regular camping site frequented by groups of ATV enthusiasts. The team's campground looked like any other ATV group encampment complete with current loud rap music, cooking hot dogs and guys tinkering with their ATVs.

Earlier that evening the *Al Zagaheer's* broadcast outlined again the significant increase in worldwide terrorist cell chatter and credible threat to a London bridge. After Alpha team had settled in their campground for the night, Meerza easily accessed the Pinterest *Allim Tiflak's* board thanks to their sophisticated high tech satellite dish mounted atop one RV vehicle. Meerza received their encrypted Pinterest orders to finish preparations and launch their attack early the following morning at 0600 hour.

Gathering the Alpha Team in the largest RV, Meerza began the team meeting with, "May Allah be praised and our work serve the greatness of Allah. May we prove ourselves to be worthy of punishing those that have enslaved our brother Muslims. Let us review for the last time the minute details of our Alpha Team attack."

This last review of the attack wasn't necessary as *Allim Tiflak* Alpha Team had spent months preparing their attack details during training at the Oman secret mining facility, and on the ship destined for Mexican waters. They knew that every detail of their mission was planned down to the smallest detail. Meerza spent six weeks reviewing the plans at the terrorist training facility in West Somerton. The team knew that *Allim Tiflak's* mission must succeed to honor the lives and service of Muslims worldwide. It was Meerza's personal responsibility to make their initial gambit succeed.

Yusra, a Yemeni 18 year old team member spoke first, "I drive my ATV to London Bridge beach at 12:30 pm and pretend to be fishing. At 1:45 a.m. I carefully slip into the water with my four explosive devices and secure them to the center pillar foundation well out of view of anyone passing by the bridge on the shoreline. I set the detonators for 6:00 a.m. and return to camp."

Raem, another Yemeni team member, taking his cue spoke in a soft tone as he pointed at the map on the RV table, "I am to enter the town from the north and take up my position here. I then await until I hear the explosion at 6:00 am before moving to my six selected targets." He pointed to each of his targets on the detailed city map of Lake Havasu.

Meerza was pleased as each Alpha team member reviewed their role and the sequence of the plan perfectly. In his heart he knew that every aspect and contingency of the plan would go off without a problem. He wondered how this small, but significant attack would be used in any overarching strategy, but knew that it would be revealed to his cell as other attacks take place. Everything was set in place, as they were the first pawns sent to initiate the first tactical opening move.

There was no doubt that the famed bridge and portions of the city would be in shambles by 6:30 a.m. The destruction of this symbol of the long-standing political relationship between the United Kingdom and the United States and their ill-gotten gains from oil, and suppression of Middle Eastern people would be momentarily lost by the American media and BBC, but eventually unveiled by *Al Zagaheer* in a detailed worldwide newscast.

The members of the *Shura* had carefully selected the Alpha Team mission and meeting site. The western Arizona open desert was where the famous World War II General George S. Patton had trained his tank brigades for the 1943 invasion of North Africa. Here is where the strategic genius of one general began plans for the defeat of the Nazis. Yassar believed that the symbolic meaning of his initial pawn's opening in this historic area might be lost on President Reynolds and the world media. If the symbolic meaning and irony were to be lost momentarily, he would have *Al Zagaheer* clarify it weeks or months later for the world after they recapped events and investigations had unfolded just to underline the terrorist leaders superior strategic and intellectual genius.

Here is where Yassar would initiate a challenge for the best minds in the intelligence and counter terrorist services of the United States, United Kingdom, Spain, France, and Israel. In this same desolate stretch of desert, *Allim Tiflak* Alpha Team would go through their preparations before executing the plan of destroying the London Bridge on the Colorado River in Lake Havasu, Arizona. An invasion strategy meant to initially confuse the British and strike fear in the hearts of America's homeland.

The small city of Lake Havasu City, Arizona was located on the Colorado River in Western Arizona. It had a population of 55,000. The community of Lake Havasu took great pride in its "London Bridge." The bridge was purchased for $2,460,000 by Robert McCullough the CEO of McCullough Oil Company. McCullough had hoped the bridge would be a new tourist destination within view of a series of casino hotels he built on the California side of the Colorado River.

The bridge was 928 feet long, and 49 feet wide spanning a portion of the river as the only egress to a small island hosting several small resorts and campgrounds. The stately five arches of solid granite in fact had been a serious problem for the City of London. It needed to be decommissioned and removed due to the deterioration of materials. The $2.5 million purchase price was a real blessing for the thin London budget killing two birds with one stone. The bridge opened in 1971 to tremendous fanfare including the dedication by the Lord Mayor of London, Sir Gilbert Inglefield. The event was to cement the long-standing relationship between the United States and United Kingdom post the Revolutionary War and War of 1812. Despite McCullough's plan the bridge became only a minor tourists attraction for the western most part of Arizona.

The inhabitants of the sleepy city were totally unprepared for any attack and much less Alpha Team's well-coordinated attack strategy, not making the connection to the televised reports of terrorist cell phone chatter and the United Kingdom's precautions to protect the London bridges. The city had benefitted from funding from Homeland Security in the post 9/11 era, but smugly assumed that there was little chance of a terrorist attack. Locals saw the federal funding as a gift for police and fire equipment. The local police presence would be no match for *Allim Tiflak's* synchronized attack on the bridge and selected targets. Alpha Team carefully assessed the response by city police, Mohave County Sheriff, Arizona Department of Public Safety (DPS – AZ State Police), and FBI resources. The earliest outside assistance could arrive was several hours after the attack, depending on the terrorist successful destruction of all communication links isolating the remote city.

Port of Los Angeles, Long Beach, CA

Allim Tiflak's Bravo team entered the United States at the Port of Los Angeles using the cover as borax and limestone shipment workers. The Greek MV Atlantikani ore ship regularly entered the Port of Los Angeles delivering high-grade limestone for steel mills in Southern California. The team picked up four used vehicles at a small storage facility outside San Pedro, CA. The eight-person Omani Baharna Arabic language team kept a very low profile as they settled into two very simple Super 8 Motels just outside Disneyland in Anaheim. They registered at the motels with forged Wyoming, Nevada, Idaho, and South Dakota driver licenses. Their immediate duty was to reconnaissance their target and map out their escape route through Los Angeles back to Long Beach. Bravo Team awaited contact by their support team on the storage of their weapons and TATP explosive devices. They utilized the motels free Internet access to check the Pinterest site for updates on their orders. Meerza, their cell leader called to confirm the team's safe arrival and ordered that they review their plan of action.

Port of Seattle, WA Foreign Trade Zone #5

Five Iraqi couples spoke the Qeltu Arabic dialect. They entered the U.S. through the Port of Seattle Foreign Trade Zone #5 using their cover as mechanical engineers on the Liberian APXL vessel. The huge container ship had a typical cargo of German BMWs, Volkswagens, Audis and Porsches. In addition the manifest contained high tech steel production machinery from Germany. The Charlie team's cover was to deliver and install the machinery in the Nucore Steel's Harris Supply Solutions subsidiary Seattle facility. After docking the team of terrorists traveling as couples caught separate busses to Oakland, San Jose and San Francisco. The day after their arrival in the Bay area, they registered and met in a room at the Oakland Marriott Civic Center Hotel. Each team member carried forged Idaho, Wyoming, Colorado Montana, or California driver's licenses to register. Meerza called during the team meeting and confirmed their daily routines until the attack. Their immediate tasks were a series of reconnaissance missions on three targets within San Francisco and reviewing their escape plan.

Chapter 14: The Increasing Intelligence Buzz
Tuesday, August 10, 1:10 a.m. EST (UTC/GMT-6)
NSA Headquarters, Fort Meade, MD

Hub Nolan, National Security Agency (NSA), Under the Signals Intelligence Mission, Director of Anti-Terrorism Division had just arrived at the NSA Headquarters. Following a rude awakening by his global network communications staff, he had driven the relative short distance along the empty Baltimore-Washington Parkway to Fort Meade in fifteen minutes. A new record certainly assisted by the lack of early morning traffic on the Parkway and Rte. 32. Entering the Anti-Terrorism conference room, Hub turned to the Global Communications Night Officer, Fred Bates.

"Fred, what do you make of the latest increase in terrorist cell communications? I thought this was a ruse, but here it is raising its' ugly head again. Big Time!"

"Hub, it can't be anything good. We have not heard this volume of chatter since prior to 9/11. It seemed that the bad guys were subverting their communications using encrypted communications used for online game technology. Their use of cell is certainly different. But there is something big going down. I'd bet my retirement that we have multiple targets and terrorist cells in operation that are attempting to coordinate their operations. I wish we had more, but as you know the CIA, FBI, U.S. Army Intelligence and Security Command (INSCOM) at Belvoir, and U.S. Army Intelligence Center at Huachuca are working overtime to sift through the strange chatter to get the real intelligence gems analyzed. Dealing with the pure volume is going to take time we do not have."

Looking at 22 pages of printouts of varied translated terrorist cell communications, from over 26 different countries, Hub asked, "If this is what you think, we may not have any of time at all. Have we coordinated with Shep at CIA or the folks over at Homeland Security?"

"Yeah, I talked with Shep, and Metz."

Pausing to read the highlighted portions of the printouts, Hub continued, "This interagency report looks like a hornets nest is about to empty into our world. I have never seen this level of cell chatter. It looks like London hits the top of the list as most likely target. Let's keep on it by increasing our asset resources. I want to call in additional analysts to break down every possible detail and pattern. Is there any word from Spencer at SIS?"

"Hub, take it easy," Fred stated in a reassured voice. "I spoke to Spencer about 15 minutes ago, he knows that you were called in and expects to talk with you upon your return. SIS have intelligence alerts from everyone on the tremendous influx of Arabic transmissions traffic originating from Pakistan and spreading to Iraq, Indonesia, Iran, Syria, Jordan, Somalia, Afghanistan, Yemen, Libya and Saudi. Director Ford is on his way in to get a quick briefing before heading to the White House. Shep said that the President, Secretary Swartz and Director Thomas were on their way to the Situation Room. When Ford arrives they will recommend to raise our Homeland Security Advisory System (HSAS) threat level to Orange (high). The British have been on full alert for months maintaining security over their bridges since this game started back in May. I anticipated that the massive increase warranted action, so we activated our off duty analysts. They are inbound and should be here within the half-hour."

Heading into his office, Hub asked "Have we gotten any coordinated verification from our allies? I want confirmation from Spencer at SIS; Goldblum at Mossad; Helmut at Bundesnachtendient; Françoise at DGSE, and Elena at CNI, ASAP. We need to know what their read is on the huge influx." Hub pausing momentarily, but pushed forward with, "Somebody needs to have something more definitive. Please get me a face–to-face video link with Sarah Mertz at CIA, her home is in Rockville. After that I need to speak with Spencer, if he is available."

Fred was unaccustomed to having Hub takeover command of the center during his overnight shift. "I just received verification, that National Security Advisor Abe Greenfeld is on his way from his home in Reston to the Situation Room via chopper. Looks like all the intelligence community heavies are heading in to review the massive increase in chatter to make a potential increased HSAS threat decision. We have also verified with SIS of the significant influx of messages mentioning London or bridge. They confirmed the chatter from their independent sources and do not seem too happy with the latest news. It is like this impending attack is going viral with a million hits on social media. Nearly a hundred thousand cell hits in the last 30-minutes. At least it is a decent hour in London. Most of their guys are well into their work day."

Hub, "The timing on this might look a little suspicious to the Senate Intelligence Oversight Chairman Nunn. Secretary Swartz, Director Thomas, and Ford are scheduled to appear before the committee in closed sessions today to request an additional $9 billion for Homeland Security designated for varied intelligence agencies.

From what I know, Nunn is like all Republicans favoring intelligence appropriations, but opposing large cities getting a larger than proportionate appropriation than smaller cities, rural areas and states that seem outside the realm of probability of an eminent terrorists attack. Senator Nunn's self interest is a problem in itself as large city targets are far more important to terrorist. Obviously terrorists target attacks against New York, Washington, London or Paris as headlines are more valuable than Jackson Hole, Wyoming. Funny coincidence that the good Senator hails from Wyoming, looking after his own rural gun wheeling constituency."

Hub found himself shaking his head as he scanned the latest printout pages with analyst comments while the printer pounded out more pages. Without looking up from the printouts he asked, "Has Senator Nunn been briefed on this spiraling increase in cell communications and the fact that the President and the NSC (National Security Council) are in the Situation Room to consider raising the HSAS alert level?"

"Nope", Fred, shook his head, and headed back to the conference room. The huge room was rapidly filling with NSA supervisors reviewing and highlighting analyst reports. The room was a packed with activity despite the hour to sift through the exponentially increasing volume of terrorist communications.

Fred yelled to Hub over the supervisor and analyst chatter, "Sarah Mertz is at Langley in a meeting. She will call back when she is available. Do you want Spencer now?"

"Please connect my favorite Brit." Walking into the conference room, Hub states, "Good morning folks. As you can see this chatter level is unprecedented. It's going to be a long day in the trenches everyone. So lets roll up our sleeves and get to work. Lives are at risk." While entering the conference room, Hub quickly stares at a cell phone communications volume graph projected on the huge screen that has jumped dwarfing in proportion from its start in May. "I want Shep and Mertz to have our preliminary report by 5 am, and a summary report before lunch. That includes all transmissions up to and including 3 am. I want theories on the terrorist motivation and likelihood of it being a specific London bridge or other targets. So let's get at it."

"I have Spencer on line 3." Fred yelled,

"Morning Spencer, has your team been up all night?"

"Middle of the night for your gang Hub, sorry our mess is putting your blokes on such alert."

Hub replies in a fake Australian accent with, "No worries, mate. Do you have any tidbits for us?"

Spencer was not amused as he might have been 37 hours earlier as the constant pressure of the damned cell calls kept increasing. "We thought that this was toning down. These nuts are playing a game with us. We have nothing of importance to report from this end. Do your chaps have anything useful?"

"Sorry," Hub replied, "Nothing here but we have teams analyzing every call. I will catch you later if we find any gems in this damn mountain of data."

"Let's check in again in a few hours," Spencer fully understood the need for time to find anything of value.

NSA Director Ford rushed into the conference room. "Hub, I need to make this brief before heading to the Situation Room. What seems to be the sequence of communication topics and the variance in the increased chatter?"

"Sir, the increase originated in the mountains of Pakistan, but rapidly spread to 15 countries over a week. In the last six hours it has grown to over 69 distinct cell areas in 26 different countries. Something big is brewing, but we still do not have a handle on it. We have drones ready to respond if they come out of their damn caves."

"Keep your feet to the fire, we need to know what is going on and really happening. It might well involve the United States. I have the Senate Intelligence Committee meeting at 10 a.m. I'd like to have something solid in a report for Senator Nunn. We need to impress that little four eyed Republican weasel, if we plan to get the funding appropriation increased for cities."

Hub hands the stack of printouts to Ford. The pile now is at 147 pages and growing rapidly at three pages per second.

"We'll do the best we can. I'll make sure you have as much valuable intelligence we can glean before the committee meeting is over. We have all hands on deck working on it here and at the Utah Data Center."

The 1.5 billion dollar Utah Data Center was a key component of the Comprehensive National Cybersecurity Initiative (CNCI) located outside Buffdale in southern Utah. It operates as a massive storage complex for all the U.S. Intelligence Community under the direction of the NSA.

The Center is a complete repository of all private e-mails, text messages, cell phone calls, and Internet searches, as well as all types of personal data trails-parking receipts, credit card transactions, checks, deposits, travel itineraries, bookstore purchases, and other digital 'pocket litter' of U.S. domestic and expatriate citizens, as well as foreign residents. Additional data streams of the same raw data were intercepted from around the world in 198 languages giving the U.S. capabilities of monitoring the world's interaction. The huge self-contained seventeen building Center campus was reliant on supercomputers capable of matching data bites to document and make sense out of data for the intelligence agencies. Their direct feed to NSA analyst at Meade was the key to helping make sense of the avalanche of data.

"That should be around 11:45. I'll ask Nunn for a few minutes at that time. After lunch I have a 1 p.m. meeting with Secretary Swartz at Homeland Security in her office on 12th Street. You can send an agency carrier with hard copies of any further intelligence directly to her office and hand it off on my arrival. The agenda is to discuss my presentation for the annual meeting of Homeland Security and the State Directors of Emergency Response Management. President Reynolds has required that all intelligence agency directors attend to show our level of cooperation and eliminate the issue of potential competition for dollars from Nunn's and appropriation committees. Thus demonstrating our effective inter-agency coordinated efforts since 9/11. The OEM and FEMA annual meeting will have Directors from all fifty states and various territories. Lucky me, I get to follow the keynote speaker in Phoenix Saturday afternoon. Why couldn't they have their annual meeting in Phoenix in January, when it isn't so damn hot? 118 degrees is not going to be fun and playing golf in that frying pan is out of the question. I should be back early Tuesday. Let's hope nothing big breaks while all the directors are in Phoenix."

———

Hub thought to himself, *how the hell could Dexter complain about a brief getaway to Phoenix. They booked the meeting at the super plush Phoenician Resort, an amazing four plus star facility.* As Hub thought about the Ford's junket, a bulletin flashed across his huge computer screen of a scheduled meeting with his analyst supervisors in five minutes followed by a conference call with the NSA Utah Directorate.

"Sounds like it might be a good meeting," Hub noted. "On another note the cell chatter may well be a subterfuge while the real target is here in the U.S.. The dam London bridges just does not make sense. You may want to mention that during your Nunn briefing."

"I had the same thought," Ford responded looking at Hub. "I already had a discussion about the possibility of a ruse with Swartz. Let's hope that the Brits security precautions prevent any attack and there are no attacks in the U.S."

The President's National Security Council and Secretary Swartz placed the country on the higher Orange HSAS alert based upon the intercepts. The change of alert status was noted on the morning news telecast and nearly crashed Facebook.

"I just received confirmation, we are at an Orange elevated alert level", Hub reported as he re-entered the conference room. "I hope the Brits are ready as something ugly is coming their way. It isn't going to be a spoon full of sugar. That is for sure. Now let's make sure a threat against the U.S. isn't in the mix." Hub stated loud enough for the entire room to hear. A few quiet giggles could be heard among supervisors at the far end of the massive conference room.

Chapter 15: Stages of System Implementation
Tuesday, August 10, 1:35 a.m. MST (UTC/GMT-8)
Palo Verde Nuclear Facility, Tonopah, AZ, 50 miles west
of Phoenix AZ

Sean selected the Palo Verde nuclear facility for the initial installation of his system for a number of reasons. First was the fact that the plant is the largest nuclear facility in the United States, housing three giant reactors producing 3.3 gigawatts. Each of the independent reactors generates enormous power, feeding the huge power grid from Los Angeles to San Diego. Second, Palo Verde's location and relative proximity to Cal-Tech's campus in Pasadena, California, where their high-powered supercomputer could simulate the effectiveness of the design system and its modifications in a matter of minutes. Third, Phoenix, Arizona was only a short 50 miles east. It had the technical clean-room support at Intel, Honeywell and Motorola facilities for any further electronic modifications and spec circuitry necessary for the project. Finally, the Palo Verde Sonoran desert location was easy for NSA satellites and drones to observe without weather related visual or electronic interference.

Sean had not spent much time in the Southwest. He was reminded of his childhood home in Buffalo, New York, which seemed so very distant and intensely compacted compared to the wide-open vistas, wondrous sunsets, evening stars and extreme summer heat of the Sonoran Desert. The Arizona wide streets and highways were much less congested as the Los Angeles area. Something about the desert appealed to Sean on a somewhat strange spiritual level. The night sky had a way of making a person feel insignificant compared to the celestial orbs and satellites racing through space. Sean drifts to thinking *there is an argument that there must be God, a supreme creator carefully placing so many planets and stars in motion in space.* For a moment Sean was jealous of his colleagues in the Cal-Tech Astronomy Department for their exploration of space and understanding of distant universes of which he had comparatively little knowledge. They must have front row seats for the galactic show he was witnessing from afar. He was struck by the illusion that you could reach out and touch the stars in the clear western sky.

This was the Cal-Tech team's eleventh onsite visit. Each visit had been well coordinated, but under a cloak of ultra-high security with all Palo Verde personnel. Some workers were given a break to vacate their work areas within the control rooms and reactor areas as the team entered to do a check. Homeland Security and NNS wanted to ensure that the thousands of Southern California Edison and Arizona Public Service (APS) personnel were somewhat unaware of the nature of the implementation of the redundancy system. Only Dr. Lawrence Grant, Director of the facility and Daniel Hoppe, Plant Security Director and most of the security supervisors knew the complex project details. Their knowledge of the project was purely so they could make the necessary arrangements to vacate necessary areas prior to the team's arrival and on site work. The security on the project was extremely tight.

The Cal-Tech team had established a pattern of arriving onsite at the beginning of the 11 p.m. to 7 a.m. graveyard shift. This permitted them to work inside and outside in the relative cool of the evening. Daylight temperatures at the facility reached 115+ degrees, but nights cooled to a relatively comfortable 82 degrees. The timing pattern permitted the completion of each phase of installation with a minimum of the facility personnel being displaced from their work areas. In fact there was little doubt that the personnel were somewhat unaware that the system was being installed and tested, thinking that the Cal-Tech team was doing some important Atomic Energy Commission modeling research for a new nuclear plant design.

Sean was pleased with the tremendous progress of the three different four-person onsite teams. The onsite teams relied heavily upon three additional offsite members working with the data streams at Cal-Tech and a NNS team interfacing the system with the NSA satellite system.

Jake Murphy, the Cal-Tech team's best computer whiz had installed the three hundred sensors that fed a constant stream of data on the three reactors and the control systems to three separate sequenced computers. Jake was now working with Sarah Hughes on the remote alternative control systems. She was able to link and upload the computer data gathered by the sensors from each reactor to the secure dedicated lines to Cal-Tech. Krishna Rashid was responsible for the NSA satellite linkup providing oversight and off site management system. In essence Sean and the team had created a system that monitored each reactor and in the event of a technical problem automatically made the necessary corrective action thus creating a redundant control system that would not permit the reactor to reach dangerous levels leading to radioactive emissions or the process leading to a meltdown.

The system prevented either an accidental act or deliberate act to set the reactor into a dangerous situation for one hour. Sean had used data from Three Mile Island and Chernobyl to run over fourteen million super computer simulations in designing this new high tech system. The system took human error or terrorism out of the picture and made a safe source of energy even safer by eliminating human intervention.

Sean was working with Craig Stevens and DeJesus Trujillo on finalizing the series of communications system. Craig was the team's communications expert, able to encrypt the real time data and audio-visual feeds. DeJesus Trujillo was the audio and visual expert, who had tapped into the facilities internal security system and installed a separate independent facility monitoring system. This provided Homeland Security and the NNS office in Washington DC with both visual and auditory surveillance abilities even when the internal monitor system malfunctioned or was turned off. The NNS would also have two systems to monitor and control each of the facilities from a special facility outside the District of Columbia beltway in Rockville, Maryland. Homeland Security and NNS had special plans to have two drones on site to provide additional outdoor evaluative eyes during the Beta testing of the system during a scheduled force-on-force exercise in November.

Back on the Cal-Tech campus Sam Ridder and Willie Two-Hawks ran the Team's simulations while Harold Fong calculated variances of automated response time and stages of correction within reactors. Thus far the data and system design had been flawless on all three reactors. Ned Toppin had finalized and installed the immobilization system in each of the reactor control rooms as a safeguard against human deliberate acts.

The entire team made tremendous headway in both the installation and the initial testing. Both Reactor #1 and #2 had already been fully installed and tested. If all went well over the next two days the final installation would be completed nearly six weeks earlier that Sean's own timetable.

The final beta test of the Redundancy System on all three reactors would be part of the next "Force-on-Force" simulation exercise scheduled for November, a full two months sooner than expected by Homeland Security. The simulation exercises were designed to enact different scenarios in which terrorists attempt to take over the facility or some other disaster occur including a deliberate direct hit of a reactor by a 777 jet aircraft. During the exercise one half of the four hundred-man security force usually acted as the terrorists while the other half defended the nuclear facility. These exercises were held in various scales every six months and rarely involved all the security personnel. The November exercise was to be an exception. It was designed as a security test with the inclusion of the Redundancy System.

Southern California Edison and Arizona Public Service had their annual stockholders meeting scheduled for December 1st. As with any power grid corporation, utilities are pressured to present plans that ultimately added value to the bottom line. Dr. Lawrence Grant,CEO of Palo Verde was mandated by both CFOs in Phoenix and Los Angeles to increase production and significantly cut expenses. Grant and Hoppe, Palo Verde Security Director had just finished a meeting about this budget issue which ended in a heated debate on how to cut the security department by either cutting the size of the force or layoff some of the higher paid more experienced security staff members.

There was a veiled threat that if cuts were not in place by the end of the fiscal year there may be a move to outsource the entire security force which was unheard of within the nuclear energy community. Clearly the size of the security force-on-force exercise would be less than in the past and perhaps cut further if the redundancy system passed the Beta testing.

Sean was located outside on the roof of the reactor control room using a specially designed landline to communicate with Craig and DeJesus inside the Control Room. Cell phones and walkie-talkies were useless given the five-foot thickness of concrete encasing the facility.

"If we can get this last system up and running tonight, I'll buy Corona's for everyone at the Buckeye Grill at lunch."

"You are on Doc, just a few tweaks and we are good to go." Craig stated in his heavy Oklahoma accent. "I just can't wait to tip a cold one with the rest of the team. I know how to put those tasty limes to use in a Coronas."

DeJesus chimed in with "That might take a bit of doing. I think Jake and Sarah are kind of into each other. They might want to be alone." DeJesus let off his crackling laugh in a manner that would drive others up the wall, but somehow the team had come to accept his humorous perspective on almost everything. "They might just want to be out under the million stars in this Arizona sky rather than in the smoke filled Buckeye Grill. Did you ever wonder why the Grill allows smoking when it is illegal in Arizona bars? They want to kill off the radioactivity on their clients glowing clothing." As usual DeJesus laughed at his joke, to a background of loud team moans and groans.

While enjoying his team's levity Sean continued, "Lets test the strength of the video and audio signal on my command. Is everyone ready? Cal-Tech that includes you."

Craig, "A ok doc. We are good to go. DeJesus, go through your count down sequence."

DeJesus "ten…nine…..eight…seven…six…five …four ….three.. two….one. We have blast- off!"

Still outside standing on the roof, Sean responds, "It is being transmitted through both the internal and external system loud and clear." Then picking up his cell phone and pressed the preset for a conference call.

"NSA, Homeland Security, NNS and Cal-Tech, This is a Dr. McMurray." Sean paused momentarily " We are initiating testing of Palo Verde Reactor #3. Do you have both the internal and external streams of audio and visual of the control room and reactor chamber? How is the data stream?"

"This is Dr. Leary at Homeland Security NNS control center in Rockville. The NSA satellite feed is loud and clear on both systems. We are also getting the reactor computer data stream and the video oversight system."

"Dr. McMurray, this is Sam on campus. We are getting the data stream from the sensors and both audio and video feeds. Fong and I will run a check on the data analysis, but from what we can see the data indicates normal operation and is coming with no interference and less than a one second delay. You have to love the NSA satellite super speed feeds. Better than the best Wi-Fi by a million times. That's not too shabby for government equipment!"

Dr. Leary's distinctive Irish accent added, "Sean, be sure to thank your Cal-Tech team for a stellar job. The next test should be simple during the "Force-on-Force" exercise. It looks like your redundancy system can do all that we expected and more. Your team has done a remarkable job. The installation and testing has exceeded our expectations. I will pass on the good news to Dr. Gibson, Task Force members and all the folks at NNS. Congratulations Sean!"

Just then Jake and Sarah appeared on the roof holding hands. They had overheard most of the conversation. Apparently, they too were more caught up in the crystal clear desert sky than the system success.

Sean acknowledged their presence with a nod, "I'd bet my entire climbing rack on its' success! We'll prove it during the "Force-on-Force simulation. Over and out from Palo Verde."

"Homeland Security, NNS and NSA signing off at 9:56 am Eastern Standard Time!"

Sam, "Doc, tell everybody that Fong and I will arrange the end of project celebration when the team returns to campus. How does a catered BBQ meal at a microbrewery in Old Town Pasadena sound? On second thought, perhaps we could reschedule our Yosemite climb. We could celebrate on the top of Half-Dome minus the food and beer."

Sean laughed, "That sounds great. I will let everyone know. I am sure they will want to party after being in the desert putting our project together."

"Let us know what you decide. Fong and I'll make the arrangements. I'll have Fong put the final data analysis printouts on your desk. We'll be more than ready for the "Force on Force test. Until then this is Cal-Tech signing off. Good thing campus security has not bugged us during this overnight project."

Sean grabbed the landline phone, "Craig and DeJesus clean up your gear. We have the green light from Homeland Security, NNS, NSA and Cal-Tech. You need to come up on the roof to join Jake, Sarah, and I. We are clear for reactor #3. The graveyard shift will be out of here in the next few minutes."

Turning to Jake and Sarah, Sean yelled, "Hey you two, these stars are phenomenal."

Chapter 16: Gambit for Mayhem
Wednesday, August 11   9:45 p.m. GST (UTC/GMT+4)
Prince Tower, second tallest skyscraper in Dubai, UAR,
Conference Room

Our jihad has reached a new tactical operational stage as the sun sweeps from the east. Yassar thought, *today will mark a new era in my leadership and mark the start of our acts of revenge. The world will soon discover that they are not engaging a crude Berber nomadic thug trapped in a cave. They ultimately will recognize my true genius and leadership on putting the Americans and their allies in their place.*

Yassar had uncharacteristically ordered an aide to call together the members of the Shura from their quarters after dinner. He had just received an encrypted Pinterest message from the *Allim Tiflak* cell. Kenji had confirmed as per the Pinterest orders, Meerza had all three Allim Tiflak Alpha, Bravo and Charlie teams ready to move on their targets. He was awaiting the final "go" order. Yassar thought that *it's ironic that that the cell teams used the same designations as elite U.S. military squad units.*

Entering the conference room, Yassar used his usual greeting, "May Allah be praised. Let our work bring honor and glory to Allah, Muslim brothers and our families. We have had contact from *Allim Tiflak.* Meerza reports that they are on schedule to move and their mission should be accomplished at the designated time."

Looking at the large projected computer screen showing Arizona, California, Spain, France and United Kingdom. Yassar's computer cursor highlighted the name of each cell, leadership, member strength, weapons, and scheduled mission sequence within the larger attack strategy, as he spoke of the multiple synchronized attack strategy.

It was far more sophisticated than anything attempted by terrorist in the past and would make 9/11 look purely amateurish as each ploy increased the pressure on the Americans and their allies. The inability to secure the safety for their citizens would bring public anxiety and distrust and destabilize the governments.

"Dakari has *Ibrabim's Dream* ready in Bilbao. Dirar reports that *Aliyah in Wonderland* is ready in Paris. Hamid reports that *Al Salwa* is patiently waiting our sequenced time in London. We will await the responses from these synchronized attacks before activating the next level of attacks. Nassar and the *Tolem* cell are ready to move into Arizona and swing into action. They are currently in eastern California. Fathi and his *Ya'qūb aš* cell have been working adjacent to the target for nearly two years. They have taken up a position west of London. The first wave will create chaos and a lack of confidence in the efforts of the counter terrorist, intelligence agencies and governments. Each of our cells are well equipped, overly trained, and in strategic position to strike. We have thought out every detail, anticipated the logical range of responses and have a high certainty of success. All we need to do is push the Pinterest boards into action and have *Al Zagaheer* broadcast their successes. Our pawns are advancing and hunting down our enemy. Their attacks will bring well thought but predictable measured responses that will fall right into out overall long-term strategy. Kenji sent the message to Meerza to start the attack."

Mousaffa smiled as Yassar finished speaking to the *Shura* in a measured manner, but with clear emotion in his voice. Mousaffa spoke in a soft tone to the Shura, "Yassar has shown us his genius again in the development of such a complex planned campaign against our enemies. May Allah and all his believers benefit from our work as we avenge our infidel enemies."

Mohammed asked, "Have the sequential messages been encrypted using our new RX56 system? We know that SIS, NSA, CIA and FBI are monitoring our bogus cell phone chatter. Our enemies are wondering why the sudden massive cell chatter given that other terrorist groups are using communication with apps and PS4 game systems. The intelligence agencies are confused and baffled by a terrorist group capable of such a wide range of cell chatter. They have not picked up on the fact that we sent ambiguous simple encrypted messages via real time to cell phones across the world to create chatter just to keep their analyst teams busy. It will be a shame that they miss the real cue of the "London Bridge" attack being located in Arizona. They have come to expect that we need to rely on the same low-tech cell chatter communication in all our attacks. It is a huge flaw in their thinking under estimating our abilities and resources."

Kenji interrupted, "I encrypted them myself. I agree that keeping them busy attempting to analyze bogus cell chatter is a pure stroke of genius. I can control the cell phone chatter from 26 countries from here in our conference room."

Yassar, "Very well Kenji! Let's give Nuru at *Al Zagaheer* the sequence slightly before each of the attacks as well as the rational background manifesto with embedded details. It is critical that *Al Zagaheer* be aware of the synchronized attacks and our assessment of the responses by their counter terrorist, intelligence and security forces. The *Al Zagaheer* broadcast will be our voice in presenting the truth about our enemies and their attempts to control what they will not understand. As a result intelligence communities will concentrate their efforts on detecting how *Al Zagaheer* got the information. The beauty of our covert operations with Nuru is its simplicity." Yassar handed over his binder of carefully sequential messages.

"The first will give *Al Zagaheer* the full scope of the *Allim Tiflak* attacks and destruction of designated selected U.S. targets. Thus bringing our enemies focus from London to Arizona. The second will present the European attacks bringing into play the revenge against the allies. Hamid's first real action has a special targeted individual. Kenji, are you sure Hamid is worthy of his important leadership position in this attack? You mentioned that he seemed a bit shaky during one of your initial meetings although he did better during his training."

Kenji immediately went on the defensive. "Yassar, he is one of the very best in the field. I know he was nervous being in my presence and having to address the depth of my questions. I personally vouch for his abilities and commitment to our cause. He sees our mission as a prelude to massive changes in Muslim countries, and is committed to the success of his mission."

"Enough said, Kenji, but I do hold you personally responsible for Hamid's role in the larger overarching plans. His cell's mission is important in the European sequence of attacks. We should be hearing verification from Meerza at any moment. Angri, has Nuru acknowledged our financial support? If all goes well with the encrypted broadcast we should look into making further financial commitments to *Al Zagaheer*."

Angri spoke in measure words, "Nuru texted me through an encrypted throw away phone to confirm the delivery of cash and to personally thank us for the opportunity to give voice to our efforts.

Without our acquisition and support *Al Zagaheer* would just have been a broken down local Arabic TV station of little importance. We put them in a powerful worldwide position eventually rivaling CNN, BBC and Al Jazeera in the Arab World. They know that we can pull the plug at any time, but I fear it will not be long before they begin to feel large enough to begin to question us as their puppet masters wanting to televise real journalism without our bias or perspective. Nuru understands that we will exercise the necessary controls to ensure that our message is vented to the Muslim world. She is our insider on their management team. I am looking forward to seeing her this weekend in Cairo."

Yassar noted as he finished a small cup of mint tea, "Angri, we must maintain our ability to dictate our position to the world, especially at this juncture as we start our strategic field operations. The world needs to know the flawless planning and eventually the symbolic clues left for the intelligence communities to decipher. Their embarrassment and failure to anticipate and prevent our attacks is very important. Let's rely on Nuru's insight and relationship with the director, *Jarid Fahrida.* Her read on him will go a long way in ensuring our ability to effectively use *Al Zagaheer.* As a contingency Mohammed find out more about Jarid Fahrida's habits, family, children and other vulnerabilities. Having that information at our disposal will ensure our ability to motivate Fahrida's continued support."

Chapter 17: Surprise Attack
Wednesday, August 11, 6:00 a.m. MST (UTC/GMT-8)
Lake Havasu City, AZ

The cell met at 4:30 a.m. in their campsite to get to their assigned approach positions outside Lake Havasu City. Each of the twelve members rode their own ATV with six explosives devices assigned to specific sequential targets within a strategically planned time frame. The attack plan had been rehearsed down to every detail. The instructions were simplified: avoid as many people as possible; fire and eliminate anyone that threatens your mission; drive up to your target; throw the explosive satchel as close as possible to the target; drive away from the target for 15-20 seconds; dial the preprogrammed code for your target # on your cell phone; and ensure that the explosive device detonated. The use of your cell phone target # will automatically indicate that number target you eliminated on Meerza's computer; and move on to your next target. When you have completed your mission rendezvous at the specified GPS location no later that 6:45 a.m.

At 6:00 a.m. the explosive devices at the base of the bridge foundation detonated within a second of each other. The heavily weight of the stone infrastructure of the bridge failed and it collapsed unceremoniously into the middle arm of the Colorado River. The twelve members of the team entered Lake Havasu City from different directions on ATVs after hearing the bridge detonation. The ATV vehicles granted the terrorists incredible mobility as they hit each of their assigned six targets.

Each terrorist carried two Glock laser sighted silenced weapons and three explosive satchels. Their explosive devices were detonated remotely using their cell phone mounted on the ATV.

192

The satchels weighed twelve pounds each and had the explosive power of five sticks of TNT. Meerza used the Vertex EVX-534 Radio UHF battery powered radio to contact Alpha team members. A short text message was sent automatically when the team member used their cell phone to detonate and destroy a target. The signal was then illustrated on his laptop by indicating the target number in red as it was eliminated. The automated system was set up to ensure that each target was eliminated in sequential order to totally isolate the city. Failure to hit specific targets would bring responses from around the state and overwhelming law enforcement resources. The team executed every aspect of their attack plan with amazing professional precision.

The residents of the city were totally unaware as the team crisscrossed the city using their Glock weapons eliminating any witness that may have seen them throwing the satchel at their target. Fifteen seconds later remotely a cell phone signal detonated the explosive charges. Each terrorist carefully watched to ensure that the target was eliminated before moving to the next target. Each of the team members knew that failure to knockout a target placed the team's mission at risk. As cell leader, Meerza did not have a roll in the execution of the attacks. He monitored as each terrorist target number turned red on his laptop. In all it had taken 18 minutes, about three minutes less than he had expected for the completion of Alpha team's mission.

The satchels destroyed seventy-two targets hitting all forms of communication including cell, landlines major exchange boxes, satellite dish communications, cable and fiber optic cable, commercial, ham radio and TV towers, and telephone lines completely isolating the small city. The airport runway, city police station and squad cars, city hall, radio transmission tower, Mohave Electrical and UNI Source Electrical facilities, cell and microwave relay towers and numerous other targets were destroyed or made inoperable.

The Mohave County Sheriffs patrol car was returning along AZ Route 95 from an area south of Parker when they saw several plumes of smoke from within the city. They attempted unsuccessfully to raise the Lake Havasu City Police, Sheriff's substation and Fire Department on their radio. They did not know that all communications were cut.

Meezra pulled his ATV into a vista on AZ Route 95 about a quarter mile south of the city at 6:20 a.m. The only team contact with law enforcement came a moment later when that Mohave County Sherriff's patrol car pulled along side Meezra as he watched the results of the attack. The four arches in the center of the bridge had disappeared into the river as the city continued erupting from secondary explosions. The city was covered in plumes of smoke and fames. The deputies found it hard to believe that the peaceful city looked like a war zone. The unfortunate deputies inadvertently pulled over at the same small vista point in Rotary Park where the tourist stopped to take pictures of the bridge. Their attention was drawn by the chaos of smoke and fire from the city center. As the deputies exited their vehicle and moved forward well in front of the ATV, Meerza simply pulled out his silenced Glock 17 custom stippling Osprey Cerakote OD weapon and eliminated the only witnesses to this part in the attack with bullets to their heads.

Before the attack Meerza had been trying to convince himself that if confronted he had the personal strength and ability to shoot anyone that stood in his way or jeopardized the team's mission. Despite the hours of training in the UK he was unsure until that very moment when he pulled out the silenced Gloch and killed both deputies. As per his training, he then eliminated the patrol car by lighting the end of a sheet of paper from the patrol car and placing it inside the squad cars fuel cap. Thirty seconds later the car exploded in a tangled mess while Meerza was well on his way escaping south towards the rendezvous location outside Parker, AZ. He felt nothing other than relief having removed the only unaccounted for law enforcement patrol vehicle in the vicinity. Meerza stopped about a mile outside of Lake Havasu to detonate an explosive device and destroy the electrical transmission line from Parker Dam. The power line was an auxiliary back-up power source for Lake Havasu City. At 6:25 a.m. the Alpha team attack was finished.

The team rendezvoused at their predetermined GPS desert site just south of the Bill Williams River National Wildlife Preserve in a dry wash about eight miles south of Lake Havasu. There they wiped clean all the ATVs and set them on fire. They got in the mini-van and Hummer, and destroyed the escape vehicle tire tracks.

Three team members drove the Hummer on the Parker Dam Road across the Colorado to Earp, CA. They took the Parker Road to CA Route 95 south to Blythe, CA. They carefully wiped down the Hummer and returned it to the A1 Car Rental agency at the airport. They boarded a private chartered general aviation aircraft at Blythe Airport (KBLH) for the short hop to Deer Valley Municipal Airport in north Phoenix.

After their arrival they caught a Super Shuttle to a small mini mall along Route 17. They walked a short eight blocks and registered at the Extended Stay America Motel on West Rose Garden Road. Their initial task completed, they needed to lay low out of sight until the next phase of the Alpha team's mission.

The rest of the team continued on AZ Route 95 in the Mazda mini van and made their way to their campsite. They packed up the campsite within ten minutes and calmly departed for Mexico listening for any radio announcements about the attack on Lake Havasu City. None of the preprogrammed thirteen radio stations were on the air, a sort of unspoken tribute to the team's effective elimination of the radio transmission tower and relay towers.

Meerza drove the Mazda mini van filled with duffle bags of weapons to a storage facility in Ajo, AZ. He deposited the weapons in a locker and picked up his white Honda Odyssey Touring Elite mini van in the Motel 6 parking lot. He posted *Allim Tiflak's* Alpha team success for phase one on their Pinterest board using the Motel 6 Wi-Fi. If all went well he would drive the short three hours on Interstate 8 into Phoenix and arrive before 2:00 p.m. During his drive there still were no transmissions from the Lake Havasu radio stations, any of the rural Arizona or Phoenix radio stations. It was weird that there wasn't a single report of the terrorist attack.

Chapter 18: News of the Opening Gambit
Wednesday, August 11   10:45 p.m. GST (UTC/GMT+4)
Prince Tower, second tallest skyscraper in Dubai, UAR,
Conference Room

Mousaffa exited the conference room to retrieve a document, ten minutes later he entered the room smiling, "Yassar, good news from Meerza on Pinterest, *Allim Tiflak* Alpha team has completed their Lake Havasu mission. The entire Alpha team has successfully escaped to Mexico and outskirts of Phoenix. The Mexican escape group should be on our pickup yacht and on the way to Cabo San Lucas to catch flights back to Phoenix in the morning to continue preparing for the next phase of their mission."

Yassar smiled, "Meerza's opening pawns will give our enemies the first insight into our existence beyond mere staged cell chatter. Now while their intelligence agencies are immersed in chaos and confusion we will inflict a series of more serious tactical synchronized attacks. All of the members of the *Allim Tiflak* cell are to be honored on their return if they complete the remaining stages of their missions.

The Shura members felt a growing confidence in the success of their extensive planning and strategy, but the celebratory mood would need confirmation by the international and local media to confirm the details of their opening ploy.

Chapter 19: The Delayed Response
Wednesday, August 11, 11:0 a.m. MST (UTC/GMT-8)
Mohave Sheriff Substation, Lake Havasu, AZ

Wednesday was the sheriff's usual day to visit the Lake Havasu substation. Jerry Shannon, Mohave County Sheriff enjoyed the weekly trip to the substation in the quiet little resort city and a quiet lunch at Cha Bones overlooking the river. The Sheriff's specially equipped white Chevy Silverado SUV with a EcoTec3 6.2-liter V8 engine was specifically equipped to provide maximum stability at high speeds in excess of 150 mph thanks to federal funds from Homeland Security. Frankly, Jerry was thrilled with having driven at speeds of more than 120 mph. He had pushed the Chevy SUV to the upper end speed limit on Arizona's traffic free wide-open interstate. It was the sheriff's newest toy, and this was the first real chance to see what it could do on back roads while on official business. With nobody around, Jerry pretended that he was in hot pursuit during a high-speed chase. Something about having the powerful SUV performing at high speed with its' blue and white strobe lights flashing still gave him pleasure beyond words.

As an elected Sheriff, Jerry was not a trained professional member of the law enforcement community. Up until the county election last November he had been a small business owner of a western boot and saddle shop in Kingman, Arizona. His business was boosted primarily by tourists from Las Vegas making the two-hour trip to the rim of the Grand Canyon. He was easily elected after running on a platform of supporting gun ownership and ending the lawlessness of the few survivalist ranches and camps in the county. Jerry ran on another big issue of setting up more speed traps on the Interstate Routes 40, 10 and AZ Route 93 to supplement the county budget. Speed traps were big business in the west and provided a tremendous source of income for the county providing serious tax relief for the otherwise economically depressed residents.

The additional speeding fines paid for seven additional deputies, which in turn wrote more speeding tickets. Jerry loved putting on his sheriff's uniform, and even wore a sidearm from time to time despite not being qualified to accurately shoot a target at close range. Being sheriff was the fulfillment of his boyhood dream. Law enforcement control over 13,500 square miles of the real west was huge for his future and already had paid big dividends for his boot business. In fact his county domain was larger than three states, the District of Columbia and all US territories. His store had a huge sign that proclaimed that it was "The Home of the County Sheriff Shannon giving the Boot to Bad Guys!"

It had taken just under thirty-six minutes to travel the sixty plus miles to Lake Havasu from his county seat office in Kingman. He was thinking about a nice steak for lunch watching the tourist on the London Bridge. At 12:10 p.m. as he approached the outskirts of Lake Havasu City he became concerned when he saw black smoke in the distance. The smoke and several small fires lingered for nearly six hours after the terrorist attack.

"This is Sheriff 1, is there a fire at the dump in Lake Havasu?" His call got no response on the police band radio. The silence was eerie. He was unable to contact the substation, Lake Havasu police, or fire department on his police radio.

As he entered the city he began passing the fire damaged remains of smoldering buildings within the city. His initial thought was that there was a serious natural gas explosion of sorts. One unit of the fire department was on the scene of an electrical transmission station so he thought that perhaps the damage was some sort of electrical surge.
As he drove further to the substation he began to consider that some form of attack had taken place. The center of the London Bridge was gone.

Jerry hurriedly pass a mangle mess of destroyed patrol cars, and private vehicles and entered the sheriff's substation, "What the hell do we have going on here, Hector?"

Deputy Hector Martinez, looked as if he was in shock, but responded, "Sheriff, there has been a series of attacks. This mess happened so quickly it is hard to remember all the pieces. I'll do my best to give you what I know or think I know." Hector was a life long resident of this sleepy little city.

"Hector, are you alright," Sheriff Shannon noticed gashes on Hector's head. "Let's get you cleaned up." Hector was clearly in some sort of daze. "Get a grip on yourself. I need to know if we have alerted the DPS, hospital, fire department, EMTs, and Red Cross."

"Sheriff our radio, cells, internet, radio stations and all forms of communication in the entire city are down. I figured that it would be best if one of us stayed at the substation. So I sent Miguel out twice on foot to assess the situation. He's given me two status reports of deaths, severe damage, and people doing what they do best in coping during an emergency. The EMTs are transporting the injured to the Havasu Regional Medical Center, and Troyer Urgent Care clinic. Both facilities are now using backup generators. All the fire department units are out on calls, but over seventy fires at the same time were far more than they could handle. They placed priorities on buildings that further threatened other buildings. Miguel is sure it was a coordinated terrorist attack given that they successfully knocked out our communication with the outside world."

"A terrorist attack here? Did we notify the DPS, or on second thought the FBI. They handle terrorist attacks."

"Yes, they attacked at 6 a.m. At 11:00 a.m. I sent Miguel in a borrowed car to Parker to notify authorities. He just returned and notified both DPS and FBI. He confirmed that help is on the way. A caravan of vehicles arrived from Parker to lend a hand. I sent him back into the city rendering assistance where he can. We still do not have any way of communicating, so we don't know when we will get outside assistance."

Jerry knew they would need very specific details, "Well, lets get it written down so we don't look like fools when the DPS (Arizona Department of Public Safety) and FBI arrive out of Phoenix. There is bound to be a lot of law enforcement folks and media pulling into town shortly. Calm down and start from the beginning."

Hector anticipated that he would be describing the series of events several times over the next day or two, "I guess it was a little before 6:00 am. Miguel and I were just about to head out of the substation to go on patrol waiting for Marge to arrive to man the substation. We had just completed our review of the evening report. There was nothing out of the ordinary at all in the report other than Frank Moore's dogs putting up their usual racket and the usual complaints about a few drunks at BJ's Bar."

Jerry pushing to learn more, "Did you, Miguel or the other deputies see or hear anything suspicious in the area prior to or after the explosion?"

"I don't know about other deputies, but Miguel and I didn't hear a thing, Sheriff. The morning started out like every other morning of the last seventeen years I've served Havasu City. It was quiet, getting hotter by the minute, but nothing at all out of the ordinary. All the deputies had arrived on time and passed our routine inspection and briefing. We had just finished our morning meeting and three units rolled out to set up a speed trap on Interstate 10 east of Blythe, another patrol to set up radar on Rte. 95 south towards Parker and Quartzite, and a patrol was on duty in the business district to keep an eye on all the tourists. Miguel and I were waiting for Marge before heading out. She was unusually late."

"Ok, then what happened? Think about every possible detail because the smallest thing might be the piece that helps us catch these bastards."

"We heard the roar of ATVs. Suddenly two of our patrol cars, SUV, three personal vehicles and our police radio tower outside exploded into a mess of twisted metal. Miguel and I went outside and were looking at the patrol cars that were totaled and on fire. We desperately tried to use a fire extinguisher to put out the fire for a short time while attempting unsuccessfully to call the fire department. All three of our gas tanks exploded. We could hear the noise of numerous ATVs buzzing between explosions. I ran back inside to check on the phone line and our police communications. Everything was out. After the initial explosion the next thing I remember was that there were fifteen or twenty more separate explosions within a few seconds.

Those detonations were louder and shook the frame of our substation building. I ran out into the messed up parking lot and walked quickly into town. All I could see was that the Lake Havasu City Hall, Police Station, Courthouse and cell towers were completely devastated and left in rubble. Then there was another series of explosions from the direction of the airport. The attacks were obviously targeted against the police, electrical facility, airport, communications system, and London Bridge. It all took about nineteen minutes. Our fire department and EMTs were doing the best they could if you consider the size of the attack. Marge never showed up, so I returned to man the substation. Sheriff, it doesn't make a whole lot of sense, not here in Havasu."

"Okay, What have you learned since the attacks?"

Hector was pensive trying to remember, "Electricity is out, and there is still smoke coming from the APS electric transmission facility and other small fires around town. I estimate that we will not have any power for the next two to three days or weeks. It usually takes them APS crews forever to get to us. Miguel and I got the emergency generator at the substation up and running. The Lake Havasu Municipal airport radio is down and runways have severe damage and totally out of service except perhaps for choppers. It turns out the bastards knocked out all seven cellular phone relay towers, microwave, satellite and land line stations both north and south of the city. Without a tower on the auxiliary power we have very limited range of a mile on what remains of the police radio communications system, but it seems so limited it is next to useless without police vehicles. The terrorists knew exactly what was necessary to totally isolate us from the rest of the world. But for the life of me I do not understand why? And more importantly who? Do you think it was one of them survivalist groups you have been trying to curtail?"

"I don't think so, but we cannot rule them out as they have the weapons, training, and probably explosives."

Jerry thought for a minute, *I don't really think it would be any of our local survivalists. They hate the intrusion of law and government control over their lives. Recently we have only had a few violent incidents when someone drinks too much. They tend to stay on their compounds, practicing and preparing for the intrusion of "big brother government. There has been no indication that they are becoming more aggressive. I just don't think they are capable of something of this magnitude. The environmentalist extremist that demonstrated against the construction of the bridge had not been in the picture for years. There wasn't any warning or threats prior to the attack that I am aware of other than the cell chatter about London.* "Tell me how bad it is. Do you have any estimate on the dead or casualties from the attacks?"

With his hands shaking, Hector dabbed at the wound on his forehead as he referred to a sheet on a legal pad, "All but one of the three on-duty Lake Havasu deputies on patrol were killed in the attack, and the one patrol car south of the city has not reported in despite their schedule. I have not been able to contact the units on sped trap patrols. The Havasu police seem to have been hit much harder. I have not been able to reach any of their units. We know that there are nineteen or more civilians dead in the center of town, with twenty-three more seriously injured, and another sixteen with minor lacerations from detonated explosives, scrapes and bruises scattered around the area. But the numbers are not firm.

We are unsure of the victims at London Bridge because of the number of tourists in the area and the fact that a lot go to see the bridge when it is cool in the morning. We always have some runners crossing the bridge early in the morning. The death and injury toll will probably rise as we get further details on aspects of the attack. I think the death toll might have been higher if it happened an hour later." Hector looked at the sheriff before continuing, his eyes began to glaze over.

"There were no deaths or injuries at the airport, but it suffered extensive damage to the runways 32/14 due to explosives placed at cement joints. The control tower suffered major damage, radar facility, navigation and communication systems were destroyed, and six of the private aircraft are in piles. The airport security fence chain lock was cut. The tower spotted an ATV rider crossing the runway just seconds before an explosive device was detonated. Both American Airlines Express and Gorilla Air have cancelled all flights. The Time Warner and Comcast fiber optic lines were cut destroying Internet access. The cities three-satellite dishes were destroyed. All fourteen Lake Havasu radio stations went off the air when our two radio towers were destroyed. The five UNS electrical substations were destroyed including the one serving the airport. They even destroyed one of the hospital back-up generators. They are operating with limited electricity and AC. All three Parker police vehicles and a fire truck arrived to render assistance. Deputy Fred Miller checked in despite being off duty. Miguel and Fred are checking out and rendering aid at the hospital as we speak. Thank goodness for the advanced first aid training last month. I am sure the hospital is overwhelmed."

The sheriff helped himself to a small cup of water, "Someone executed a full blown terrorist plan to deliberately isolate us. We are going to need help big time. Let's assess the entire city and see where we can render the most assistance. Can you take my SUV to Parker to see if you can get a more detailed message out to DPS and the FBI updating them of our dire situation? Try to get an estimate on when they will be arriving." The sheriff recognized that Hector was going into shock, so he decided that sending him anywhere wouldn't work. "On second thought, I am sure aid is on the way and will be here shortly. There is no need for you to drive to Parker."

Twenty minutes later there was a huge noise outside the substation, Jerry watched out the front window at a sleek black Bell Jet Ranger chopper setting down adjacent to the mangled sheriff patrol cars. Three sun-glassed men in dark suits entered the substation. Not your typical substation visitors by a far stretch of the imagination. The first man entering the substation identified himself as FBI Special Agent David Foster of the Phoenix office as he flashed his credentials. He introduced agents Brown and Grindell as some FBI technicians unloaded their gear. Both agents flashed official FBI identification. The Feds had arrived. Jerry knew that his role would soon be redefined, but if he played his cards right he could still be in the media spotlight for weeks. Jerry and Hector shook their hands.

Jerry stepped forward, pushing out his chest as if to impress the agents with his physique. "I'm Jerry Shannon the Sheriff of Mohave County. You are in my jurisdiction. At this point we are verifying survivors of the attack and have not confirmed the death count.

This is our first priority. We will do everything possible to support you boys, but we need to take the important lead position in the investigation. Nobody gets away with shit like this without personal payback by my local law enforcement team. After all, we were the ones attacked."

Foster got right to the point, "We flew over the entire city to assess the damage. Given the state of destruction of the electrical substations, city hall, and other sites we classify this attack status as a major terrorist act and major crime scene. As such it falls well within our FBI jurisdiction. We'll need a large space in the city to act as the FBI operations center for our field investigation. We have thirty agents inbound from Phoenix, San Diego and Los Angeles by choppers, and a caravan of mobile crime equipment and forensics lab coming from Phoenix. We are going to need to set up a command post, communications facility, area for storing forensic evidence, and several witness questioning areas. Do you have any suggestions?" Foster had blown by the statement by Sheriff Shannon as if it was nonexistent.

Shannon was aghast as he reacted to Foster's request, "I and my team want to ensure that the perpetrators get what they rightly deserve. We need to be the center of the investigation. If you agree to our taking the lead, I'll arrange to have a place for your operations headquarters. I think the Thunderbolt Middle School will work best because of its' availability due to ongoing renovations, size and central location."

Foster seemed a bit perturbed, "Sheriff Shannon, I don't need to get into a pissing contest with you as you marked out your territory. I cannot guarantee what your role will be in the investigation.

Frankly you don't have the equipment or the resources to properly investigate this mess. All I know is that while you are standing here jabbering the terrorists are escaping." Foster's voice became significantly louder, "Please stay out of the damn way of my FBI team of investigators! I can guarantee that who ever did this will face federal justice. We don't take kindly to acts of terrorism! Now where is this Thunderbolt School, so we can set up our investigation center?"

Jerry took the rebuff as expected, recoiling a bit, almost appeared to be indignant, but recognizing that Foster was correct. He stepped back and pointed out that the school was two blocks North of the sheriff substation. He offered to drive the FBI team to the school facility in his SUV.

"There shouldn't be any problem getting to use the school given the nature of the districts renovation situation. I'll call Doug Williamson Superintendent of the Lake Havasu Unified School District to get his approval and have someone meet us at the school."

In the back of his mind, Jerry thought perhaps he was over matched for this situation after all this wasn't what he expected as part of the job. He'd better let the professionals do their thing and just stay in the frame when the television cameras were rolling. The reporters would be arriving shortly. Acts of terrorism in a small sleepy city like Lake Havasu City would shock little cities across America. He could envision CNN and network teams focusing on this attack for weeks.

"That's a more helpful attitude on your part Sheriff. Why don't you have your men assess what remains of Lake Havasu and meet us at the school in half an hour? I have several semi-trucks with generators, communications equipment and vehicles arriving within 30 minutes." Foster stepped out of the substation to answer his ISatPhone Pro satellite cell phone. It was a call from the FBI Area Chief for Phoenix, Neil Fischer.

Foster gave an extremely brief summary and added, "This is going to be a mess getting to the bottom of this situation given the time of the attack and constraints of the local sheriff and local talent. How soon will the rest of the team arrive?"

"Dave, seven more Phoenix agents are less than 10 minutes away. The agents from San Diego are 22 minutes away. The LA field office is sending eight agents that should be there in just over 50 minutes. I'm sending you all I can spare. I need some of the Phoenix agents to secure the Homeland Security, OEM, and FEMA conference facilities. Get me as much information as possible, and let me know what your resource needs are el pronto. The Director is going crazy in Washington. Thomas thinks that our Phoenix field office dropped the ball again after failing to follow-up on the early clues when the 9/11 terrorists were getting their flight training at the Goodyear Airport. Thomas has an elephants' memory but the finesse of an jackass wearing roller skates."

Foster did not comment on the barb, "Will do Neil, but don't hold your breath. I have a feeling our terrorists are well out of the area. Given the cell phone chatter about London Bridge, I'm 99% certain that we are dealing with well-trained foreign terrorist. I think we will need NSA and CIA support on this case. I expect the next invasion to be the media folks in their remote broadcast vehicles."

"You have NBC, ABC, CBS, CNN, radio and the press caravans coming your way. I am sure Interstate 10 out of Phoenix and LA are huge traffic jam filled with media vans and journalist." Being rather flippant Fischer continued, "I bet even PBS, HGTV, Comedy Channel and the Disney Channel are joining the huge traffic jams. I'd expect some news choppers momentarily. I'll try to get there myself via chopper within the next hour. That should put me onsite at the same time as most of the media hounds set up their circus. You hold them off until I get there. I'll handle the media folks. You and the early response team concentrate on figuring out as much as you can before evidence is tainted and destroyed in the cleanup. I will get there as soon as possible. The Director has asked for a full assessment of the attack by 6:30 p.m. EST. We need confirmation of whether the terrorists are foreign as expected or homegrown ASAP. There is a sizeable number of survivalist camps in Mohave County and the bridge itself was opposed by environmentalists before and during construction due to lack of a full environmental impact study. They need to be ruled out completely, but I agree with your suspicion that the attack was not by a homegrown variety of terrorists. London Bridge went down, but not on the Thames."

Hmmm, I'm glad he will be handling the media, Foster thought, "Will do Neil. I really appreciate your handling the media. One thing about this situation is that Londoners can probably relax and take a deep breath as the terrorist pulled a switcheroo. These terrorist bastards were probably playing mind games with the Brits misdirecting their resources. I will have a quick summary of what we have thus far for you in a few minutes. You can brief the Director. See you in a bit. Please hurry the media will be anxiously awaiting your press conference."

Ten minutes later Fischer received a quickly prepared summary report: *Between 6:00-6:25 a.m. MST a group of an estimated 8-15 terrorists on ATVs used automatic silenced weapons and explosive devices to attack Lake Havasu, Arizona centered around London Bridge. The city suffered severe damage to numerous structures, communications and electrical services and the iconic London Bridge was destroyed during the synchronized attack. At this point authorities are investigating the scene. Early estimates are that 30+ died and numerous people were severely injured during the attack. That is a preliminary estimate and may change. The wounded are being treated at the Regional Hospital and clinics under difficult conditions. At this point no group has claimed responsibility for the attack. The FBI agents on site are attempting to confirm that the attack was the act of foreign or domestic terrorists.*

Fischer picked up his secure landline and called the Director to update the information from Fosters initial report. Fischer spent the next ten minutes speaking with FBI Director Frank Thomas on the attack and then an additional five minutes on the security preparations for the Scottsdale OEM conference.

"Frank, I just texted you Foster's on site preliminary summary of the attack. The attack probably is the eminent cell chatter threat against London. It could be something important, but on it's face value it is pretty small potatoes compared to any of the bridges across the Thames or in other US cities. It may well be a single incident, but our ongoing investigation will determine the significance in the context of any potential bigger picture. You know, I really don't need this in my backyard when NSA Director Ford, DCI Dessile, SHS Swartz, Senator Nunn and all the state Directors of Emergency Management from the entire country are coming into town.

But then again what choice do I have. I will call you for a lunch briefing around 7 am when I return to Phoenix. I hope to have something solid for you to convey up the DC food chain."

The first of the TV media trucks arrived as Foster was giving assignments to the newly arrived FBI agents from Phoenix. It was nearing 1:45 p.m. A soft groan preceded a comment under Foster's breath, "How do these news hounds get on location so quickly. Fischer better hurry." He slowly began getting into the Sheriff's Silverado yelling to the reporter rushing towards the SUV, "No comment at this time. Neil Foster the FBI Area Field Chief from the Phoenix office will give a full briefing when his chopper arrives in about an hour."

The SUV spun around with lights flashing as Jerry Shannon smiled to himself after seeing the first of the media caravan arrive. He planned to return to the media truck and give them an in depth interview. Shannon wanted to project his control of the situation and power while the media was looking for details. If he played his cards right he would be on magazine covers, and every television across the United States. Given the fact that the attack was probably from foreign terrorists, perhaps he would get international exposure within the next few hours. This could ensure his reelection for decades.

Chapter 20: International Media Reports a Terrorist Attack

Thursday, August 12 3:45 a.m. GST (UTC/GMT+4)
Wednesday, August 11, 11:35 pm ADT (UTC/GMT+3)
Al Zagaheer Television Studio 1, Doha, Qatar

"Good evening, this is Nuru Monaga reporting breaking news from our *Al Zagaheer* studio in Doha, Qatar. We are following up on a terrorist attack against the United States in Lake Havasu City, in western Arizona. The attack took place early Wednesday morning, FBI officials in Phoenix, Arizona began investigating a terrorist's attack that severely damaged a large portion of this small city and destroyed their famed London Bridge. The bridge spanning a portion of the Colorado River was a huge tourist attraction along the Arizona and California border. Robert P. McCulloch purchased the stone bridge built over the Thames River in 1831, from the City of London in 1968. This is the same bridge that is the focal point of the English children's song "London Bridge is falling down." In fact London had scheduled the bridge for demolition prior to being purchased, tediously moved stone by stone and reconstructed in Arizona. Despite considerable environmental opposition to the project, the Arizona "London Bridge' was constructed in 1971, and opened to traffic in 1973. The bridge was the key attraction for an economic development plan including casinos and resorts for the Colorado River area. The granite span connected the city to a small deserted island. A year following the bridge construction the Beachcombers and London Bridge resorts, Crazy Horse Campground and Islander RV Park were built as part of the development plan on the island." Nuru's voice continued over a file video showing the bridge and the long-term historical relationship of the U.S. and UK including their joint efforts in destabilizing Iraq and laying the foundation for the war against ISIL terrorism focused in the Middle East and other Islamic countries.

"The bridge and a vast portion of the small community of Lake Havasu City were reportedly destroyed in an early morning terrorist attack. Details of the attack will be forthcoming in a FBI briefing at 3 p.m. local time. The initial reports indicate that several government buildings including the city hall, police and fire stations, and airport were destroyed; all communications and electrical services were also cut completely isolating the city. The initial report did not indicate the number of deaths or casualties. No terrorist group has claimed responsibility for the attack. It is interesting that the attack took place in an area of the Sonoran Desert where General George Patton prepared his tank brigades for the battles in North Africa during World War II. International intelligence agencies were fully aware of the threat as cell phone chatter over the past few weeks monitored around the world forewarned of the attack against "London Bridge". The extreme United Kingdom precautionary security efforts seem in vain as the attack took place in the Southwestern United States in the middle of the Sonoran Desert. The bridge stood as a symbol of the extraordinary relationship that exists between the US and the UK. That relationship has expanded as the UK supported the invasion of Iraq and Afghanistan, support attacks against ISIS, and assisted the US in the "War on Global Terrorism. Perhaps the destruction of the bridge is a message from the terrorist that not all international relationships are good for both nations. This is Al Zaga the number one news source in the Middle East."

The *Al Zagaheer* broadcast was followed by a real estate commercial that had a brief scene of a male teacher reading the Quran to his class of boys.

Thursday, August 12   3:45 a.m. GST (UTC/GMT+4)
Prince Tower, Dubai, UAR, Conference Room
Yassar and the Shura leadership reviewed specific details of
the *Allim Tiflak's* four phased plan projected on a large wall
video screen showing California and Arizona. As the initial
phase went into action the members of the Shura monitored
the *Allim Tiflak* cell's progress and initial media reports of
success attacks through their board on the Pinterest web site.

Additional details of the planned attack were fed through
secure encrypted hand written notes passed to Nuru Monaga
at *Al Zagaheer* via a water delivery man, on the back of his
bogus invoice. The invoice was destroyed shortly after it
was received. The terrorist network wanted to demonstrate
the unprecedented nature of their threat, capabilities to strike
foreign targets much like 9/11. In mounting an attack in the
United States they created an element of fear making
intelligence agencies seem inadequate in securing their
borders. The attack also demonstrated incredible resources,
sophisticated reconnaissance, elaborate detailed planning and
professional expertise in the military like operation. The
point was that they were motivated in response to attacks
against Muslims worldwide to launch strikes on U.S. soil in
retaliation. The attack was no rag tag operation run by a
splinter group. There was no doubt that the terrorist had
created confusion and chaos in the U.S. and UK over why the
remote London Bridge was selected as a target. The
upcoming *Al Zagaheer* televised report would also question
why the terrorist would use cell chatter to expose the London
Bridge as a target and face increased security making the
mission nearly impossible within London. *Al Zagaheer* was
given the news item before the attack was initiated. Follow-
up encrypted communiqués updated details of the successful
attack.

After hours of monitoring the international media the first reports began to surface. Yassar was confident that everything went as planned, but with little to be learned from the repetitive nature of the media, he decided to retire for the evening. It had been a long night awaiting the attack confirmation.

Yassar arose from his lounge chair facing a bank of large screen televisions, "Now if you do not mind, I will make my way to my quarters. May Allah keep you and our teams well." He felt the excited eyes of his Shura team diminish at the thought he would not continue to share in the vicarious success of their operation through the media.

Yassar quickly exited at 3:45 a.m. while the other members of the Shura turned to see what CNN, BBC, World, Nile TV, Al Jazeera, CNC China, BBC Haryana, NTV News24, CNBC Pakistan, France24, FOX, Sky News Australia and *Al Zagaheer* were reporting on a wall of huge flat screen HD televisions. Initial reports on CNN showed a map of Lake Havasu City, showed file footage of the bridge, and a brief description of a series of explosions that brought down the very popular London Bridge tourist attraction. They reported the attack damaged several other key locations within the rural Arizona city. They had dispatched a team that would be reporting from the scene within the hour.

CNN reported, "The attack in Lake Havasu City is in such a remote location in Arizona it seems such a very unlikely terrorist target. At this point no group has taken responsibility for the London Bridge attack and other targets within the city. Local officials initially suspect survivalist and extreme environmentalist who had opposed the construction of the span across the Colorado River.

Secretary Swartz of Homeland Security was unavailable for comment, but unofficial sources within the FBI stated that there may be a link to the earlier international cell chatter posing a terrorist threat on London Bridges."

The *Shura* enjoyed the repetitious coverage by the media for an additional three hours to assess the impact the attack had internationally. Each report seemed to expose that the intelligence agencies had centered their security precaution efforts on bridges crossing the Thames River in London. The media explored the possible link between the international cell chatter and the attack. Several terrorism experts went as far as postulating that the attack was outside the capabilities of al-Qaeda and ISIS, thus bringing an unsettling pall of fear over the United States in not knowing what or who they were dealing with.

Yassar was in his quarters quietly enjoying the success of the first opening foray in this complex chess game, and especially in confusing the enemy. The master had his successful opening. Now it was time to await the anticipated United States and United Kingdom responses.

Earlier.........

Chapter 21: Alpha Team's Feign an Escape
Wednesday, August 11, 9:00 a.m.
Thursday, August 12, 2:00 p.m. MST (UTC/GMT-8)
Yuma, Arizona and Cabo San Lucas, Mexico

An important part of the Alpha Team mission was to misdirect to the intelligence agencies, law enforcement and military units investigating and pursuing their escape. Dividing Alpha Team and leaving false trails that end in dead ends was critical for the success of the follow-up phase of their attack.

Three remaining parts of Alpha team had driven the slower moving RVs down AZ Route 95 to Quartzite, AZ stopping for fuel and then on to Yuma, AZ. Two RVs headed west on Interstate 8 to Calexico, California crossing the border into Mexicali. The crossing into Mexico was much easier than their earlier entry into the United States. The U.S. Border Patrol inspectors were focused on the flow of weapons and cash back into Mexico. Once in Mexico the team felt relaxed as they drove south on the Federal Highway 5 to San Felipe. They carefully sanitized the RVs and sold them to the owners of Kiki's Campground. The quiet town had a reputation for great seafood, so they enjoyed a nice meal at La Hacienda de la Langosta Roja restaurant with a beautiful view of the small seaport on the Sea of Cortez.

The last unit of Alpha team drove the last RV south from Yuma crossing the Mexican border at the San Luis crossing. Once in Mexico the team drove east on Mexican Federal Highway 3 along the coast to Puerto Penasco (Rocky Point). About thirty minutes outside of town they used the RV's 40 channel Bearcat CB radio to contact the Dot Commer crew.

"Hey big buddy," Jalal smiled as he attempted to raise the crew, "we are have a great time in the dunes. We will be in for lunch in about an hour."

"Dude, you always head in when hunger gets the best of you," laughed a member of the crew. "The chow and beer will be ready when you arrive. Out."

They joined the larger crew of *Dot Commer* encamped on the beach. The group spent fifteen minutes carefully sanitizing the RV before pouring gasoline throughout the interior and setting it on fire sending up plumes of smoke on the deserted beach a quarter mile south of Tessoro at Las Conchas.

The group immediately boarded the *Dot Comer* yacht and got underway. The luxury yacht made the quick thirty-mile trip to pick-up team members at San Felipe in less than two hours. Just then the news of the attack broke on the yacht's television. Once the team was reunited, they set off for the Isla San Lorenzo, a famous local scuba dive site. *Dot Commer* joined several other groups of divers from as far south as Cabo San Lucas in single tank dives. Shortly after 2:30 p.m. they departed on the long 200-mile leg to Cabo San Lucas when they heard the first CNN reports from the scene of the Lake Havasu attack. *Dot Commer* arrived in Cabo San Lucas at 2:00 a.m. to take on fuel.

The yacht crew dropped off Alpha team with scuba gear and immediately departed the marina at 3:30 a.m. heading out into the Pacific. Turning off all exterior lights under the cover of darkness, *Dot Commer* once again rendezvous with the empty Greek MV Atlantikani loaded with steel girders headed to Khaliifi Bin Salman Port in Bahrain.
The *Dot Commer* crew sanitized the ship before boarding the large freighter. They remotely engaged the engine setting the crewless yachts course due west into the open ocean. The *Dot Commer* had a preset explosive device timed to explode in twenty minutes. The yacht would eventually become a dead end for the pursuing U.S. military and intelligence agencies.

Not long after the freighter got underway they saw a flash and faint sound of the explosive marking the end of the multi-million dollar yacht. The Atlantikani sailed south stopping in the port of Lima, Peru before rounding Cabo de Hornos (Cape Horn). It would take another nine days before it reached its final destination and the *Dot Comer* crew disembarked safely.

Meanwhile at 9:00 a.m. a shuttle bus transported Alpha team and their scuba equipment the short twenty-two miles to the San José del Cabo International Airport (SJD), BS, Mexico. They joined groups of other scuba enthusiasts and boarded American Airlines Flight 446 at 12:43 p.m. back to Phoenix, AZ posing as being part of the larger group of scuba divers returning from their open water dives. Each team member had an expertly forged U.S. passport and matching drivers license from different states. It was well known that the INS passport security at the Phoenix airport was somewhat lax. The only concern the team had was the required thumb-scan upon entry. The team passed through passport and customs without incident. Upon exiting Sky Harbor airport members of Alpha team rented three cars from different agencies at the huge Phoenix Car Rental Terminal. Each of the team registered at inexpensive motels spread out over the Tempe and Scottsdale area posing as students arriving to find apartments for the upcoming semester at Arizona State University. They watched various news reports with interest on their successful Lake Havasu attack and varied reports of attempts to identify the ATV riders from rather poor videos taken by several ATM and security cameras within Lake Havasu City.

Nearly 24 hours earlier Meerza had escaped to the Phoenix area. He used a forged Des Moines, Iowa driver's license as he registered in the Mesa Motel 6. His cover was as a baseball scout assigned by the Chicago Cubs to work with several prospects for their AAA Iowa Cubs during the summer development baseball league. He needed to lay low for a few days to assess the responses to the Lake Havasu attack and begin preparations with Alpha team for the next phase of attacks.

Chapter 22: London Takes a Breather
Thursday, August 12, 8:00 p.m. BST (UTC/GMT)
10 Downing Street, London UK

Thomas Graham was seated in his study with a pot of his favorite Makaibari Estate Darjeeling imported tea, thought to be the most expensive tea in the world at near 125 € per kilogram. It was his favorite evening ritual when the sound of a summer rain beating against the windowpanes took his attention from the pile of NSA and SIS reports. His ritual was a serious break in 10 Downing Street traditions, as most PM indulged in a snifter of brandy or single malt scotch in the evening. Thomas loved the nuance and sheer decadence of the tea given as a gift by the Prime Minister of India.

The past 24 hours brought an audible sigh of relief from the nine million plus residents of Central London and the adjacent shires. It started when both the BBC and CNN broke the initial news of the terrorist attacking the old London Bridge in Lake Havasu City, Arizona. It just missed the Wednesday evening papers, but was the talk of the town as Londoners made their commutes home and sat in their favorite pubs. Thomas was sure there were numerous jokes being made about the old bridge that was scheduled for demolition prior to being bought by the American millionaire finally meeting it's dismal fate and serving the UK once again.

Three months of precautions for what seems to turn out to be a terrorist ruse as the Admiral had suspected early on. The terrorist had proven that they were capable of hitting the old bridge in a small isolated city, but undoubtedly were thwarted by the thought of attacking an actual bridge in London proper under the massive security precautions put in place.

Perhaps they altered their plans knowing that London was more than prepared while the old London Bridge sat essentially unprotected. At best the destruction of the bridge was a symbolic victory metaphor of the destruction of the U.S. and UK relationship.

Only hours after the attack at Graham's 7:00 p.m. staff meeting all the members of the cabinet and intelligence community had concurred in a decision for significantly reducing the security forces protecting the bridges and end the stoppage inspection of busses and trains. The reductions would start immediately and continue over a week to the pre-alert levels of last April. It made financial sense to have the military units cut substantially and lessened on a daily basis over the next few weeks. It seemed silly having such a visual force in place when the real target had been destroyed and the intelligence cell chatter buzz had ceased completely. In retrospect a review of the cell chatter never had any mention of United Kingdom or London as targets. It just mentioned London Bridge not specifically the UK. It would be a pleasure to eliminate the threat level and have Londoners feel more secure as they traveled the city. But at the same time he wondered whether there might be more security issues to come. The slight pall of fear seemed to permeate his thoughts despite escaping the most recent threat.

Helena and Graham planned to celebrate Helena's success directing the Tate. She had the London art world all a buzz about the finalized Tate's December Wassily Kandinsky exhibit. The Daily News had two full pages on the importance of bringing together such a large worldwide assembly of pieces from private collectors and museums. That article was more than complimentary of Helena listing the Tate's numerous accomplishments including significant exhibit patronage and increase in permanent collection acquisitions due to donations during her tenure.

She looked smashing in the two London Times pictures with selected Kandinsky paintings. Perhaps more impressive was her comments in an incredible interview on the size and importance of bringing over one hundred and twenty Kandinsky pieces together from museums and collections around the world. London and UK Travel Bureaus were placing advertisements in International newspapers offering special tours and tickets for the exhibit. All and all it reflected well on Helena's leadership, vision, and passionate work at the Tate taking it to a new level rivaling the world's best modern art museums.

Thomas Graham thought *Helena and he could get away for an extended romantic weekend distancing themselves from their complex schedules and heavy work demands. He immediately thought of a small romantic St Ives manor along the coast of Cornwall. He would call Helena immediately after hearing from the Admiral. It felt good to be thinking of something other than the possibility of a terrorist attack, security precautions, and budgetary issues. He felt Londoners feeling the same relief as the security alert was lessened more than an hour ago. Life needs to go back to normal, if indeed that was ever possible.*

As the summer rain pounded the windowpane more intensely, Graham's cell phone rang. The digital display indicated that the Admiral was calling.

"Good evening Admiral"

"Good evening Mr. Graham, I'm relieved to report that my SIS, FBI and NSA sources indicate that the Lake Havasu attack had little to do with the UK other than the damned tourist bridge." The comment was followed by the Admiral's short chuckle. Johnson obviously was feeling better as the whole stressful situation passed, and his theory that it was a ruse was proven to be true.

Graham could sense the Admiral's dismissal of the event as a non-event and return of his sense of humor. "That is excellent news. Is there any new developments on the search for the terrorists?"

There was a slight pause, "No Sir. It seems as if all of NSA's technology was of little use, as the terrorists seem to have escaped to Mexico on a pleasure craft out of the Sea of Cortez into the Pacific and disappeared. The U.S. Navy, Coast Guard and Air Force are conducting a coordinated search of the Pacific. They are reviewing the NSA and CIA satellite recordings of the vast Pacific area."

"Is there any indication of any further threat to the UK?" Graham posed.

"The cell chatter has stopped completely and our combined intelligence communities do not foresee any further threat. We can all breathe a huge sigh of relief. My chaps at SIS are cutting back to our normal staffing unless you think otherwise."

"That seems prudent. Please give Spencer and his sector my appreciation for their extraordinary efforts dealing with the threat ordeal."

"Will do so sir," the Admiral paused. "Spencer is still somewhat perplexed by the unlikely Arizona target of no strategic importance. His perception was based on the odd extreme remoteness from the more likely targets in the United States. Accordingly, the Lake Havasu attack made no logical strategic sense, especially after the generation of the massive volume of international cell chatter.

Spencer voiced that he had a very uncomfortable feeling that the attack was just a precursor of something much more serious. This is certainly not a shared feeling among my senior staff. But Spencer has been right on such premonitions in the past."

"I have had the same mild, yet weird feeling too, but perhaps not as strong as Spencer. It is like this was to easy to prevent and something else is about to happen in the U.S." Graham responded.

The Admiral replied immediately, "As I mentioned all fourteen of my senior staff, all experts in the intelligence field do not share Spencer's unsettled sense over the strange attack. I think the plan we have devised to lessen the precautions over time will serve us well. It is not as if we will be leaving our defenses down completely. That said I think it is time to relax. My wife and I are off to our cottage in Sussex for the weekend. I am sure our garden is a bit overgrown and needs some serious attention. I will be available as always by cell. Do you have plans?"

Graham reflected on the Admiral's comments about Spencer, and replied, " Helena and I are thinking about a weekend in Cornwall. Enjoy your weekend Harold. Please give my best wishes to Emily. Here is hoping that the weather holds. If this rain continues all weekend your gardening plans may need to be set aside."

"I will pass along your good wishes to Emily. At some point we would love to host Helena and you at our cottage after saving our garden. Cornwall should be amazing at this time of year. I hope you have a restful weekend."

The Admiral's call with nothing new in the updated information shared by U.S. intelligence sources gleaned from the early analysis of the Lake Havasu attack and subsequent investigations. After months of tedious work attempting to analyze the terrorist cell chatter for naught, setting in place the massive precautions on London bridges, the Admiral seemed much more relaxed and attempting to return to his normal lifestyle and routine. The issue of over extended cost of the precautions would wait until next week.

Spencer's intuition on the obscure terrorist attack location should not be disregarded completely. After all, Spencer's innate intuitive sense, internal radar or sixth sense on such matters that had served him well throughout this extensive intelligence career. Spencer had obviously warned the Admiral and the staff of his lingering intuitive feeling, but was scoffed at for being "overly cautious." Despite the Admiral's reaction, Graham's sense was to take those perceptions more seriously. Like Spencer, Graham hated being played with by an unknown enemy in some sort of unspoken game unaware of the opponent's next move. But then again that was the counter-terrorism game. He hoped his shared sense of uneasiness would not impact the weekend with Helena. A smile crossed his face thinking about a weekend relaxing the secluded St Ives estate in Cornwall.

Chapter 23: Initial FBI Assessment
Thursday, August 12, 5:35 p.m. MST (UTC/GMT-8)
Lake Havasu City, AZ Thunderbolt Elementary School
The devastation of a sleepy tourist city like Lake Havasu City was completed well before being reinforced by FBI and other law enforcement teams arrived on site. The media RVs arrived in mass. They set up a media camping area along river north of where the bridge once stood. The FBI quickly set up a site management location in the Thunderbolt School on the edge of the city. The media were like vultures awaiting any further updates from the FBI, police and city and state officials. Swarms of reporters spent hours with Sherriff Shannon, Deputies Hector and Miguel, interviewing every person they could find including the tourist that were trapped on the small island on the western end of the destroyed bridge. Several campers at the Crazy Horse Campgrounds and families registered at the Beachcomber Resort had to rely upon pleasure boats to get back to the Lake Havasu City leaving their vehicles on the island. Reporters descended on the families as if they were celebrities.

National media giants ABC, NBC, FOX, and CBS coverage paled compared to CNN and BBC in depth coverage. The CNN news pieces included an interview of the Lord Mayor of London on the tremendous loss of the historic bridge. The CNN researchers unveiled that Robert McCulloch thought that he had purchased the iconic Tower Bridge and was somewhat shocked to find that he purchased the granite stone London Bridge. The BBC then focused their coverage on the announcement of the slow removal of the security precautions protecting London's bridges, a few Conservative Parliament members blasted the PM for his decision to spend huge amounts on securing the bridges when the attack was in the U.S., while others criticized the PM for removing the security so quickly putting Londoners at risk.

The FBI was working behind a severe time delay due to the lapse between the attacks and awareness by the outside world. They had immediately coordinated with Homeland Security and NSA in an attempt to gather data from passing satellite images on the movement of vehicles in Mohave County area. Unfortunately, it would take days to analyze all the stored images. The huge time delay hindered the efforts by the Border Patrol to secure the U.S.-Mexico border. The Arizona Department of Public Safety (DPS) set up roadblocks on every highway in the directions of Phoenix, Los Angeles, San Diego, Kingman, and Las Vegas. The same time delay was more than sufficient for the terrorists to escape without being detected.

FBI Director Frank Thomas was feeling the heat by the administration and members of both Senate and House Intelligence Committees. As usual the media were expecting immediate apprehension of the terrorists in this remote isolated area and pointing fingers at a lack of intelligence forewarning of the potential attack. Begging the question why not one of the seventeen intelligence agencies thought that the London Bridge attack could be the Arizona London Bridge. He though *that immediate apprehension was highly unlikely, but felt confident that the terrorist would eventually pay the price for their attack, much like Bin Laden.*

Director Thomas called Neil Fischer to share the heat, "Neil we need to catch these asshole terrorists like yesterday. Congress and the President are chewing my ass. Are there any additional resources that you need?"

Neil fully understood the pressure, "The early evidence shows a well planned and coordinated effort on ATVs vehicles. It was very professionally planned and executed. At this point we have completely eliminated any homegrown survivalist or environmental terrorists. This had to be part of the international cell phone chatter that led us to believe that London was the target. We are concentrating on a likely escape into Mexico. We are following up with the Federales on several potential leads. I have more than my hands full of state and local resources. Our teams are doing their best, but it is highly unlikely that we will catch the perpetrators in the next few hours, days or perhaps weeks. This is going to take time as we run down leads."

"We don't have the luxury of much time." Thomas barked in an unusually loud and irritated tone, "Reynolds wants the terrorists caught because the terrorist attacked a small city on our soil regardless of the insignificance of the damn bridge. They had the balls to attack us on our soil."

"All we can do is our best. Resolving this attack might be like our efforts that led to catching *Bin Laden*, it might take years." Neil tried to remain calm under the mounting pressure; "My real fear is that the attack is the prelude to something much bigger."

Frank seemed to understand and calmed a bit, "I hope not. Keep me posted on any leads so I can deal with he media in Washington. I was scheduled to be on the "Meet the Press" this Sunday prior to the attack. I now have a request by "Face the Nation" and "State of the Union" this Sunday from a remote Phoenix feed at the conference. I need some progress to report on Sunday, anything at all will help. I am considering recommending the cancelation of the Homeland Security and FEMA Conference in Phoenix until we have a handle on this situation. What do you think?"

"Frank, I know what your are going through, I am dealing with the blood sucking media here and in Lake Havasu. We are doing our best." Neil thought about the upcoming conference in his backyard, "I think it is premature to cancel the conference over what could be a very low level insignificant attack. If we cancel the terrorists have won a small victory and impacted government operations. Just think of the reaction to the one shoe bomber on a plane. I've got to run to a forensics team meeting. I will keep you updated Frank."

The FBI and five other agencies were attempting to piece together as much evidence and leads from the Lake Havasu London Bridge attack in the midst of the overwhelming media presence and constant interference. A number of factors contributed to delaying the response by authorities. The attack used the element of surprise in a very remote area, and isolating the city through precision targeting power and communications. Unfortunately, an Arizona monsoon cloud cover prevented NSA satellite surveillance to provide specifics on the vehicle movements within the area prior to and following the attack. NSA analysts were reviewing the spotty periods that the satellites were able to record. The general public in their attempts to be helpful were reporting hundreds of situations that in the end complicated the FBI investigation. There were a numerous anomaly's that were being investigated including: high speed SUV vehicles travelling on Interstate 10; burn out ATVs outside Parker, AZ; a RV vehicle pulling two ATVs travelling at a high rate of speed towards Kingman, Arizona and towards Las Vegas; a RV fire on a beach outside Rocky Point; shots heard just outside Parker, AZ; reports of several armed men travelling towards Flagstaff; and suspicious looking men at the base of Hoover Dam.

The good citizens were trying to help by being vigilant, but each report led teams on wild goose chases. At this point it was too difficult to determine if any of these leads would lead to the terrorists, all the reports needed to be checked out. Forensics had numerous partial fingerprints on remains of several of the explosives that did not match any of those within their massive system. Fischer felt the building pressure to come up with something substantial. That same pressure was felt within the investigation teams on the ground, forensics teams, and the analysts reviewing video footage. Everyone wanted to find the single piece of evidence that results in the identification, capture and eventual confrontation with the terrorists bringing the group to justice.

As lead FBI Special Agent in Phoenix, Neil was placed in charge of all the federal agency resources. He was delegating the authority to coordinate the investigation efforts into geographic sectors, pushing the forensic team for evidence and managing the huge media presence. All agencies seemed frustrated with lack of solid leads, unlike their work on the Boston marathon and Atlanta bombings where significant information became available almost immediately.

Gayle Swartz, Secretary of Homeland Security, Frank Thomas FBI Director, Abe Greenfeld National Security Advisor, Senator Rex Nunn Chairman of the Senate Intelligence Committee, and General Ralph Shoemaker, Director of National Security Council were having a serious discussion among high ranking administration officials on the potential cancellation of the Scottsdale Homeland Security, Office of Emergency Management (OEM) and FEMA conference.

President Reynolds and the Cabinet made the ultimate decision to go forward with the conference to show that the United States was not intimidated by the attack and in consideration of the conferences huge non-refundable expenditure tied to the fear of public outrage when the media revealed the wasting of funds due to the isolated attack. The President hoped that the Homeland Security, OEM and FEMA agencies could use the terrorist attack as a key topic in the conference breakout sessions thus making use of real situation rather than any simulation.

Chapter 24: Planning a Three-Pronged Attack
Thursday, August 12, 10:00 pm PST (UTC/GMT+9)
Los Angeles, Oakland, CA and San Francisco CA, and
Wickenburg, AZ

Following the attack, two Alpha team members dropped off Meerza off in Ajo, AZ to pick up his own vehicle. They drove the tan Mazda 5 mini van on back dirt roads to outside Wenden, AZ where they wiped it clean, deserted it in a wash area well off the road, and switched into a dust covered white Toyota pickup truck hidden under a tan camouflaged tarp. Their tanned unshaven faces completed their American appearance along with dirty jeans with worn leatherwork gloves hanging out of their butt pocket, tattered cowboy hats, tee shirts, and well-worn work boots completed their disguise intended to blend them into the relatively small town. The pair drove to a dude ranch safe house just outside Wickenburg Arizona. The terrorists extensive training and planning had worked well beyond expectations.

The *Shura's* recruiter, *Akaman*, had an incredible eye for detail ensuring that each selected cell member met the criteria for avoiding the typical prejudicial and racial profiling by small town Americans and the law enforcement. As part of the recruitment process all candidates were required to shave their beards, change their hair color and styles, and begin wearing some of the paraphernalia worn be typical Americans including crosses, U.S. flags, tattoos, belt buckles, and jewelry.

Kaji Hassam, a Saudi, known to locals as Kevin Gregory, was the owner of Los Amigos Dude Ranch located six miles north on AZ Rte. 89 on the outskirts of Wickenburg, Arizona. He had been a crucial agent for the *Shura* for the last six years. His primary role was a key to the success of the next three strategic attacks.

His first role was to obtain the sophisticated weapons necessary for the next phase of *Allim Tiflak* cell missions, from varied mail order and gun shows in Utah, Arizona, Nevada, Montana, Idaho and California. He knew it was an easy task given the Americans fascination with firearms, and their protection of their precious Second Amendment right to bear arms. He attended gun shows acquiring over 60% of the sophisticated arms without a background check. The other weapons were purchased via the Internet using the names of the various transient dude ranch workers and using VISA gift cards he purchased with cash.

When the two members of *Allim Tiflak* arrived at the ranch in their pick-up truck they were amazed to find a fully outfitted tourist bus full of arms, ammunition and explosives in an old barn in the back of the property. Kaji had acquired a 24-passenger tour bus, which he customized with heavy-duty suspension and armored sides and heavy tinted bulletproof glass. The frame and design of the tour bus required major support to handle the added weight of the arsenal. Modifying the bus was a simple project given Kaji's remote barn location and distance from the nearest neighbors. The bus was completely full of various weapons and munitions, including three .50 caliber BMG sniper rifles, and rocket propelled grenade launchers (RPGs). Kaji's biggest accomplishment was salvaging scrap pieces of nine different Browning M2 twin .50 caliber machine guns from three salvage yards and putting together this highly illegal military grade, automatic, belt fed weapon. The machine gun was mounted in the tour bus with over 5500 rounds. The ammunition for the weapon was secretly acquired by paying off a San Diego Naval CWO2 Ordinance Officer.

The officer reluctantly made the deal to cover a huge gambling debt owed to a bookie noted for violence. The normal 105 round of boxes fed ammo were specially linked to allow over 1000 rounds to be fed into the deadly weapon before a need to be reloaded. The pair from Alpha team spent the next two days cleaning and preparing the tour bus and huge array of weapons for their entire team's next attack.

Kaji's second role was to actively obtain information about the logistics of the Homeland Security conference at the Phoenician resort using the assistance of his family. It was as simple as having his son, Nelson take a position as a busboy. He was surprised how much information his son gathered about the conference events from picking through trash from a dumpster and talking with various valets, maids and banquet staff members. Kaji maintained careful records of the local tour busses, their typical schedules and locations in the Paradise Valley and Scottsdale area. He had his brother, Sam, park the modified tour bus in regular Paradise Valley locations that would be used in the attack so local neighbors would be accustomed to the presence of the bus. Kaji rented a 5,000 square foot house on East Vista Drive and N 64th Street that had a large RV parking area from the rear and provided a perfect 600-meter rear view of the Phoenician Resort. His brother Sam and Nelson lived in the house on and off for the past five months. Sam and Nelson eventually picked up Alpha team members when they dropped off their rental cars at the Phoenix Sky Harbor Rental Terminal, and moved them into the East Vista Drive house. From time to time they parked the modified tour bus at the rear of the property so neighbors would become accustomed to seeing its presence.

Kaji third role was to acquire vehicles and additional weapons for both *Allim Tiflak's* Bravo and Charlie teams and another second level cell. He stored the weapons in three rented storage facilities in Torrance, California south of Los Angeles; Burlingame just south of the San Francisco Airport along Rte. 101; and the largest cache of weapons at a storage facility in Quartzsite AZ. His biggest logistical coup was acquiring three experimental Tomahawk cruise missiles armed with conventional W80 (1000 pound high explosives) with the v2 TWCS "green screen" mobile launching system, three LaWs advanced laser weapon from a Weapons Logistical Officer, at the China Lake Naval Weapons Research Facility. The laser was capable of slicing through concrete walls as if it was butter.

Victor, Kaji's youngest brother, played a critical role taking a job as a field hand on a farm west of Buckeye, Arizona for the past year. He deliberately created a number of friendships with employees of the Palo Verdes nuclear power plant by hanging out at the local Longhorn Grill and Tact Bar. These friendships included members of the plants internal security force. Victor's final piece of reconnaissance intelligence had provided information on the coded internal security lockdown system, and specifics on an upcoming November force-on-force security exercise at the plant that would play right into the Shura's next level attack plans.

Kaji obtained important details of the Palo Verde plant security systems, security guard automatic weapons, electronic security lock-down system key pad locations and codes, electronic "explosive sniffer sensor" devices, and methods to bypass the electronic identification card operated turnstiles, at Palo Verdes by bribing Derek Taylor, the vendor's poorly paid installation expert. Taylor had supervised the installation of the sophisticated Palo Verde security system and was responsible for updating the code changes.

More importantly Taylor taught Kaji how to enter the Palo Verdes security system administrator's account and use of the manufacturers password to bypass the entire sophisticated lock-down system. Kaji had Victor stage Taylor's accidental drowning in his own Jacuzzi to eliminate any direct link to the terrorist organization. The local authorities and Homeland Security concluded their investigation of the incident reporting that Taylor's blood alcohol concentration (BAC) level of .43 at the time contributed to his accidental drowned in the heat of the hot tub. There was no evidence of foul play.

Yassar's gambit strategy in western Arizona ensured that every federal agent, state and local law enforcement officer that could be spared were busy in Western Arizona chasing Lake Havasu terrorist to dead ends. In fact FBI agents and teams from San Diego and Los Angeles were also assisting in checking the hundreds of investigative leads in Lake Havasu, Parker, San Diego, Kingman, Flagstaff and Rocky Point, Mexico. Yassar had planned on using the developing chaos surrounding the Lake Havasu attack, anticipated carefully measured law enforcement delayed responses as a way to slip *Allim Tiflak*'s Alpha team back into the Phoenix area on flights from Blythe, CA and Cabo San Lucas.
Needless to say the FBI and other security agencies were looking for terrorists leaving Arizona and not re-entering the state. A relatively smaller security force would be left to provide support for the joint Homeland Security, Federal Emergency Management Agency (FEMA) and Office of Emergency Management conference. The conference was a ripe target with nearly 500-attendees from all fifty states, all territories and included several top federal officials.

A successful attack would significantly decimate the U.S. ability to respond to emergencies and breed new public anxiety about national safety. He had accurately predicted that the administration and federal agencies decision not to cancel or reschedule the conference in light of the minor terrorist attack.

The two Alpha team members regularly used the tour bus to familiarize themselves with the escape route they would take following the next phase attack. The team was now within easy striking distance for the final part of the Alpha Team mission.

As planned *Al Zagaheer* reported that the suspected terrorist group claiming responsibility for the Lake Havasu City attack had escaped on *Dot Commer*, an expensive yacht that was spotted leaving Cabo San Lucas and heading out into the Pacific Ocean in a special breaking news broadcast. U.S. Navy and Coast Guard resources were searching an estimated 7,000 square mile grid to find the vessel. The broadcast was fully scripted by the Kenji Habbi, the Shura's Head of Communications. The telecast had its predicted impact as enormous FBI and NSA resources further investigated all aspects of the report and assigned surveillance on the Al Zagaheer facility and personnel tapping their phones, monitoring their e-mails, and tailing their every movement.

After verifying the placement of Alpha team in the East Vista Drive house, Meerza drove his own white Honda Odyssey Touring Elite mini van and parked in the Phoenix Sky Harbor Preflight covered parking facility on 44th St. He took a 4:00 p.m. flight to (LAX) Los Angeles to meet briefly with the eight-man Bravo team in the back room of Molly Malone's, a small neighborhood Irish pub off Wilshire Blvd.

Bravo Team looked like a group of college students out for a night on the town. Meerza and the team spoke in mildly coded terms as if they were an athletic team, so anyone passing by could not overhear their conversations. They expressed that they were anxious to play their game. The Bravo team was tired of laying-low in their Anaheim motels for two weeks especially after the news of the successful Lake Havasu attack hit the media. They wanted to get into the game.

Three hours later, after ensuring the tactical details, Meerza caught a flight from LAX to Oakland Airport and met briefly with Charlie Team's five couples. He knew that Akaman had been extremely professional in recruiting and training Charlie team. They were a wide range of heights, weights, hair colors, lengths of hair, etc. The group had dressed to look like tourist couples that frequented the small Black Bottle Coffee bar in Oakland for coffee. They took the simple precautions to arrive and leave separately and quietly to ensure that they were not seen. The bar, owned by Kaji Hassam, was always closed on Thursdays. Following the meeting the six members of Charlie team took different BART trains to their Burlingame Embassy Suites hotel. One couple picked up their special blue-coated 2015 Chevrolet Express 3500 LS van at the parking lot outside the bar and drove to Kaji's Burlingame storage facility. The storage facility locker was equipped with Charlie team's weapons and explosives. An hour after the meeting with Meerza the team reassembled in their waterfront suite with a view of approaching SFO bound aircraft. The purpose of the meeting was to review the complex stages for their complex attack and confirm that were fully prepared for their attacks.

One Iraqi brother and sister couple had undergone additional extensive indoctrination to ensure that they could successfully complete a special suicide mission. Their path to being radicalized was filled with personal tragedy. Their father, Moriffa Ghazzi was an esteemed Lt. General Farefo (فَريق) in Saddam Hussein's Republican Guards responsible for hiding the dictator in their country home in ad-Dawr, outside Tikrit. Assen, their mother, served as a Colonel Aqeed in Saddam's personal bodyguards. Both were heavily sought after aces in the U.S. deck of Iraqi most wanted cards. When their home in Baghdad was surrounded, the couple decided to fight it out rather than being captured and disclosing Saddam's location. The Iraqi brother and sister watched from upstairs as members of the U.S. First Battalion of the 5th Special Forces broke into their home and killed their father, mother and inadvertently youngest sister during an eight minute bloody gunfight. Following the incident they had repeatedly vowed to avenge the deaths of their family. The young couple left the meeting to do reconnaissance on opposite sides of the San Francisco TransBay tunnel and study Bay Area Rapid Transit (BART) schedules. Shad Ghazzi spent time in the West Oakland BART station to observe trains travelling to San Francisco, while Dleen, his sister did likewise at the Embarcadero station for trains travelling to Oakland. As planned Meerza did not accompany Bravo or Charlie teams on their missions, knowing full well that Bay area and LA extensive video surveillance would be searched and carefully scrutinized for any additional team members accompanying the terrorists' suspects before and after the attacks.

As he reviewed the five-pronged attacks again, he was confident that the teams were well prepared, in place and the missions would be successful. He relaxed at the San Francisco International Airport's Lark Creek Grill bar watching the CNN updated report on the Lake Havasu attack, awaiting his flight back to Phoenix. Meerza smiled to himself as he thought *if the Americans only knew that Lake Havasu was a small tip of an iceberg and a massive glacier was about to hit their homeland hard.*

After arriving at Phoenix Sky Harbor Airport, Meerza picked up his mini van and held a short meeting with the Alpha team members at the East Vista Drive house. The team reviewed the scenario for the next attacks and their precise timing. Later that evening Meerza drove the forty-two miles to the dude ranch outside Wickenburg to meet with Kaji and his extended family. He rewarded Kaji with the secret account number and access code for a Swiss bank account holding $15,000,000 for his family's efforts. Kaji and his immediate family had a 7:40 p.m. British Airways flight BA 0288 direct from Phoenix to London, from there they would travel by private bus to Istanbul and separate to escape into several Middle Eastern countries. Meerza then rendezvoused with the entire Alpha team at the East Vista Drive house at 2:00 p.m. on Friday afternoon.

Chapter 25: The Old Guard
Thursday, August 12, 8:00 a.m. MST (UTC/GMT-8)
Office of Emergency Management in the State Office
Building, Phoenix, AZ

Rod Harris had a long history of being involved in emergency planning going back to his first days as Civil Defense Coordinator for the City of Phoenix in 1976 during the height of the nuclear arms race and Cold War with the Soviets. He graduate from Arizona State University in 1975 and used his fraternity connections to land what was considered a cushy low paying and low stress civil service position working in the old basement of the Phoenix City Hall.

As the Soviet nuclear threats declined due to the Strategic Arms Limitation Talks (SALT) marking the slow march to the end of the Cold War, his position as Director of Office of Emergency Management (OEM) morphed from running monthly air raid drills in schools and public buildings; constructing and stocking secure bomb shelters; storing water and food to feed thousands to dealing with a wider range of natural emergencies. The most pressing of these Phoenix area emergencies were the annual Salt River flooding that occurred during the August monsoon season dangerously turning the city's dry washes into raging torrents trapping vehicles. During his time in emergency management he had to deal with seven floods that were lightly termed 100-year floods by the media as they only were only suppose to happen every hundred years. He was relieved when the U.S. Army Corps of Engineers designed flood controls and basins that eliminated a part of the threat. Recently the *haboobs* or dense dust storms attributed to climate change, presented a new threat to the Phoenix area limiting visibility and causing huge waves of vehicle accidents and heavily restricting private and commercial air traffic.

Rod had been a longstanding joke among his lifelong friends. He was the guy responsible for making the local TV and radio stations test their emergency broadcast system each month with their annoying alerts. That annoying shrilled alert sound drove Rita, his wife, and all of his relatives' crazy especially as it interrupted favorite television shows or football games. As the years passed Rod became more and more deeply committed to streamlining the city's 911 and OEM systems. After 9/11 he designed detailed coordinated disaster plans with the fire department, police, first responders, and medical facilities. The plans were for everything from earthquakes, dust devil tornados, to rattle snake and scorpion infestations. He was going to miss his single lifelong job when he retired in December. However, the idea of having time for fishing on the small lakes around Showlow, AZ was very appealing on numerous levels.

The OEM Directors were heading to Phoenix for the conference and Rod, as Arizona Director of OEM, was the designated host. He had been up to his ears in a million details organizing golf tee times and reserving luxury boxes for the Arizona Diamondbacks games. The Homeland Security, FEMA conference included all the Directors of the Office of Emergency Management from all fifty states and three territories, and a sizeable group of influential federal officials. Rod and most of the OEM Directors had been close friends for nearly 42 years going back to their old Civil Defense days.

Rod was an old fishing friend of Senator Rex Nunn. They were close fraternity roommates for four years at Arizona State University, and maintained that close relationship. The good senator had spent several cool days up on the Mogollon Rim fly-fishing the streams outside Rod's cabin just a few miles north of Showlow.

Likewise Rod had frequented the trout brooks at the base of the Teton Mountains of western Wyoming and into Montana. The two friends loved to give each other a lively ribbing about their inability to catch a cold much less a single trout, or the only bite they got was a mosquito or deer fly bite. But the reality was that each night there was always an abundance of fresh trout in their frying pan.

Rex had amazing power within the Senate that he exercised to ensure that every state had an equal share in the fund appropriations for Homeland Security, CIA, NSA and OEM much to the chagrin of major cities and urban areas. The fact was that the best-trained and equipped emergency response team was Rex's hometown of Laramie, Wyoming. Their equipment and training easily rivaled New York City and other large metropolitan cities despite the locales highly unlikely targeting for any terrorist attack.

Following the Lake Havasu City attacks three days earlier things had radically changed as Rod's office provided support for the small community. Rod was busy attempting to deal with the various spins placed on the attack by the huge pre-conference media presence and various conference attendees arriving at the Phoenician resort. Suddenly every small town in Arizona felt a revived pressing need for more protection and material support. The additional national and international media in Arizona covering the attack added more pressure on Rod and his staff. The presence of high-ranking administration and intelligence leaders would add another dimension to the conference in Scottsdale. Rod thought *the conference was going to be a headache well before the attack. Now it seemed it was becoming an unmanageable three-ring circus.* The trail of the terrorists was getting colder hour by hour and day by day.

The FBI seemed embarrassed at not having found major evidence on the terrorist, planning, and escape, much less capturing the culprits. Unfortunately the NSA and CIA spy satellites were of little help as the Arizona desert was not a high priority for their video files and Arizona's typical August monsoon storm coverage had severely limited their effectiveness.

Rod knew the recent situation in Arizona would be a tremendous asset for Rex to strengthen his position for localized Homeland Security fund disbursements as in the past. Nobody disputed that small rural areas did not need the funds as much as large cities given the final death toll at Lake Havasu City was six times larger as a percentage of the city's population than the 9/11 attack in New York City. Despite all of this, Rod was looking forward to seeing his OEM friends at the annual conference at the plush Phoenician resort in Scottsdale.

There was a rumor circulating among the various OEM Directors that the annual meeting might have gotten postponed or cancelled due to the Lake Havasu attack. They feared that due to the proximity of the attack, the powers in Washington might pull the plug on the conference. Rod knew that nothing could be further from the truth. The cost of the conference was amazing even at Arizona's off-season summer rates. There was no way to reschedule or cancel the conference at this point without an issue of huge financial waste being exposed by the media. President Reynolds also expressed his firm conviction that cancelling a government event played into the hands of terrorists. A vast majority of the conference attendees were arriving on Friday and departing on Monday.

As the local host Rod and Rita, his wife, planned on greeting arrivals at the resort with Stetson cowboy hats and silver and turquoise inlaid Bola ties created by Zuni artisans for Directors and their significant others. Rita played a vital role as the hostess for the spouses and significant others during the three conference days. Later Rod and Rita would host a BBQ, rodeo, line dancing and good old fashion square dance. A small team of OEM assistants from various state offices had been recruited to assist in doing some of the conference grunt work. One of Rod's staff was extremely busy gathering information on the situation in Lake Havasu, to update members during the conference.

The final expense tab for the three-day official meeting for 485 official participants and spouses or significant others exceeded well over $2,100,000. The fact that an era of terrorism gave Homeland Security and the Office of Emergency Management the funds for such a lavished annual event chaffed Rod's conservative DNA and made him feel very uncomfortable. After all he was raised in a frugal conservative western family with parents that lived through the meager means of the depression years. He knew the value of a dollar and thought the conference at the taxpayers expense could have been a simple well-structured Webinar. But on the other hand this conference did serve a personal secondary purpose of giving him one last hurrah with his cronies, making all the work worth it.

Rod met two of his oldest friends at Sky Harbor Airport to take them up to scenic Pinnacle Peak at the top of Reata Pass for a late mesquite grilled steak lunch. A big part of the old cowboy restaurant tradition was for some pretty young cowgirl waitress in cutoff denim shorts tight cutoff shirt to suddenly flirt with an unsuspecting overdressed male visitor.

248

Just as the waitress sat on the male's lap, she turned and cut off half of his tie. This happened quickly much to the absolute horror of the typical patron as she stepped up on the table in her far too short cowgirl outfit and nailed the end of the tie to the ceiling beam. The tradition was all in good fun, but Rod did not want to take a chance that one of his friends would have on a favorite or very expensive tie. He had several old ties in his pocket for their use and distributed them before they reached the restaurant.

Rod was working with the Phoenix Police, Scottsdale Police, Maricopa Sherriff's Department, U.S. Marshalls, Arizona Department of Public Safety (DPS), and FBI to secure the conference site, three off resort general events, and three events specifically for spouses and significant others. The Lake Havasu attack and ongoing investigations of leads had over half of the originally planned conference law enforcement presence occupied with their investigations. Rod was going to have to do with the limited available personnel. He was feeling confident that everything that could be done was finished. He hoped that the next day being Friday the thirteenth would pass without incident despite the "old wives" superstition.

Chapter 26: Enjoying The Perfect Evening
Friday, August 13, 7:00 p.m. BST (UTC/GMT)
10 Downing Street, London, UK

Upon returning from Cornwall, Thomas Graham planned a perfect outing with Helena after enduring weeks of tension and stress from awaiting an imminent terrorist attack. Graham thought *Helena looked stunning in her Sara Carr evening gown, four-inch heels, and blonde hair pulled up in a fashionable bun.* They attended a late afternoon welcoming reception for the new Spanish Ambassador at the Spanish Embassy in the chic Belgravia area of London. They left the reception early to catch a 7:30 p.m. performance of *Spamolot*. Graham was unimpressed by the revived satirical musical after having seen the original cast, but caved to Helena's wish to see the production. After the performance, the couple enjoyed an incredible five-course meal at the Winter Garden in the Landmark Hotel. Minutes after placing their order, Chef Rex Poytonio made a special appearance at their table presenting them with a wonderful Armagnac liqueur apéritif from Gascony, and fully describing the details of the preparation of their meal. The meal was an extravaganza lasting two hours with amazing wines served with each course. Shortly after 11:30 p.m. they settled into Graham's Downing Street quarters. Their nightcap was interrupted when Graham received a cell call and quickly excused himself to take the call in his study..

"Sir, Spencer here. I'm afraid we have another sudden drastic increase in highly likely terrorists chatter. The chatter does not mention any specific targets or countries. On another note, the intelligence news from Arizona indicated that the terrorists had made good on their escape despite a massive effort by the U.S. It may take some time for the Americans to run the terrorist down."

"Thanks, Spencer, both are somewhat disturbing, but I don't see that there is a need for any immediate action on our part. Please keep me informed if there are any further developments." Graham felt his temples throbbing slightly, a sure sign that the internalization of stress had returned. Spencer's news was unsettling, but Graham decided to keep his thoughts to himself and enjoy sharing a Jean Fillioux La Pouyade Cognac. They retired to his bedroom to enjoy their cognac followed by an amorous ending with Helena deciding to spend the night.

Chapter 27: The Annual Homeland Security Conference Junket

Friday, August 13, 1:00 p.m. MST (UTC/GMT-8)
The Phoenician Resort, Camelback Rd, Scottsdale, AZ

The Homeland Security and Emergency Response Management directors looked forward to their annual junket conference and meetings. It was always held in a plush resort with great food, fun activities and more than adequate time for relaxation. The fact that these luxurious junkets were paid for by taxpayers in the Homeland Security budget seemed to be more than justified by the directors as small compensation for their relatively low salaries. The planned format of the conference was a keynote address on Friday by Gayle Swartz, Secretary of Homeland Security, and then three hours of general sessions on Saturday and Sunday. The spouses had optional events during the course of the day and special events each evening.

The security for the conference included a five-member Secret Service detail for Cabinet level officials, FBI agents, Phoenix Police, Scottsdale Police, Arizona State Department of Public Safety troopers, Scottsdale Auxiliary Police, and hotel and personal security assigned for specific officials. Neil Fischer was responsible for coordinating all the units while also managing the terrorist investigation in Lake Havasu. He felt overworked and a bit frantic worrying about the possibility of another attack within the state under the very noses of numerous top federal officials.

The majority of the meeting participants arrived early on Friday to take advantage of the pampering spa, swimming, tennis, and golf packages put together by the Arizona hospitality committee. Several spouses looked forward to exploring the incredible shopping in the adjacent Scottsdale Fashion Square mall.

The Phoenician Resort was built atop a small hill abutting the base tail end of Camelback Mountain. The long eighth of a mile palm tree lined driveway wound up from Camelback Road past amazing desert plants, fountains, and scrubs to the lavished circular valet parking area at the top of the resort. The gigantic resort reception and check-in area had a massive covered terrace and bar overlooking the pool to the south. Entering the resort reception area, guests had a spectacular view of Scottsdale, Phoenix, and the numerous aircraft landing at Sky Harbor Airport ten miles away.

The desert sun had burned off the last wisps of cool air lingering in vegetated neighborhoods in the Valley of the Sun. It was going to be another scorcher as the temperature hit 99 degrees at 8:30 a.m. Rod Harris thought how *some of his friends are going to bake this morning with tee start times after 9 a.m.* Golfers playing the Phoenician Resort course normally sought the limited shade on the back end of Camelback Mountain and from the few saguaro cacti lining the course. Rod's hospitality committee had arranged for them to have three golf carts with huge coolers of iced beverages and iced towels. He knew most looked forward to playing rounds at the five-star resort. The golf arrangement was a minor aspect in the work Rod had accomplished over the past five months.

Rod Harris was an old school type of guy. He was a bit weather-beaten but in fair physical shape for his 67 years. Common sense and the value of a dollar had always been part of his very being. Rod hated the fact that his younger OEM Directors took advantage of the conference situation year after year without a second thought. It was the topic again and again around the Harris household. The only aspect he loved about the meetings was the opportunity to see friends from far and near.

The conference content was usually fairly minimal. Rod hoped that the leaders in Washington would tone down the expenses and put more of the funding to expenditures that actually improved the OEM's ability to respond to varied natural and human caused emergencies. He planned to bring up the issue on his next fishing trip with Senator Nunn, who held the power to make such changes. Senator Nunn's aide-de-camp called to confirm that the Senator had altered his calendar to attend all three days of the conference and stay an additional two days to fish and hunt on Rod's Showlow property. Rod had nothing to lose with bringing up issue with Rex as the Arizona State Legislature had forced his December retirement after formally acknowledging his incredible public service. Only three of his remaining friends had been in the emergency response business going back to the old Cold War years. Over the past ten years, friends kept retiring on Rod as he became the oldest remaining Civil Defense guy on the list of OEM Directors. Rod just didn't feel it was time to get the rocking chair out on the back porch and retire, but the legislature and his wife Rita said otherwise. The conference was served as his swansong. Having time with Rex was a huge bonus. Rod could hardly wait to show Nunn the classic Winchester rifle he recently purchased on eBay.

Rod and Rita stationed themselves in the resort's spacious open lobby where officials and their guests registered upon their arrival. A mix of Arizona and Washington state personnel staffed the hospitality tables. They gave each participant and spouse a gift bag, information folder, Stetson cowboy hat, and choice of western kerchiefs or bola ties. Rod knew that each swank bag and hat cost in excess of $200, which just fueled his feelings of unnecessary government waste. The hospitality staff was on their last legs as the shaded open-air foyer was not air-conditioned and there wasn't the slightest breeze to move the hot dry desert air.

As Rod pondered over the excessive expense of the conference, a motorcade of six black Mercedes limousines arrived in the canopied entrance. The first and second contained the entourage of Homeland Security Secretary Gale Swartz. The next dropped off the National Security Agency Director Dexter Ford and nine of his staff., followed by three stretch limos with CIA Director Gary Dessile and FBI Director Frank Thomas and their executive staffs. The last portion of the convoy was three black Ford Exposition SUVs with heavily tinted black windows contained the National Security Advisor Abe Greenfeld and four of the National Security Council members and staff. Their police motorcycle escort lined the long driveway up the hill from Camelback Road. These important federal officials always travelled in style. In the back of his mind, Rod wondered how many sleek government jets were parked on the tarmac at the Scottsdale Airport and Sky Harbor. Most of the big shots just didn't travel in commercial aircraft like the lesser attendees and their families who had arrived via the usual domestic airlines.

Arizona Governor Ann Hargrove and Scottsdale Mayor Madeline Frazer had been waiting in the lounge sipping iced Irish coffee. Hargrove was making an appearance and personally welcoming the most recent group of arrivals. One of her aides must have given her the word via her cell phone as she appeared next to Rod when Secretary Swartz entered the reception area. The roar of the police motorcycle escort leaving ricocheted off the south rock face of Camelback Mountain. It was deafening and the fumes made several guests gasp for air. The Governor was all show and of little substance, an ultra conservative Republican from Rhode Island transplanted in the Sunbelt.

She looked more at ease in her usual Tom James business suits and heels than the western outfit she had donned to welcome the group of dignitaries. Rod stifled a laugh as Hargrove offered her hand to Secretary Swartz with a warm, "Howdy, welcome to Arizona." Years of attempting to put Phoenix on the map as a major modern high tech city were swept away by the impression created by this political clown trying desperately to act western. Rod stepped away from the governor and put his arm around Rita, who appeared a bit nervous as she fidgeted with her hair. Rita refused to wear the complimentary Stetson hat. Given her very nature greeting top federal officials was a real difficult task for her, but as usual Rod knew she always rose to the challenge. All the formality of introductions, greeting strangers, and the security presence in the resort made her very uncomfortable. She bared it with a smile knowing full well that these were Rod's colleagues and a part of his retirement party.

Rod hated portions of his role as host. He knew there would be the side trips to the Fort McDowell casinos and even discreet official requests to visit the few nude strip joints on Washington Street. In a conversation with Rita on the short drive over to the Phoenician, both had agreed that Tuesday could not come soon enough for either of them. Both looked forward to enjoying a few days at their rustic cabin in the cool pine covered Showlow hills. Rod couldn't wait to test his new Winchester and unwind fishing with Rex.

Chapter 28: All Hell Breaks Loose
Friday, August 13, 4:00 p.m. MST (UTC/GMT -8)
Phoenician Resort, Camelback Road, Scottsdale, Arizona, United States

Meerza held a final meeting with Alpha team to give a brief motivational speech on the importance of their mission as retribution for the terror the U.S. had spread across the Muslim world. After a brief prayer, he left the staging area at 4 p.m. as his role during the attack was as an observer of the law enforcement response and giving assistance and directions during the team's escape. Alpha team relied heavily on their reconnaissance and Maji's intelligence notes to initiate the attack. They ensured that residents in the area received an official resort flyer warning that there would be fireworks at 6 p.m. to kick off the Homeland Security Conference after the keynote speech. A majority of the team began preparing the tour bus parked at the rear of the East Vista Drive house. The bus had a specially built rear window that propped up sufficiently for their protruding twin .50 caliber machine guns. A black plastic screen camouflaged the barrels, making it impossible for roving eyes on the golf course or resort grounds men to spot the deadly weapon. A team member trained specifically on the twin machine guns, capable of firing 1000 rounds per minute. Another team member served as a spotter using Celestron SkyMaster Giant 15x70 Binoculars on a tripod, to give the command to fire and direct adjustments at targets 650 yards away. The machine guns were intended to inflict the most damage during the attack.

Their location gave them a perfect range of fire over the entire Phoenician resort. The other team members took sniper positions on the second floor of the East Vista Drive house. The large Scottsdale home had a huge open backyard with an unobstructed view of the resort. The snipers were highly trained and skilled, wearing only black to make them invisible to the naked eye. Their task was to fire out the slightly opened windows, cleaning up targets that escaped the rain of .50 caliber bullets. Their position also gave them a clear view of N 64th Street, allowing them to hit any potential law enforcement response. The plan was for the attack to only last six minutes, devastating the conference, and shattering the sense of security within the entire U.S. Other teammates were launching a simultaneous attack on the spouses' trip in the Scottsdale Fashion Mall.

The conference started with an invocation in the ballroom and a short introduction of Secretary Swartz. The immense foyer area outside had an elaborate white Carrara marble floor and huge balconies at both ends that looked out over the golf course, swimming pools, and lush gardens. The foyer walls were decorated with large Anasazi and Hohokam designs with additional pictures of Casa Grande and Montezuma cliff dwellings that gave an interesting culture context to the ultra-modern resort facility. Homeland Security, OEM, and FEMA hung their official seal banners along the hallway between massive potted trees.

At exactly 6:00 p.m., Gayle Swartz, concluded her keynote presentation to thunderous applause. Within five minutes, the conference participants poured out into the immense foyer to enjoy a free open bar and gourmet finger food. Groups of attendees gathered and mingled; several wore their Stetsons and Bolas.

The resort catering staff had three bar locations and ten different tables full of delicious assortments of cheeses, shrimp, mini roast beef sandwiches, veggies, tacos, nachos, chips, dessert items, ice water, and coffee. Several servers circulated between attendees with trays of appetizers, glasses of wine, bottled imported beer, and champagne. A seven-piece mariachi band played, adding to the festive occasion as music filled the air. Outside, the conference a fireworks display shot skyward over the resort and Camelback Mountain with numerous thunderous booms. Several of the attendees strolled onto the balcony to view the spectacular show over Camelback Mountain. After another five minutes, members of the Washington VIP entourage joined the massive mixed group of state OEM and FEMA attendees in the foyer.

Alpha team waited patiently, observing the crowd until Secretary Swartz and Senator Nunn exited the ballroom. The team's spotter grinned seeing his VIP targets. نار "Fire!" he yelled. The twin .50 caliber machine guns opened up a deadly barrage as shell casings littered the bus floor. Suddenly the noise of the fireworks and music was drowned out by the initial burst of .50 caliber bullets shattering the foyer. The noise was deafening as the machine gun fire shredded the first group of victims perched on the balcony. The M21 sniper rifles joined in, picking off easy targets, splattering blood across the walls of Anasazi and Hohokam designs. People fell, dropping wine glasses, beer bottles and china plates where they stood. Bullets ripped through flesh like it was paper, piercing through bodies, and fracturing the marble wall tiles. The crowd attempted to run or crawl for cover behind the large potted trees and under the catering tables. Others attempted to reach the two stairwells. The death toll rose as the relentless volley of bullets hit their targets.

Rod had taken shelter in the stairwell, grabbing, and pulling as many of the attendees as possible out of harm's way. Neil Fischer appeared down the stairwell and began helping get conference attendees to safety. Recognizing the direction of the gunfire, he used his two-way radio to call Ken Fowler, the DPS Captain in charge of DPS conference security detachment. "Ken, this is Rod!" he yelled over the sound of the fireworks, chaotic screaming, and unrelenting gunfire. "The conference is under terrorist attack! Heavy weapons are firing from the north over the golf course. Call emergency responders and send patrol cars up North 64th Street. Be careful, these guys are heavily armed."

"Shit," Ken responded. "I'll alert the EMTs and dispatch units. Do the best you can to save others. Good luck!"

Despite the continued gunfire, Rod crawled across the blood soaked marble floor, cutting his hands on shards of broken glass. He felt sick as he recognized several dead friends and colleagues among the bodies. He pulled several of the wounded attendees back to the stairwell out of harm's way. His years of training seemed to go on automatic as he sadly recognized that subconsciously he was carefully prioritizing victims and selecting only individuals that looked as if they might survive their wounds. The sounds of screaming, weeping, and shouting could barely be heard over the continuation of the massive fireworks exploding overhead and bullets continually raining down the foyer. *The damned fireworks are endless and cover the attack*, Rod thought, watching as a reporter pull Gayle Swartz's dead bodyguard off her blood soaked body. Swartz seemed unharmed, but her eyes betrayed her absolute panic-stricken fear. Rod pointed to the alcove back into the ballroom. The reporter nodded her understanding, crawled off in that direction, and dragged Secretary Swartz by the nape of her Armani business suit jacket.

The fireworks ended, bringing hope that the rain of bullets would subside. The last person Rod saved from the foyer was his lifelong friend Rex Nunn, who was bleeding profusely as his arm dangled uselessly from his shoulder held on by small shreds of tendon and muscle. Rex's face conveyed his fear of dying as the artery sprayed squirts of blood with each panic filled heartbeat. Rod immediately applied his belt as a tourniquet hoping to save his friend's life. The two slowly made it to the stairwell, sliding across pools of blood and around motionless bodies.

When the gunfire started, Chris Leffler, one of the security guards at the valet station, recognized the sound of the twin .50 caliber machine guns. He had served three tours in U.S. Army Special Forces in Iraq and fully understood the deadly nature of the attack. He ran to the security command center as several DPS vehicles screamed down the driveway to respond to the attack. He found Neil Fischer taking a phone call from the Secretary Swartz's assistant. Leffler interrupted him to explain that he knew the extraordinary firepower of the .50 Caliber machine guns. The weapon was superior to any of the weaponry at the resort. Neil immediately contacted the Scottsdale SWAT team being held on standby less than four miles away.

The conference security detail at the resort was unprepared for this particular type of massive attack from the rear of the resort. Most of their presence was concentrated on the single southern access road up from Camelback Rd. As the attack continued, Ken Fowler led four other DPS vehicles left from the resort onto Camelback Road and immediately left onto N 64th Street.

As the terrorists anticipated, the DPS units turned onto the street adjacent to the golf course north towards East Vista Drive. The police sped less than a hundred yards when they came into the redirected line of fire of the twin .50 caliber machine guns. The bullets tore through the vehicles as if they were made of tin foil. In seconds, the vehicles were engulfed in flames and completely blocking N 64th Street. DPS Captain Fowler was able to get off a quick radio message describing the attack as originating from the rear of a black tour bus before being silenced by the deadly line of fire.

Several curious neighbors on East Vista Drive stood outside watching the fireworks display in the early evening twilight. When the show ended and the gunfire continued, they scurried home to call 911. Because of the ongoing loud sound of discharging weapons, the neighbors took shelter within their homes and carefully watched out their windows.

Rod Harris heard Fowler's last words before the radio message ended with the horrible sound of bullets striking his vehicle. Rod realized he had sent the DPS team to their deaths. Seven minutes of unrelenting gunfire on the resort and less than thirty seconds on the DPS vehicles, the gunfire finally stopped, creating an eerie quiet.

Several emergency responders, carrying medical equipment, raced down Rod's stairwell and provided immediate aid that was critical in saving lives. Soon additional EMTs appeared down the other stairwell and poured into the foyer. The growing number of EMT's set up a triage system using strips of colored tape: black for dead, red for critical, yellow for serious, and green for minor. It was a simple time saving method to prevent another EMT from assessing the same victim, thus saving critical minutes.

The large foyer was a mass of activity attempting to save as many lives as possible. Several of the wounded slowly made it up the stairwell on their own to the reception area, while others helped rendering assistance and comforting the severely wounded. Hotel staff appeared with towels and first aid kits. Seconds later, police officers and fire fighters appeared to assist the EMTs in moving the critically wounded to ambulances in the circular driveway entrance just as two medical choppers landed in the parking lot.

Meanwhile the Alpha team gunner and spotter removed their earplugs, closed the bus rear window. The snipers calmly exited the house and boarded the bus with their weapons. One terrorist opened the large gate to check outside. He found the street deserted, so he waved to the bus driver, and hopped into the bus. The bus pulled out of the driveway onto East Vista Drive and took an immediate left turn north onto 64th Street. They could hear the distant sounds of sirens from various emergency vehicles and two choppers moving towards the resort. They knew that the wreckage of the DPS vehicles totally blocked any pursuit vehicles from coming in their direction.

Rod immediately called the Paradise Valley Police Chief, Paul Cooke, who was just leaving his police headquarters in an unmarked police vehicle in response to reported gunfire from the residents on East Vista Drive. He was unaware of the events taking place a mile and half away when his cell phone rang.

"Hello, Rod," he answered. "How are you?"

"Paul, it's a fuckin' blood bath at the Phoenician!" Rod shouted, yelling over the screams of victims and responders around him. "We're dealing with a horrible terrorist attack at the OEM conference. They hit us with heavy automatic weapons fired from somewhere up in Phoenician Estates and off 64th Street. I got a report from DPS that the terrorists were last seen in a black tour bus heading your way. Given their firepower, it's best that you do not engage them. I repeat, do not engage them. Swing around and follow them at a safe distance. They already destroyed several police units. Let Special Agent Neil Fischer know where the bus is headed. Use your cell phone. The terrorists are more than likely monitoring the police radio. I'm sending you Fischer's contact number now. Good luck!"

"Holy Shit! Will do Rod!" Cooke looked at his driver, Officer Sam Kraft. "We have some terrorists heading our way in a black tour bus. Let's roll slowly towards the Phoenician Resort and turn west on McDonald Drive." Cooke immediately called Neil Fischer. He had met Fischer three years earlier at a conference on gathering evidence at the FBI office near Deer Valley Airport. At that very moment, he spotted the tour bus coming directly at them.

Neil Fischer was back in the security command center just outside the reception area trying to muster a response to the attack. He had just hung up his landline phone when Cooke called. "Fischer here," he answered immediately.

"Neil, this is Paradise Valley Police Chief Cooke, I have a visual on the suspected black tour bus involved in the Phoenician terrorist attack."

"Great news, Chief. Use extreme caution. The terrorists have heavy-duty weapons. Stay on the line, I'm patching you into a conference call with Scottsdale SWAT."

The fact that they had identified the terrorist location and may be able to tail the terrorists was extremely important as it provided Neil with sufficient time to act decisively in formulating a response plan. Rod's next call was to Scottsdale Police Chief Rebecca Kelson. Kelson had earned an amazing record as one of the first women in the Navy SEALs prior to completing her master degree in Criminal Justice and being appointed the first woman police chief in Arizona.

"Chief Kelson here," an assertive female voice answered.

"Kelson, I have PV Chief Cooke on the line. He has a visual on the suspected bus. His eyes can help coordinate a plan to stop these assholes."

"The bus just turned right from 64th Street East onto East McDonald Drive," Cooke interrupted.

Cooke's driver turned in the opposite direction of the bus to throw the terrorist off. After a hundred yards, they made a quick U-turn and began tailing the tour bus at a safe distance east to Scottsdale Road.

"The bus is acting normal," Cooke continued, "driving well within the posted speed limit and stopping at the traffic light on Scottsdale Road. They seem unaware that we are following them. Their right blinker is on. They'll be heading south towards Old Town, traveling in rush hour traffic."

"They're heading right for us," Kelson responded. "We'll be ready."

The well-equipped Scottsdale SWAT teams prepared for an intercept as the tour bus continued slowly towards them.

Friday, August 13, 6:00 p.m. MST (UTC/GMT -8)
Scottsdale Fashion Square Mall, Camelback Road,
Scottsdale, Arizona

Before the terrorist attack on the Phoenician resort, a separate four-man team of armed terrorists with 9mm silenced Glocks in shopping bags were in the process of slowly hunting down the party of conference spouses at the Scottsdale Fashion Square. The terrorists dressed in shorts, tee shirts, ball caps, and sandals, looking like other young men walking through the packed mall. The group quickly separated to cover more ground through the vast shopping mecca. Each wore ear buds to maintain cell contact with each other.

Rita Harris, Rod's wife, led the group of 29 spouses and significant others on an excursion to the elaborate Scottsdale Fashion Mall. She was somewhat surprised when Rod called, assuming *he would be much too busy enjoying his friends and acting as the conference host to call her.*

"Rita," Rod gasped. "Listen, there's been a vicious terrorist attack at the resort. It's very important to not bring the spouses back to the resort. The situation is very fluid and they do not need to see the terrible carnage. I'm sure some of their loved ones will be wounded or dead."

"Oh my God, are you all right, Rod?"

"I'm fine. But keep the spouses away until I tell you otherwise."

"This is horrendous. What can I do?"

"There are a lot of attendees who were killed by gunfire and others who are going to be lucky if they survive." Rod had a sudden flash of clarity that turned to panic. *The terrorists might attack the spouses in the mall.* "Exactly where are you in Fashion Square?"

266

"Uh, We are on the second level, near Barney's and the Harkins Theater. Why?"

"Listen carefully. You need to order your security detail to immediately escort your group into the Harkins movie theater farthest away from the entrance and have them secure the perimeter."

"What's going on?"

"Sorry, there might be a chance that you and your group might be a target."

"Jesus, what the fuck, Rod?" Rita had to be upset as uncharacteristically her words flowed underlining her point.

"Just do it! Please!"

Rita hastily alerted the security officers. They marshaled the confused group into the newly remodeled Harkins Theatres and led them into the most remote auditorium. They posted four Scottsdale police out of sight at the entrance and another two at a rear door. Rod remained on the line with Rita until she confirmed she and the group of spouses were safely secure within the theater.

The four terrorists roamed through the massive multi-story mall, searching for the group of spouses among the throngs of Friday shoppers. They had pictures on their phones to identify five of the highest priority targets: Elizabeth Nunn, Georgina Thomas, Janis McGowan, Betsy Ford, and Anne Hargrove. They planned to eliminate the group's security detail, take the most prestigious spouses and the governor hostage, and force them into the approaching tour bus outside.

Their search was unsuccessful in locating their targets for over twenty-five minutes. Time was running short as the resort attack was over and the bus was on the way.

Realizing their opportunity had slipped away, Jalal Hamundi reluctantly called Meerza, and "I know calling is against our protocol, but you need to know that we have not been able to locate our guests." What should we do?"

"The group are there somewhere," Meerza responded. "You have failed us." He paused with anger and disappointment. He was tempted to leave his men in the mall, but decided they had spent too much time training them to lose them. "Collect your team and meet at the extraction point on Scottsdale Road. The bus is on the way. You are going to have to rush to meet it."

Meerza was in his minivan just outside Fashion Square. He was upset by the call and failure to capture hostages. The mall hostages were an integral part in Alpha Team's escape on a chartered jet from the Phoenix-Mesa Gateway Airport. Meerza immediately called the tour bus and ordered them to pick up his mall team immediately. To help with the extraction, he continued monitoring the police radio band. The chatter had been filled with endless chaotic calls from first responders and police at the resort, revealing they were totally overwhelmed with the huge aftermath of the massive attack. Meerza finally smiled, satisfied with the damage Alpha team had inflicted during both attacks.

The tour bus pulled over on North Scottsdale Road just before the intersection at Camelback Road. The individual mall team members appeared separately over a span of less than a minute and loaded into the bus.

"Neil, this is Cooke. The bus pulled over on Scottsdale Road just north of Camelback. They are picking up four additional male individuals carrying shopping bags."

"Did they come out of the Fashion Square Mall?" Neil Fischer asked.

"Yes, I can confirm they have picked up four men exiting from the mall. The bus is now entering traffic driving south down Scottsdale Road, stopped at the intersection."

Rebecca Kelson broke in on the call. "We're ready. We have a well-structured SWAT response barricade in place just south of their current position. I'm sending two of my armored vehicles to close the trap behind the bus. My security detail has also secured the group of conference spouses within Harkins Theatres. They are awaiting for instructions."

"That's great news," Neil said with relief. "We'll move the spouses to a secure location outside the mall when we are sure the time is right. We will have to sweep the mall for possible explosive devices. Our sole focus needs to be on the tour bus and ending any further threat of these assholes."

"Affirmative."

As Neil thought of the bus picking up additional men from the mall, a cold chill ran up his spine. He feared the worst-case scenario that the terrorists left explosive devices to create further havoc within the mall. He immediately called mall security and dispatched three police units to force an immediate evacuation. He called the Scottsdale and Phoenix bomb squad sniffer canines into action to clear Fashion Square, hoping beyond hope that this was not too little too late.

The carnage of multiple bombs in the mall on a Friday night might exceed the deaths and destruction at the conference.

The Scottsdale police had six dark blue AAV-7 (LVTP-7) armored vehicles given as part of a special grant from Homeland Security. The amphibious vehicles had been primarily used in various parades and for water rescues in various washes during Scottsdale's monsoon season. They were stationed at the Police Headquarters on 75th Street and already on standby before the start of the conference. When the call came in, it took them three minutes to organize and travel the short five blocks to Scottsdale Road and plan an interception of the tour bus.

Chief Kelson had attended a two-day special military training exercise in the effective use of the armored vehicles at Fort Bragg three years earlier. She continued monitoring Cooke's stream of communication and plotted an intercept to happen at East Shoeman Lane. The fact that bus maintaining the same route south was truly a blessing. It simplified the plan to thwart the terrorist by having four of the armored vehicles completely block all four lanes in both directions south of Scottsdale Road. Once the road was totally blocked, they moved in Viper spiked tire-strips and a massive barricade of police vehicles. The fifth and sixth armored vehicles sat a block east on Camelback Road, waiting for the tour bus to pass before following behind the bus to block any terrorist effort to escape to the rear.

Meerza's police band radio came to life with the Scottsdale police ordering the final set-up of their SWAT team trap just south on Scottsdale Road and East Shoeman Lane.

He realized that it was too late to warn Alpha team as he watched the bus cross Camelback Road, followed closely by two armored vehicles pulling in behind them. The police radio became extremely active as the barricade force spotted the bus approaching towards them. Within seconds, Meerza understood the dire situation and knew he had to prevent Alpha team from being captured.

Shortly after the bus crossed a small canal bridge, Jalal, the driver, spotted the huge police barricade ahead. In an instant, he looked in the rearview mirror and spotted the two armored vehicles pulling in behind the bus. He recognized that Alpha team was in a no win situation. Their biggest fear of being captured was becoming reality, and their only option was to inflict as much death and destruction as possible.

"Open up the machine gun!" Jalal shouted an ordered. "Everyone arm yourselves! Kill infidels for the glory of Allah!"

Alpha team opened up the rear window for the twin .50-caliber machine guns and began firing at the armored vehicles behind the bus. The other terrorists used automatic weapons on the police barricade in the front. They received an immediate barrage of return gunfire from the forty-nine law enforcement officers hidden behind armored vehicles and police cruisers.

Like all of the Shura's tactics, there was a well-conceived contingency plan. Meerza fully understood the desperate situation, and recognized his ultimate responsibility as cell leader. He called a special cell number and activated the detonators for two explosive devices that Kaji built into the frame of the tour bus: one adjacent to the two gas tanks, the other beneath the container of ammo belts feeding the twin .50 caliber machine guns.

When the explosives detonated, the bus ripped completely apart, shredding the occupants, sending flames skyward, shattering building windows, and sending deadly shrapnel everywhere.

Friday, August 13, 6:21 p.m. MST (UTC/GMT-8)
Old Town Scottsdale, Scottsdale, Arizona
The tour bus explosion suddenly terminated the gun battle and removed any further threat from the terrorists inside the bus. The sheer force had spread deadly debris in all directions with an ear-shattering boom, killing three officers in the nearest armored vehicle, and flipping one of the police squad cars along the barricade. The downward force of the explosion created a small crater in the pavement and severely damaged the small canal bridge.

"We've neutralized the terrorist bus," Chief Kelson reported over the police radio. "Officers down! Officers down! Send all available EMTs to our Scottsdale Road location ASAP." There was a small tremble within her deep feminine voice underlining the urgent need for assistance. Kelson had been hit by shrapnel from the bus explosion.

The uninjured police officers set up a triage area and gave aid to the most seriously wounded. Most of the Scottsdale and Phoenix emergency units were already occupied at the Phoenician Resort. Several doctors' appeared out of nowhere from local offices, and then first responders from Tempe and Mesa arrived within minutes. The scene looked like a war zone. The police suffered a huge loss as five officers were killed, four remain in critical condition, eight in serious condition, and an additional eleven with minor wounds and hearing loss. Their swift action had annihilated the tour bus loaded with terrorists, leaving the officers a sobering weird sense of euphoria as a small consolation.

Friday, August 13, 6:45 p.m. MST (UTC/GMT-8)
Interstate 10 between Phoenix and Tucson
Meerza listened to the chaos on the police radio band as he drove south to Tucson. After fifteen minutes of freeway driving, he switched to KTAR commercial radio that reported live on the scene from outside the Phoenician conference attack and from the Scottsdale barricade location. After a short time the on scene report was interrupted with reports of additional attacks in Los Angeles and San Francisco.

Meerza felt his heart throbbing with adrenaline pumping through his body. It was one thing to spend months studying and preparing for the coordinated attacks, but it was another thing to see the cell's hard work being successfully completed. He hoped the attacks in California by Bravo and Charlie team were as successful.

He arrived in Tucson and stopped at the Hyatt Place hotel near the airport. Once comfortably settled in, he called for room service while watching the incredible media coverage of the coordinated Arizona and California attacks. He knew the *Shura* would be monitoring the news and will hopefully be pleased with his work. Given the completion of *Allim Tiflak's* mission, Meerza used his laptop to confirm his cell's successful efforts with one final covert entry on the cell's Pinterest board.

Chapter 29: Simultaneous Attack in Los Angeles
Friday, August 13, 4:48 p.m. PST (UTC/GMT-9) and Phoenix time
LA County Museum of Art, Wilshire Blvd, Los Angeles, CA

At precisely 4:49 p.m. PST, the eight-person Bravo team arrived in four different vehicles outside the Los Angeles County Museum of Art. They parked near West 6th and Fairfax Ave. The team dressed in blue maintenance staff overhauls and calmly walked the short distance. They carried concealed silenced Glock automatics under their loose shirts and explosives in their knapsacks and toolboxes.

Bravo team's attack was planned to go operational on a special gala night at the museum for the opening of an *Andreas Gursky* exhibition. The museum had closed at noon to prepare for this 5 p.m. special event for three hundred top donors. As per their attack plan, Bravo team separated to cover the museum's four structures. Working in pairs, they ignored the closed signs and entered the Ahmanson Building, the Broad Contemporary Art Museum, Hammer Building, and the Arts of the Americas Building.

Gloria Hecht, a LACMA Assistant to the Executive Director, heard strange language shouting outside her office. Peeking out a small vertical shaded window, she saw two gunmen gunning down a security guard exiting from the adjacent office. Ducking quickly, she quietly locked the door, hid under her desk, and remained motionless with her heart pounding with fear. After a few minutes the shouting and shooting stopped, leaving only the cries of the wounded. She finally reached up on her desk for her cell and called 911.

"This is 911. What's your emergency?"

"Terrorists are attacking the LA County Museum of Art," Gloria said, using an extremely soft tone from her hiding spot. "They're shooting everyone. Please god, send help."

Bravo team moved swiftly through the varied art galleries, setting detonators on their TATP explosives for exactly 5:10 p.m. PST.

The dispatcher asked, "What is your name?"

"Gloria Hecht. Please help us."

"Gloria, are you hurt? Are terrorists around you?"

"I'm not hurt, but I've seen several of our staff gunned down in cold blood."

A series of loud explosions could be heard over the phone. Gloria felt the building shake as the explosions rattled the museum complex.

"Did you hear that? They're setting off explosives!" Gloria crawled further under her desk fearing the collapse of the roof as ceiling tiles dropped down in her office.

Rita West, the dispatcher, had undergone years of extensive training in dealing remotely with a huge variety of emergencies. She remained calm as she utilized her dispatch console to alert the Los Angeles Police West Bureau of the attack, followed by an alert call to both the LA SWAT and bomb squad. Her final call was to alert LA Fire Department and medical units.

"Gloria, please remain on the line, stay calm, and stay out of sight until help arrives. I have dispatched LAPD and LAFD to your location. My GPS tracking system indicates your location on the grounds of the LA County Museum of Art. My console also indicates we have a fire alarm going off at your location. Where specifically are you within the facility complex?"

"I'm in a small administrative office behind the ticket office in the Grand Entrance."

The trendy Los Angeles art crowd was extremely light since the majority had not yet arrived. The security guards at entrances were taken by surprised and eliminated easily by the silenced Glocks. The terrorists ran through the various galleries of each building on a rampage. Taking mere seconds to killing museum personnel, guards, a few donors, and a number of scattered catering staff. They stopped only to place explosives devices at critical structural locations according to their mission plan. The focus of the attack was the art not the taking a massive number of lives. As the timers ticked, the team vacated the buildings and drove off in four different directions. The entire attack actually took less than Shura's planned six minutes.

Rita's final alert was to warn the LA Fire Department and EMT response teams of armed terrorists at the LACMA location, instructing them not to enter the buildings until police gave them an all clear.

"All the alarms are going off. Oh my god, please hurry. People are dying. I can smell smoke."

"Gloria, emergency responders will be arriving in a minute. Is there anyone else with you?"

"No, I'm by myself."

"It'll help if I can get more information from you. How many terrorist did you see?"

"I, uh . . . Only saw two, but I heard bombs going off in other buildings, so there must be more terrorists."

Ten minutes after leaving the museum, the four Bravo team members drove into separate covered parking facilities and abandoned their stolen vehicles. The team's plan relied upon the police traffic surveillance video system to identify their initial getaway cars and create a massive LA County wide search for those four vehicles. Each member of the team had a specific task. One of the pair wiped down the stolen car and switched to another older model purchased car, while their partner used the silenced Glock to destroy the video cameras at the exit prior to their departure. Within three minutes they exited the parking garage. This ploy gave the terrorist sufficient time to get lost in the massive rush hour traffic as they travelled south on the 405, 110, and 710 expressways towards Long Beach.

The LA police vehicles arrived at LACMA in mass from all directions to find the museum complex in flames and with a huge amount of obvious structural damage from collapsed roof. The responding units of the LA Fire Department watched helplessly as they awaited the police "all clear." The LA SWAT "B" and "C" platoons arrived and immediately secured the parameter while "A" Platoon set up the Operations Command Center RV on the lawns behind the facility on W 6th Street. As soon as the Bomb Squad sniffing dogs cleared the Grand Entrance, two SWAT team members rescued Gloria from her office. There were four dead bodies near the entrance of the building, another two outside her office, and three critically wounded staff members found behind the ticket counter.

Sixteen minutes after Gloria's initial 911-phone call, FBI Assistant Director Margaret Reynes arrived on the scene with a specialized rapid response team. An FBI agent obtained Gloria's somewhat sketchy description of the two dark haired male terrorists dressed as maintenance workers. She was so rattled that her information about the terrorists attack was fairly useless. Then one of the two other surviving staff members described two additional terrorists in the same manner and thought she heard them talking in an unfamiliar foreign language.

After waiting for the sprinkling system to subdue the fire, the SWAT teams searched each building and discovered fourteen bodies of guards, catering staff, and museum donors. It took the bomb-sniffing dogs almost 50 minutes to clear the area. The buildings had sustained significant structural damage and the expensive collection of art was totally destroyed.

As Yassar had accurately predicted in a Shura meeting nearly six months earlier, the police had spent almost an hour clearing the museum of any potential unexploded devices, which prevented the LA Fire department to enter and extinguish the few remaining fires, and getting EMT medical teams to remove any surviving victims. The Medical Examiners vans appeared and began the gruesome task of documenting the forensic evidence before removing the dead and burned victims. Wilshire Blvd was a mess as rush hour traffic was routed around the crime scene.

Bravo team parked their vehicles in an area frequented by local fisherman near the Port of Los Angeles. The terrorists piled into a van with tinted windows and traveled three short miles to Berth 227. They calmly parked the van, cleared the port's security check point, and boarded the *MJ Pffeiler* container ship docked at berth 227 by 6:15 p.m. PST.

The U.S. owned and registered ship was scheduled for a 7:00 p.m. departure for a twelve-day trip to Shanghai, China carrying automotive parts. All the members of Bravo team were exhilarated after successfully completing their mission and escaping. Ralfi, the oldest member, texted Meerza that the package was loaded, and then tossed his prepaid cell phone into the water as the ship slowly exited the harbor.

The FBI determined that terrorists had obviously reconnoitered the museum before the attack as they were aware of the centralized security office location and easily destroyed the museums sophisticated video recording system. What the terrorist did not realize was that a second off-site video system had captured the attack from numerous camera locations. Several FBI agents were able to collect those recordings and additional video from eight local ATMs and seven traffic control video system cameras covering the three-block area. They delivered the footage to the FBI Technical Support Center just off the 405 Interstate. An hour later, the FBI had quality pictures of the entire Bravo team and descriptions of their four escape vehicles. At 7:15 p.m. an all-points bulletin was issued for the entire LA basin. TSA was alerted to watch for any of the terrorists trying to escape using commercial aircraft. INS was ordered to intercept any suspects at all border crossings.

The FBI evidence team took samples of the bomb material residue, shell casings, and additional forensic evidence. They brought in Dr. Pia Swanson, a UCLA Ethnologist Linguistics expert. She was able to listen to the off-site video footage and identify the terrorists' language as a form of *Omani Baharna Arabic*, typically originating in Oman. At 9:15 p.m. the LAPD Information Technology Bureau had used traffic light video surveillance recordings to track all four vehicles to covered parking garages in different areas of the city.

The exit security cameras at the garages were destroyed. However, one system had an additional internal camera that caught one pair of terrorists changing cars. Using enhanced technology, the bureau was able to produce quality pictures of their single escape vehicle. A special order was issued to stop the vehicle and prevent it from crossing the border to Mexico. The alert was extended to four surrounding states.

Another FBI twelve person team reviewed the video footage of Los Angeles airports (LAX), Burbank (BUR), Ontario (ONT), Long Beach (LGB) and San Diego (SAN), while another team checked flight plans and passengers of all the local general aviation airports to ensure that the terrorists had not escaped by air.

Slightly after 12:25 a.m. a Long Beach police patrol found the identified terrorist escape vehicle with three other vehicles in a parking area frequented by local fisherman. Forensics on the scene found good prints of eight individuals in those vehicles. The sets of fingerprints were sent off to INS. Using the FBI and INS fingerprint identification system they were able to identify the eight terrorists and locate their point of entry into the United States. The vehicle thumbprints matched those of seamen that arrived off the Greek registered *MV Atlantikani* on August 9th that had not returned to their ship for its departure, on August 12th. Immediately NSA and FBI began investigating the movement of the ore ship, and all ships departing from the Port of Los Angeles after 5:00 p.m. in the small hope of intercepting those vessels and identifying any other potential terrorist plot entering the U.S from the *MV Atlantikani*. A total of eleven ships had departed the Port of Los Angeles between 5:00 p.m. and 8:00 a.m. the following morning. It was a small but viable lead.

At the same time as the Scottsdale and Los Angeles attacks.......

Chapter 30: San Francisco Bay Area Attacked Simultaneously

Friday, August 13, 4:10 p.m. PST (UTC/GMT -9)
Downtown, San Francisco, California

Earlier that afternoon, Charlie team had picked up Kaji's white Chevrolet Express 3500 LS extended passenger van with heavily tinted windows from their vehicle storage garage. The 12-passenger van had a glossy paper-thin dark blue coating to conceal the real color of the van. The glossy cover was easy to remove in less than a minute and would play an essential part during Charlie team's planned escape.

The entire team made arrangements with the hotel staff to have their luggage delivered to SFO at 6:15 p.m. They spent the mid-afternoon reviewing the mission, selecting their very realistic looking masks, and preparing their weapons and explosive devices. They drove the van on the short trip from Burlingame to a storage facility on Beale Street in San Francisco. The van dropped off the Ghazzi couple at 4:25 p.m. to give them sufficient time to pick-up their bicycles and move to their separate designated BART attack locations. The van then drove along the Embarcadero to waste time before moving to their first attack location.

The van proceeded to the loading zone for Marc Jacobs Designer store on Maiden Lane at 4:50 p.m. Abdel Fattah, youngest male member of Charlie team entered the nearly deserted *Xanadu Gallery* precisely at 4:45 p.m. He used his silenced 9mm LazarMax Glock to quickly kill the three staff members and planted a series of four triacetone triperoxide (TATP) explosive devices on varied levels of the circular gallery structure. The detonators were preset to detonate at precisely 5:00 p.m. PST.

He then placed the closed sign on the door, locked the gallery door using the keys obtained from the manager's desk, discarded the keys in the curbside dumpster and jumped into the awaiting van. Within minutes the blue van travelled the short five blocks to the San Francisco Museum of Modern Art (SF MOMA) and parked in the rear of the museum on Natoma Street.

Seven of the eight remaining Charlie team members entered the San Francisco Museum of Modern Art (SF MOMA) at 4:55 p.m. The realistic masks and overhauls were necessary to avoid being recorded by the museum's video security system and identified later by INS or FBI facial recognition software. The first entering team member used his silenced 9mm Glock to kill the two guards posted near the entry and two ticket sale personnel. The second team member dashed to the security office in the rear, shot the lock and killed the startled guard inside before he could use the silent police alarm signal. He placed an explosive device adjacent to the video security system hard-drive with a detonator set for six minutes. That team member emerged from the security office dressed in a guard's uniform taken from a locker, and took position inside the main entrance door after posting a prepared sign. "MOMA closed for plumbing repairs until 7:00 p.m. We apologize for any inconvenience." A third team member had moved the bodies of the guards behind a counter so they could not be seen from the window or entry door. The remaining four-team members swept through the museum eliminating museum personnel and the few scattered visitors alike. They placed numerous ten-kilogram TATP explosive devices on critical weight bearing support beams on each of the three levels of the museum. Each device was preset to detonate at exactly 5:05 p.m., precisely engineered with sufficient explosives to absolutely destroy the support beams.

Preparations and Execution of BART TransBay Attack

Earlier Shad and Dleen Ghazzi entered the storage facility to pick-up their bikes with their deadly explosives. Each bike had saddlebags loaded with explosives. They quickly rode the five city blocks to the Embarcadero BART (Bay Area Rapid Transportation) station. Shad boarded the very first train heading across the bay to the West Oakland station to get in position for his suicide attack on a return train. At 4:56 p.m. Dleen boarded the first car of a BART Yellow line 14-car train to Pittsburg/Bay Point at the Embarcadero station. Shad boarded the first car of the 4:56 p.m. Red 14-car train to Milbrae at the West Oakland station. The Ghazzis looked like typical campers carrying large backpacks with visible sleeping bags. Their twin saddlebags showed Canadian flags to put other BART passengers at ease. Each backpack was filled with additional explosives. As usual both trains were packed to capacity with rush hour commuters. The detonators were attached to their backpack belt level waste straps.

San Francisco Xanadu Gallery Explosion

At precisely 5:00 p.m. all hell broke loose as the explosives detonated in the Xanadu Gallery. The street side windows of the gallery exploded and the force shattered windows on both sides of Maiden Lane. Two SF Police cars responded to the 911-cell phone call from a passing pedestrian that was injured in the blast. The interior of the gallery suffered structural damage and was on fire when the first fire engine arrived on the scene. The fire captain suspected a gas leak explosion. It was eleven minutes before the fire was subdued and the SF Fire Chief entered the gallery and discovered the murdered charred staff member bodies and the evidence of a detonated explosive device. Police detectives were dispatched to the scene to begin the tedious and gruesome task of gathering forensic evidence as the Medical Examiner attempted to document the location, positions and identity of the murdered bodies.

San Francisco MOMA Attack

At exactly 5:05 p.m. the SF MOMA museum explosive devices detonated simultaneously. The structural integrity of the museum's upper levels failed and crashed portions of the structure to the ground level 80 feet below. The front facing windows of the MOMA museum exploded outward over 3rd Street and shattering two windows in the Moscone Center a block away. The blast sent shards of glass everywhere injuring numerous people on the street and causing an accident between two passing vehicles. Several tourists outside the Yerba Buena Center for the Arts were injured by flying glass 147 feet away. The bombs enormous boom echoed and bounced off numerous downtown skyscrapers. Some locals thought it sounded much like the sonic boom caused by the Blue Angels flying over downtown during Fleet Week.

At 5:07 p.m. the San Francisco fire department engines from the Howard Street station responded to the MOMA fire alarm a short two blocks away. The SF Police already on the scene were certain that the incident was an explosive device, and expressed their concern that additional explosive devices might still be unexploded within the museum rubble. The SF PD prevented the fire department from entering the museum until the bomb squad had confirmed that it was clear. The bomb squad arrived at 5:18 p.m. and using bomb sniffing dogs determined the remains of the building were free of additional devices at 5:40 p.m. The fire department extinguished the small remaining fire and attempted to determine the locations of the detonated explosive devices. They found that the force of the explosions piled level upon level of rubble sandwiching several bodies between each floor level. It wasn't until they removed some of the rubble, that the police discovered that the victims died of gunshots.

Two witnesses claimed that they saw several people exit MOMA and enter an awaiting a large dark blue van at the corner of Natoma Street just before the explosion. The San Francisco police had blocked off 3rd Street and were controlling busy rush hour traffic around the MOMA scene. KGO-TV used a location at the corner of 3rd and Howard Street as an on-scene reporting location. KPIX used their traffic helicopters to begin broadcasting the breaking news that terrorists had detonated explosives destroying the San Francisco MOMA museum, and that there were apparently other explosions downtown. The city was under what appeared to be a well-coordinated series of attacks.

The main body of the MOMA terrorists had escaped in the blue van. It took them three minutes to drive the eight blocks on 3rd Street east to AT &T Ball Park parking lot. They parked in a remote area of Lot A. The van was the very first vehicle to enter the lot. The four female terrorists quickly removed their mask and changed their overhauls in the van, while the males striped the blue coating off the van. The van coating was placed in trash bags, while the males changed in the back of the van. The females spent the next ten minutes wiping down the interior of the van as the males disposed of the trash bags containing the masks and overhauls in three different trash containers located within the huge parking lot. One male quickly dumped another trash bag weighted with the cells weapons into the adjacent San Francisco Bay.

The four couples quickly walked across the huge parking lot carrying their small carry-on luggage to King Street. The couples separated as they exited the parking lot at 5:21 p.m. as it was just beginning to fill with some SF Giants baseball fans arriving early for the pregame batting practice and game starting at 7:30 p.m. Each couple waved down a separate cab freed as fans were dropped off for the Giants game. Each couple ordered the cab to head south to SFO International Airport.

The cabs took 25 minutes in rush hour traffic using the 280 Interstate and the 101 to arrive at SFO. By 6:15 p.m. the four Charlie team couples had retrieved their hotel luggage, and were checking in for varied international flights to Amsterdam, Auckland, Tokyo and London scheduled to depart within an hour after 8:00 p.m.

BART TransBay Attack

The *BART TransBay Tunnel* was an engineering marvel connecting the San Francisco spurs with the entire East Bay areas. It was constructed of six metal sections on land and lowered by crane onto the floor of the bay. Once in position the section was connected to other sections and covered in sand and gravel unlike tunneling through rock saving both time and millions of federal dollars. The six mile long BART *TransBay Tunnel* was 136 feet below sea level under the San Francisco Bay.

At precisely 5:00 p.m. the couple yelled "For Allah and all worshippers" as they reached for their detonators. When the Ghazzi's suicide devices exploded in the lead train cars the engineers and occupants of the first train cars were killed immediately. The first two cars at the front of the trains veered off the tracks and slammed into the metal tunnel section. Luckily the rest of the trains remained on the tracks and luckily the explosion did not cause a rupture leaking SF Bay water into the tunnels. A serious leak would have drowned all surviving passengers on both trains. Both tunnels were totally blocked in both directions. Panic struck the estimated 600-passengers in each train as they were aware that the explosion derailed the train and hit the side of the tunnel perhaps causing a leak.

The 1000-volt power rail, making escape in a total dark tunnel nearly impossible, powered the lengthy BART trains. Most of the tech savvy passengers pulled out there cell phones and attempted to call loved ones, but no signals were available at the 130-foot depth, so they used the phone's flashlight feature to assess their situation. The passengers understood that the explosion was in the front of their train, and were unsure if BART Central Control recognized that their train had stopped within the tunnels.

Ted Faust, BART Embarcadero Station Master, heard the twin explosions and contacted Central Control, which already recognized the stoppage of the trains on their huge system display wall panels. Immediately BART shutdown the power in effected sections and activated their emergency protocols to begin rescue operations from both ends of the tunnels. San Francisco and Oakland police, firemen and emergency responders were immediately pressed into action.

Chapter 31: U.S. Media Coverage
Friday, August 13, 8:15 p.m. EST (UTC/GMT-6)
CNN Center, HLN Studios, Atlanta, GA

At 8:15 p.m. EST CNN interrupted regular programing for "Breaking News" on a somewhat confusing development that there were reports of a terrorists attack on the Homeland Security Annual Conference in Scottsdale. The United States had been the target of numerous lone wolf attacks but nothing as well coordinated and equipped as the terrorist attack on numerous federal officials. The details were very sketchy but numerous deaths brought a mind dulling feeling of fear, anxiety and rising anger. The newscasters droned on without much detail.

At 5:18 p.m. PST, KPIX channel 5, a San Francisco television station owned and operated by CBS, interrupted their regular evening news programming for a special report on the bombing of the San Francisco MOMA museum. At 5:24 p.m. KPIX 5, interrupted the coverage of the MOMA attack to report that two BART trains travelling in opposite directions were reportedly damaged in San Francisco TransBay tunnel blocking the entrance and egress from San Francisco and an explosion and fire in a small downtown art gallery. Police and emergency teams had entered both tunnels searching for survivors and hoping to assist with possible rescues. Initially the media reported that there were no confirmed deaths, but as the reports continued the death toll rose with reports of deaths in the three San Francisco attacks. The rescue mission under the San Francisco TransBay tunnel was well underway, but slow in reporting the situation. SF Police and FBI agents were following up on the few sketchy descriptions of the terrorists and their vehicle.

At 9:35 p.m. EST, "This is a special Breaking News bulletin. I'm Maria Espandoza, in the CNN Center in Atlanta GA.

We have just had confirmation that five separate terrorist attacks have taken place in Scottsdale Arizona, Los Angeles and San Francisco California. Geraldine Hoffman, our CNN correspondent was covering the Annual Homeland Security, FEMA and Office of Emergency Management conference in Scottsdale when the terrorist attack took place. Geraldine?"

The TV camera shows Geraldine standing adjacent to the Phoenician Resort sign on the north side of Camelback Road with Camelback Mountain in the background. "The joint Homeland Security and Office of Emergency Management conference came under deadly automatic weapons fire shortly after 6:00 p.m. as the conference attendees, including high ranking federal officials, exited the keynote address by Homeland Security Secretary Gayle Swartz. The resort was under extremely high security prior to the attack, but an anonymous law enforcement source noted that much of the FBI and law enforcement security scheduled for the event had been reassigned to investigate the Lake Havasu terrorist attack. At this point the Phoenician Resort is in sheer chaos with numerous dead and wounded conference attendees. In the words of several resort employees the human carnage was unbelievable and the resort suffered major damage. The access road behind me leading up to the resort is cordoned off with emergency vehicles making multiple trips to local hospitals. We have not received any figures on the deaths or extent of injuries to conference participants and other victims. The police source noted that they are setting up a triage system and moving the dead to within the massive resort ballroom. As per their protocols they are withholding the names of the victims until their families have been notified. We know from a reliable source that Senator Rex Nunn was among the seriously wounded. He will be undergoing surgery at the Mayo Clinic Scottsdale facility in an attempt to save his left arm.

We also learned that FBI Director Frank Thomas suffered a minor flesh wound in the leg during the attack. Following the initial attack several DPS police vehicles attempted to pursue the terrorists on N64th Street. Those DPS officers and vehicles were completely destroyed by the terrorist automatic weapons. We have confirmation that five DPS and two Phoenix police officers were killed during that failed attempt to end the attack." A hand appears and gives a sheet of paper. "Excuse me, I have just been handed an update. The Scottsdale SWAT team set up a trap for the terrorist vehicle. The terrorists were attempting to escape in at tourist bus travelling south on Scottsdale Road. The SWAT team set up a well-coordinated barricade roadblock on Scottsdale Rd south of Camelback Road. The terrorist's vehicle was stopped and neutralized by the Scottsdale SWAT team. The report states that after less than a minute of intensive gunfight the terrorist's tour bus exploded killing the group of terrorists. Several police behind the barricaded roadblock were killed and suffered life-threatening injuries. The explosion caused serious damage to adjacent building, Scottsdale Road and bridge over the Arizona Canal. Arizona Governor Ann Hargrove will be giving a news briefing at 10:00 p.m. local time to give details of the attack."

"Thanks Geraldine, please keep us advised of any further developments on the horrendous Scottsdale attack. In the meantime we also have a report on another terrorist's attack in Los Angeles. Josh Mecker, our LA correspondent is on the scene of a devastating attack against the Los Angeles County Museum of Art. Josh?"

"Maria, a small band of terrorists entered the four different buildings of the Los Angeles County Museum of Art slightly before 5:00 p.m. PST. The museum generally open on Thursdays was closed to the public this evening for a special donor event. The terrorists reportedly entered dressed as maintenance workers carrying toolboxes and backpacks. The terrorist killed guards, staff members and early arriving donors before placing several explosive devices in and destroying the Grand Entrance, Art of the Americas Building, Ahmanson Building Modern Art Gallery, and Broad Contemporary Art Buildings. The recently refurbished buildings suffered serious damage along with over an estimated $350 million of their modern art collection. LACMA reportedly had over 250,000 pieces of art in their collection on display and in a secured storage area that suffered major damage. Although no information has been released about deaths or casualties of the staff, or donors, the police and emergency services have blocked off Wilshire Boulevard for four blocks to permit access for ambulances, and fire apparatus. The LA Police Department SWAT team established a command center in the area outside the LA West building. Two units of the Los Angeles Police Department's Special Weapons And Tactics Team (SWAT) and LA Bomb Squad are on scene in the process of sweeping building by building to ensure that no terrorists or explosive devices pose any additional threat. We have not been able to confirm if the terrorists escaped in the midst of the chaos. California Governor Mark Jeffers, FBI Assistant Director Margret Reynes, LA Police Chief Hal Gerry, and Los Angeles Sheriff Doug Trout will be giving a joint press conference at 9:30 p.m. PST local time."

Maria, "Thanks Josh, we look forward to your updates as information becomes available. Let me point out that the Scottsdale and LA attacks happened at exactly the same time as those in San Francisco given the one-hour time difference. I want to turn our attention to Nancy Nobel, our CNN correspondent in San Francisco. Nancy?"

The telecast shows Nancy in a park with the shattered windows and devastated MOMA museum in the background, "I am in the park across Yerba Buena Lane from the severely damaged San Francisco MOMA museum. You can see the shattered windows and rubble remains of the San Francisco Museum of Modern Art behind me. San Francisco police and fire department continue combing the building for any possible survivors of this brutal terrorists attack. According to witnesses a small group of terrorists apparently wearing mask entered the building just prior to 5:00 p.m. and exited shortly before the building exploded. Within minutes several explosions brought down the upper levels of the contemporary art museum destroying the collection of modern art. At this time authorities have not issued any statement about the deaths or injuries from the terrorist attack. There has not been any confirmation of any terrorist being killed or captured. We are waiting for a special briefing by San Francisco Mayor Alice Craft and Police Chief Robert Cortez which is scheduled for 9:30 p.m. PST."

Maria, "Thanks Nancy, please remain on the line should any additional information become available. San Francisco had another attack in the BART TransBay tunnel under the San Francisco Bay. Our CNN Correspondent John Duran is on the scene outside the Embarcadero BART Station. John?"

The camera is focused on John at the BART entrance at street level on Market Street adjacent to the Hyatt Regency, "The BART Embarcadero Station is absolutely chaotic as emergency responders and police enter the two tunnels attempting to rescue victims and survivors under the San Francisco TransBay tunnel. The Embarcadero station has been cordoned off so first responders from local hospitals and recuse teams have access to transport victims to various medical facilities. At this point the only details we can report is that two separate explosions took place at precisely 5:00 p.m. PST damaging two BART trains traveling in opposite directions fully blocking the tunnel under the San Francisco Bay. Both of the trains would have been jam packed with rush hour passengers. BART officials are planning on a press briefing at 11:00 p.m. PST at the Embarcadero Ferry Building to give updated details of their ongoing rescue and recovery operations and early investigations of the explosions. BART officials confirmed that the TransBay appears to have maintained its integrity with no apparent leaks from any of the leak monitoring sensors. They also noted that the other spurs of the BART system are in full operation with additional police protection and precautions. BART has arranged bus transport to and from key BART stations including Powell St, Montgomery, and City Center to Oakland until further notice.

John continued, "The city of San Francisco accustomed to dealing with earthquakes disasters is attempting to deal with this tragedy at the hands of unknown terrorists. As if that was not enough, we have been monitoring the police radio band on a bizarre terrorist attack on the famous small Xanadu Gift and Art Gallery. Given the magnitude of the other attacks there has been little information about the 5:00 p.m. gallery attack and explosion that killed several employees and demolished the gallery designed by Frank Lloyd Wright as a model for the Guggenheim Museum in New York. At this point there is no definite connection with the two other bombings, but unofficial sources are confirming that the precise timing may prove that if the simultaneous incident is a bombing, the BART attack may be an extension of the two other San Francisco terrorist attacks. "

"Thanks John. We will keep it here to bring you the latest in the series of coordinated terrorist attacks. Keep tuned to Headline News for the breaking news on these massive coordinated attacks. We are following what appear to have been five separate synchronized terrorist attacks in Arizona and California. Please stay tuned." A huge graphic flashed across the screen reading "American Homeland Under Heavy Attacks." The programing gave way to another talking gecko GEICO car insurance commercial.

The ongoing CNN coverage reported that the coordinated attacks apparently had no cell chatter warnings indicating the potential for an attack, which in itself was unusual according to FBI and Homeland Security agents, except for the earlier heavy chatter about the "London Bridge." A panel of CNN security and terrorist experts reported that the intricate planning, weapons, and explosive devices used in the recent attacks appeared to be much more sophisticated than *al-Qaeda, ISIS* or other terrorist organizations could muster.

The CNN panel tried to make sense of the attacks against the Lake Havasu's London Bridge and art museums as both seemed to be extremely low priority targets. Clearly the attack against the Scottsdale Phoenician conference and BART trains were more troubling as they required significant planning and effort to hit these higher priority targets. The United States is under attack without warning despite the massive number of intelligence and counter terrorist agencies efforts to protect America.

Friday, August 13, 9:30 p.m. PST (UTC/GMT-9)
Public Safety Building, San Francisco, CA
At 9:30 p.m. San Francisco Mayor Alice Craft, BART CEO Craig Williams, San Francisco Police Chief Robert Cortez, and FBI Special Agent Greg Tremont started a joint televised press conference in the Public Safety Building conference room adjacent to the San Francisco Police Headquarters.

Mayor Craft began the press conference setting the stage that they would be reading statements and would not be taking questions at this briefing. "Between 4:50 and 5:15 p.m. a series of terrorist attacks took place at three locations within San Francisco. Judging from evidence the first attack was at the Xanadu Art Gallery where the terrorist killed the gallery staff, used an explosive device and set the gallery on fire. The second attack took place at exactly 4:58 p.m. when seven terrorists entered the San Francisco Museum of Modern Art, killing the museum staff, security guards and visitors. The terrorist planted explosive devices that caused major structural damage to the integrity of the upper levels to fail onto the ground floor of the museum. Video evidence shows that those attacks were mounted by the same group of terrorists. The final attacks were bombings of two BART trains travelling in opposite directions within the BART TransBay Tunnel at 5:00 p.m.

We are not giving information on the current number of deaths and seriously injured as teams of first responders are still clearing the BART tunnels. Information on the victims will be forthcoming in our next briefing after we have notified victim families. Our condolences and prayers go out to all the victims and their families and loved ones. We give special thanks to the quick response by SF police and emergency crews. At this time BART CEO Craig Williams will give his statement."

"Thank you, Mayor Craft. The entire BART system administrators, and employees offer our condolences and prayers for the victims and loved ones of the attacks. At precisely 5:00 p.m. our Control Center was alerted by a very sophisticated sensor system indicated that both trains had suddenly stopped within 100 yards west of the Yerba Buena island. At the same time the Embarcadero Station Master heard the unmistakable sound of explosions from both the east and west bound tunnels. Immediately the TransBay Tunnels electrical third rails were shutdown and the BART Emergency Response Team was activated with alerts to both the San Francisco Fire and Police Departments. Our current focus is on the ongoing rescue and recovery operation of the occupants of the BART trains. Our initial report was that only the front portions of the 14 car trains were derailed hitting the walls of the tunnel. The front two cars on each train sustained the brunt of the explosive devices resulting in numerous deaths and various serious injuries to the occupants. Despite the serious terrorist event, there was no leakage of water into the tunnel. The potential for any further deaths or injuries from the high voltage third rail was automatically ended by our computerized shutdown system. We are thankful to the first responders and assistance of the medical units from varied hospitals for their efforts in onsite initial treatment, evacuation, and transportation of victims needing additional medical attention.

All victims were transported to the Embarcadero station. As you can understand with an operation as large as this we are awaiting a final assessment of the attack. The FBI investigation, assessment of damages to the BART TransBay tunnel, removal of damaged train cars and debris, repairs to tracks, and resetting the system could take a week or more. My understanding is that the FBI has an investigation team on the scene gathering video evidence and forensic evidence. In the meantime BART is running busses to and from San Francisco and Oakland. We will give an update of the entire situation at the next briefing at 11:00 pm in the Ferry Building and constant updates on our webpage. At this time San Francisco Police Chief Robert Cortez will give his statement."

"Thank you, Mr. Williams. Our investigative teams are working on sifting through the forensic evidence of the three attacks, interviewing witnesses and reviewing the critical footage of video taken by numerous security cameras prior, during and after the attacks. We have video evidence of the male and female suicide bombers on bicycles entering the Embarcadero Station prior to the attacks on the BART trains. We have video footage of the terrorists entering and leaving MOMA, and escape in a blue van prior to the detonation of the explosive devices. Eyewitness reports confirm that the same blue van was used in both the Xanadu Gallery and MOMA attacks. At this point we have an all points terrorist bulletin issued for the blue van that was used in the attacks, statewide, western region and border crossings into both Canada and Mexico. Details on the attacks will be more fully described in our next briefing. At this time FBI Special Agent Greg Tremont will give his statement."

"Thanks Chief Cortez. At this point no terrorist group or organization has claimed responsibility for the coordinated attacks. The FBI is working under the assumption that due to the precise timing of the coordinated attacks in Scottsdale, Los Angeles and San Francisco that they were planned and executed by a single terrorist organization. A Joint Terrorism Task Force (JTTF) was created to ensure that all the numerous federal intelligence, state and local law enforcement agencies bring to bear their coordinated resources, shared evidence data, and investigative abilities on every aspect of each attack. The goal of the JTTF is to bring those directly involved and supporting the attacks to justice. There will not be a corner of the world where those responsible can hide. I can assure you that we will get them. The public can assist law enforcement with any video or leads on the attacks and help locate the terrorist blue van driving south of the museum. I want to warn the public that the terrorist occupants of the van are armed and extremely dangerous." A picture of the blue van taken by a video camera was flashed across the screen with a FBI phone number. Please contact the JTTF at the number on your screen if you have any information that will help us in the pursuit of these terrorists."

Mayor Craft stepped forward, "The city will be officially mourning the deaths of the victims in a special Day of Remembrance on Sunday, August 15th on Civic Center Plaza. There will be another full briefing tomorrow at 9:00 a.m. at which we will respond to media questions. Again our condolences and prayers go out to the victims, families and loved ones." At the end of the conference the four officials left the room quickly and refused to answer the deluge of media questions. Media journalists scrambled to report on the briefing.

Chapter 32: San Francisco FBI Investigation
Friday, August 13, 9:14 p.m. PST (UTC/GMT-9)
San Francisco FBI Office, 450 Golden Gate Ave, San Francisco, CA

At 9:14 p.m. the FBI team and SF PD Information Technical Bureau had finished their review of video footage of 27 BART stations and located high quality video of the Ghazzi's with their bikes and backpacks entering the BART Embarcadero station. The bikes slipped past security during the 4:30-7:00 p.m. bicycle restricted period and entered the prohibited first cars of the BART trains. Other street videos showed the couple riding at the corner of Beale Street and Folsom Street. Twenty agents were visiting every building in the area attempting to locate where the couple were prior to those videos.

Additional video footage gave the investigators an excellent picture of the masked solo assassin entering the Xanadu Gallery and fair pictures of the still masked terrorist within the blue van. Another team reviewing intersection videos located the blue van traveling from the Maiden Lane attack, picking up the masked terrorist and escaping down 3rd Avenue. That linked the two attacks. A traffic camera looking south from Market Street captured a distant image of the team entering and leaving the SF MOMA building before the explosion. The footage did not reveal whether they were male of female or reveal any physical descriptions as they wore *Dickies* long sleeved coveralls. Unfortunately, due to a huge power outage caused by a "N" light rail train accident and a bus hitting a power pole with a transformer, the police lost sight of the van from four key traffic cameras in the area. FBI agents were checking with local traffic copter footage to see if any caught footage of the van during their normal rush hour coverage.

Hours Earlier........

Chapter 33: Phoenix Media Coverage
Friday, August 13, 5:45 pm MST (UTC/GMT-8)
Phoenician Resort, Scottsdale, AZ

Sandy Jacobson, a twenty-five year old rookie KPNX television news reporter had been assigned to cover mostly traffic accidents, human interests and school related stories in the Phoenix area over the past year. When a senior colleague was seriously injured in a rush hour traffic accident on the AZ51, she was reassigned to the OEM and FEMA Scottsdale conference. She presented a short segment on the Good Morning Phoenix news covering the conference preparations. Her big chance would be the keynote presentation by Secretary Gayle Swartz and other high level Federal officials at the joint conference. Following the speech, Sandy and her cameraman were following the Secretary's entourage exiting the ballroom with hopes of doing an interview.

Sandy was standing within seven feet of Secretary Swartz desperately hoping to catch a follow-up interview when the first sniper shot ripped through the Secretary's shoulder throwing her to the tile floor.

That same instant, the security detail surrounding Secretary Swartz were killed and dropped in place. Instinctively Sandy and the cameraman crawled back into the small alcove entrance to the ballroom with the camera rolling capturing the carnage as the massive rain of bullets reeked havoc on the mob of participants in the lengthy hallway.

Quickly recognizing that Secretary Swartz's three-man security team were neutralized and unable to assist her, Sandy put her life on the line and crawled back into the hallway to grab Swartz by her exposed hand.

Using her good arm she worked hard to push off the dead body of a Secret Service guard shielding Swartz.

Camera rolling behind her, the young reporter used all her physical strength to secure the Secretary's hand, slowly sliding and pulling her inch-by-inch through pools of blood back to safety.

The graphic nature of the video capturing the ongoing attack and numerous heroic acts within the hallway would be of little use to the KPNX station. However the recording would later document important details including a short 20-second shot north down the hallway towards the terrorists firing position across the golf course.

Sandy happened to be in the right spot, at the right time. Her heroic act of saving the life of the Secretary Swartz was a news reporter coup. For the next three hours she and the cameraman fed live coverage to the NBC national network of the emergency responders and efforts to deal with the horrendous attack. NBC had a huge team of editors working to edit the extremely graphic footage for useable film, yet thankful to have a team in place at the scene. Viewership of the event could only be compared to that of 9/11 coverage.

Working carefully like a more experienced reporter, Sandy was careful not to interfere with first responders, but was able to get interviews with Swartz and several officials. She concentrated on gathering facts with a human twist as her breaking news story was preempting regular programing. The video of Sandy pulling Swartz to safety was posted on YouTube and went viral with 12.4 million hits in less than 30 minutes. The network was setting record ratings as her detailed reporting of the attack was paired with the edited video of the attack.

In light of the well-coordinated professional attacks in Phoenix, Los Angeles and San Francisco there was media frenzy that recapped the coverage of the New York September 11th attack on the World Trade Center Twin Towers. Over 80% of the coverage focused on the Scottsdale attack due to seriousness of the attack on high-ranking administration officials responsible for national security and responding to emergencies.

Chapter 34: Presidential News Briefing
Saturday, August 15, 12:42 am EST (UTC/GMT-5)
White House, Washington, DC.

At 12:42 a.m. EST, breaking news telecast interrupted all network television and radio stations across the United States. The televisions of America showed a variety of graphic banners "America Under Attack," "Terrorist Attack America," "Deadly Terrorist Attack on U.S. Soil" etc., as a voices announced: "We are interrupting normal programming for this special briefing by President Reynolds. The President will address the nation momentarily." A live view of a vacant White House pressroom podium comes on with a message scrolling across the bottom of the screen, "U.S. President Reynolds Briefing." After a few seconds, a very somber, casually dressed President Reynolds appeared through a door to the left and approached the podium.

"Good Evening my fellow Americans," Reynolds appeared uncomfortable as he began reading his prepared statement off the teleprompter, "It is with a heavy heart and tremendous sadness that I report that terrorists have perpetrated six coordinated attacks within Arizona and California. Our nation's deepest condolences go out to the families and loved ones of the victims of these horrendous attacks. Several of my administration officials attending a joint Homeland Security and Office of Emergency Management conference in Scottsdale and law enforcement officers sacrificed their lives and were severely wounded in their effort to protect others from further harm. The Scottsdale SWAT team killed all the known terrorist perpetrators during their attempted escape. " President Reynolds' face looked drawn and white as he paused before continuing.

"In a separate attack numerous civilians were murdered and wounded in an armed attack against the Los Angeles County Museum of Art. In a series of three other attacks the San Francisco Museum of Modern Art, two BART trains, and a small art gallery were attacked with a number of citizens killed and wounded. Rescue and recovery efforts are still underway within the BART TransBay tunnel under San Francisco Bay. These coordinated attacks are an attack against each of us. Our entire nation suffers a blow when one of us is a victim of such a terrorist attack." Reynolds appeared somewhat emotional as he paused, "We give special thanks to the numerous law enforcement officers that prevented the terrorists from additional attacks in Scottsdale and have responded to each of the other attacks. We appreciate the efforts of first responders and medical personnel that continue to render aid to the victims. We have thousands of FBI and law enforcement officers working as I speak to find those responsible for any portion of the attacks or supporting in any way the terrorist attacks. While we are still dealing with the horrendous aftermath of the attacks, I wanted all Americans to know that we will be utilizing the tremendous resources of all federal agencies, state and local law enforcement in conjunction with our international intelligence agencies of allies to find and bring each terrorist and their leadership involved in these attacks to justice. We have formed a Joint Terrorism Task Force (JTTF) to coordinate these massive efforts. There will be no safe haven in the world for those involved in terrorism on United States soil or on our citizens and facilities throughout the world. I want those involved in these attacks to know that there time is limited and we will get everyone responsible for the heinous acts. In light of this new terrorist aggression, I am asking Congress for an additional 4 billion dollar appropriation to support our war against terrorism. At this time I would like FBI Director Frank Thomas, who was present and wounded during the Scottsdale attack, to give details on the attacks and answer questions on specifics."

The television screen switched to show FBI Director Thomas standing before a Phoenician lectern. Frank Thomas had escaped the onslaught at the resort thanks to being on a cell call near the ballroom stage regarding a high-level corruption investigation of a noted Congressman from New Jersey. He was slightly wounded when a ricocheting bullet pierced the flesh of his right thigh. Thomas had three aids gathering details of all the recent attacks. He knew the media would draw parallels to the New York September 11th attacks on the Twin Towers. His briefing was extremely thorough. At it's conclusion 55 minutes later, Thomas answered as many questions as possible with the information he had at hand regarding all the attacks. At the conclusion of his briefing

Thomas made the observation, "These sophisticated coordinated attacks were well beyond the capabilities of any known terrorist group. These attacks demand that we develop new technology, investigative techniques and abilities to monitor suspected individuals. It was my recommendation to President Reynolds that Congress restore the powers rescinded in the revised Patriot Act to NSA and the FBI to protect our citizens and country, and additional funds be appropriated to fight terrorism. Personal liberty may have to suffer in the short run for some for the safety of all Americans." Thomas concluded his comments and took several questions before bringing the briefing to a close. He astutely and carefully deflected those questions that would reveal the significant details that would impede credible ongoing investigations.

The nations media had been fed a series of events that clearly had the potential to capture the news cycle for months with special in depth reports years later. The media went into an unprecedented frenzy.

Behind the scenes researchers created files of footage from before the attacks, electronic 3D models were constructed of the Phoenician Resort, BART TransBay Tunnel, LACMA and SF MOMA.

Needless to say the entire nation shared the horrendous shock that the terrorists had access and resources to execute highly planned, brazen and coordinated professional style deadly attacks in major US cities. The fact that a terrorist group had successfully attacked urban areas in Arizona and California brought new fears and anxieties to the U.S. and heightening media criticism of our intelligence and counter-terrorism efforts. The fervent hope was that all the terrorists would be killed or captured as soon as possible as the nation mourned the loss of the victims and more so their sense of national security. The media knew just how to feed those fears and anxieties with an overdose of exaggerated reality that raised the network ratings. The networks capitalized on the situation by raising the cost of commercials during their special reports.

Chapter 35: Arizona Follow-up
Friday, August 13, 8:45 p.m. MST (UTC/GMT-8)
Phoenician Resort, Scottsdale, Arizona

As a result of Sandy Jacobson's personal heroic act, presence of mind in the midst of the attack, quality of reporting the on scene and numerous interviews, she learned of Rod Harris's heroism. His interventions had saved over twelve lives in the line of fire pulling participants including Senator Rex Nunn to safety. He was also credited with using common sense to anticipate the terrorists escape route and alerting the PV Police, which permitted law enforcement to monitor the terrorist attempted escape route. This on the spot surveillance gave the Scottsdale SWAT team the sufficient time necessary to set-up the barricade trap that stopped the terrorist's escape. As Sandy furthered her investigation it became clear that Rod had anticipated and perhaps prevented the second terrorists target against spouses and family members in the Scottsdale Fashion Square. There was no doubt that his decision to protect the group of spouses prevented the terrorist from adding additional victims to the toll of dead and injured in the horrendous attack. Rod's training and preplanning efforts lessened the impact of the resort attack by immediately initiating the Arizona Division of Emergency Management protocols that activated the well-planned sequential responses credited with saving additional lives. Sandy's televised report on Rod's actions was preempted by sporadic short news of the Los Angeles and San Francisco attacks. She reported that there was a true hero working within the midst of the chaotic aftermath of the attacks. Sandy reluctantly relinquished her report to take her first break in over six hours.

"This is Sandy Jacobson of NBC reporting from the Phoenician Resort terrorist attack sending you back to NBC News Headquarters in Rockefeller Center for further breaking news." As Sandy signed off she received a call from NBC Vice President Lenard Goldstein.

"Hello Sandy," inquired a female voice. "This is Denise Gerry, Executive Assistant to NBC Vice President Leonard Goldstein." Without hesitation, Denise continued, "Would you please hold while I put Mr. Goldstein on the line?" Not waiting for a response, the call was transferred to her boss.

"Sandy this is Leonard Goldstein," a warm voice greeted Sandy. "The executive staff has been very impressed with your professional coverage of the Scottsdale attack. Your heroic act is trending like crazy across social media. We want you as a lead guest on the Today Show here in New York tomorrow morning. As a follow-up I would like to schedule a meeting with the NBC executive management team." After a brief pause to give her a moment to digest the invitation, Leonard continued, "All of your arrangements have been made, first class air, hotel and limo. The executive team and I are looking forward to meeting with you."

"Mr. Goldstein," Sandy responded, "I'd love to come to New York. But I would like to do a follow-up on my report there is so much still going on here in Scottsdale."

Pausing for a second, "You can do the follow-up report on your return to Phoenix. You don't want to pass up this extraordinary professional opportunity."

"You're right," Sandy was quickly convinced. "Please send me the details for the trip. Thanks for giving me this opportunity."

"Great, I will have Denise text you the details. You will have Denise's cell number, let her know if you have any questions or concerns. I look forward to meeting you tomorrow morning. Have a great trip." Without another word, the line went dead and Sandy got a text with the travel details.

In fact Leonard Goldstein had another assistant calling Rod Harris to see if he would be willing to come to New York or be interviewed remotely from Phoenix. Rod had his office voice mail full and had his cell phone turned off. He was just trying to process the reality of the past few hours.

Friday, August 14, 10:00 p.m. MST (UTC/GMT-8)
Arizona State Capitol Building, Phoenix, Arizona
An hour after the Presidents address, Arizona Governor Ann Hargrove, FBI Phoenix Field Chief Neil Fischer, Arizona Department of Public Safety Director Harry Freeman and OEM Director Rod Harris held a joint press conference under the gold dome of the Arizona state capitol building. The smart looking governor dressed in an Anne Klein black business suit showed subtle signs of stress and sadness on her face as she approached the podium microphone.

"Good Evening, unfortunately, it is with tremendous sadness that I report the death of nearly a hundred government servants and numerous Phoenician hotel personnel in the attack on the Phoenician resort, eight Arizona Department of Public Safety officers killed in the line of duty attempting to stop the conference attack, and deaths of nine additional Scottsdale police officers in the successful blockade that eliminated the terrorist tour bus. In addition numerous conference attendees and members of our law enforcement community lay in local hospitals fighting for their lives and suffered serious multiple injuries. Our hearts go out to these victims and their loved ones as they deal with the aftermath of this horrendous attack." Ann took a moment to breathe before continuing, "A special morgue area has been established within the Phoenician Resort to process the dead bodies from the Phoenician attack and Scottsdale police barricade.

Local hospitals were initially under staffed, but off duty members of the larger medical community have amazingly responded to this incredible challenge for the sheer volume of nearly two hundred extremely injured and wounded victims. We thank the EMTs, doctors and hospital staffs for their extraordinary efforts in saving untold lives. Unfortunately in attacks like this the number loss may increase over the next few days due to the serious nature of the wounds. All the conference spouses and families have been transported and secured in a different resort under the protection of a huge security team. They are being kept informed of the status of loved ones lost and injured in the attack by a group of psychologists and grief counselors. I want to thank the citizens of Arizona and the nation for their massive support during this tragic event. On a better note, I am able to declare that the second portion of the terrorist attack on a large group of conference attendee spouses at the Scottsdale Fashion Square facility was prevented by the actions of Rod Harris, the Director of the Arizona Office of Emergency Management. As the media has reported, Rod is a real hero for his swift and decisive decision-making and actions. He will be addressing you in a few minutes. At this time I would like to have FBI Phoenix Field Chief Neil Fischer report on their ongoing investigation of both the conference and barricade."

Neil had been standing to the governor's right, immediately stepped forward to the microphone as the media continued to take pictures and televise the press conference.

"Thank you Governor Hargrove." Neil looked at the notes he had prepared for the briefing and began detailing the facts that had come to light in the past five hours. Teams of forensic specialists were combing every inch of the Scottsdale Road barricade site for the smallest evidence to give insight into the terrorists and the organization that planned and executed the attack.

Another team was within the East Vista house used by the terrorists and using the fingerprints obtained to check the FBI and INS databases to identify the individuals involved in the attack. A specialized FBI team was pulled in from the ongoing investigation of Lake Havasu attack to review the two hours of surveillance video from within the Scottsdale Fashion Square in an attempt to identify the four terrorists that had roamed the mall. As a precaution the Scottsdale Fashion Square was cleared of any potential terrorists and explosive devices by police teams and the bomb squad's sniffer dogs repeatedly crossing every inch of the massive facility. The team did not find any evidence within the facility. The mall will be reopened for normal business on Saturday. Concluding his portion of the conference Neil asked for one last question. A reporter asked if there was any connection to the Lake Havasu, Los Angeles, or San Francisco attacks. Neil simply shook his head, "At this point it is too premature in our investigations to determine through concrete evidence that the attacks in Arizona were by the same individuals nor whether the coordinated attacks in Arizona and California were initiated by the same terrorist organization. That does not however exclude the possibility that they are all connected in some manner. I am certain that at some point in our exhaustive investigations we will conclusively answer your question. Due to the precise timing of the events it seems highly likely that the attacks are related, but I reserve that judgment until we have real evidence. Thank you." Neil looked relieved, yet tired as he immediately stepped from the microphone, despite the numerous reporters that had raised their hands, Neil clearly declined to answer any further questions as Rod Harris stepped to the microphone.

"I am Rod Harris the Director of the Arizona Office of Emergency Management. My wife, Rita, and I served as host for the joint Homeland Security, OEM and FEMA conference. "

"My wife and I wish to express our deepest condolences to families that loss loved ones in the Phoenician Resort and successful Scottsdale barricade. We lost close personal friends and colleagues. We feel a huge personal loss of friends after forty-five years of working with our national network of OEM and FEMA Directors, members of our local law enforcement and emergency responder communities. Numerous members of those same groups are in our local hospitals critically wounded from the attack. Our personal hopes and prayers are that they recover from their injures."

Rod referred to a sheet in his hands. "I thank Governor Hargrove for her gracious comment, but I certainly do not feel like a hero as some of the media have reported in light of this horrendous attack. The heroes were the slain and injured DPS officers attempting to stop the conference attack, and Scottsdale officers that prevented the terrorist from escaping or using their weapons on another site. My OEM office has established an important system to provide information to any of the immediate families of the victims. The system provides specific information on all the two hundred victims under medical treatment. The system provides the victim's location, hospital room, status, name(s) of attending physicians with contact information, and expected release if available. The system can be found at **www.AZ.OEM/emergency/status.gov.**"

The webpage link flashed up on viewer television screens as Rod continued. "This secure system can be accessed utilizing the last four digits of the victims Social Security number. Please call my office listed at the bottom of your TV screen if you are having any difficulty.

"I want to express my sincere appreciation for those responders saving lives and currently involved in dealing with the horrendous aftermath of the attack. I know that our nations resources will investigate, pursue and bring to justice all those terrorists involved regardless of the level of involvement. Thank you." Rod did not take any questions as he simply stepped back from the microphone. In the back of his mind he wished for the peaceful serenity of fishing up in the coolness of the pines of the Mongollon Rim.

At that point Governor Hargrove stepped up to the microphone announcing that another scheduled briefing with the opportunity to ask questions was scheduled on Saturday at 9:00 a.m. Hargrove, Fischer and Harris immediately retreated into an adjacent office. DPS immediately secured that door to ensure that no members of the press follow them.

The huge media presence then spent the next hour rehashing again and again, embellishing on the information presented and areas of the conference attack and SWAT barricade not covered by the briefing. A few of the crews were planning on spending the night to ensure a good location for their cameras at the next news conference.

"Well that went as expected," Neil gave a small groan. "There is a delicate line between giving the media transparency and a full disclosure of all the facts for public consumption and crossing the damned line into factors and aspects that will hinder our investigation forewarning the terrorist of what we know and what we are following up on. I much prefer keeping the media in the dark. I have to run this is going to be endless days and nights of work. I will be back around 8:30 to give you an investigation update prior to our next briefing."

"Thanks Neil," Ann was a bit preoccupied trying to process the events of the past five hours. "I'm afraid I am still shaken by the whole attack. Just hours ago I was welcoming everyone to the conference and now a sizeable number of the Homeland Security, OEM and FEMA folks are dead or in hospitals. I really appreciate how the FBI and law enforcement has responded in addressing the attack. Please let me know if there is anything my team can do to help the FBI. I am going home a have a decaffeinated double Irish coffee. See you in the morning."

Neil called his driver and had him pull around to the West Adams Street side of the building. He nearly sprinted out a side door evading the lingering contingent of press camped in the front of the Capitol.

"Goodnight Rod," Ann gave him a small hug. "You were amazing today in making a terrible situation a bit better. Thank you."

"Goodnight Ann, I hope the Irish coffee does the trick and helps you get some well deserved sleep."

"I hope it works too. I don't usually drink hot coffee in August, so I am making this an exception with a double shot of Jameson's to calm my nerves." Ann quickly entered into her private office suite and had her DPS security officer call to have her official black Yukon XL1500 pulled up to the usual side door.

Rod reached for his cell phone. He noticed that there were 66 voicemails from numbers he did not recognize. He would try to get back to them in the morning. He called, Claire, his assistant in charge of the staff at the Phoenician Ballroom to get information on Senator Nunn's status.

"Hi Claire, how are you and the team holding up?" Rod asked, but immediately regretted asking. He knew well that his staff were dealing with the ugly reality of the dead, wounded and pressure of inquiries by loved ones over the past four hours.

"Hi Rod, we are hanging in there, but just by a thread." Claire was always pretty blunt with Rod. "The past few hours have been emotionally wrenching. I think we are running on pure adrenaline to kill the numbness."

"I have a contingent of eight state administrative staffers heading your way to give your team relief. Please take them under your wing and orient them to our system." Rod paused, "Please give me an update on Senator Rex Nunn."

Rod heard Claire working her usual magic on her computer keyboard, Claire responded, "Senator Nunn was one of the lucky ones. He is at the Mayo Clinic resting peacefully after three hours of surgery that hopefully saved his arm. The latest hospital report at 10 p.m. states that he should be coming out of the sedation around 3 a.m. He is in room 435. The hospital noted that he is being protected by his special U.S. Capitol Police detail. His wife, Elizabeth was with him before and after the surgery. She is staying at the Boulders in Carefree Room number 234. She left the Mayo about an hour ago, so she is probably at the Boulders by now."

"Thanks Claire, I just need to check in with Rita and I will be heading your way. Please ask the staff if they need anything that I can pick-up on the way. Under the circumstances some comfort food might hit the spot. I will stop off for a couple dozen Crispy Creams donuts."

"Rod, as good as that would be, there is no need, Xavier the Phoenician Director of Food Services has his staff providing enough comfort food to feed an army. We will see you when you get here."

Chapter 36: The Scottsdale Investigation
Friday, August 13, 11:45 p.m. MST (UTC/GMT-8)
FBI Command Center, Scottsdale AZ

The FBI had the overarching responsibility and incredible expertise to immediately responding, organizing resources, gathering and analyzing evidence from within the conference, terrorist's house and barricade crime scenes perimeters. They had teams working within the Phoenician resort foyer identifying and photographed victim bodies. Once that process was completed they marked off the body outline in their exact location prior to having the medical examiner move the body to the temporary morgue. Once within the temporary morgue, teams of Arizona county medical examiners systematically verified the victim's identity again before tying on the toe-tag, listed and stored the victim's valuables in sealed plastic bags. They then examined the body, determined the exact cause of death, recorded and photographed forensic evidence, and placed the bodies in military body bags with appropriate identification on the outside of the bag. A vast majority of the victims were ultimately to have closed coffin services due to their extensive deadly wounds. A team of Arizona OEM staffers were pressed into duty to enter the processed information into the Arizona OEM website system to inform the victims loved ones. The database also listed the contents of the plastic bag containing the victim's valuables and requested family members to give instructions as what they wanted done with the personal effects. Another team monitored each individual in the database for request from loved ones. They were tasked with making arrangements for transporting the body home and contacting local funeral directors for final arrangements. Every attempt was made to ease the horrendous trauma for the victims loved ones. Rod Harris had demanded that the process be as humane as possible and aware of the raw emotional feelings that loved ones were experiencing, but also the toll on his staff.

A FBI team of investigators processed the crime scene on N64th Street where six DPS officers were slaughtered by the massive barrage of machine gun and sniper fire. Once they completed their investigation the bodies were moved to a special area within the temporary morgue. That team was then tasked with gathering forensics evidence from the East Vista Drive terrorist home. The house was a valuable treasure trove of fingerprints and DNA evidence. Team members were assigned to download the phone data from the landline, access the local cell tower data for the past year, obtain utility bills and payment records, copies of rental agreements, and a host of other items that potentially had links to the planners and leaders of the terrorist group. All the evidence would be processed and analyzed by specialists at the *FBI Command Center*. Other technical teams were providing support and working on various leads at FBI Headquarters in Washington, DC and Quantico, VA lab facility.

Once established the crime scene perimeter of the Scottsdale barricade covered eight square blocks. The Old Scottsdale area was cordoned off to permit the team to secure and gather potential evidence before thrill seeking spectators and businesses entered and tainted it.

A Denver FBI forensics team flown in to Scottsdale Airport by government jet arrived shortly after the last remnants of smoke cleared the blockade area. This highly specialized technical team experienced in processing massive explosions immediately began processing the chemical composition of physical evidence. It was tasked with clearing the actual scene and gathering, processing and analyzing the huge amount of evidence.

The team established a local *FBI Command Center* in a large 12,000 sq. ft. empty two-story office space on Shoeman Lane. The Command Center would host a 12 person IT team bringing several fully equipped semi-trucks of communications equipment, computers and other forensic lab and technical equipment from Los Angeles.

Their initial forensic finding was unclear as to what caused the tour bus explosion. It took the FBI forensics team three hours to confirm that two explosive devices exploded simultaneously within the bus. They were unable to determine whether a terrorist within the bus or another terrorist outside the bus detonated the explosives. It seemed logical that the terrorists within the bus would have attempted to inflict as much damage as possible in their no win situation shootout. The bus explosion cut that short and destroyed most of the evidence within the bus and mutilated the terrorists beyond recognition. The explosive devices detonated ammunition and exploded the three fuel tanks creating minute mixtures of terrorist body fragments and shrapnel spread over four blocks.

The FBI forensics team was attempting to gather as much physical DNA evidence as possible to match against the evidence from within the East Vista house. The raw mixture of terrorist body fragments made their identities nearly impossible. The FBI specialized forensics team with the assistance of the Phoenix Police and Arizona State Forensic personnel continued to gather as much DNA and physical evidence as possible combing the crime scene inch by inch. As in all terrorist attacks the hope was that the slightest piece of evidence would lead back to others that may have been involved and ultimately the leaders that planned the attack. Fragments of two burner cell phones were found in tack within the perimeter.

After six hours the Paradise Valley Police Chief Cook and his driver were able to use surveillance cameras within the Scottsdale Fashion Square to identify the four terrorists they saw board the tour bus. Those separate frames of identified terrorist gave the FBI team eighteen high quality pictures of the terrorists. The pictures were immediately matched to image sophisticated recognition systems within the Immigration and Naturalization Service (INS), NSA and CIA to determine their criminal past and potential points of entry into the United States.

The FBI was working under a tremendous amount of political pressure from the administration, congressional delegations, and the media. Time was not their friend. Each passing hour gave the terrorists the opportunity to mount another attack or escape out of the U.S.

Chapter 37: FBI Briefing in Lake Havasu
Saturday, August 14, 8:00 am MST (UTC/GMT-8)
Lake Havasu City, Arizona, Thunderbolt Elementary School

After more than seventy-two hours the federal, state, county, and local authorities still had little to give the media as a follow-up report on the initial devastating terrorist attack. The second official press conference was held in the multipurpose room of Thunderbolt Elementary School.

The five hundred plus members of the press corps, and TV journalists that initially booked up RVs and hotel rooms for over one hundred miles in Western Arizona and across the river into California were gone. Those numbers had dwindled substantially as the OEM Conference, Los Angeles LACMA and SF MOMA/BART attacks took on greater importance involving major city centers. NBC News had set up a temporary center in Las Vegas and used three helicopters to move their news personnel to all of the more recent attack sites.

The initial media frenzy had been unprecedented as helicopters circled the Lake Havasu to take film footage of the London Bridge rubble, and follow official vehicles deep into the Sonoran desert. At that point the lack of international and domestic news had the media stuck focusing on Lake Havasu. Those same journalists and reporters were diverted by the more recent attacks. Given the norm for another "breaking news" situations suddenly drew the blood-sucking members of the press onto greener pastures. David Foster and his FBI team couldn't wait for their departures so they could continue their detailed investigations.

The FBI and media had interviewed all of the senior citizens of the city in hopes that they may have seen any aspect of the attack. The retirees had a local tradition to walk along the river in the cool morning hours and then taking their coffee at the London Bridge café at 5:30 a.m. The fact was that the Lake Havasu attack began at 6:00 am in nearly 93 degrees heat and most of the seniors had sought the shelter of their air-conditioned homes.

At 8:00 a.m. on a Saturday morning, the school's multipurpose room was jammed packed, like a can of sardines, into the sticky, hot, airless school facility. The FBI spotted three reporters and estimated more than a hundred and fifty locals. Clearly a majority of the people in the room were locals interested in hearing details of the attacks and ongoing investigation. Despite efforts by the FBI and school officials, the air conditioning unit was inoperable making the situation well beyond unbearable even at this early hour. Most of the curious crowd decided to stay for the briefing despite the stifling stagnant oppressive air.

FBI Area Chief for Phoenix, Neil Fischer had been scheduled to fly in from Phoenix to conduct the press conference, but was preempted by the scheduled Phoenix Capitol briefing. Agent Foster stood in using a time-tested formula giving a brief statement followed by varied team members reporting and a short period for questions. The highlights were when he indicated areas that had been attacked on an electronically projected Smartboard map of the city and the expanded area. He followed that with pictures of the major damaged sites with a basic timeline of their sequential destruction during the attack. Foster spent ten minutes using a map projection of how the terrorists on ATVs approached their targets, and the varied escape routes.

He then turned to the grim basic statistics on fatalities, confirming that the Mayor Joyce Vern, Police Chief Jimmy Grant, eighteen other police and city workers, and seven county sheriff deputies and staff members were fatalities in the initial firefight and bombings. An additional thirty-four citizens were shot during the attack. Five fatally, eight with life threatening wounds, and sixteen remain hospitalized in Lake Havasu, and three were transported to Phoenix for special surgery facilities. His finale was a short grainy video shot by a citizen's cell phone of a helmeted terrorist riding through the city on an ATV wielding a silenced weapon and transporting satchel charges. The video was shot just after the rider had destroyed the Lake Havasu Police station. The video was followed by several pictures of ATV riders taken from ATM machines and business security cameras throughout the city. A security video camera at a shop near the London Bridge did capture short video segments of three different terrorists on ATVs pausing momentarily to view the destroyed London Bridge. The fact was that the terrorists operated openly and reeked havoc on an unsuspecting American small town was terribly upsetting and terrifying. David Foster underlined that every effort would be made to bring those involved to justice, like the 9/11 attackers and Boston Marathon bombers. At this point the FBI and other investigators could not positively link any of the physical evidence to the Lake Havasu London Bridge attack to attacks in Scottsdale, Los Angeles, and San Francisco California, but further investigation evidence might provide the link.

After thirty-four minutes, the press conference had a brief question and answer session.

Agent Foster gave numerous comments like "That is still under investigation" or "I cannot comment on that at this time." When asked repeatedly if the Lake Havasu attack was linked to Scottsdale or the attacks in California, he gave an ambiguous response, "I cannot speculate on the possibility of any link to the other attacks, but investigators are pursuing that as a possibility." At the end of the briefing, Foster apologized that he needed to head back to a forensics meeting.

The audience clearly expected more information and hopefully evidence that would lead to the capture and justice for the terrorists. The small contingent of the media found that the briefing provided little for their TV networks, newspapers, blogs and magazines.

Aidan Harper of CNN was quoted off the record as saying "This was a classic example of the FBI stonewalling the media. They have to know more than they are revealing. That is a story in itself, but nothing compared to what is happening with the other attacks. I hope the news conference in Phoenix, LA and San Francisco are more forthcoming."

After the briefing Foster reviewed the FBI forensics lab reports. He found that all individuals had been shot with the some form of Glock laser sighted silenced automatic weapons using the same ammunition. The deadly accuracy of the assailants indicated that they were exceptionally well-trained marksmen able to hit targets while moving on their ATVs. The pinpoint accuracy of the sequence of the attack indicated that the terrorist had spent months planning and practicing the attack. FBI scuba divers determined that the explosive devices on the abutments of the bridge had different timer detonators, from explosive devices used on other structures in the city, which were set off by a detonator contacted by cell phones.

———

As expected small details and leads were beginning to dominate their investigation. Analysts assumed that the attack had to have involved ten to twelve or more terrorists to execute the attack in the estimated thirteen minutes. Experts examined ATV tire tracks found near the site of two dead police officers south of the city. Numerous ATV tracks around the city led to a site where twelve ATVs had recently been destroyed by fire. Forensics had obtained several partial fingerprints off the charred ATVs. The NSA, CIA, FBI and INS were processing those fingerprints. The FBI could not accurately determine which vehicle tracks belong to the terrorists because the location was such a popular area for ATV riders. The residue of C4 used in the attack matched the small amount of residue on the ATV's, which was a formula identified as being sourced out of Idaho. The Lake Havasu C4 did not match the TATP residue used in recent Los Angeles and San Francisco attacks. After extensive modeling they ultimately proved that the twelve destroyed ATV's were the vehicles used in the attack. The primary investigation had focused on the terrorists, their escape routes and attempted to identify the organization and purpose of the attack. The sad fact was that there really was not much more that the FBI had at this time.

The FBI knew that much like the Lochabee, Scotland bombing of Pan Am Flight 103 in 1988, it would take months or perhaps years to get everything they needed to catch-up with the terrorists. That was true for the intelligence efforts to locate and eliminate Bin Laden. Efforts were in place to analyze the satellite images of the area to determine the exact escape routes. Due to the remote desert location and delay in responding to the attack, the roadblocks to Las Vegas in the north, Blythe, California in the west, and Phoenix to the east were extremely late, the first being established almost six hours after the attack.

David Foster commented to Frank Thomas, "At least the roadblocks kept the Arizona DPS and Mohave County Sheriffs occupied and out of the way of our forensic teams and investigators. Those local guys are a gun happy group ready to take-out any suspected terrorists."

The police roadblocks covered every possible direction yielded nothing to help the authorities. The FBI agents joked to themselves about the inept roadblock efforts of the local police and Sheriff Shannon, and State Department of Public Safety. They assumed that the terrorists could have used back roads to reach Los Angeles or Tucson before the first roadblock was in place. At best the roadblocks slightly impeded the media and gave the local authorities a sense of serious involvement in the case. The FBI analysts examined all 47 legal border crossing video from El Paso, Texas to San Diego, California, but initially finding nothing substantial as it was like a needle in a haystack. The FBI and Border Patrol played and replayed thousands of hours of recordings of all vehicles carrying ATVs crossing out of and into Mexico. Mexican authorities reported nothing suspicious as most of the RVs crossed the border pulling only two to four ATVs. But that was to be expected as only 1 in 1,000 ever gets fully inspected entering or exiting the US. In a typical year nearly 45,000 RVs cross into Mexico and return back into the US. After over forty-four hours of searching the videos the team of analysts found the crossing of Martha Chase and identified three of the young men pictured in Lake Havasu videos as terrorists. The agents determined that it was a critically important development and returned to Lake Havasu City to begin using NSA and FBI resources to find Martha Chase.

The FBI expanded its investigation by sending a few agents into Rocky Point, Mexico to the site of a suspicious RV fire on a beach south of the city. The Mexican authorities reported that a group of six men departed on a yacht not long after the RV fire. But upon further investigation the agents had witnesses state that the men had been staying in local hotels and drinking on the beach when the Lake Havasu attacks took place. The yacht reportedly had a destination of Isla San Lorenzo, Mexico, a well-known scuba dive location. Tracking the ship they found that it had been to Isla San Lorenzo, Mexico and travelled on to make a brief fueling stop in Cabo San Lucas before heading out to sea. Investigators in Cabo were attempting to determine as much as possible about the yacht crew and any passengers. At this point satellites were unable to locate the yacht on the Pacific Ocean. The US Navy and Coast Guard had dispatched ships and planes into the area in hopes of spotting the yacht.

That night Foster held a teleconference with Director Thomas and Neil Fischer to summarize what the team had learned from their multifaceted investigation in Lake Havasu and Mexico. The essence was that for some odd reason the terrorists had taken out a tourist attraction bridge that had little importance other than to the local economy. There was no evidence linking it to any of the twenty-two survivalist and environmental extremist groups in Arizona. They found no direct link to international terrorists except the persistent international cell phone chatter and *Al Zagaheer* anonymous sourced report of a London Bridge target. Their investigation was following up on the possible escape via a yacht out into the Pacific. They confirmed that the *Al Zagaheer* news reported that the Lake Havasu London Bridge was destroyed was actually aired sixty minutes before the FBI was on scene in Lake Havasu.

Thus indicating that *Al Zagaheer* had direct prior knowledge and likely contact with the terrorists leadership or the organization. NSA and CIA would follow-up on that possible direct link to the terrorist organization.

There did not seem to be any form of economic motivation in the Lake Havasu attack. No religious link that supported the attack was by radicalized Muslims. No terrorist network had claimed responsibility for the attack. Each of the fatalities though tragic, showed no discernable link to the attack. Perhaps this was the most significant target the terrorist felt capable of attacking successfully at the time or it was a prelude to the next attacks. Most likely the Lake Havasu attack was a practice run for the Scottsdale and California attacks. If it was *al-Qaeda* the attack spoke volumes about their newly developed ability to mount a damaging attack on the U.S. soil. NSA seemed to discount this line of thinking because the attack was extremely well equipped and planned well beyond *al-Qaeda's* capabilities that had been degraded by constant drone attacks. Perhaps this was just a real under fire training run as the target was of such low importance. The speculative nature of the report was not very complete. It certainly left serious doubts about their ability to understand the "psyche" and motivation of the terrorist leadership and provided little light on information that could be linked to the other attacks.

David Foster was uncomfortable with the rate at which the Havasu investigation was moving. He felt at odds, as he needed more resources than those being sent his way. He knew that the Scottsdale, Los Angeles and San Francisco attacks were of much greater importance, but wanted to understand why the Lake Havasu attack happened and thought that the investigation could provide links to other attacks and help prevent future attacks. In reality Foster's pleas with Neil for additional resources went acknowledged but unheard. Neil had the Scottsdale conference attack in his backyard. The newer major focus was on the larger urban attacks with the same illogical targeting of the art museums and the somewhat higher priority conference and BART attacks. The attack on the Scottsdale conference was a much higher priority target given the involvement with high-ranking federal officials charged with protecting the United States and reacting to such attacks and natural disasters. The brazen attack, use of highly effective weapons, and gunfight with armored vehicles were bound to be the center focus of the media for a much longer news cycles.

At the end of the FBI meeting Neil expressed his frustration, "I wish the Scottsdale conference had been cancelled or postponed for a few weeks. We needed to get the Lake Havasu terrorists and not have to deal with the political implications from the conference and California attacks that are front and center."

When the FBI Interim Report reached FBI Headquarters, NSA in Fort Meade, and CIA at Langley, Ken Shepherd "Shep" and Hub Nolan were certain that the Havasu attack should eventually be linked to the same extremist terrorist group. They wanted to spend time analyzing the evidence to determine the motivation for all the attacks.

What were the terrorist leaders thinking in selecting the obscure targets? Why had they given the impression that it would be a bridge in London? What were they really after? Are the attacks over or will they continue? How did a group plan such a well-synchronized series of attacks in major U.S. cities without intelligence detecting the threat?

Homeland Security felt that the Lake Havasu attack put greater pressure on their responsibility to secure and protect even small communities. Secretary Swartz said in private "I cannot imagine or project what the ultimate security cost implications of these well planned escalating attacks might be for the United States. Now every little hick town will want resources to protect and defend their citizens from terrorists."

That very thinking would play into Senator Rex Nunn's conscious decision on the appropriations formula due September 8th. Military Intelligence and NSA agreed with Langley that the attacks must be somehow linked. Dexter Ford, the National Intelligence Director ordered that all agencies concentrate on communications to and from the known *al-Qaeda* and *Al Zagaheer* sources to preempt any subsequent attacks. How the hell did they miss the recent attacks? These attacks were an embarrassment that should have been prevented. He had planned on getting everyone together in Phoenix to formulate a comprehensive plan for Homeland Security, Intelligence Agencies and Emergency Management. Now they were dealing with the horrendous aftermath of the synchronized attacks and the huge media spin that despite the huge federal expenditures the United States was no safer than before 9/11. There were major intelligence failures.

FBI Director, Frank Thomas, was preparing his statement for the media follow-up to the Phoenix news briefing. The conference attack hit a very vulnerable U.S. target that would have greater impact than the other attacks. The Scottsdale attack was a strike targeted at the very leadership providing security and responses for emergencies. The terrorist leadership had carefully mounted the series of attacks to build anxiety and lack of public confidence, embarrassing the intelligence community, illustrated the vulnerability of targets on U.S. soil and had agencies spread thin focused on attempting to respond to numerous attacks. Clearly the administration had underestimated the abilities of this terrorist organization and it's leader.

Chapter 38: United States Conference and Museum Attacks Reported
Sunday, August 15, 8:00 a.m. ADT (UTC /GMT+3)
Al Zagaheer Television Studio 1, Doha, Qatar

"Good Morning, This is Nuru Monaga reporting from our *Al Zagaheer* studios in Doha, Qatar. U.S. news sources report that a coordinated attack on the Los Angeles County Museum of Art (LACMA), San Francisco Museum of Modern Art (SFMOMA), and Bay Area Rapid Transport (BART) TransBay tunnel under the San Francisco Bay and a attack of the joint Homeland Security and Office of Emergency Management conference in Scottsdale, Arizona all took place shortly after 6:00 p.m. PST. The two museums contained pieces of contemporary and modern art that appeared to conflict with traditional Muslim values. A separate attack on the Bay Area Rapid Transport trains in the tunnel under San Francisco Bay has blocked the tunnel in both directions. The FBI Director, Frank Thomas, and field agents in charge will conduct a televised briefing on all the attacks within the next hour. There were no terrorist survivors of the Scottsdale conference attack after being trapped by the Scottsdale law enforcement SWAT Team. FBI Special Agents of the LA and SF Field Offices, state and local law enforcement are exploring possible leads and requesting the public for assistance in providing further information. All major city bridges, rail systems and art museums in the U.S. have been placed under heightened security with huge local police, military and National Guard security. The public panic in the Western United States has reached a new height given the major cities involved in the attacks and the inability of U.S. Homeland Security to capture the anonymous terrorists under the constant scrutiny of unprecedented television coverage. The U.S. media blames the administration for failed security breaches, and congress for budget cuts to the Homeland Security budget.

A short segment was shown of Senator Rex Nunn, Republican Chairman of the Senate Intelligence Committee wounded and having survived the Scottsdale attack, making a statement from his Mayo Clinic hospital bed after the amputation of his left arm, "The attacks underline the importance of funding national security, counter terrorism and intelligence agencies. I support President Reynolds request for the additional appropriations to fight terrorism. We need to secure our boarders especially with Mexico. We will put all our resources and efforts into capturing and holding those responsible for these attacks." Reports for San Francisco are coming up next. Stay tuned. This is Al Zaga the number one news source in the Middle East."

CNN, BBC, and *Al Zagaheer* were following up on the problem of lax security on the U.S. border with Mexico which was amplified after CNN released information of the escape of the Lake Havasu London Bridge terrorists on *Dot Comer* through Rocky Point and Cabo San Lucas, Mexico. The remains of the Dot Commer vessel were found by a Mexican fishing boat and released to U.S. Navy at a location 489 miles southeast of the Big Island of Hawaii. The Navy reported that the residue on the debris indicated that an explosive device had been used to destroy the yacht. The fragments were being taken to awaiting FBI investigators in Honolulu, Hawaii and on to the FBI forensic lab in Quantico, Virginia.

The ownership of the vessel was traced to Mikhail Khodocasky, CEO of Rusneft, and Russian oil billionaire tycoon. The ship had been dry docked four weeks earlier for repairs at Baejela Shipyard in Montenegro, on the Adriatic Sea. The ship was last seen in the dry dock as repairs were completed and the ship readied for a return to the Black Sea home base. Perhaps the most interesting aspect was that the captain and crew of seven assigned to be with the ship during repairs were also missing. An international manhunt was underway to find the Dutch ship *Captain Erich van der Schlotten,* and the professional crew.

The broadcast cut away to President **Mark Reynold's** news conference in which he stated, "Our nation mourns the death of all the individuals in the recent terrorists attacks. Let me underline that like *Osama Bin Laden* and the Lockabee terrorists, those involved in the recent U.S. attacks will be found and held responsible for the deadly attacks. A $15 million dollar reward is offered for information leading to the capture and successful prosecution of the terrorist leaders." Stay tuned for further developments as we carefully follow the varied aspects of the terrorists' attacks. This is Al Zaga the number one news source in the Middle East."

The televised report was followed by a commercial showing a mother in a burka reading to the two young children seated on her lap under a tree.

Chapter 39: Synchronized European Attacks
Monday, August 16, 8:00 a.m. CEST (UTC/GMT+1)
Bilbao, Spain, Solomon Guggenheim Modern Museum
The terrorist attacks in the western United States turned the
focus of international intelligence and counter terrorist
agencies on the Americans.

The *Ibrabim's Dream* cell received their operational orders
from **Dakari Essa**, the thirty seven year old Syrian cell
leader, after he reviewed entries on their Pinterest board. A
naturalized citizen carrying a Spanish passport, Dakari had
been living in Bilbao, Spain for the past three years. His
covert cover was as the coordinator of a major international
study abroad program. He coordinated programs and hosted
students to learn Spanish from over thirty-two different
countries for twelve universities and eight language schools.
It was very common for Dakari to have contact with visiting
foreign professors and students. Authorities thought nothing
of the common foreign visitor staying in Bilbao for 3-6
weeks of intensive language studies. Thus the group of
individual members of the *Ibrabim's Dream* cell arriving in
different intervals over the past four weeks slipped under the
Spanish (CNI) intelligence agency radar.

As the cell leader, Dakari was responsible for coordinating
the cell's two-pronged attack against three major bridges
spanning the *Ria del Nervion O del Bilbao* and the world
famous *Bilbao Guggenheim Museum.* The attack was set to
go operational at precisely 8:00 a.m. to destroy the museum
and disrupt the early morning traffic into the Basque city. He
and a team member Diego were responsible for setting the
TATP explosive devices on the foundations of three bridges.
They planted the explosive devices late the night before, but
in checking the remote detonator that morning they found
that one device on the bridge overlooking the Guggenheim
Museum was malfunctioning.

The device did not respond to repeated attempts to activate it. In a last minute attempt to ensure that all the devices went off as planned, Dakari went to replace the device at 7:50 a.m. the morning of the attack. A passing bank teller noticed Dakari and the strange bundle under the structural support of the bridge and called the local police.

The local police Chief Alejandro Madray, Direccion General de la Guardia Civil Bilbao, received the phone tip from the teller. The tip reported that Basque ETA terrorists in a white Renault were spotted placing explosive devices on the Salbeko Zubia Bridge at 7:52 a.m. Chief Madray dispatched eight well-armed Guardia units within seconds to protect the bridge. The Guardia units arrived at the south side of the bridge too late. As at precisely 8:00 a.m. the explosive brought the bridge down in full view of the units approaching the bridge. At that precise moment there were several other explosions. The closest was an explosion in the adjacent museum.

Minutes earlier, the Bilbao Guggenheim museum staff had been making normal weekday preparation for the normal museum opening at 8:30 a.m., when seven heavily armed terrorist cell members burst through the glass doors. The terrorists armed with laser sighted silenced Glocks immediately slaughtered the four unarmed guards and thirteen of the museum staff. Placing one team member dressed as a guard at the entrance, the rest of the team raced through the museum placing a series of explosive devices at preselected structural support walls to destroy the upper levels of the ultra modern Guggenheim Museum. Each device was set to detonate at precisely 8:00 a.m.

The team had just gathered in the front foyer to escape when they heard the bombs outside on the bridge detonate. As they left the museum a second later their devices exploded causing the upper structures to implode and collapse onto the main level. The exterior of the museum showed little physical signs of the attack other than the shattered doors and windows. The team turned momentarily to watch the explosion and the aftermath.

The Guardia units, unable to stop the bridge explosion, witnessed the museum explosion and responded within seconds arriving in time to see the terrorists entering two awaiting Fiat Doblo vans. The Guardia unit disabled the vans by shooting out their tires. The terrorists were caught in a deadly crossfire pinned within their vans as it was riddled with bullets. Dakari watched the dire situation from a vantage point across the river. He reached for his phone and called a pre-set cell phone number. The call immediately remotely detonated the explosive devices planted on the frames of both vans. It was imperative that none of his cell be captured alive.

Chief Madray received telephone reports that two additional bridges had been destroyed within Bilbao. He recognized that the attack was much more insidious as Bilbao was under a major attack, so he contacted *Centro National de Intelligence (CNI)* informing them that a series of terrorists attacks had taken place. The CNI initiated their established protocols immediately closing their international border with France and Portugal, closed all airports in Northern Spain, requested Interpol assistance and began monitoring all cell phone chatter from all the cell towers within 20 miles of Bilbao.

Agents of Spain's *Centro National de Intelligence (CNI)* arrive on site by helicopter within 20 minutes. It was a short trip from Madrid. The highly trained national intelligence agents were a huge contrast to the somewhat incompetent local CNI agents primarily responsible for monitoring *Basque Euskadi Ta Askatasuna (ETA)* separatist terrorist activities. The team of seven agents arrived on site were ill prepared for the human gore in the remnants of the vans outside. The remains of the vans were totally unrecognizable. They walked through shards of glass into the Guggenheim amid the fallen beams and remains of crumbled walls were the human remains of seventeen individuals they assumed were targets of the terrorists plot. Luckily the museum was not open at the time of the attack, so there were fewer deaths. The team of CNI agents began their tedious investigation into the forensic evidence of the attack.

Dakari and Diego responsible for the destruction of the bridges escaped Bilbao in their white Renault. Despite detailed planning the attack had not gone off as planned. They attempted to cross the frontier into France just north of San Sebastian. The French border at Biriatou was closed when they arrived, so they immediately turned around and sped back to San Sebastian. They parked their *Renault Mégane* in an employee parking lot adjacent to *Chorizo Borda Berri* meat packing facility. Dakari spotted an empty cattle truck leaving the facility. Quickly the pair of terrorist ran across the lot and mounted the rear of the truck. They hid in the open back of the empty truck covering themselves with straw and manure. The truck travelled the 360 km of back roads into the Pyrenees Mountains and crossed the international border into at the Duana de Sant Julia de Loria into the country of Andorra. Dakari and Diego exited the truck without being discovered by the driver, and took refuge in a vacant sheep barn in Juberri. They needed time to ensure that the Spanish intelligence and law enforcement authorities were not on their trail.

Aldana Ibarra, the CNI agent in charge, and **Martin Escalar** Basque Regional Agent with the assistance of an Interpol drone from San Sebastian spotted the Renault vehicle which suspiciously turned around after attempting to cross the French frontier border at Biriatou and sped back to San Sebastian. Moments later the drone circled the suspicious parked vehicle at the meat packing facility, but missed seeing the terrorists board the rear of the cattle truck. Arriving at the parked Renault, they questioned potential witnesses in the area. No one seemed to know anything about the parked vehicle. At the end of the workday a worker curious about a la policía squad car in the employee lot, asked what was going on. The CNI agents said they were looking for the owners of the Renault. The slaughterhouse worker said he saw two men leave the Renault and jump into the back of an empty cattle truck from Juberri, Andorra.

Six hours later the CNI and *El Cos de Policia d'Andorra* conducted a house-to-house search of the Juberri area. Dakari and Diego fearing that they would be captured decided to shoot it out as they watched the police approach their shed. Minutes later both terrorists were dead. The remote sheep shed near Camillo, Andorra became the focus of an international investigation. Forensic teams from Madrid were busy investigating every centimeter of the sheep shed, cattle truck, and bodies of the dead terrorist. The Spanish armed intrusion by CNI with the aid of Francois Geuterre, Andorra Head of State was a small matter for the Spanish Prime Minister, Hector Susarez. Agent Ibarra gave credit to the *El Cos de Policia d'Andorra* for their immense assistance in finding and eliminating the international terrorists.

Ibarra sent CNI Director Fernando Bea details of the terrorist attack after the success of the manhunt into Andorra. Bea shared details with Shep at the CIA, Hub at NSA Intelligence and Spencer at SIS. The fact that terrorists attacked another art museum was an emerging pattern that could not be ignored. The strange attack only further confused the international intelligence communities. Why were the terrorists attacking obscure targets?

The terrorist attack and elimination of the terrorists hit the world media through Spain's EFE, spread within minutes to CNN, BBC and is quickly picked up by *Al Zagaheer,* despite the fact that they already had more specific details of the attack directly from the Shura leadership. The Shura fully understood that *Al Zagaheer* would be under physical and electronic surveillance by intelligence agencies, so they passed notes to the studio via the bottom of their trash bin that was replaced daily.

Monday, August 16 6:00 am CEST (UTC/GMT+1)
Pont de Grenelle, Pont Bir Hakein, Pont Royal,
Pompidou Museum and Musee d'Orsay, Paris, France
The **Aliyah in Wonderland** terrorist cell, led by **Dirar Issa,** had been in preparation for their mission for over two years. Dirar had worked for the Paris Cite Ministry of Public Works for the past ten years. He had divided the cell into Alpha, Bravo and Charlie teams. Dirar had been awaiting the Pinterest board orders to go operational for six weeks as the news of the coordinated U.S. attacks was covered by in the France 24 News telecast, followed by the eighteen other French stations and local radio stations. When the orders were finally posted the cell had ten hours to initiate their synchronized four pronged Paris attacks against three major bridges spanning the Seine River and two Paris art museums.

Dirar and Heba, his wife, made up the Alpha team. They used an official Ministry of Transportation Roads Directorate truck and cover of pitch darkness of the night to plant the explosives on the three Paris bridges. The explosive devices were preset to detonate at 8:00 a.m. They walked along the Allée des Cygnes to reach the center abutments of the Pont de Grenelle and Pont Bir Hakeim. At midnight they drove their truck to the Pont Royale adjacent to the Louvre where they installed a barricade blocking the bridge and installed Ministry of Transportation Roads Directorate official flashing lights. Dirar as a respected Director within the Ministry had given official notification of the bridge closure well in advance to the local TV and radio stations. Dirar and Heba then placed explosives under each end of the famous bridge set to detonate at 8:00 a.m. At exactly 7:59 a.m. the bridge bombs detonated causing confusion and catastrophe for the morning commuters as onlookers gawked at the missing bridges and ensuing traffic jams.

Bravo team was composed of ten heavily armed bombers assigned to attack the beautiful *Musee d'Orsay.* The team was dressed in black uniforms of the paramilitary gendarmerie. The museum scheduled to open at 9:00 a.m. was slowly coming to life as the staff arrived. Bravo team quickly neutralized the three guards meeting around the museum entrance awaiting the arrival of a bogus shipment of art. The team entered the museum's worker entrance and herded the staff into a small office space on the first floor. In the meantime several terrorists scoured the three floors to find the specific displays of modern art targeted for the attack.

They attached numerous explosive devices to destroy large portions of the upper floors of the *Musee d'Orsay.* Before the bombs detonated at 8:00 a.m. the terrorists locked the staff in the small office space, exiting the main entrance. Eight terrorists immediately filled a large Ford 350 Cutaway delivery truck parked on the one-way Rue de Lille. The other two terrorists crossed the *Place Henry de Montherlant* to take the RER D'Orsay train to Versailles.

A unit of the National Gendarmerie stationed at the *Place Saint Thomas d'Aquin* responding to the bridge explosion blocked *Rue de Bac* cutting off the Rue de Lille. Upon hearing the additional explosions in the d'Orsay they had their police van speed down the *Rue de Lille* in the wrong direction catching the terrorists as they entered their van. The National Gendarmerie armed with automatic machine guns quickly sprayed the Ford truck with bullets quickly killing the terrorists trapped inside the windowless van. **Jaques Beaumont** Field Agent of *Service de Documentation Exterieure* (French Intelligence External (SDE) and **Clemenau DuPoissant**, Agent of *Direction Centrale du Renseignement Interieur* (French Intelligence Internal (DCRI) arrive at the d'Orsay site by SUVs within eight minutes hearing the final hail of bullets into the terrorist's truck. The terrorist had been dead long before, but the gendarmeries were venting their anger on the van and its terrorist occupants.

Charlie team made up of nine armed bombers dressed as maintenance workers entered the freight elevator of the *Pompidou Museum at 7:45 a.m.* prior to the normal museum opening at 10 a.m. The terrorist had forged official Ministère de la Culture documents for the removal of several walls and installation of newly arrived art. The terrorists quickly eliminated the four guards at the entrance and in the security office as well as three guards roaming the museum galleries. The museum's regular staff rarely arrived before 9:00 a.m. Two of the team covered the entrance while the team planted a series of RATP explosive devices on all four levels of the *Pompidou Centre.* At 8:00 a.m. the series of bombs exploded and echoed throughout the busy Parisian Le Marais district. Units of the National Gendarmerie stationed in trucks at Hôtel de Ville and a huge contingent from the Préfecture de Police arrived at the Pompidou Centre just as the terrorists were exiting the building down the exterior escalator. In a heated automatic weapons battle the three National Gendarmerie soldiers, two police officers and all nine terrorists were killed.

The SDE investigators began examined the d'Orsay Musee security videos and realized that two of the terrorist had not been in the van, but entered the RER d'Orsay train station. They quickly identified the remaining d'Orsay Musee terrorists from security video footage. A nation wide alert was televised with pictures taken at the RER station of the two terrorists. Using the extensive security video footage the SDE and police began to search the *Rue Cler.* A phone tip from the owner of a small hotel placed the terrorist in their third floor room. Assembling a massive force on the small street disrupted the normal walking street market activity. Minutes before assaulting the hotel there was a series of gunshots. Within minutes the SDE entered the small hotel room finding the terrorist bodies after their apparent suicides.

Jaques Beaumont Field Agent of *Service de Documentation Exterieure*, began the immediate national security response by closing all train stations, metros, highways around Paris, all three airports, and begins the detailed investigation of the two museums. These precautions remained in place for three hours until the SDE was certain that there were no additional terrorists. After investigating the strange unauthorized closure of the destroyed Pont Royale, the SDE sends out a national and Interpol international alert for Dirar Issa. Earlier that morning at 5:30 a.m., before the time-delayed detonations on the bridges, **Dirar** and his wife, **Heba** successfully escaped Paris undetected as tourists on the Eurostar train to London. **Jaques Beaumont**, of SDE shared information with Spanish CNI, Shep at CIA, Hub at NSA Intelligence, and Spencer at SIS. The attacks on museums and bridges still seem to make little sense as there were numerous higher priority targets.

Chapter 40: Striking London

Monday, August 16, 7:00 a.m. BST (UTC/GMT)
Hopton Street, and Tate Modern Museum, Southwark,
London, UK

After an initial meeting in a small car park garage on *Rennie Street* in the Blackfriars Bridge area of London, the members of *Al Salwa* prepared their weapons and planned to take-up their positions in stages moving into their attack mode from the Bankside Gallery in the heart of London. A key additional element of the attack was Alec Nuba, British citizen born in Nairobi, Kenya, and devout Muslim. Nuba had had been radicalized and recruited by Akaman. He obtained a position as the evening guard for the well-known Horton Street Art Gallery less than 100 meters from the cells target the Tate Modern Museum. Part of his benefit package was a fourth floor small loft flat. The gallery sales and office staff never arrived before 10 a.m. so Nuba easily granted access to each of the twelve other members of *Al Salwa* between three and six a.m.

Hamid was first to arrive and first to leave the gallery taking a walk across the famous Millennium Bridge over the Thames at 3:15 a.m. The area on both sides of the bridge was absolutely deserted. By 3:37 a.m. the two TATP explosive charges were set to detonate at precisely 8:00 a.m. in the midst of the morning foot traffic rush hour. A magnetic fastener attached the charges to the bridge well out of sight of any casual passerby. It was a more sophisticated device from the earlier bombs used in the London Tube attack 2005. Hamid was back in the gallery before the last member of *Al Salwa* arrived at 4:25 a.m.

After a final check of their silenced Glocks and TATP explosive charges, *Al Salwa* reviewed the plan one last time using the original plans of the Tate Power Plan updated to the Tate Modern Museum in 2009. The preparations were followed by 20 minutes of prayer. They asked for Allah's help in the successful completion of their mission. Their mission was well planned down to precise details and timing, but there always was an unforeseen chance of something going wrong. *Al Salwa* had jointly decided that they would fight to the death rather than chance capture by British authorities.

At 7:45 a.m. the group poured out of the gallery. They immediately approached the Tate Modern Gallery covering both the main and service entrances. The staff of the museum had fallen into an observed set routine for the past eight months. Hamid had created detailed notes from observing every museum staff member's arrival and departure routine for weeks that he shared in the briefings with *Al Salwa*. They knew the name and position of every staff member working the typical Monday morning shift.

At exactly 8:00 a.m. the Curator MS. Helena Hassler, usually presided over a meeting of the entire staff including security guards, except the guard posted at the museum entrance. The staff meeting was to review the coming week and details on special events, large groups, and major donor visits. The Director conducted the meetings in pretty much the same way, a brief review of the days' and weeks' events, odd issues, and congratulation to employees for birthdays, engagements, anniversaries, newly born children, and news of new acquisitions or exhibits. They always met in the large second floor hallway just outside the executive offices. The scheduled meeting made *Al Salwa*'s work easier as they would not have to scour the building to round up stray museum personnel. Thus eliminating a significant issue of prematurely setting off security alarms.

The planned attack had several elements of importance. The first was symbolic as the very modern Millennium Bridge was a symbol of England's transition from the glories of the past Empire into the future of the 21st Century dedicated just before January 1, 2000. The walking bridge spanned the Thames between St. Paul's Cathedrals (1710) and Tate Modern Museum (2000). The cathedral on the north bank above Ludgate Hill was a remarkable symbol of the glories of the past while the museum on the south bank marked a new future and acceptance of modern art since 1900 in a relatively conservative British art culture. The second reason was the decadence of modern culture symbolized by the art within the Tate Modern. The art or so called art conflicted with those values dearly held by Muslim Ulama, Alimah and devout followers. The third reason was Yassar's token clue to counter intelligence agencies. Tate Modern was formerly an old coal burning Barkdale Power Plant converted to oil to lessen the infamous London soot. The sooty old power plant was phased into oil and then closed for environmental reasons as the United Kingdom became more and more reliant on nuclear power and nuclear weapons. The final reason was the abduction of the Curator Helena Hassler. Ms. Hassler was the subject in a well-publicized romantic relationship with Prime Minister Thomas Graham. Unofficial sources in the social world of London had the couple getting married prior to Easter. Capturing Helena would be very helpful in ensuring *Al Salwa*'s escape and seriously effecting Graham's decision making.

A silenced bullet placed right between the eyes killed Kent Whitham instantaneously, the fifty eight year old sole guard posted at the main entrance. The killing shot was fired at close range using a silenced Glock automatic 9mm with a LazerLyte rear aiming system and a thirty round clip. The unarmed Whitham was dead before the second member of *Al Salwa*'s had reached the main entrance door. The team quickly moved Whitman's body behind a counter and Alec Nuba dressed in the same guard uniform took over Whitham's position at the main entrance.

Within twenty seconds the entire assembled staff were being held hostage and laying face down on the hallway floor. Four *Al Salwa*'s members began checking the group to identify and isolate Ms. Helena Hassler. Something was very wrong. Helena was not among the assembled staff.

Hamid stepped forward and shouted in a demanding voice, "I need the Director's assistant to come forward before I shoot this lady." Hamid had his Glock pointed at the middle-aged woman lying directly to his right.

A gray haired man in a gray ill-fitting vested suit raised his hands, "I am Reginald Smyth, the Director's personal assistant. Please don't shoot Vivian. She only works in the museum business office as an accounts clerk."

Hamid asked in an agitated booming voice, "Where the hell is Helena Hassler?"

Reginald replied, "I'm not sure, she should have been here for the Monday morning staff meeting. I do know that she was shopping for a gift for her niece this morning. She is scheduled to attend her niece's birthday party at 11 a.m. this morning in her sister's home near Regent's Park. She may have been delayed in traffic."

Hamid understood that happenstance might have permitted their "primary" target to elude the attack. Regardless of her presence or absence the plan was to place explosive charges in the four floors of galleries to destroy the symbols of world cultural decadence. He alerted Alec Nuba that Helena Hassler was not in the facility and may suddenly appear. If so she he was to capture her and contact him. Hamid hoped that Ms. Hassler would appear, but knew that his team needed to begin setting the explosives as soon as possible before the bridge was detonated. Everything had to be synchronized for precisely 8:00 a.m.

What the staff and terrorist did not know was that Helena had opened the Museum Shoppe located near the entrance and locked herself inside at 7:35 a.m.. She was looking for some appropriate gifts for her niece and lost track of the time. Just as she was about to leave to join the staff upstairs, she witnessed the terrorists moving Kent Whitham's dead body to a small alcove outside the shoppe. Shaken by the attack, she tried to remain calm as she secluded herself within the book section of the shop farthest from the windows and glass doors. Helena had always prided herself in being able to have her wits about her in serious and stressful situations. She wondered how she would handle this crisis as her heart pounded with fear. As Helena's heart pounded, she found that she was having difficulty breathing. Anxiety was a real enemy to remaining calm under the circumstance.

She told herself that she must remain calm and positive. "On the bright side this was not going to be a day where she faced the typical pressure of donors, or art critics panning the Tate Modern exhibits." She thought to herself. "Today may be my very last day, so I will make the best of it." Reaching for her cell, Helena turned on the device to the alarming message *extremely low battery*.

Before Reginald identified himself, Helena had already placed a mobile phone call to the Prime Minister Thomas Graham. She hoped she would be able to catch him before he made his trip to Parliament at 8:15 a.m. It wasn't all that easy to get through on Thomas's personal mobile. She knew that as a matter of courtesy he screened his mobile phone calls during his meetings, which usually began slightly after 6:00 a.m. If she was able to get through he could certainly get the quickest police response. Her life and perhaps the lives of her entire staff depended on a quick response and immediate assistance. Thomas picked up on the second ring.

"Good morning, Helena. How are you this morning?"

Without thinking Helena responded, "Thomas listen carefully, something has gone off very wrong here at the Tate. I'm safe for the moment, but in great danger. Some men with drawn weapons have taken over the Museum and murdered a guard in cold blood at the entrance as they stormed in about four minutes ago. They have all gone to the upper levels except one guard on the main entrances. We need help immediately!" Just then the explosives detonated on the Millennium Bridge sending a chill up her spine.

"Oh my god! Helena, what was that explosion in the background?"

"I'm not sure where it is coming from, but it is close. Thomas, hurry, we need help. I think these may be the terrorist you have been worried about over the past few months."

Graham fearing for Helena's live, "Helena, where are you in the building? "

"I've locked myself in the rear of the museum gift shop on the first floor adjacent to the main entrance. I'm lying on the floor in the book section. I think I'm safe for the moment, but the sound of explosives being detonated seems so close. I'm not sure but it sounds like it is outside." Helena could hear what sounded like the fire brigade responding to the explosion outside. Her phone went dead suddenly ending the call.

Just then a series of screams rang out as Hamid shot Reginald in the back of the head as a measure to instill fear and control over the museum staff.

Hamid ordered, "Now shut the hell up! I will shoot the next person that says a word."

The cold-blooded murder was to ensure that none of the staff gave his team even the slightest bit of trouble. Hamid thought to himself, "These Brits rarely see weapons and acts of violence except on the telly. It is much too common in my world. It is time to teach them a lesson or two."

Hearing the fire brigade respond outside, Helena got a brilliant idea on how to help her staff. She didn't know how long it would take before help would be arriving, so she felt compelled to act immediately. She slowly crawled over to the north interior wall of the gift shoppe behind the cashier's counter and pulled the combined security and fire alarm.

When the Tate Modern was recently refurbished at the cost of twenty-five million €, the retrofit included the installation of a modern fire prevention systems and security system. When the alarm was pulled the solid fireproof security doors automatically closed cutting off each gallery and floor into relatively small sections of a room or two. She had hopefully trapped some of the terrorists in various galleries and parts of the building away from her staff until help arrived. She could hear the sound of both the fire brigade and police getting louder off in the distance.

The explosion of the small Millennium walking bridge took seconds as it disappeared under the Thames River. As each of the *Al Salwa*'s team wasted precious time searching for Ms. Hassler in the massive museum, they set explosive devices and individually reported back negative results on their coded walkie-talkies. They continued to plant explosives as they searched and traveled from gallery to gallery. The cell members on each of the floors reported that they had heard the explosion destroying the bridge outside. The last team member to report had reached the café and reported that he actually saw the bridge supports explode and the span disappear into the murky water of the Thames. All the explosive devices set to detonate at 8:20 am were in place in the galleries. When suddenly there was a loud alarm, and the security system locked most of the terrorists in various galleries. Those team members were trapped in their galleries with explosive devices set for less than a minute. Hamid was hoping beyond hope that Helena would appear, when the alarm went off. He realized that the triggering of the security system trapped his team within the galleries on the floors above him.

What Helena had not thought about was that the fire and security alarm panel was just outside her office, where the terrorists were holding the staff. The alarm panel was in easy access for the night security guards. The panel lit up with numerous blinking red lights and one blue light showing the exact location where Helena had pulled the alarm. Hamid and one other team member were with the staff outside the executive offices when the alarm isolated the rest of his team. He quickly spotted the panel and noted that the alarm originated in the Museum Gift Shoppe on the ground floor. The chaos on the walkie-talkie was terrible as every team members reacted to the locking of the galleries trapping them inside. The security system had worked as designed isolating areas from fire or other dangers.

Grabbing the nearest staff member, an admissions booth attendant, Denise Flower, and putting his Glock 9mm to her head, he asked in a very threatening voice, "Now how do we override your damned fire alarm system?"

Robert Gibbs, security guards replied, "Denise doesn't know. It takes two keys, one from security and another from the fire brigade or police. I'm afraid your men are trapped and the fire brigade and police are on their way. Here is my alarm key, but it will be of little use." Robert showed Hamid the key on a silver key chain.

Hamid hated the thought that after all the months of planning and sacrifices a simple thing like the newly installed fire alarm and security system negatively impacted the cell's mission. Without hesitation he shot Denise, and then he shot Robert for his truthful but upsetting comment, as they served no further purpose. The abrupt action caused a few of the staff to cry out again momentarily. They quickly silenced themselves remembering Hamid's stern threat and obvious short temper.

Hamid decided that he wanted to punish the person that had pulled the alarm and foiled *Al Salwa*'s mission. Alec Nuba was their guard at the main entrance. The map of the first floor plan showed Alec's position at the front entrance was less than thirty meters from the gift shoppe location where the alarm had been pulled.

Hamid spoke clearly into the walkie-talkie, "Everyone, I am working on getting the alarm reset. I need you to shut up. Alec, listen carefully, forget about the front entrance. I want you to check out the gift shoppe and bring me the person who pulled the damn alarm. The fire brigade and police will be coming through those doors at any moment. We need to make the person sounding the alarm pay for screwing up our mission. Bring that person to me. I'm up on the second floor hallway outside the executive offices."

Helena felt a slight pause of relief as she watched the terrorist, posing as a Tate security guard, moving away from the front entrance. Her first thought was perhaps he saw the police approaching the museum entrance. That thought was short lived as he ran directly towards the door of the Museum Gift Shoppe. After trying the locked door, he aimed his Glock at the locked double glass doors. The silenced weapon spit a bullet that shattered the shoppe door on impact. The terrorist quickly reached in and unlocked the door, entered the dark shoppe stepping on the shards of broken glass.

Helena was a short ten meters from the terrorist. She could hardly breath knowing that at any moment she could be shot. Her heart and mind raced knowing the dangerous position she was in crouched behind a large display counter. There were ten counters of various objects d'art and books that offered some modest concealment. The fact that the terrorist failed to turn on the lights was a slight advantage in the dimly lite shoppe. Despite her feeling of terror, she decided to take off her heels and slowly work her way around the various counters opposite the terrorist as he worked his way through the large dark shop. The sound of the terrorist foot crunching and kicking glass was unsettling. If the opportunity offered itself she would dart for the shattered door and then sprint to the main entrance. As the terrorist turned to look into an alcove Helena threw a large heavy Art Deco book across the shop well away from her hiding place. As she expected the terrorist moved quickly to the area where the book landed. His weapon in the ready position unaware that he was stalking the museum director.

Helena saw her opening and bolted for the door. The terrorist realizing he had been duped, dropped to the floor whirled around, wildly aimed the red laser beam of his weapon and began firing in Helena's direction. The six silenced shots shattered vases, framed prints, and one leaded glass window facing out towards the grand hallway entrance. One stray bullet grazed Helena in the leg. She winced in pain, but was able to maintain her balance as she ran thru the shattered glass door. The shards of glass severely cut and became embedded into her bare feet. The piercing glass in her feet matched the pain in her leg. The soles of both of her feet bled profusely, making it hard to even walk without slipping and falling on the mixed blood on the marble floor.

The freedom of the main entrance was a mere twenty meters away. She limped significantly slowing her pace due to the stinging pain and lacerated cuts on her feet. Helena hoped that the terrorist running behind her was not an excellent marksman. The terrorist saw his prey and thought carefully about Hamid's desire to deal with the situation, fired warning shots at the feet of the limping woman. Three more shots whizzed by smashing the tiles near Helena's bleeding feet. Fearful to look behind her Helena continued half walking as fast as possible. The immense pain was unbearable.

Shots rang out again, louder and in a short burst from a different direction. Less than eleven meters to her right an armed Protect Command agent wearing a bulletproof vest was covering her escape. She thought she was free when one last bullet spit out of the terrorist's silenced Glock hitting her back knocking her to the floor.

Helena knew that the bullet had hit her torso. Before she passed out, she gazed up into Thomas's crystal blue eyes. She wondered if he was really holding her or was it a dream. Helena wondered whether her relationship with Thomas had made her and her work place a prime terrorist target as she slipped into blackness. Graham had her in his arms, shaking with fear as he attempted to shelter her blood soaked body.

At that instant the explosive devices in all the galleries exploded in a huge deafening crescendo as shots rang out within the interior of the museum galleries. At that same moment the shots rang out in the upper galleries as varied cell members hear the arrival of the police and seeing the hopelessness of their situation then took their own lives rather than being captured by authorities.

Thomas Graham and members of his Protection Command security team whisked Helena away with the assistance of several helmeted armed police officers, while twenty armed uniformed officers with bullet proof vest ran past Alec Nuba's bloody body lying in the long first floor entry way.

Hamid hearing the gunfire from the entrance hall and the area outside the gift shoppe ran down into the long hallway. As he entered the great hall entry way he was hit by two shots by the Protect Command officers and dropped to the floor. The cell member controlling the staff, watched in horror as Hamid dropped to the floor spewing blood. He turned his Glock on himself, placed the barrel in his mouth, looked at the terrified staff, took one last breath and fired.

Chapter 41: European Attacks Reported
Monday, August 16, 11:45 p.m. ADT (UTC /GMT+3)
Al Zagaheer Television Studio 1, Doha, Qatar
"Good evening, Nuru Monaga reporting from our *Al Zagaheer* studios in Doha, Qatar. We are presenting a special news report on a series of well synchronized terrorist attacks against bridges and modern art museums in Bilbao, Spain; Paris, France and London, UK. Our correspondents will present comprehensive details of the attacks within the hour as the declared "war on terrorism" has taken a drastic turn for the worse as terrorist attacks hit areas in the heart of Europe. We have film footage covering the attacks, responses and the ongoing briefings by authorities in each city. Officials report that all the terrorists involved in the attacks were killed or committed suicide. At this point no terrorist group has claimed responsibility for the attacks, but unofficial sources postulate that it was a new jihadist group fighting the U.S. and her allies as a response to the "inhumane war against Muslims."

Nuru paused, "I have Abdul-Baqi Rashad, our Madrid correspondent in Bilbao, Spain." The segment begins with split screen footage of the ruins of the interior of the world famous Guggenheim Art Museum and file footage of the Bilbao bridges prior to the attacks.

"The chaos here was caused by the simultaneous bombing of three critical bridges crossing the *Ria del Nervion O del Bilbao* within the city center and the well coordinated attack against the ultra modern Bilbao Guggenheim Museum. Agent **Aldana Ibarra** of Spain's *Centro National de Intelligence (CNI)* reported in his briefing that at exactly 8:00 a.m. a series of bombs destroyed the three bridges without causing any deaths or fatalities." The screen changes to an angle showing the missing spans of all three bridges. "At the same time, a large band of an estimated ten well armed terrorists forced their way into the Guggenheim Museum killing guards and staff; and wounded several other personnel prior to the museums scheduled 10 a.m. opening. The terrorists then detonated a series of well-placed bombs that caused the buildings integral vaulted second and third upper levels surrounding the atrium to collapse onto the main floor. The famous curved exterior was able to support itself, but was filled with rubble and the remains of the modern art collection. Agent Ibarra's report indicated that the attack destroyed a large portion of the building an estimated 1.9 Billion Euro or $2,280 million dollars of modern art from the Guggenheim permanent collection and some pieces on loan from private collections. The terrorists involved in the museum attack were stopped and killed during their attempt to escape by the immediate response of the local police. Those terrorists had no identification and acid scarred fingertips making identification nearly impossible. Two of the terrorist involved in the bombing of the bridges escaped in the back of a cattle truck into the mountains of bordering Andorra. **Martin Escalar** Basque Regional CNI Agent with the help of a tip from a witness was able to track down and kill both terrorists on a farm near Camillo, Andorra. The Guggenheim Museum Board of Trustees scheduled an emergency meeting in New York City on Tuesday to deal with the human tragedy in response to the attack. It may take months for the Board to assess the damaged museum and decide on whether the famous 32,000 square-meter Frank Gehry designed building will be restored. A team of insurance investigators and art specialists from Lloyds of London will comb through the site to determine the extent of the damage to the art collection and structure. Curator Francisco Juan Moroso stated that the building was a 50% loss and none of the art survived the attack. Our interview with the Bilbao Director of Municipality Public Works, Diego Gomez estimated eighteen to forty months to repair the damaged bridges. The loss of the three bridges is a major issue for this thriving Basque city. A special briefing by CNI and local authorities is scheduled for Tuesday morning at 10 a.m. This is Abdul-Baqi Rashad reporting for Al Zagaheer from Bilbao, Spain."

"Thank you Adbul-Baqi. I have Nimr Farouk Armiri reporting from Paris." As Nimr began his Paris report there was five minutes of footage of the d'Orsay and Pompidou Museums and the three Paris bridges destroyed in the attack.

"Thanks Nuru, at exactly 8:00 a.m. a well coordinated attack destroyed three famous bridges over the Seine River in the heart of Paris, and staged a bold attacks destroying a large portion of the *Musee d'Orsay* and three levels of the *Pompidou Museum* in the heart of Paris. Both of the art museums displayed important world contemporary art. **Jaques Beaumont** Field Agent of *Service de Documentation Exterieure* (French Intelligence External (SDE) gave an extensive briefing indicating that the ten terrorists involved in the *Musee d'Orsay* attack were killed by elite gendarme *Préfecture de police de Paris* as they exited the building and attempted to escape via a delivery van on the Rue de Lille.

Agent Beaumont indicated that the d'Orsay suffered incredible damage to the interior of the historic architectural structure, but more importantly total destruction of a large portion of the irreplaceable world famous art collection. There were nine security guards and museum staff killed in the attack and several severely wounded were taken to local hospitals. Initial estimates placed the loss at over 3.5 billion €." The screen focused on earlier footage of the Musee d'Orsay.

"The terrorists involved in the *Pompidou Museum* attack were killed exiting the building. Our initial information has twelve museum personnel killed at the hands of the terrorist and numerous wounded. Estimates placed the losses of the *Pompidou Museum* art and building damage at over 1.1 billion €. Paris police, *Service de Documentation Exterieure agents* (SDE) and agents of *Direction Centrale du Renseignement Interieur* (DCRI) are following up on leads of one suspected terrorist that destroyed the three historic bridges. The most disturbing aspect was the fact that the attacks were synchronized with attacks in Spain and United Kingdom showing masterful planning, coordination and resources. French Prime Minister Claude Moreau will be giving a statement at 9:00 a.m. on Tuesday. This is Nimr Farouk Armiri reporting from Paris."

"Thank you Nimr. We are reporting on extraordinary terrorist attacks. These attacks seem to be threatening the heart of Europe and the UK. I have Arthur Dennis for a report from London. Arthur"

"The city of London has been in the middle of a war of wits with the terrorists for months beginning with the incredible cell chatter warning of an attack on London Bridges. The UK responded with tremendous military precautions to protect all the bridges, when the old London Bridge in Lake Havasu, Arizona was attacked and destroyed. Authorities slowly lessened the security precautions only to have London attacked this morning as part of the synchronized attacks in Spain and France. The UK terrorists used an estimated fourteen explosive devices to destroy the upper floors and galleries of the Tate Modern Museum. The attack took place at 8:00 a.m. prior to the museum opening. Helena Hassler, Tate Museum Curator, a personal friend romantically linked to Prime Minister Graham and six museum staff members were pronounced dead at the horrendous scene. However the integrity of the Tate structure withstood the explosion with little damage. Lloyds of London estimate the value of the minor structural damage and extensive modern art collection at 900€ million. Unfortunately Ms. Hassler perished at the hands of terrorist's gunfire during the attack and police counter attack. The Tate security system that isolated each gallery in a lock down and assisted the quick response by authorities is credited with saving the rest of the Tate staff. In a desperate effort most of the terrorists were trapped by the security system and died at their own hands or from detonated explosive devices in the galleries. While responding authorities shot three terrorists. Prime Minister Graham is expected to make a speech on BBC regarding the attacks later this evening. On a lesser note the terrorists destroyed the London Millennium Bridge, a steel suspension walking bridge for pedestrians crossing the River Thames, linking Bankside Tate Museum with St Paul's Cathedral in the heart of London. In reality the bridge had been a bit of laughing stock, nicknamed the "Wobbly Bridge" as it swayed during a charity march shortly after it's opening and had to be repaired and reopened in 2002. The success of the attack has Londoners more than a bit anxious.

The question that they seem to be asking themselves is just how this could happen after all the security precautions? Is London safe? This is Arthur Dennis reporting for Al Zagaheer from London."

Nuru, "Thank you Arthur. I have Fadima Jarret reporting from San Francisco." The introduction featured Fadima's voice reporting over 11 minutes of footage of the LACMA, MOMA and BART.

"Arizonans and Californians were shocked by the highly coordinated terrorist attacks against the Homeland Security Scottsdale Conference, Los Angeles County Museum of Art (LACMA), San Francisco Museum of Modern Art (MOMA), Bay Area Rapid Transit (BART) TransBay tunnel under the San Francisco Bay and the Xanadu Art Gallery. At exactly 6:00 p.m. PST Friday, several teams of terrorists put in operation a series of well coordinated attacks on seemingly low level art museums and gallery targets and then hit the much more significant joint conference killing scores of U.S. Federal government officials and then a major transport system for the San Francisco Bay area. The attacks themselves had fewer victims than the 911 Twin Towers and Pentagon attacks, but demonstrated that the terrorist had the skills necessary to plan elaborate attacks, muster resources and adequate training to successfully hit major United States cities. Thus ending the false sense of security Americans held over the years. In the wake of the attacks Americans are manifesting more anxiety, insecurity and more anger with the fact that the war on terror has struck home on U.S. soil, while the Reynolds administration has been reporting that the Islamic terrorist capabilities have been severely diminished after massive series of drone strikes. The FBI and other agencies have launched major investigations to identify, locate and eliminate those responsible for the attacks. This is Fadima Jarret reporting from San Francisco, California."

Nuru, "Thank you Fadima, please keep us updated on any other further developments of this story. I have Mohammed Tarik reporting from Phoenix, Arizona." As Mohammed gave his report there was a montage of video footage of the Lake Havasu Bridge, Phoenician resort, Scottsdale Fashion Park, and the street scene where the tourist bus exploded in Scottsdale.

"After the unexpected earlier attack on the Lake Havasu London Bridge nearly 120 miles west of Phoenix, Homeland Security and OEM officials gathered for their annual conference in Scottsdale, Arizona when a violent attack struck the plush quiet resort on Friday. The upscale resort became the scene of a precise deadly attack on the conference, and ended in Old Town Scottsdale where the estimated ten terrorists were eliminated at a massive law enforcement barricade. Police sources report that the attack was from deadly machine gun and automatic snipers firing from well outside the resort grounds. The heavy military weapons fired for an estimated ten minutes. During the deadly resort attack another group of terrorists attempted to attack a group of conference spouses and significant others at the adjacent Scottsdale Fashion Square.

Rod Harris, Director of Arizona Office of Emergency Management was credited with foiling the terrorists by having the Scottsdale Police and Paradise Valley police intercept their tour bus as it departed from picking up terrorists at the mall. The ensuing gun battle with the bus was cut short as the police SWAT team set up a roadblock of several armor vehicles to the front and rear of the bus. The area of the blockade was in Old Town Scottsdale, the only small stretch of Scottsdale Road with few businesses and limited population. Shortly after the gunfight began there was a massive explosion, shredding the bus and killing the terrorist. Neil Fischer, FBI Area Field Chief Phoenix reported in a briefing that at this time investigators are unsure if the explosive device was detonated inside or from outside the bus. When questioned by the media about available FBI and AZ Law enforcement resources, Fischer made the point to note that a significant force had been involved in pursuing the Lake Havasu attack. Gayle Swartz, Secretary of Homeland Security and Senator Rex Nunn Chairman of the Senate Intelligence Committee, who were conference speakers, have a press conference tomorrow morning after the families of the deceased have been notified. Regardless the boldness of the well planned, resourced and executed attack on federal officials has Homeland Security and the administration rethinking their counter terrorism efforts. Residents in the U.S. are angry to have the war on terror erupt in their backyard. This is Mohammed Tarik reporting on the Phoenix attack."

Nuru, "Thank you Tarik. This concludes our special broadcast on the increase in terrorist attacks in Europe following attacks in the U.S.. As we end the broadcast, Haruid Masama, one of our expert terrorism analysts, has pointed out that the museums attacked seemed like low priority or soft targets, but did display pieces of modern western art that are extremely confrontational and in direct conflict with the traditional held Islamic values. The attacks have international security officials and politicians scrambling to investigate the attacks, catch the remaining terrorists and leaders, and hopefully uncover any additional plots. This is Al Zagaheer the number one news source in the Middle East." Following the broadcast an oil company commercial showed a short scene in which a child was reading a famous Arabian fairy tale.

Chapter 42: Fighting the Radicalized Terrorist
Monday, August 19, 12:00 p.m.   AST (UTC/GMT+3)
Muhammad Bin Saudi Islamic University, Riyadh, Saudi Arabia

Halalani Des Sauid, the twenty year old princess, daughter of King Abdul ben Aziz, sat at a conference table in a large elaborate teleconference room. She had the opportunity to complete her bachelors and masters degrees at King's College London, and was working on the doctorate at Muhammad Bin Saudi Islamic University in Riyadh.

Halalani is an out of the mold royal feminist amid a religious culture that institutionalized the oppression of women within her culture. As such she openly rebelled against numerous common Islamic practices and was outspoken privately with her father.

Some of the commonly held practices and restrictions against women included: need for a husbands permission to apply for a passport; a woman's life or "*Deyeh*" is valued only half as much as a man's life; required wearing the Islamic Hejab in public; restrictions on the use of make-up; a woman cannot leave her home without her husband's permission, even to attend her father's funeral; a husband may ban his wife from any technical profession that conflicts with family life or her character; a man can divorce his wife by verbalizing "I divorce you" whenever he so chooses and does not have to give her advance notice; woman cannot open a bank account without her husband's permission; women needed to be accompanied by a male guardian known as a "*mahram*" whenever they leave the house; a woman may not enter a gym or swimming pool used by men nor even look into such a facility; there is no official law that bans women from driving but deeply held religious beliefs prohibit it; women are strictly prohibited from trying on clothing in shop dressing rooms; and some areas of Saudi Arabia severely limited women's access to education. The life of Islamic women under "sharia" law interpreted by local mullahs placed extraordinary pressure on women and Islamic men frequently acted as religious police to enforce the multiple laws and levels of the religious restrictions. The result was that Islamic women developed higher percentages of depression and had suicide rates significantly higher than Islamic men. Halalani's education in the United Kingdom and cultural awareness created an ever-increasing cynical view of the governmental institutionalization of arcane religious restrictions. She recognized that changes in this area were coming at an incredibly slow rate and her energies would be better spent in other areas.

She was tired of watching 97% of all Muslims stereotyped in many areas of the world as supporting the acts of terrorism by the few. It upset her that peace loving, law abiding devote Muslims were stereotyped and discriminated against for the heinous actions of the 3% on the radical fringe. That radical fringe used an ideology that was contrary to the Quran and beliefs of all mainstream Muslims. That ideology held that all infidels or non-believers in the teaching of the Quran needed to be eliminated in the creation of a Muslim Caliphate or state. ISIS was using the ideology to recruit others and physically oppressing people in Syria, Iraq and Libya. ISIS follower's practices of beheading, caged drowning, massive firing squads, forced suicide bombings, and dismemberment confronted the morality and civility of other areas of the world. As terrorist attacks spread through varied parts of the world, huge populations fell into the trap of assuming that all Muslims were like those barbarians portrayed in the media. The result was the roots of prejudice growing within countries and reports of more and more discrimination against Muslims that did not hold or respect the ISIS ideology.

In Halalani's view a few radical leaders with tenuous religious backgrounds twisted the use of ideology and *jihad* as a motivator for recruiting uneducated, unemployed, and poverty stricken Muslim youths, and waved the dream of an idyllic life in a Muslim caliphate. Terrorist leaders presented the worldwide responses aimed at ending terrorism as attempts to attack all Muslims. Those leaders fed their followers egos as warriors and martyrs supporting terrorism on multiple levels in the name of supporting all Muslims. Thus creating an untenable cycle that perpetrated the violence without a foreseeable solution. She fully understood the form of scapegoat thinking used to blame others for their dire living conditions, death and destruction in Muslim lands as well as the hope that the Caliphate would be a sort of nirvana for all Muslims.

Halalani felt compelled to do something to make things better for all Muslims, so she approached her father with the concept of creating an international student action organization to oppose the ISIS ideology and deal with prejudice and discrimination against Muslims. She was surprised when her father gave not only his blessing but committed to financially support his favorite daughter for the benefit of Muslims worldwide. King Abdul understood the complexities of modern society and the necessity to permit structured change. His support raised criticism amongst Saudi Imans, Mullahs, and other Muslim political leaders opposed to change. This was a bold step indeed on his part.

That was two years ago, during which the Halalani created an organizational charter and structure. She set up goals for countering terrorism attached to Muslims, and the stereotypical prejudice and discrimination that followed terrorist attacks. Each terrorist attack further attached all Muslims to being radicalized, intolerant, irrational, and prone to abhorrent acts of violence. It was nearly eight months since starting the organization. In light of the recent terrorist attacks in the United States and Europe, Halalani felt it was a perfect time to formally launch her new international student organization. At this point she had invited two hundred university organizations to participate, a little less than half that were present in her first videoconference. She spoke clearly into the microphone welcoming the student organizations to the first meeting of the Students Against Radicalized Muslims (SARM). She stepped forward as a woman among men willing to demonstrate her leadership, intelligence, and commitment to changing misconceptions about Muslims worldwide. It was time for the silent majority of Muslims to counter the radical fringe.

Halalani articulated the tenets of the SARM charter. The video-conferencing attendees responded positively to concept that their actions had the potential to change the course of history for all Muslims. She inspired young Muslims to become proactive in countering jihadist recruiters in mosques, universities and communities. The proactivity would be through monitoring radicalized rhetoric, countering radical flyers and literature, attempting to oppose recruitment efforts, and encouraging clerics, Imams and Mullahs to condemn the use of violence, and terrorism. The essential acts of exposing plans for terrorist attacks, and establishing social media that revealed the truth about terrorist leaders would counter the undercurrent within Muslim communities. The basic foundation of SARM was to ensure the tolerance of other cultures and religions, respect life and abhorrence of violence, to oppose those that preached violence and revenge, and acceptance of the beliefs and ideals of others.

The videoconference was a call for action asking for student organizations in Europe, Americas, Asia, Africa, Australia, and the Middle East to commit to act against the Muslim radicals. The steps were fairly simple. Each student organization was required to direct communicate* potential terrorist situations or issues with the SARM Riyadh office. The office would process the information and take appropriate steps to counter the situation. The structure eliminated some of the local danger connected with being proactive against radical terrorist within the whistle blowers community.

Halalani recognized that there was a huge risk for her father in supporting her organization, not to mention the risk to her own life. She was passionate in her leadership and commitment to promoting change for the betterment of Muslims. She hired a professional staff of ten women and ten men to work regional desks using their SARM website, social media and direct phone contacts to understand the complexity of reported situations. Once a situation was reported to a regional staff member, it is processed and presented to the five person administrative group that determined the best course of action. SARM was a full time commitment to proactively counter terrorism and making life better for the average Muslim.

Chapter 43: Dealing with Reality
Monday, August 19, 1:00 p.m. BST (UTC/GMT)
10 Downing Street, London, UK

The Admiral's SIS agents and The New Scotland Yard explosive specialists had ensured that the Tate Museum was clear of terrorists and unexploded explosives. The scene was a mess as the entire Museum staff was severely physically and emotionally shaken by the attack. Witnessing the savage deaths of staff members and Helena had taken a real toll. The museum was closed as forensic specialists gathered every minute shred of evidence

Despite the terrorist's pact to fight to the end or commit suicide if the attack went wrong, only twelve of the thirteen died during the failed attack. The terrorist posing as a guard was the first to die, shot six times by Protect Command agents. Only ten of the thirteen ended their own lives by detonating the explosives in their assigned gallery space or using their Glock weapons on themselves. All of the permanent collection of art in eleven galleries, and three special larger exhibit rooms were destroyed in the attack. A total of eighty-nine pieces were destroyed. The facility itself was closed during painstaking evidence gathering and the extensive repairs.

The Tate Museum Foundation Board of Directors estimated that the work could take several months. The board felt compelled to reopen the facility as soon as possible to show their resilience and spirit of the British to worldwide terrorists. Plans were made to install a plaque honoring the slain staff members and Helena Hassler at the eventual reopening. If all went well as expected, the reconstruction would be in time for Helena's final Kandinsky Exhibition. Lloyds of London had a team assessing the damage and making plans to cover the reconstruction expenses, and cost of the lost art owned by the Tate, or on loan from numerous donors and other museums.

The police response team and the PMs own Chief of the Protect Command detail was extremely curt with Thomas for the manner in which he risked his own life to get to Helena before the area of the building was properly secure. His actions did however get great press from the BBC TV and radio networks, CNN Headline News, legitimate papers and the tabloid rags. Thomas Graham was a hero rising to new heights in popularity worldwide.

Thomas Graham had been in a state of absolute shock for the last twenty-four hours. He felt that it was going to be hard to shake the feeling of tremendous loss. Rarely had the slightest feel of depression permeated his thoughts. It took a tremendous effort to focus on his work.

The terrorist attack was staged in the very heart of London thus increasing the public sense of angst and anxiety. The Millennium Bridge's destruction and damage to the Tate Modern was staged under the very nose of UK security forces and SIS intelligence efforts. That was less troublesome for Thomas than dealing with thoughts of Helena's critical wounds. The fact remained that he had unwittingly put her in harms way by letting news of their relationship leak out into the media. *How had he been so stupid?* As he thought about their growing relationship he had come to the conclusion that she was more important than the power and prestige of being Prime Minister. In that period of reflection he discovered how deeply he loved and cared for Helena. He told himself that *she had to recover so he could tell her just how much she meant to him.* The bits and pieces of his responsibilities seemed to pale in comparison to what needed to happen on a personal level.

He barely remembered carrying Helena to the waiting med-evacuation helicopter. They were flown to University College Hospital near Regency Park. UCH had maintained an outstanding reputation in London for their success in dealing with severe bullet wounds. Given the lack of firearms in the UK, bullet wounds were somewhat rare. The UCH team was an assembled group of experts that had significant military experience in Iraq and Afghanistan. A team of Britain's six best surgeons spent six hours in the operating theater dealing with Helena's abdominal and spinal injuries. The team warned that the tumbling 9mm bullet caused significant internal damage. The bullet had passed through major organs and exited cleanly out her back. It was within a millimeter of her spinal cord. If the bullet had passed a fraction of a millimeter in either direction it would have paralyzed or ended Helena's life. She survived the surgery much to the surprise of the attending surgeons. The Chief Surgeon, Dr. Raymond Fagan had operated on numerous similar fatal wounds while serving in the Royal Army Medical Corps (RAMC). As a weird twist of fate, Hamid, a terrorist that led the terrorist attack on the Tate Modern was treated by the same UCH doctors and was hanging onto life by a weaker thread in the same heavily guarded facility.

After a very brief stay in the surgery recovery area, Helena was secretly transferred to a special SIS government medical facility just outside Oxford. It would be weeks before they would be certain of her long-term prognosis due to the complicated intestinal damage. The entire UCH hospital staff were sworn to maintain the strictest secrecy about her condition during and after her operation. At some point there would be an announcement by Dr. Fagan that she had succumbed to fatal gunshot wounds inflicted by the terrorist. The body of an unidentified homeless female killed in a motor accident was placed in the UCH intensive care unit for a brief period. She would be pronounced dead and moved to the morgue bearing Helena's name.

Arrangements had been made to have the body of the homeless woman placed in a coffin and placed under a secure guard detail at F.A. Albin & Sons Funeral Home, Arthur Stanley House at 545 Culling Court Rd relatively close to the Tate Modern Museum. The funeral home was selected as a convenience for museum staff and friends. To further embellish the impression, arrangements were made for a closed coffin wake and funeral. The dailies would be provided with her approved photo, obituary, and details of the private service at St Martin-in-the-Fields. The Anglican Church on the northeast corner of Trafalgar Square would host the brief by invitation only ceremony. The PM's office focused on staging full preparations for a dignified funeral. An amazing flood of condolences and flowers poured in from state dignitaries and the public rivaling that of Princess Diana. A small area at the corner of Whitehall and Downing St and another outside the Tate Museum main entrance became shrines to honor Helena and her staff. The public outcry was overwhelming.

Thomas met with Helena's only living relative to ensure that she knew the reason behind the elaborate staged death. Her Aunt May was relieved to hear that at the moment Helena was still in critical state and resting peacefully under doctor's care. She agreed to play the important part of the grieving aunt in the charade. The staged death provided Helena with greater security should there be another team of assassins embedded within the country.

In the back of his mind Thomas knew he had to deal with the ugliness of the terrorist situation and the potential backlash if Helena survived and the rouse eventually became public. The very public facade that Helena was deceased seemed to buy him some additional time in the public eye as he privately dealt with his loss. Thomas, with his liberal background, ethically never subscribed to the use of torture under any circumstance. He had been outspoken in criticizing Tony Blair for the use of water boarding in Iraq War. His position changed after he watched the Tate surveillance camera footages of the cold-blooded murders of the Tate staff members and attempt on Helena's life. The footage of Helena being shot was more than he could stand. Hamid the sole surviving terrorist did not deserve humane treatment after his ruthless use of violence.

In the meantime SIS had Hamid the only surviving terrorist r in captivity in hopes of interrogating him in a secret SIS location outside the preview of the London media. The press ran with the SIS story that all terrorists had been killed or committed suicide after being locked in various galleries.

Spencer and his SIS team had their work cut out for them in tracking down the few leads from each of the thirteen terrorists. In examining the bodies of the dead terrorists there was no identification papers or driver licenses. None of the team had a cell phone in their possession. Two had bus transfers indicating a time on which they had boarded specific double decker busses and been issued the transfers at 3:00 a.m. One terrorist had a small imprinted napkin from the Maroush Restaurant. All of the terrorists except one were active in four different mosques in London, Brixton, and Shepherd's Bush. The very common clothing worn by the terrorists were purchased at Primark stores. Dental impressions were made of two terrorists that had significant dental work in hopes of identifying their country of origin or provide a lead to their identification.

Thumbprints of the terrorist were processed by the UK Border Agency and the entry records forwarded by the Home Office to Spencer at SIS.

Spencer held a meeting of the expanded SIS team, "We need to keep the media at safe distance as we attempt to glean information from our captive and follow every lead. They need to be kept at a distance and out of the Tate Modern. You need to be aware that the media may be following you so use extraordinary precautions. Needless to say our work has the potential of saving lives and restoring the public's faith in our ability to provide security. I want hourly reports as you investigate your leads."

Thomas Graham met shortly with Admiral Johnson and Spencer Wendell prior to a meeting with the United Kingdom's National Security Council in the Cabinet Room.

Graham took his seat at the head of the conference table, "Well we are in the midst of a media frenzy. They want the latest details on the attack of the Millennium Bridge and Tate Modern Museum. They always have a morbid fascination with the gory details. I want the fact that Helena survived the attack and that we have one of the terrorists maintained as absolutely top secret. Everyone involved in the Tate attack handled one-on-one to ensure that there are no possible leaks. It is a matter of national security. We need to sanitize all the information regarding the attacks so the terrorist leadership and organization are left in the dark. I do not want the public to know details that might jeopardize Helena's safety: our captive or further hamper our investigative efforts. In a weird way I feel as if the Tate attack may have been the result of my relationship with Helena. It's critical that the country remains calm as we follow through on finding and dealing with the terrorists and ultimately their leadership."

Admiral Johnson cleared his throat, "Mr. Prime Minister, if I may assert that Helena knew full well the enormous risk of being a public figure. You should not blame yourself. " After a pause he continued, "I already met with the Tate staff, law enforcement that responded to the incident, UCH staff, and our own medical facility staff to ensure that everything is kept under wraps as a top state secret. I had a Geoffrey Collins, a senior member of the SIS executive staff member, write a well-crafted speech that underlines that we are using all our resources to deal with the incident, and our ongoing investigation. Your staff can review and edit the speech. I can assure you that we will get the job done, but despite our efforts there may eventually be a leak."

Graham seemed in a trance as he stared out the window, "I must admit that I have been a bit unraveled since the Tate attack. I need to have you give a briefing to the National Security Council and assist when I make the BBC presentation this afternoon. I am relying on SIS to manage all the details and most importantly get those responsible."

Spencer hands the PM a copy of the draft BBC speech. "Mr. Prime Minister, you can rely on SIS to manage the witnesses, secure the information, and give the National Security Council the essential facts without bogging them down with minute details."

Just then Thomas cell phone vibrated. As he looked that the screen, "Please excuse me, I am going to need to take this call." Thomas stepped into his study. "President Reynolds I only have a minute as I am about to address our National Security Council."

"I will be less than a minute. Thomas I want to express our sincere condolences for your loss of Helena and the other Tate staff members. Susan and I were dismayed to hear she was a victim of the attack. I speak for all Americans in expressing our deepest sorrow and offering our condolences. Please have someone within your staff contacts us with details as we would like to support you at the service."

"Thank you. I appreciate your sincere sentiments. In fact Helena is in critical condition in a secure location. We are hoping to get information from her on the terrorists attack. You need to keep the fact that she survived an absolute secret. We also have the critically wounded leader of the terrorist cell. I will have Spencer of SIS contact your NSA if we learn any further intelligence. I apologize for the time crunch, but I do need to hurry to my meeting. Thank you Mark, for your compassion and making the time to call. I will let you know if Helena's condition changes."

Members of the National Security Council composed of Deputy Prime Minister; Chancellor of the Exchequer; Secretary of State for Defense; Secretary of State for Foreign and Commonwealth Affairs; Secretary of State for Home Department; Secretary of State for Energy and Climate Change; Chief Secretary of the Treasury; Chief Superintendent Scotland Yard; and General Chief of Staff entered the Cabinet Room. After a brief time to chat, Thomas Graham asked the council to take their seats.

Graham took a moment to gain his composure and began, "As you know the attacks followed shortly after the removal of the extraordinary security precautions on London bridges. Apparently the terrorist leadership played us as if in a game of chess. Leaking the potential for a London bridge attack, striking Arizona, watching us remove our security and finally attacking what seemed like low priority targets. Public anxiety and outrage at the brazen attack in the heart of London has reached a new high and placed the government in a rather precarious position thanks to the extended media coverage. I have asked Admiral Johnson and Spencer Wendell of SIS to brief the Council on the attacks and their investigation. Admiral Johnson."

Johnson took the cue, "Thank you Mr. Prime Minister. I want to underline the importance of the intelligence community to uncover several important aspects of the Millennium Bridge and Tate Modern Museum attacks. We hope to gain the upper hand with the unknown terrorist organization leadership. I have asked Spencer to give a full accounting of our investigation under the code of secrecy. No member of the Council can speak of any of the facts presented in this meeting. Spencer you may precede with your presentation."

Spencer gives a full account of the bridge and Tate attacks and ends with the fact that they have the wounded terrorist leader in a secret location, but does not disclose that Helena survived the attack in critical condition. Following the presentation he gave a brief summary that disclosed the following: 1) They recognize that the new terrorist leadership was able to secretly coordinate synchronized attacks around the world well beyond the abilities of *al-Qaeda* or other terrorist organizations. 2) The terrorist leaders had access to significant funding and resources. 3) We assume that the recent attacks are a prelude to attacks on more significant hard targets worldwide. 4) The operational terrorists are from the Middle East and Islamic countries thus an implication that the attacks are an international form of jihad. 5) SIS and the military are working together to further secure what we see as higher priority targets. 6) We have increased the surveillance of mosques and infiltrated some of their social settings. 7) We have asked Students Against Radicalized Muslims (SARM) to assist us in gathering information on radicalized individuals and any further terrorist plots. As the National Security Council meeting ends members file by Thomas Graham and offer their sincere condolences on the loss of Helena Hassler. Thomas is gracious in accepting their condolences.

The print media, radio, television and social media focused their pressure on the Graham's Labour Party government to increase efforts to prevent further attacks, and to find and hold the terrorists' leadership responsible.

Spencer and a team of SIS doctors attempted to interview Hamid without success as he went in and out of consciousness. During one segment Hamid moaned the term "Al Salwa." Spencer and the SIS analyst were assessing everything that may render a clue. They determine that the term was the title of a common Arab children's book. Admiral Johnson and senior SIS staff had a significant discussion of possibly using water boarding and sophisticated truth drugs, but at the conclusion decided against it due to the changing moral climate within the UK. In fact Hamid is much too weak to withstand either. The SIS dilemma was trying to extract information now to prevent another attack, or wait until they are sure Hamid can withstand a full interrogation. In the end the SIS team is determined to extract intelligence using their time-honored techniques when his condition permits. The SIS team expressed their ongoing concern that Hamid might die before disclosing anything about the terrorist leadership, organization, funding, communications or other planned attacks.

Spencer and SIS analysts reviewed the individual border entry data on each of the terrorists in an attempt to determine the possibility of developing a gestalt picture of the attack and terrorist organization. He assigns SIS agents to investigate each border entry.

The security forces within the UK and the Border Agency had immediately tightened all forms of transportation in and out of the UK. They posted alerts with all their localized police precincts, as per the Admiral's plan to cover the possibility of capturing any other terrorists.

Helena continues to be in critical condition, slipping in and out of consciousness. Thomas Graham was in constant contact with the staff of the SIS hospital facility treating both Helena and Hamid. Despite the pressure and challenges of preventing the next terrorist attack, Thomas secretly leaves London to visit Helena. The attack ordeal has brought him to the realization that his relationship with Helena means so much more to him. He has difficulty seeing himself in a life without her. She has to survive the attack so he could express his feelings.

Chapter 44: Worldwide Man Hunt Launched
Tuesday, August 20, 9:00 am EST (UTC/GMT-6)
Central Intelligence Agency Headquarters, Langley,
Virginia, USA

CIA Director Gary Dessile received a call on his the secure phone in his Langley office. Gary's direct outside line is primarily used only by Directors of Intelligence in similar positions. The caller was Admiral Harold Johnson, an old friend from the years Gary spent in the U.S. Naval Intelligence. Dessile had provided Johnson with some vital but very sensitive intelligence on the Argentine Navy during the 1982 Falkland War. That intelligence ultimately was credited with shortening the conflict and saving the lives of countless British seamen. The Admiral had a strong sense of reciprocity and knew that if the opportunity presented itself he would not hesitate to repay Dessile.

Gary noted in a kidding voice, "Harry, I thought you were up at your cottage in the Sussex tending your flowers." Their friendship had gotten to a point that Gary called Harold by his childhood nickname. Dessile was only one of three people that ever had that opportunity.

"You know that even British spooks cannot get away over a weekend much less during the week. We are a hard working lot. It seems to me that you rarely use your beautiful weekend home on Oak Point overlooking Chesapeake Bay. We are in the same sinking boat at the moment. My people tell me that you rarely visit it and your wife's vegetable garden is becoming overgrown. It seems like we have wasted our money on homes away from our offices that we rarely if ever use. I guess they will serve as retirement retreats."

"One day we'll both retire and let the world see if it can function without us. You will have time to tend your rose gardens and write your memoirs, and I'll write my best selling spy thriller, do a bit of sailing on the bay and tend to the grandchildren."

Harold laughing, "You know damm well that I detest roses. My garden is a traditional English garden sans any form of roses. What are you going to write about? Your government will not let you write a book dealing with real intelligence issues for thirty years. Gary the only other thing you could possibly write on is your coin collection."

"You have hit the nail on the head, as they say on this side of the pond. My collection of Roman and Greek coins might well be worth writing about." Gary laughed slightly, "All personal life aside Harry, how are things going with the terrorist you captured at the Tate?"

"We have made some progress despite his critical condition and inability to remain conscious for more than a minute or two. We are running down as many leads as possible. I'm sure the terrorist leader thinks that we are in some sort of game and he is the master of the board. He appears to be holding his cards fairly close too the chest. We still do not know where he is operating from or any sense of his identity. Do your blokes have anything to share?"

"That doesn't surprise me in the slightest. These terrorist characters have a natural distain for our profession. I'm sure that he thinks he can outwit our best analyst and super computers. It seems to me that at some point we can exploit that flawed over confidence, or at least use it to our advantage. Until then my CIA teams are still in the dark."

Harold had reached the same conclusion, "This organization has units operating in regions on a very tight schedule. They must have an extensive training facility and enormous resources. We were able to use facial recognition technology to identify our captive as Hamid Kouri, a 34-year-old Saudi. We have completely combed his Herron Tower office and South Kensington flat. Nothing in his phone or computer records indicated being involved other than normal business for an Omani Mining company. He was an expert in limestone used in the production of steel. It appears that our attack may have been in the works for less than a year as he entered the UK on December 17. Obviously he and his leader put all that preparation time and work into what amounts to relatively small and unimportant targets like a bridge and art museum. Why would they do that?"

"I think they want to distract us into thinking that this network is unable to hit something significant. Then again our OEM Scottsdale conference, BART and Helena were significant targets. I think they are playing a waiting game and assessing our responses before striking something larger."

"Ah, precisely what we have concluded at SIS. But that begs the question of where will the group go from here. What will be the leader's next target or series of targets? Will they continue to attack soft targets or go for higher priority hard targets"

"Shep, and his team in the Counter-Terrorism Section think the next attack is bound to be something much more serious, perhaps a dirty bomb in a crowded city event or small drones taking down commercial aircraft. This group is just warming up. We are going to need to be preemptive if possible or face another 9/11 situation with very serious consequences."

"Spencer Wendell and our Counter-Terrorism section arrived at the same conclusion. Our inclination is to use the scant information from our terrorist to the maximum. One piece that might help you is that the attack unit was planning to remain in the UK. Perhaps they intended to participate in another mission. We did learn a curious factoid that the terrorist moaned the name *Al Salwa*. That is the name of a famous Arab children's book. That might lead somewhere. We should know more if our captive lives. On another note Helena Hassler is alive in critical condition but showing minor signs of improvement. This is highly classified. We have her in a protective hospital setting. I'll call when I know more."

"That is helpful. I'll have Shep look into Arab children's books. We have confirmed that the Conference terrorists were the same group that hit our London Bridge. They doubled back from Cabo San Lucas to hit Scottsdale. We think we have some of the California terrorist cells still around waiting to initiate another higher priority mission. We have not been able to find where they disappeared, so it is likely that they may still be here in the U.S. That is if they follow any set pattern. Then again there may be no similarity at all in patterning one plan to that of another. I want to set up a videoconference session with the international counter-terrorist and intelligence community to hopefully gain more intelligence and widen our manhunt. Are you up for it?"

"Absolutely, I will let my people know. You are spot on! Let's hope that neither of our countries faces another tragic event at the hands of terrorists, but I know that will not be the case. Take it easy Gary. If you ever finish the book on your coins you might like to take up gardening. Your Oak Point home really does need help. If I were free to travel I would gladly lend a hand." Harold gave a slight chuckle. "There is something very therapeutic about getting your hands soiled in dirt rather than in our usual dirty business. Do try to get out of your office at a decent hour. Cheers!"

Gary held the phone for a moment thinking about the tips provided by the Admiral. It meant that there was a likelyhood that the Havasu cell, the California attack cells might be waiting for orders to hit their next higher level targets. A more significant terrorist target would mean that he and the entire intelligence community had their work cut out for them. The summer home just south of Annapolis, in Oak Point, Maryland seemed farther away than ever.

Gary called Shep and Hub to share the SIS tips.

The recent terrorist attacks have counter terrorism and intelligence agencies whipped into an absolute frenzy. Two hours later during the videoconference of CIA Director Gary Desille; NSA Director Dexter Ford; FBI Director Frank Thomas, SIS Director Admiral Harold Johnson and Spencer Wendell, they shared details of what they have learned from the attacks.

Desille noted, "Our international assets have not been able to identify the terrorist group that operates in the source areas of the cell phone chatter nor make any headway in monitoring contacts by phone, fax, internet etc. with *Al Zagaheer*. They obviously had pre-knowledge of attacks so they are a likely a major lead to the terrorist organization. We have eyes on all their employees and their families."

Thomas added, "At this point our Havasu investigation has drawn an unfortunate dead end as it seems the terrorist group involved in the Havasu attack were the same as those killed in the Scottsdale tour bus explosion. The DotCommer yacht was commandeered right out of dry dock. We were hot on the trail of Martha Chase a major player in the units initial border crossing. Her body and her husbands were found in the burnt remains of a small house in the village of Sayula, Mexico. We have a team investigating this lead about 50 miles south of Guadalajara. We have an international alert for the missing crew of the Dot Commer yacht, but little to report on that lead. We were able to use photo identification technology to identify the two BART terrorists from video surveillance as jihadist. They were Shad and Dleen Ghazzi, a brother and sister team from Iraq, entering the U.S. legally off the Liberian APXL limestone ore ship in Seattle. We are checking all immigration from the port of Seattle over the past six months. Our best physical evidence is from the Scottsdale Homeland Security Conference attack. We are using facial identification technology on four of the terrorists that were in the Scottsdale Fashion Mall and killed in the bus explosion. We are investigating the extensive work completed on modifying the tourist bus. Most of the vehicle identification on the bus was removed, however extensive lab work revealed the VIN number on one piece of debris despite the clever effort to remove it from sections of the vehicle frame. We have the remains of the bus and traced its' sale to Kevin Gregory, the owner of a dude ranch in Wickenberg, AZ. Kevin and his family recently left the U.S. and were traced to Turkey. CIA teams are tracing the whereabouts of the Gregory family through eastern Turkey. We have varied terrorist weapons serial numbers and are checking on the point of sale sources for the weapons. Our forensics team gathered excellent sets of fingerprints from the East Vista house that matched with the partial prints from the terrorist in the tour bus. INS initially ran those prints through their system with negative results, but later eight prints were matched passengers of a flight from Cabo San Lucas to Phoenix. The group must have entered the U.S., probably along the Mexican border with Martha Chase for the Lake Havasu attack. We did find DNA and partial fingerprints of another terrorist at the East Vista house that was not with the remains of the other terrorists in the tour bus. That leads us to the conclusion that there is a terrorist at large and likely to be the leader."

Thomas stopped his briefing for a minute when he received a phone from Jerry O'Toole, President Reynolds's Chief of Staff. "Hi Jerry, I am in an international video conference. I will call you as soon as it is done. That will probably be in another 45 minutes."

Thomas put down his cell and picked up where he had left off. "We are following up on leads on the group that attacked LA. Fingerprints on the cartridges and in abandoned vehicles match those of seamen that entered the U.S. on the Greek MV Atlantikani ore ship at the Port of Los Angeles delivering high-grade limestone for steel mills in Southern California. They stole a series of vehicles that were used in their escape. Several of the stolen cars ended up near the Port of Los Angeles. We are following up on the security camera footage of crews departing from the port shortly after the LACMA attack. We are going to be intercepting the eleven ships that departed the Port of Los Angeles at their next port of call. The terrorists in the San Francisco MOMAs attack stripped their van of the blue coating and left it in the AT&T fan parking lot A.
We were unable to recover fingerprints, but have several samples of DNA from clothing left behind in the van. The DNA markers indicate that half were female. We do have four cab driver accounts of various couples waving them down to get to San Francisco International airport and security video showing them within the airport and taking flights to various international destinations.

We have their passport records, and footage of them prior to leaving on international flights. We have FBI teams following the trail left by each of the couples, but at this point it is going to take time to track them down and bring those responsible for the San Francisco attacks to justice. At this point I wish we had more, but be assured that our teams will get to the bottom of every attack. We are certain that the terrorists are a well-funded radicalized Islamic group with significant support within the United States. The leadership meticulously planned each attack for maximum effect using the media coverage. It appears that each attack target and the timing were so precisely pinpointed to create maximum chaos with law enforcement resources, counter terrorism and intelligence agencies. This is no ordinary terrorist group or leaders. They are well beyond the resources and planning of al-Qaeda or ISIS."

Admiral Johnson was taking notes, "The attacks in Europe fit the same modus operandi. Definitely Middle Eastern Islamic, well funded, and extremely well planned. We just cannot fathom the reasoning behind attacking bridges in the heart of cities and art museums when we have a huge number of much higher value government, energy grid and infrastructure targets.
All the terrorists in the Tate were without identification and had the tips of their fingers removed through a very painful acid process. We used photo identification technology to identify their point of entry into the UK. At this point we have been successful using our immigration, police data files, and Interpol resources. We are in the process of interrogating the single captured terrorist who remains in critical condition. Our analysts and international assets have not been able to identify the group responsible for the flurry of cell chatter calls, nor likely group responsible for the attacks. Given the timing and tactics we have concluded that this is a very different breed of leadership.

Undoubtedly the leadership has a well-planned strategy to cause our agencies to respond as he expects. We are determined to resolve the mystery and counter with some major form of retaliation."

" My FBI team is looking for any pattern that we can exploit. We need to anticipate the leader's next move and then respond in a way that puts him off his game. I think we should share what we have to date with other counter terrorism and intelligence agencies. Bringing other intelligence agencies up to speed with detailed knowledge of our leads might end up leading to their giving us one missing piece that completes the puzzle and brings the terrorist organization down. On the positive side I have been in contact with an international Muslim student organization called SARM. They are opposed to the effects each attack has on normal Muslim communities and are working to provide information on radical recruitment efforts, terrorist activist and issues within their communities in thirty-six different areas of the world. Hopefully they will render some solid leads."

Dexter Ford looked at his Blackberry momentarily, "I have the NSA super computer pulling all data connections with Al Salwa in hopes of finding a link of the London attacks to our U.S. terrorist cells. Let's send off a joint summary and follow it with a video conference call. We might get lucky and one of the other agencies comes up with that missing puzzle piece. We need to find the terrorists within our midst and root them out. The public has been inundated with media coverage, bombarded with fear mongering, and becoming more anxious while losing confidence in our ability to protect them on our own soil."

"I agree we have the same issue in the UK. Who will distribute the summary and host the video conference?" Admiral Johnson asked.

"NSA has the best technology, I will have my folks create the summary and organize the video conference."

Hub Nolan had the summary submitted within three hours and organized the video conference with Elena Blano Suarez, (Spanish Director Centro Nacional de Inteligencia, CNI); Françoise Etiene, (French DGSE Direction Générale de la Sécurité Extérieure); Helmut Roetzerberg (German Bundesnachtendient BND); Rubin Goldblum, (Israeli Mossad); Leon Rostankovich (Russian SVR & GRU); Jans Huise (Belgium, Director of Service Général du Renseignement et de la Sécurité (SGR); Marco Tancredi, (Italian Director Agenzia Informazioni e Sicurezza Interna_(AISI); Bati Ugelnal (Indonesian Badan Koordinasi Intelijen Negara - BIN); Geng Wen Ping (Chinese Ministry of State Security (MSS); and Goro Miyoshi (Japanese IAS).

Hub Nolan used sophisticated NSA technology to present the timeline and details of all the U.S. and European terrorist attacks. The counter terrorism group is somewhat frustrated by the lack of knowledge pointing to the terrorist leader responsible for the growing number of attacks. They agree that the terrorist leader must have his sights set on something of a much higher target value and that the future attacks may involve other nations. Hub challenges each country to make a list of the twenty-five most likely terrorist targets and steps they should consider to protect their assets. The joint resources of all the intelligence and counter terrorism agencies are challenged to comb through resources and assets worldwide for any leads on the coordinated attacks and the terrorist leadership. Each attack group was apparently self contained, within itself and dead ended investigations. The terrorist suicides, altered appearances, falsified passports, acid treated finger and palm prints, and the lack of credible eyewitnesses frustrated the agencies.

The international media continued to ramp up world fear and anxiety. Extreme pressure is placed on the world's political leaders, governments, and intelligence communities of all countries to protect the public from further attacks. There is a massive outcry to bring the terrorist groups involved to justice on the world stage. Other domestic, economic, environmental and international issues seemed to fall by the wayside as the media pushes governments to focus on safety and security as the highest priority.

For the next several months the intense worldwide manhunt continued with NSA intelligence reports on the progress of the clearing of 12 ships until the Shanghai ship carrying the Los Angeles LACMA terrorists makes port. An elite unit of thirty CIA and Chinese MSS teams intercepted the *MJ Pffeiler* container ship only to find the group of terrorists already dead due to self inflicted wounds in a container. Three of the San Francisco MOMA terrorist couples were identified and tracked on different routes to Turkey, Aden and Yemen. The final couple was tracked to New Zealand where the trail turned cold when the couple departed on a small 42-foot sailboat. The weapons used in the SF MOMA attack were traced to Gregory's ranch workers in Wickenburg, Arizona. As in past terrorist attacks the counter terrorism units needed to stay focused on following all leads and piecing together the network of teams and cells in hope of somehow leading back to the organizationleadership.

Chapter 45: Upping the Ante in a New Gambit
Tuesday, August 20, 7:45 p.m. GST (UTC/GMT+4)
The Prince, Skyscraper, Dubai, United Arab Emirates

Yassar had been carefully monitoring the flood of television and newspaper reports analyzing the terrorist attacks in Europe and United States. A wall filled with twenty-six different international television stations, and news online sites within his residential area gave him the ability to view wide varieties of reports. Those same monitors had a PIP (picture in picture) of varied Prince Tower internal security channels, and video messaging throughout most of the modern world. The news telecasts indicated that the targeted countries remained in a state of chaos over the sequence of soft targets, and fear over possible hard targets, and the illogical motivation of the terrorist leadership.

Londoners could not believe that despite being alerted well in advance about the potential for an attack against a London bridge the security forces were unable to prevent terrorists from taking out the Millennium Bridge, damaging the Tate Modern and slaughter of the museum staff.

President Reynolds was dealing with the fallout of the Scottsdale attack and major concerns of congress over national security set before the media in Intelligence Committee hearings. The time honored U.S. arguments over appropriations for security and budget cuts to other domestic programs was ongoing and gaining traction. These attacks led to a growing lack of confidence in the British, French, Spanish and U.S. governments. There was an extensive ominous cloud of fear throughout the Western world despite a short hiatus without recent attacks.

Yassar enjoyed the immense power he derived from creating chaos with just a hand full of well trained devoted followers strategically placed and using his plan. The most developed countries in the world were living in the shadow of fear, unsure of when or where of the next attacks. Time was on the side of terrorist plots. The power grew out of being able to affect the lives of political enemies despite their incredible depth of economic, military, and intelligence resources. There was a surge of excitement in knowing he was matching wits with the intelligence agencies, and their technology. His opponents were hunting him internationally and frustrated by their lack of success. The thought of targeted nations bringing to bear every resource within their arsenal to unsuccessfully find him excited him more than anything else he had experienced in life.

Each mission's success was addictive in supporting Yassar's modus operandi of the sleek agile chess master capturing and killing piece after piece in the strategy was to ultimately cripple or destroy the enemy. As the Master of Deception was playing mind games and enjoying every aspect of keeping the opponent guessing where and when the next attack would be coming. The *Al Zagaheer* news would be reporting that an unnamed Muslim splinter group claimed full responsibility for all the U.S. and European attacks. His plan was to keep the intelligence agencies focused on finding the news organizations sources and ultimately ties to terrorism.

The Shura continued secretly sending large quantities of cash to *Al Zagaheer* through a wide variety of legitimate businesses for advertising. Some of the cash purchased high tech encrypting equipment to thwart much of the NSA electronic surveillance of phones and Internet. A special cement lead and magnetic lining shielded the *Al Zagaheer* studios to prevent heat detection equipment. They installed a unique designed German device creating huge waves of white noise thwarting internal and external ear dropping efforts. A security team provided constant sweeps of the facility and personnel for planted listening devices. All *Al Zagaheer* personnel were required to use burner cell phones purchased in seventeen different countries.

The *Shura* was headquartered in a modern fortress with the secure luxury of incredible technology and creature comforts. The Shura facility was a unique complex of seventeen floors and sixty-five rooms including a private restaurant, multiple storage areas, small arms firing range, ultra high tech encrypted communications center, recreational center, and individual *Shura* member apartments. The complex had a state of the art security system and three levels of armed guards with multi-faceted fingerprint, voice, retina, and facial recognition technology. Constant security sweeps, reflective glass on the windows, automatic scrambling of voice transmissions, encrypting both text and e-mail messages on integrated secure servers designed by talented hackers with quadruple monitoring for intruders. The security precautions were understandable given Yassar's status, wealth, financial interests and position within the Arab world.

Yassar scheduled an 8:00 p.m. evening meeting of the Shura. The agenda of the meeting was to: 1) review the result of the varied cell attacks; 2) adherence to the initial strategic plan; 3) necessary follow-up or action; 4) security of cells within the field during the short dormant respite; and 5) concerns about potential clues, leads or loose ends leading back to the Shura prior to moving to the second level of attacks on hard targets.

Yassar entered the conference room dressed in a flowing *thoub* robe, and traditional head covering *ogal, tagiyah* and *shumagg*. He had just returned from visiting the Jumerirah Mosque. "Good evening everyone" (مساء الخير جميعا). Over the past six years Yassar's friends and associates had witnessed his slow but growing use of traditional dress and deepened religious commitment. They suspected that it had to do with the death of his loved ones and Amal, his daughters, upcoming wedding into the UAR royal family.

Kenji Habbi, was the last to arrive for the briefing. He obviously had been watching the televised reports of the commotion and chaos in the U.S. and Europe. In a small way the success of *Al Salwa*, despite Hamid's death, was a reflection on his own leadership within the *Shura*.

Kenji, "Yassar, I take it that you have seen the varied media reports of our attack on London. The massive cloud of fear and anxiety has captured the entire United Kingdom. They were powerless in avoiding *Al Salwa*'s attack despite their initial defensive stand. Your masterful switch from threats on London Bridges to focus on U.S attacks, and back to Europe was brilliant. Graham is obviously shaken by the death of Helena Hassler. He may be highly motivated by revenge making his decisions and responses easier to predict as we shift to our next level of attacks."

"I have monitored the reports just before retiring to my quarters last night." Yassar, paused momentarily, "*Al Salwa*,'s attack was a real psychological blow to those who defile Islamic values and punish our Muslim brothers. We are making some real progress. It is a shame that the *Al Salwa* cell did not escape the Tate with Helena. There had to have been something that we underestimated or missed in our detailed planning. I would like Nuru to use her *Al Zagaheera* international media connections to investigate what we may have missed. I need to avoid any such mistakes in any of our future attacks."

"I will have her make discreet journalistic inquiries." Kenji seated himself on Yassar's right. "I hope you plan on continuing to move forward with the sequenced higher priority targets. Thus far the plan has accomplished what we intended striking fear into the U.S., UK, France and Spain and confusing the intelligence agencies of our enemies. The destruction of each soft-targeted bridge and art museum was a blow against decadent Western modern thinking and aesthetics. You have proven again and again that you are an amazing strategist in devising the overarching plan, but we need to accept that things happen in the field of combat. The most important thing is the overall success of our missions and the chaos it has created for our enemies."

Yassar turned slightly to Kenji, "*Al Salwa*, has proven themselves to be valuable members of our plan, however their elimination means that we will need to recruit replacements and puts us slightly behind schedule for the third level. I never intended to use and then dispose of cells. The *Al Salwa* cell's sacrifice should be rewarded. We need to involve highly trained cells in extended missions like *Allim Tiflak*. I appreciate your loyalty Kenji. It is very important for you and Akaman to recruit men like Hamid to lead our cells that follow orders without question down to the last minute detail of our tactics and strategy. We also need the pawns that are willing to sacrifice their lives for our cause and avenge the enemy's war against Muslims. You certainly have your work cut out for you."

Mohammed and Angri enter the conference room hotly engaged in a conversation about the success of the attacks in Europe.

Yassar's eyes darted towards the men full of a somewhat unusual impatience and indicating that the meeting was about to begin. Both men quickly recognized his mood and took their seats at the round table. Yassar observed that even the members of his *Shura* were creatures of habit always sitting in the same seats despite the openness of meeting seating. Habits are not a good thing because it provides your enemy with insight and makes you more predictable. Habits make us more vulnerable. This could be a real problem if we are being hunted by security, anti-terrorism and intelligence organizations worldwide and have posted the 75 million dollar bounty for information leading to our capture or death.

"In Allah's name, we begin our briefing. Let's give special thanks today for our successful operations to date, and that our future plans continue to be as successful."

Yassar stopped for a moment to show a brief BBC video clip of the bridge and Tate Modern. "Mousaffa will not be here today. He is in Oman inspecting a new addition to our operations training facility. Over the past three days he has been contacting some of our friendly drug dealing warlord donors of recruits in Afghanistan, Iraq, Oman, Yemen and Qatar. He will join us in a few minutes via video conferencing. It is amazing to think that over 40% of our operations are unwittingly paid for in part by the heroin and cocaine addicts of the United Kingdom and the U.S. That stream of money is twice the amount given by donors to various mosque charities that flows to other terrorist groups and 50% of the funds ISIS gets from the sale of their limited oil production. Angri, I'd like to have the drug lords increase their contributions. We should be able to capitalize on their celebrating our success in recent attacks. Do you have any suggestions that you could pass on to Mousaffa?"

At that moment there was a familiar beep, as Mousaffa jointed the meeting on the massive monitor at the far end of the room. He was obviously within the center of the Shura's remote mining operation in Oman. "Praise Allah, for the success of our attacks and avenging the deeds of our enemies."

Yassar smiled, "Welcome, Mousaffa. Indeed we have initiated steps down a road that is full of success. We were discussing how to extract more donations and recruits from the drug lords."

Angra, "Let us suggest that the drug lords transportation system is extremely vulnerable to attack by Interpol, American DEA, or a team of well organized thugs. If need be we can have thugs underline their vulnerability with a few token attacks. Then we can provide them with the necessary protection of their resources and transportation routes. They'd get the message. A bit of extortion can work wonders in expanding their willingness to fund for our cause. The benefit of additional recruits will underline their support."

Yassar smiled at Angra's assessment, "The BBC has reported *Al Salwa*, success in London. The SIS, NSA and CIA are confused and chasing dead ends. They are patiently anticipating the timing of our next attack. My son-in-law Nassar is anxious to begin *Tolem Series's* mission. *Tolem Series* is by far the largest cell that we have deployed to date. Nassar reports that boredom has caused some petty bickering amongst his cell as the cell members work in the fields of California. They are ready to swing into action and hit their primary hard target west of Phoenix. *Tolem Series* will be linked in a strange way with *Allim Tiflak* attacks in Arizona that will further terrify our American opponents and cause outright panic. The public will not accept another attack in Arizona under the very noses of their increased law enforcement and anti-terrorism efforts. Three attacks within a relatively small area with a clear escalation to harder targets will slam the Reynolds's administration."

"Yassar, has *Kaji* gotten the weapons to supply *Tolem Series*'s team?" asked Angri Kafti.

"The whole next sequence of our operation depends upon Nassar and *Tolem Series* having the weapons they need to get the job done. I still cannot get over how Kaji was able to purchase a complete military arsenal within the United States and Canada for less than the $11.3 million dollars we had allocated for the operation. But by far the most impressive was obtaining three new design cruise missiles by paying off the gambling debt of an officer in the China Lake Naval Weapons Research facility. Why would we chance bringing weapons in from outside the U.S. if they were readily available within their loophole filled legal system?"

Angri and Kenji laughed at the comment and the harsh reality that Americans hold their right to *bear arms* to the ultimate degree allowing high powered military weapons to be sold under a varied gun shows and by straw buyers from gun owners. Their acquisition of the missiles was a bonus that had taken nearly two years, but added to the odds of their successful second level attack.

"I wish it was true of all our targeted countries." Kenji added without a second thought.

Yassar interceded, "*Šarūnī, Ya'qūb aš* is working on the second level target site in the Midlands of England. He and his men are waiting for the security around the UK to relax. He reports that he may be short handed due to the deaths of *Al Salwa*. The elimination of Hamid's *Al Salwa* cut the *Šarūnī, Ya'qūb aš* manpower by one third. Let's review our timetable and the sequence for the second level attacks once more."

Throughout the entire three hours and forty-five minute meeting the group sipped traditional Moroccan mint tea. Each member of the *Shura* loved the tradition of having the wonderful mint tea. It was served on a silver and gold inlaid tray with a *Sala* teapot. Each member sipped from small ornate silver and glass *Taj* tea glasses. This small indulgence was a symbol of friendship and trust among numerous Arab peoples and tribes. The tea had a calming effect on the Shura and gave them the ability to really focus on minute details of the next attacks. Jurgurtha Messina, a Muslim follower from Berber Morocco, prepared this delicious tea treat using an old family recipe. Jugurtha also prepared a tray full of tasty *Mafruka, Murgasgas*, and low fat *Mohallabiah*

Once Jurgurtha left the conference room, Mousaffa started his presentation on another large high definition screen. There was significant progress made in Oman, Yemen, and Qatar. The fact that Mousaffa had already collected over 15 million Euros for the cause on the short trip reflected well on the various warlords support of the *Shura*.

Mousaffa reported on the preparations of the current trainees within the Oman mine-cave facility. The highlight of his report was the level of training that his security and operational forces had undergone in the past few days. He also noted that they had installed a special high-speed exhaust fan system in the sealed laboratory producing Sarin nerve gas. "The issue of any potential Sarin gas accident in the complex is finally put completely to rest."

"That should make us all feel better." Yassar responded with a slight smile. Next, Yassar asked for a full financial report from Angri.

"I'm pleased to report that with all the payments to Pakistani officials and current operations worldwide. The *Shura* had nearly 981 million Euros for future expenses. This does not include the funds that Mousaffa just collected for our cause. "

"That is excellent Angri." Yassar paused and added, "We have many operations that have gone as planned. The focus of this meeting is to review aspects of each cells mission in detail." Pausing a moment, "We will start with *Allim Tiflak*. Mousaffa , please review each of the multiple prongs of the *Allim Tiflak* cell attacks?

Mousaffa used the remote control on the massive 6 meter by 5-meter screen on the south wall of the conference room to project images from the *Al Zagaheer* newscast as he began his summary. "The *Allim Tiflak* had the most complicated of missions. Meerza Saliba served as the cell leader. Alpha team successfully destroyed the London Bridge over Lake Havasu and returned to Phoenix to successful attack the Homeland Security Conference in Scottsdale. Meerza was forced to eliminate Alpha Team with two contingency explosive devices within their tour bus. There were no loose ends for the operation. Bravo team had successfully destroyed the modern art collection of the LA County Museum, escaped to the Port of Los Angeles, and were presently at sea. But as the U.S. and Chinese counter intelligence forces boarded their ship they sacrificed themselves for our cause. Charlie team successfully destroyed the Xanadu Gallery, modern art in the San Francisco MOMA and created mass confusion by detonating explosives in both directions of the BART San Francisco TransBay tunnel. Charlie team escaped on international flights and are being tracked by counter terrorism units in four countries. The *Allim Tiflak*'s overall missions were a total success confronting the Homeland Security conference, destroying decadent art, disrupting transportation in a major U.S. city, causing confusion, anxiety, fear and increased concern among Americans about terrorism on U.S. soil. Are there any questions or concerns?"

Mousaffa completed a summary of each of the three remaining cells over the next hour. There were little questions or concerns, but general comments on the ingenuity of the strategy and fantastic results of excellent recruitment, training, and support. The summary was an assessment of the progress of FBI investigations of the Lake Havasu, Scottsdale, Los Angeles, San Francisco; Spanish CNI in Bilbao; French SDE in Paris, and British SIS London attacks.

———

The final piece of the assessment covered any possibility of clues or intelligence leads that might lead back to the Shura. At this point the varied attack successes spoke for themselves and there was no concern about anti-terrorist organizations identifying or following information leads back to Dubai.

The Shura took a moment to recognize the sacrifices of the individuals in the cells involved in the successful attacks.

Yassar asked, "What have we done to support the families of the remaining live cell members to date?"

Angri Kafti distributed a summary sheet listing each of the cell members in groups by cells. Next to each name was an indication that a specified family member was given an untraceable sum of 400,000 United Arab Emirates Dirham.

Angri began, "As you can see the families of each of the cell members were rewarded an untraceable package of cash beyond the individual's lifetime expected income. The packages were delivered under tremendous secrecy, well received with detailed instructions on limited spending. The sum will more than support those families. The actual funds were kept in a separate charitable fund funneled and provided for by 17 of our corporations. Any questions or concerns?"

"Thank you Angri." Yassar paused before continuing. "The aforementioned attacks were pieces of a much larger multi-phased strategy to do irreparable damage to the United States and her allies. We are committed to the second level of higher priority attacks. If all goes as planned we will have the U.S. thinking about something other than Thanksgiving turkey." A slow grin crossed Yassar's face as he relished the thought of raising the stakes in his mission of revenge to avenge the deaths of his family and acts against all Muslims.

The Shura put into motion their second level of their strategic plan in Arizona and United Kingdom. The early successes of attacks reinforced their confidence that the next level of higher priority attacks would meet with similar results and much more serious consequences for their enemies. The members ended the meeting confident in taking the attacks to the next more deadly second level.

Months later..............

Chapter 46: Design Implementation Phase
Monday, October 16, 1:35 a.m. MST (UTC/GMT-8)
Palo Verde Nuclear Facility, Tonopah, 56 miles west of
Phoenix Arizona

The Cal-Tech team redundancy system installation work was nearing completion. The system installation had been in total secrecy after 11 p.m. over the past nine weeks. The Sonoran Desert temperatures reach there highest during August with daytime highs averaging 129 degrees with overnight lows averaging 92 degrees. The Cal-Tech team worked on a very tight schedule, despite the uncomfortable conditions. They expected to be ready for the final Beta testing of the entire system during a scheduled *force-on-force* security drill in November. The concept was that testing the system during an actual simulation of a terrorist attack would be far better than simply putting the system under a series of random tests. Sean was pleased with the project's progress as the team completed the installation of their equipment. They completed Beta testing of the internal system and satellite linkups at Palo Verde Reactor I and II, and were 58% through the installation on Reactor III. Sean had confirmed with the NNS task force the projected scheduled completion of work, without any unforeseen issues on Reactor III within a month. He submitted weekly reports to NNS and maintained contact with the Task Force team through Dr. Powers. The feedback from NNS and NSA on both Reactor I & II was extremely positive. The U.S. felt increased pressure on securing nuclear reactors was furthered by the NSA evidence pointing to ISIS terrorist interest in a Belgium reactor and meeting with a Tier 4 Nuclear Electronics Technician from the facility.

Sean and Kathryn were using FaceTime to communicate during the day and nightly given the two-hour time difference. Going beyond their initial reaction to the series of terrorist attacks, loss of lives and destruction of art, they spent time discussing the utter anxiety and fear prevalent internationally and nationwide. They concluded that the media played a major role in amplifying the hysteria through 24-hour coverage of terrorism. As information became public about the terrorists in the BART attack, they recognized a pattern. Individuals in dire situations were basically unemployable due to poor education and disadvantaged economies, could become Muslim heroes, provide for their families and get international media notoriety going out in a blaze of glory as terrorists. They both reviewed recordings of specific news broadcast each night so they could analyze their content and create a dot matrix "fear mongering" scale of each news report. Both FOX News and CNN seemed the largest culprits as fear mongers making news by expanding and emphasizing the fear elements in nearly every news story. The constant news coverage of terrorism was twenty times worse than the Ebola and Zika threats to the U.S.

Sean and Kathryn made plans to get together in November just prior to the final testing as a form of celebration and meet in Pasadena in December during Kathryn's winter break. Their relationship had developed on many levels as they shared time apart.

"I have been hoping that we could share some time doing some rock climbing on the red rocks of the Sedona – Oak Creek area and explore areas of Northern Arizona." Sean was hoping that Kathryn would learn to share his passion of the sport. "There are some great climbs for a first time rock climber. Are you game?"

"I will have to do some more indoor climb training before November, but want to share the adrenaline rush you get from climbing. I want to be sure that you will also find time for some more difficult climbs that challenge you and your team." Kathryn was a bit anxious about challenges a rock face presented, but wanted to give it a serious try. "My Aunt Grace spent a week on vacation in Sedona and raved about the sheer beauty of the red rock outcrops. I am looking forward to seeing you in November and exploring parts of Arizona."

"Don't worry about me. My team and I have been exploring the 5.10 climb up Coyote's Tower. That will be more than enough to feed my rock climbing inner soul." Laughing, " I want you to enjoy the experience and understand the challenge that feeds my passion for the sport."

"I have three experienced rock climbers in one of my Global Strategic Communications class. They promised to take me out to the SportRock Climbing Center in Alexandria, VA. It is supposed to be the best rock climbing gym in the DC area. I hope to be better prepared to do some real red rock climbing. I am sure Coyote Tower is out of my league, I just don't want too build up your expectations too high on what I can challenge myself to climb."

"No worries, I just want to have you give it a go and give you an insight into what makes me tick. Regardless it will be great spending time with you rather than on my laptop or IPad app. I have to run, part of my team is ready for the final night installation on Reactor II. Let's chat during your Wednesday lunch break."

"Wednesday at 12 p.m. EDT works for me. Have fun tonight under the million Sonoran stars. I will be thinking of you trying to get cool atop on of the plant cooling towers looking at the night sky." Laughing out loud.

"I usually don't perch myself on those towers. I prefer the AC in the control room. Noon your time is great.... wish I were there to hold you and give you a kiss. Got to run! Goodnight!"

Chapter 47: Analyzing Terrorist's Mind Games
Friday, November 22, 8:45 a.m. PDT (UTC/GMT-8)
Watson Laboratory, California Institute of Technology
Campus, Pasadena CA

After nearly seventeen weeks in the scorching daytime sun and cool nights in the Arizona Sonoran desert, Sean and the Cal-Tech team finish the installation of the Redundancy System in Reactor III. As was the norm the team met in the spacious lab upon their return to Pasadena to update any system installation details, issues, and review the data downloaded with the on campus team.

Craig and DeJesus arrived at Sean's lab very early on a smoggy Friday morning. They were in a heated discussion over the past terrorist attacks in Arizona and California and the series of attacks in Europe. They had printed out the web pages of CNN, LA Times, Washington Post, London Times, Herald Tribune, La Monde, BBC and NY Times trying to piece together as much detailed information as possible. In the past, a major part of their relationship with Sean and the rest of the team had been a variety of intellectual mind game exercises. Factual information was gathered, processed, and analyzed to formulate connections and hypothesis. The group would then attempt to prove or disprove their hypothesis. Both Craig and DeJesus hoped that they could use the data from the attacks as the basis for an early morning team mind game exercise before starting the meeting agenda. It would serve as a great way to engage the installation and campus teams.

Craig was intrigued about the fact that the Lake Havasu City attack had been about 60 miles Northwest from their redundancy system project at Palo Verde nuclear facility and the Scottsdale attack 55 miles East. He thought that Sean would be interested to learn the close proximity to Palo Verde, which was smack in the center between the attacks. Sean had been following the few known facts about the Lake Havasu City attack, but had been busy crunching data and not really heard details on the LA and San Francisco or the three European bridges and modern museums attacks.

DeJesus was drawing a mind map on the whiteboard, when he came to a revelation "I find the proximities of the terrorists' Lake Havasu London Bridge and Scottsdale conference attacks coincidently close to our Beta project in Palo Verdes intriguing. But there is more to this than meets the eye. The terrorist leader was obviously playing a mind game with the counter terrorism agencies by leaking the misleading cell chatter that the target was the "London Bridge." That set off the huge response from the Brits in London."

As the two sifted through various printouts, entering information and comparing notes they began to see a number of flaws in the reported attacks. As part of their exercise they listed facts and parallels between the U.S. and European attacks on a large whiteboard creating a timeline. Both felt that seeing the information in a huge mind map made it easier to understand, process and analyze the varied events. They hoped that the entire Cal-Tech team would use the attacks as a focus for their mind game exercise.

Sean arrived a half-hour early for the team meeting. "Hi guys, what do we have here?" He began to process the information on the whiteboard mind map and timeline. The three knew that the process became easier each time they engaged the larger group in the mind game exercise as multiple minds added different facts and perspectives to the map and helped the analysis. Sean and the two Cal-Tech graduate students became so engrossed in the exercise of postulating questions and hypothetical answers that they lost track of the time and the slight modifications for the redundancy system they had intended to work on that morning before the team meeting.

At 11:45 a.m. most of the Cal-Tech team including Ned Toppin arrived for the meeting. As each entered the lab they became interested in confronting the maze of facts spread across the whiteboard dominating the room. Shortly after noon Sarah and Jake arrived from Manhattan Beach. They faced the usual ongoing good-natured kidding about their budding romance from Craig and DeJesus over the past month. The team started teasing the couple on why they were late hoping to get some reaction. Sean intervened with a comment that they need to get to work and projected the meeting agenda on the screen, and sent it to their individual laptops.

"I am pleased with our final installation on all three reactors. If all goes well we can wrap this meeting up in an hour. Once the real work is complete we can enjoy the challenge of a new mind game. As you can see Craig and DeJesus have set up the parameters for an intriguing and challenging game.

For the next hour each Cal-Tech team member reported on their area of responsibility and answered questions from other team members. Sean reviewed the data downloads with the campus team members.

The team activated the remote NNS video access to the three separate control rooms and confirmed the NSA satellite connections. A series of fifteen satellites were networked to ensure that the nuclear plant redundancy system had constant contact with the new NNS facility built to monitor it and any eventual additional facilities. Ned described the formula for concentrations of gas to fit the individual control room and the remote controls for the system. Just after 1:20 p.m. Sean thanked each team member separately acknowledging his or her individual efforts and contributions. At that moment Jake and Sam returned wheeling in a cart of different pizzas and drinks.

"That is it for the formal part of the meeting. Let's enjoy a quick lunch and jump into the mind game if you are up to it." The expected response was unanimous including Ned. "Let's have Craig and DeJesus lead us through what they have already on the white board."

Craig deferred to DeJesus to get the ball rolling. For the next twelve minutes the team listened intently to the collection of relevant bits of information on the terrorist attacks and helped in adjusting the notes on the mind map.

Sean took the floor "Thanks guys, it sounds like a great opportunity for us to explore facets of each attack as if each contributed to the whole in a mega picture. Stepping back, adding information, seeing parallels, analyzing the events and attempting to get that gestalt picture. The mastermind terrorist leaders may be leaving a trail of breadcrumb clues that will lead us to his motivation or what his next target might be. Are we game?"

"Bring it on. I love these mind games. Do any of you guys have more to add?" Willie responded and picked up a marker ready to add information.

Sarah looked at the whiteboard mind map full of data and notes and asked, "Well it looks as if you guys were busy earlier this morning assembling most of the obvious facts?"

DeJesus pretended to take a bow, "We started the exercise by creating a comparison of the initial U.S. attacks to the European attacks, and now we are attempting to find more connections, answering our own questions, and hopefully make predictions about future attacks. Our exercise is much like putting together fifty pieces of a five hundred-piece puzzle, and trying to guess what the picture would be like when it was completed. How does one piece connect to the whole?"

The game was a challenge as each piece pushed the other team members to provide major or minor facts, spot relationships and to analyze the data. Synthesizing the varied parallels between what was known about each attack and seeking meaning from the information to form their overall thesis.

First, they hypothesize that a bridge brings two or more landmasses together like an alliance. Each of the attacks was against allies in the war against terrorism or in the view of some Muslims under the auspice of fighting terrorism while slaughtering hundreds of thousands of Muslims, destroying significant cities and mosques, and attempting to gain footholds in the politics of oil.

Second, was the simple fact that each of the U.S. attacks were initiated at exactly MST 6:00 a.m. and PST 5:00 p.m. showing precise timed planning of the coordinated attacks. The European attacks were initiated in three countries at precisely 8:00 a.m.
It would be highly improbable that unrelated terrorist attacks would begin at the same time that maximized the chaos and confusion for responders.

Prior to the attacks, the targets were not considered as priority targets by intelligence and counter terrorism agencies and had high public visibility.

Third, the terrorists had used the same silenced Glock 9mm automatic weapons and chemical composition in the TATP explosives in all attacks. It was highly unlikely that terrorist would use the same weapon given the wide range of other alternative automatic weapons used commonly by terrorist including the Bersa, Ruger, Sig, Browning, and Desert Eagle. The attacks were connected and perhaps used the same resources to obtain weapons. The weapons might also be a link to the fact that all the terrorists used the same weapons in training.

Fourth, the terrorists had demonstrated a remarkable level of planning, execution of their plan, and at this point escaped pre-attack detection. The personnel used were precisely trained to accomplish each mission. The attacks also had sufficient pre-knowledge of the targets and obvious access to resources. These attacks were not a series of random terrorist acts. The seemingly soft targets must have some importance in the overall attack strategy. The attack mastermind also accurately anticipated the responses by authorities creating diversions that drew the intelligence agencies from the UK to Arizona and back to Europe.

Fifth, the terrorists had shown a cold-blooded ability to murder innocent civilians. There was no thought involved in each of the executions nor the aftermath of the bombings. The terrorists were accustomed to violence. What motivated the terrorists was not necessarily material gain, but revenge or political gain over an enemy, perhaps against the collective group of allies involved in the war against terror.

Sixth, the terrorist leader had engaged their enemy in a series of mind games by threatening action against London bridges as a way to keep British citizens in a shadow of fear, and causing British security to act in a predictable security response. They then switched and attacked the remote Arizona "London Bridge." When the table of fear reversed to a small town in America, the mastermind switched the game again focusing on three major U.S. urban centers showing the organizations extensive capabilities. When the focus centered on western U.S. cities, the Brits responded by incrementally lessening their security. The leader then reversed again to the urban heart of Europe by attacking bridges and art museums. Thus creating another parallel to the U.S. attacks.

"We've got it right. The attacks were a series of planned diversions. Not anyone in their right mind would think that global terrorists would be after the Lake Havasu tourist bridge. Why destroy the London Bridge in Arizona or Millennium Bridge? Obviously other London and Paris bridges were more historically important like the Tower Bridge, Golden Gate Bridge, Verrazano Bridge, Westminster Bridge or Albert Bridge. Other bridges had more importance in London, Paris and U.S. and transported more people? Why select a tourist bridge? Why an obscure basically walking bridges?" Willie posed to the group.

Henry shook his head and immediately responded, "I saw an *Al Zagaheer* reference to the area around Lake Havasu that noted that General Patton used the Sonoran Desert area as a tactical training location for his tank brigades prior to being deployed to North Africa. Could the mastermind think that the area was the perfect place to begin to prepare for a new era of terrorists attacks?
Does Lake Havasu symbolically represent the strong relationship of two allies? It looks like one great tactician mirroring the actions of another.

Ergo the London Bridge is a symbolic soft target located in the U.S., perhaps because both the U.S. and UK worked hand in hand in the Iraq War. Bush and Blair started to stir up a hornets nest."

"Perhaps the outdated London Bridge pointed to the old British Empire and colonial domination. Perhaps the Millennium Bridge as the newest of London's bridges had something to do with the direction of the UK since the year 2000 when it became involved in supporting the U.S. in Iraq, and Afghanistan. The UK entered the war on terrorism that the Muslims see as a war against their religion and way of life." Craig took a marker and made two entries on the mind map.

Sean paused and contributed, "Interesting insight.....once the leader had cell chatter focusing on London the terrorist targeted the actual attack on the obscure Arizona target. The Brits then breathed a welcome sigh of relief as suddenly more important U.S. targets including San Francisco, Los Angeles and Scottsdale conference were hit maintaining the focus on the U.S."

"The United States had all their intelligence and law enforcement resources focused on the coordinated attacks in major California cities and really dropped the attack in Lake Havasu, Arizona as being relatively insignificant. Then to add insult to injury they attacked the OEM and Homeland Security conference back in Arizona, perhaps their real hard target all along. The implication being that you cannot protect little towns nor the U.S. top security and emergency response officials on homeland soil. Thus taking terrorism to a new level on U.S. soil. The terrorists have us by the nuts. I bet the attacks seem to be leading up to more important harder targets."

Sarah noted, "Krishna has a point. Just when the FBI focuses on the more serious domestic U.S. attacks, the terrorist leader moves the focus away again to attack Spain, France and the United Kingdom. Each allies in the war on terror."

Harold gets out of his chair and walks to the white board, "Assuming that there is a pattern of more serious attacks after having started with the low priority bridges and art museums, to hard targets like the Homeland Security conference. The EU countries and the U.S. are now focusing on protecting other more important bridges and art museums, while fearing what might be the next higher priority European target. Logically the terrorist leader might be setting up another change of focus perhaps logically back in the U.S. The leader is playing a game of chess, taking minor pawns while his real targets are of much higher value." Harold took a marker and corrected two spelling errors.

Sam looked wide-eyed at the whiteboard and quietly added, "I had a thought that supports your idea that the terrorist leader was leaving a clue about setting up another higher level attack in the U.S. The Paris bridges that were attacked are interesting in themselves. The Pont Royale is near the heart of the city and the Louvre Museum, which was not attacked. The Pont de Bir-Hakeim is at one end of a small island Ile aux Cygnes while the Pont de Grenelle is at the other end of the island adjacent to the Statue de la Liberte. I think the terrorists were pointing directly back at the U.S."

"Why were art museums attacked? Almost all the museums contained modern Western Art. It seems to be more deliberate than just a cultural clash over modern art. The Tate Modern Museum stands out from the rest, as Helena Hassler was a high priority target unlike any of the other museums. Why was the Tate part of their attack? How does it fit into the terrorist strategy? What is there about the Tate that might help us understand the leaders' mind games? What is there about the most recent attacks that would leads to a hypothesis about where they would be potentially attacking next?" Willie rubbed his chin as he postulated a series of questions to the team.

Sarah immediately responded, "I think I can add something about the Tate Modern that you have not mentioned, or put on the board. While I visited my sister in London last summer, I learned that the Tate Modern is housed in an old coal burning power plant. The building was retrofitted from coal to oil and then decommissioned as England moved more and more to being reliant on nuclear power. The Tate Modern houses only modern art unlike the Tate Gallery that houses old Masters. Another interesting clue left by the terrorists is that the terrorist hit the Xanadu Gallery in San Francisco. I once visited the small little gallery. It was a unique prototype designed by Frank Lloyd Wright in 1948. The gallery was Wright's physical prototype, or proof of concept for the circular ramp built in full scale at the Solomon R. Guggenheim Museum in New York City. The attack against the Xanadu Gallery was like another "breadcrumb clue" forewarning about the terrorist Bilbao attack against the Guggenheim Museum. The Guggenheim family were involved in mining, smelting, investing in power plants, and transportation. We will need to keep that in mind. The Pompidou Museum was named after George Pompidou, President of France in the sixties bring France into the nuclear age. Perhaps that is another clue about a future attack against political leaders."

"Ah, beauty, body and brains. Don't you just love the combination Jake?" Craig quipped with a chuckle. The entire team laughed.

Jake, grins, "Sarah has it all. She isn't number one in all her classes and likely valedictorian for nothing. She puts the rest of us nerds to shame."

"Sam and Sarah, I think you've hit upon something and put us on a new track of thinking. The Lake Havasu City's London Bridge was a clue pointing to the Bilbao, Paris and London Millennium Bridges. That bridge was a clue pointing directly to the Tate Modern. The Tate Modern is a clue more than likely pointed at nuclear power plants. The Paris bridges point back to the U.S. I'd guess probably power plants back here in the U.S. and in Europe. What power plants in the US and Europe would hold the greatest interests for terrorist?" Sean draws a series of arrows and numbers them before continuing. "Logically the trend with the Tate was coal to oil to give way to nuclear. If our hypothesis is correct the trail of "breadcrumbs" leads us to reverting back to the U.S. with likely targets in energy, mining, transportation or aeronautics, which if we were correct in our assumptions would be followed by a more serious attack in like areas in Europe. My intuition points to nuclear. Why steal nuclear materials for a dirty bomb that affect small areas when you have nuclear facilities that are far more dangerous and have a larger potential for wide spread public panic."

"That would naturally agree with the premise as a nuclear scientist, but on that thought, there are currently one hundred and three nuclear power plants in the U.S. alone." DeJesus stated, "How can we narrow that list down to likely targets for the next level attacks?"

"That does not include the other thirty-seven reactors that are not used to generate power nor areas storing vast amounts of nuclear waste that can taint water supplies." Sarah took a drink from her aluminum water bottle.

"I'd guess they would be more interested in a nuclear facility and probably a big or important one." Willie began writing on the only available space on the whiteboard. Within minutes he had produced a listing of the ten biggest nuclear power facilities beginning with Palo Verde in Phoenix Arizona, Three Mile Island, Waterford 3, Wolf Creek 1, and South Texas, etc." Craig stopped when he had listed the top ten based on operational year, and exact generation of millions of megawatt hours, much to the astonishment of the team.

"What nuclear power plant would have the greatest effect on the U.S. if it were to shut down or worse went into meltdown?" Sean asked.

Craig circled Palo Verde as his number 1. "I bet Palo Verde because the three reactors were on the same facility. The loss of power would hit Arizona and Southern California, and the potential of a radioactive cloud would spread across the U.S. due to prevailing winds."

DeJesus jumped into the discussion, "I disagree, it depends on whether you are considering the lack of power to large populations, in which case Connecticut with 51% of their power being nuclear for most of New York City. I would go with the Connecticut Yankee facility. Second, South Carolina is the state with the largest number of reactors. But on second thought my money would be on Palo Verde because it is the biggest generating facility and gives power to the power grid of two states, impacting Southern California the hardest. If you are looking for radioactive waste Arizona has over 359 areas that store or are contaminated by nuclear materials. The fact that most Americans know is that nuclear reactors produce enormous amounts of power, but fail to understand that in producing energy the reactors spent fuel also create radioactive waste by-products that are quickly becoming a curse that may eventually end civilization, as we know it. If a plant melts down like Chernobyl, people will be dealing with a real "Simpson's" issue for thousands of years."

"Simpson's really!" Sean laughed out loud. "Okay DeJesus, you can get off your glowing soapbox. We are well beyond a full understanding of the spent fuel issue. I think we have a viable line of thinking and plausible hints as to the next targets. We've hit on why it is so critical that we complete the final beta testing of our redundancy system and eventually install the system in other facilities. So lets hit it! The Force-on-Force is coming up on Sunday."

While the group disbursed, some headed to their computers and reviewed the data of their latest transmission, Sean pondered what had just transpired. He thought that it might be worth a call to Dr. Gibson, Office of National Nuclear Security in Washington, DC. Initially he thought she might like to hear the nature of the Cal-Tech team's newest hypothesis and thinking. However after a minute he thought she would probably not give much credence to the musings of his team of students, despite their incredible talent. Surely the FBI or CIA had puzzled over the same factual data and reached their own connections, hypothesis and conclusion.

Sean took a few minutes to call Kathryn. He was hoping to catch her as she finished with her classes for the day and began working on her dissertation in some remote office in the Edmund A. Walsh School of Foreign Service, Intercultural Center. He missed her and wanted to catch her before heading back to work.

Kathryn answered on the second ring.

"Hi Kathryn, how is my favorite grad student TA doing today?"

"Fine, it is nice to know that I fall into being one of your favorites among the throng of Cal-Tech grad students." She paused to hear if there was a reaction. "I'm just trying to spend a bit of the pittance I get for being a TA on a new California outfit and heading to a late lunch. Oh my God, it is time for an early dinner. I'm with Ellen, a doctoral candidate friend, shopping at the Shops at Georgetown Park and pondering going out for a salad at the Bean Counter on Wisconsin Avenue. What are you and your team up to?"

"Well frankly we completed the prep work for our force-on-force beta testing on Sunday about an hour ago. So the team decided on playing one of our mind game exercises dealing with the recent terrorist attacks in the U.S. and Europe. We developed some interesting connections and hypothesis about the terrorist organization and potential next targets." Sean spent the next 20 minutes going over the team's collaborated collection of data, observations, analysis and conclusions.

Kathryn listened intently. "Sean, I think you have something there. Have you shared it with Grace?"

"No I thought she might think it was aspects of the attacks that the FBI, CIA or NSA already had considered and projecting."

"You might be right, but I will let it slip out when I see her on Monday. She is away in Rhode Island working with a regional security team for the New England nuclear plants." Pausing for a moment as she reflected on their relationship. "I miss you and cannot wait to see you again. I am afraid that you are working too hard and some of those nerdy Cal-Tech coeds will get you in their analytical nerdy clutches."

The inference caused an outburst of laughter from Sean and Kathryn, as the reality was that less than 700 women and 1500 males on campus were so intensely involved in their studies and research that relationships on campus were extremely rare, but did happen on occasion working closely on projects.

"I will defend myself by beating them off with my laptop.' They laughed, Sean continued. "I will call later so we can FaceTime about 10 p.m. your time tonight. I miss you and wish we could be together more often. I cannot wait until you arrive tomorrow. It seems like we have not seen each other in months."

"I know, but absence makes the heart grow fonder. I cannot believe I just said that. It is a cliché that Grace uses from time to time." Kathryn laughed.

"I have got to get back to the team. Left alone they probably have figured out the name, phone number and location of the terrorist ring leader and his next five targets."

"I miss you too, but tomorrow we will be together. I'll text you if my flight is delayed, and as I deplane. I look forward to meeting you at the baggage claim area. I think your team may have unraveled something here. Take care until later tonight, I have a Cobb salad that is calling my name!"

They said their goodbyes quickly.

After the final intense meeting confirming that the system was on track for the Beta testing late on Sunday, the team went their separate ways planning to reassemble for their final van trip at 4:00 a.m. on Saturday for the final system review before the force on force test.

Chapter 48: Expert Reports on Terrorists Attacks

Friday, November 22, 8:00 p.m. AST (UTC /GMT +2)
Al Zagaheer Television Studio 1, Doha, Qatar

"Good Evening, This is Nuru Monaga reporting from our *Al Zagaheer* studios in Doha, Qatar. We have a special guest, Clinton Myers, the former British Director of the Secret Intelligence Service Counter-Terrorism Section online."

"Clinton, thank you for agreeing to appear on our special terrorism segment."

"It is my pleasure Nuru."

"What patterns do you see in the number of recent terrorists attacks in Europe and the United States since August?"

"The recent terrorist attacks in the United States, Spain, France and United Kingdom appear to be the work of several well-equipped teams or cells coordinated by an unknown terrorist organization and leader. They have demonstrated capabilities that are well beyond those of known organizations like al-Qaeda or ISIS. My anonymous UK intelligence source reported that UK immigration authorities revealed that the terrorists eliminated in the Tate Museum attack entered the country using high quality fake identity passports and from different points of entry over a period of five years. Interpol had conducted a search of their enormous database using the terrorist fingerprints and DNA to identify their entry points and country of origin. The attacks have resulted in authorities in all four countries significantly increasing security on all points of entry. Considering that Europe has open borders there is little immigration data except at airports and border crossings into the UK from other European countries.

Those same countries are increasing security of government buildings, national monuments and other high priority facilities, bridges and now protecting huge number of art museums."

"Do the anti-terrorism authorities have any indication of the group responsible or the country supporting the attacks?"

"My sources have not shared that information with me, but I assume that to date there are no solid leads back to the group, leadership or country of origin supporting the attacks. I feel that we are just touching the tip of the terrorist iceberg. I think more violent attacks on higher priority targets are inevitable. It is a slippery slope as intelligence agencies efforts to clamp down on radical Islamic extremist gives non-radicalized Muslims a reason to react and support terrorism. There will probably be more attacks on higher priority hard targets until the organization cells and leadership are neutralized. But as we play the waiting game, it appears that time is on the side of the terrorist. They set the rules and timetable."

"Thanks Clinton for sharing your expertise. It still seems unbelievable that the terrorists are masterfully avoiding detection and are capable of such brazen attacks against the U.S. and her European allies. "

The next full hour of the special report focused on video footage from each of the attacks, followed by reports from correspondents reviewing the extraordinary security at the Golden Gate, Tower, and Verrazano Narrows Bridges. "This is Al Zaga the number one news source in the Middle East."

Immediately after the sign off, a drug company commercial followed the report featuring a father reading a nighttime story to his children and turning out the light.

Chapter 49: The Preliminary Beta Test Verification Trip

Friday November 22, 4:00 a.m. MST (UTC/GMT-7)
Palo Verde Nuclear Facility, Wintersburg, Tonopah, Arizona, USA

The weekend prior to Thanksgiving, Sean and half of the Cal-Tech team gathered at 3:45 a.m. so they could escape the weekend LA traffic and travel in the cool of the early morning. The final trip to Tonopah, Arizona was to demonstrate the redundancy systems effectiveness during the ultimate Beta testing during the facilities Force-on–Force internal security exercise. Sean dove alone in his new jeep and led the team van. They had booked seven rooms in the Holiday Inn Express in Avondale, AZ about thirty miles east of the Palo Verde nuclear facility. The other half of the team remained on campus to monitor the sensor data from all three reactors and the quality of the satellite linkups with NNS, Homeland Security and NSA.

The Cal-Tech team's numerous installation trips on the facility was kept top secret and known only by Dr. Lawrence Grant, Daniel Hoppe and a small group of three night security captains and the operations managers for each of the three reactors control rooms. Sean and the Cal-Tech team were confident that the Beta testing verification of the redundancy system in all three reactors would get NNS approval for full system installation in the remaining U.S. facilities pending Congressional appropriations. If successful funded perhaps provide like access to nuclear facilities worldwide.

The usual extremely summer hot day temperatures exceeding 119-degrees and cool 92-degree nights on the Palo Verde facility had been a real physical test for the Cal-Tech team during the installation phase.

They were looking forward to experiencing the much cooler 75-degree day and 39-degree night on their Palo Verde force-on-force test visit. Following the test there would be several follow-up meetings with NNS in Washington and a summary meeting for the Palo Verde staff.

The team planned to add a rock-climbing outing to Sedona the following week after the Beta testing on Sunday evening. The outing would be their first outing after beginning the high paced NNS Redundancy System installation in May. The opportunity to climb would serve as a team celebration. Sean was excited about his new blue Jeep Wrangler Sports S Hard-Top with all the bells and whistles including a large metal lock box to store his climbing and camping equipment. He loved the rugged look of the Jeep. It would be perfect for their outing into the high desert wilderness and later during climbs in the Sierras Nevada Mountains.

Kathryn flew into Phoenix Sky Harbor on an American Airlines Flight 1826 out of Regan National Airport (DCA). She was anxious to spend a few days with Sean and explore aspects of his work as well as exploring parts of Northern Arizona. She was anxious to see Sean. Kathryn sent a text message to Sean at 12:32 p.m., while she exited the plane. It took her nearly twelve exasperating minutes before she took the escalator down to the packed Terminal 4 Baggage Claim area. Sean was at the entrance to the area waiting with open arms. After a long embrace and kiss they found the area where her flight's baggage was to be delivered. Sean picked up Kathryn's single black Samsonite bag and showed her to the elevator back up to the parking garage. He seemed excited as he rolled the bag in one hand and held Kathryn's hand in the other. She was surprised when Sean stopped in front of the blue Jeep Wrangler and gave her a kiss. Both smile at each other and wrapped their arms in a big hug. Kathryn pushed back looking at the jeep.

"Did you rent a Jeep?"

"No, I bought it as a sort of celebration gift on completing the Palo Verde project. We are going to use my jeep on its virgin climbing trip up to Sedona."

Kathryn loved kidding Sean, "I didn't think you would go the Sports Utility route. The jeep has such low gas mileage performance. You could have rented a real car or a mini-van. Then again you are not the mini van type of guy." She said laughing to herself and waiting for his response.

Sean retorted after reading Kathryn's eyes, "I was going for an American vehicle to disguise our liberalism in this Arizona's bastion of ultra–conservatives. We also needed a vehicle that could handle the Arizona and California outback. We can certainly have you rent your own vehicle if you like. I really don't think you are ready for a mini van either." Sean caught Kathryn in his arms and kissed her again more passionately. He relished the scent of her hair as he held her lifting her slight body a few inches off the ground. "I have been waiting too long to have you in my arms. I was waiting in the baggage claim area for nearly 45 minutes."

After a few minutes Kathryn pushed back looking into Sean's eyes. "Well the jeep will have to do if we are incognito liberals surrounded by Arizona's crazy politics fed by the initial conservative tradition of Barry Goldwater. Arizona has been leaping leaps and bounds to the Alt-Right due to reaction to the illegal immigration issue. I would not want us to end up in one of Sherriff Joe Arpaio's jail tents."

"Touché. Well played. Sherriff Joe still has his jail tents as a deterrent to illegals, criminals and perhaps the straying liberals." Sean helped stuff Kathryn's single bag atop climbing gear box in the back of the jeep. "Are you ready for some lunch? I know a great little restaurant in Buckeye that serves "real Mexican." That is not Tex-Mex or Cal-Mex. It is the real thing. I hope you like jalapeno peppers!"

Kathryn admitted that jalapenos were well beyond her ability to eat Mexican food then added. "Great let's get some grub partner. I am so famished I could eat a coyote." Kathryn tried her best to speak with a western drawl accent. Both laughed at the feeble attempt from an easterner.

"Ten minutes in Arizona and you are talking like a local. Next you will want me to get a gun rack, and rifles for the jeep."

Both laughed as they left the terminal and got on Rte. 51 North. It was a cool crisp early afternoon in Phoenix. Thirty minutes of driving through Phoenix's urban sprawl along Interstate 10 to the West, Sean pulled off on to AZ Rte. 86 and minutes later into Ramiro's parking lot. Kathryn and Sean had talked non-stop the entire way about a number of topics and their weekend plans. Sean was looking forward to introducing Kathryn to rock climbing on the famous red rocks of Sedona after the system tests. Kathryn was excited to get on real rock after practicing on the artificial rock-climbing walls at SportRock Climbing Center in Alexandria, VA.

During lunch discussion they underlined their mutual concern that nuclear power presented to society. Sean was vehement that steps like his system made nuclear facilities safer, but gave in on the fact that decommissioned nuclear facilities and the nuclear waste posed an environmental nightmare in growing parts of the world. Following lunch they explored the agriculture belt around Buckeye before heading back to Avondale to freshen up at the Holiday Inn Express.

Minutes after entering Sean's room they fell onto the king size bed. Their afternoon was the prelude to an evening of sex beyond their vivid erotic dreams. Neither understood how much they had missed the intimate physical contact. Initially Sean played the role of aggressor and Kathryn the willing submissive. During the course of their love making the roles reversed as the passion soared throughout the night.

Early Saturday morning they met the Cal-Tech team for breakfast at Tony's Cafe. Sean and Kathryn were the brunt of several joking comments about thin hotel walls and appearing to need some sleep. Sarah and Krishna had a humorous dialogue about the scorpions and snakes driving the rest of the team to tears of laughter. Sean carefully laid out the plan for an early dinner and 5:00 p.m., suggesting that everyone get a restful night of sleep as the *force-on-force* exercise and system Beta test would demand that everyone be fully focused and at their best.

Before dinner Kathryn asked to see the Palo Verdes facility during daylight hours, so Sean noted that they would run by the plant well before the team met for breakfast the next morning. That evening was like their first night together, except for Kathryn zonking out around 1 a.m. as her body was still on Eastern Time.

———

440

The following morning they took a 20-minute easy drive along Interstate 10 to Tonopah. The Sunday traffic on the main route to California was fairly sparse. The Wrangler's air conditioning was being tested for the first time as the temperature rose to 81 degrees. Unaccustomed to the heat, Kathryn fiddled with the control trying to get the AC system to work better before giving up and rolling down her window. The landscape was beautiful and expansive as miles of mountain behind endless desert scrub and rock underlined the expansive isolation of the area. Sean exited the highway at N 379th -road and headed south along South Wintersburg Rd. Kathryn had Sean stop at the Tippy-Top Bar and Grill, so she could use the restroom facility. Sean ordered two cans of Coors Lite and two bottles of ice-cold water. When Kathryn exited the Ladies room, she smiled and guzzled the bottle of water saving the beer for after her parched throat was fully sated. Sean smiled and ordered four more bottles of water and watched as Kathryn slowly savored her beer. The bar was a local dive with good food frequented by plant personnel, ranchers and local bikers.

"I kind of like this bar despite the inflated prices. There isn't another little restaurant within eight miles of the plant. I must warn you that you may find yourself in trouble if you let anyone overhear your liberal ideas."

"I had my suspicions after seeing the portraits of the Ronald and Nancy Reagan, George H and Barbara Bush, and George W and Laura Bush as the decorative touches of the interior design, amid the flags and items supporting our troops. Although I can see that the wall is missing a picture of Jeb Bush to complete the Bush dynasty. You do take me to the finest places." She laughed and finished her beer, and reached for another bottle of water.

"Let's hit the road we are getting pretty close to the facility and the shift changes in less than an hour at 3 p.m.."

Once back on the road Kathryn could see the Palo Verde facility cooling towers looming in the distance. She assumed that the facility was at the same intersection with the bar. Sean drove the final four miles towards the massive complex. Kathryn began talking about the incredible size and the toxic nature of the radioactive elements used in producing power at the facility. Sean centered his focus on the important role the facility played in powering most of the electrical grid for Southern California and Arizona. As they passed a massive lake, Sean explained the incredible balance needed for millions of gallons of water from the Colorado River to cool the reactors. A sizeable amount of the water was visible as steam vented skyward from each of the three cooling towers and the rest of the water was recycled into two separate ponds. A major issue of the plants desert location was the natural evaporation of water in both the intake lake and the recycling ponds. A major fear was the depleting of water from the Colorado River and the challenge caused in competition for every gallon with the huge agriculture belt in the Imperial Valley of California. The Colorado River water was over subscribed, which meant that eventually there would be huge lawsuits over water rights.

Kathryn was extremely quiet as Sean talked in detail about the facility. She was clearly shaken by something she had not expected or saw coming. Finally she spoke.

"I am afraid I'm having a weird reaction to the nuclear plant's incredible size and hazard to humanity. It is spooking me out. It is one thing to intellectually recognize the positive need for non-fossil fuel energy in modern society that mandated a nuclear facility. However my thoughts of death to huge populations from fallout, poisoning of the land or water near nuclear waste storage, and dealing with the half-life decay of nuclear waste are causing a freaking strange reaction. How could a civilized society build this monstrous plant so near a major city? Weren't there fears of what could happen if there was an accident?"

She had intellectually dealt with her aunt Grace on the nuclear concerns and efforts to make the form of energy safer over the years. Her aunt had assured her of the ability to produce safe nuclear energy, but seeing the monstrous Palo Verde plant this close was well beyond anything she expected. Her mind was acting on a very visceral level to the horrid realization of all her fears.

"Sean, you are going to hate me. I know this is going to be a shock and disappointment, but I just cannot stay here. I have got to get out of here, I mean out of the hotel in Avondale, out of Phoenix and Arizona. I know that it isn't rational, but I really cannot explain how much seeing my first nuclear facility is viscerally freaking the hell out of me. Can you drive me to the Phoenix airport?"

Sean knew that the reaction was relatively uncommon, but from time to time when someone saw a nuclear facility and was knowledgeable about the social and environmental issues the nuclear power presented, they became panic driven and fearful. But he was hoping beyond hope that Kathryn would understand on an intellectual level and be able to handle it given his lifelong passion.

"Kathryn, I fully understand the foundations of your fear. I have come across it with others over the years. I must admit that I am disappointed and wish you would stay, but understand your need to leave. We all have self-defined limits on what we can and cannot do. We can stop at the hotel and pick-up your bag and be at the airport by 4:30."

"Thanks for understanding. I wish I could stay, but I know that my mind is racing on a million issues caused by the nuclear program. Perhaps it was from watching 60 Minutes repeated coverage of the devastation caused by the Chernobyl disaster and the governments of the world cover it up to defer the extent of the impact on the Ukrainians and the environment."

Two hours later Kathryn departed on American Airlines Flt 1091 to Dallas and Flt 1581 to Washington DC. She deliberately took the red-eye to escape her fear. Intellectually she was upset with herself for what she knew was an unfounded fear, and ruining the weekend with Sean. She sent a text message to Sean from Dallas at 12:30 a.m., but knew he would be busy with preparing for the force-on-force exercise.

"I hope you can forgive me, and your final Beta testing goes well. Give my best to your team. Call me Monday. Love you." Kathryn was undergoing some serious self-examination hoping to determine the depths of her sudden aversion to the very sight of the Palo Verde facility.

Sunday November 24, 8:00 p.m. MDT (UTC/GMT-7)
Palo Verde Nuclear Facility, Tonopah, Arizona, USA
As in all the previous entries into Palo Verde, Sean and his Cal-Tech team appeared at the western most gate of the nuclear facility at exactly 6:00 p.m.. The entry was always under the cloak of secrecy to ensure that facility personnel were unaware of the installation of the redundancy system.

444

It had taken 25 minutes on Interstate Highway10 to reach the exit from their hotel. The six-mile drive in a van unequipped for driving off-road on an unimproved dirt road seemed to have taken what seemed like forever. In reality it was eight minutes of being jostled around as the van slipped and slide on the mixture of gravel and dirt for the final short six miles. Twice the van had nearly ended up in dry washes. Each time Sean wished that he were driving his more suitable jeep. Obviously the old construction road had fallen under disrepair even since their last trip a week earlier.

"Sarah, I wished we'd brought some ice cream and chocolate milk. This trip would have been better than a blender for making a great shake. You know like the real shakes at In-an-Out Burger." Jake liked to kid and tease Sarah as a form of fore play.

Sarah retorted, "Jake, is food all you are thinking about?"

"At least he isn't thinking about his weak kidneys. Doc, I need to stop and take a leak." DeJesus chimed in.

"Hey Trujillo, are those Coronas from last night getting to you? Craig Stevens added with a laugh.

"We'll stop for a minute. I think we are finally coming up on the security gate." Sean applied the brakes and the van rolled to a stop spraying some gravel.

Stretched before the van as far as the eye could see in the vast desert was a twelve-foot high fence. The top of the fence had three tiers of evil looking razorblade sharp barbed wire and periodic video security cameras. After five minutes, they spotted the locked gate. Signs on the gate and along the fence informed trespassers that it was highly electrified and of the $150,000 penalty for trespassing into the facility.

"Each time we pass this sign it gives me the willies." DeJesus commented, "Man, it looks like they don't want anyone except desert rats in this place. Do you think if I had pissed on the fence their entire electrical system will fail?"

"DeJesus, if you pissed on that fence the electrical current would have been conducted right up the stream of urine and fry your little thing." Craig never cut any slack for his close friend. Everyone in the van joined in laughing.

"What do you mean little thing? That would be one hell of a shocking experience. I would get a real jolt out of it." DeJesus laughed along with the rest of the team.

The gate was unguarded, but as with the entire facility it was under video surveillance. The video security system afforded the security command center the ability to watch the movements as small as a jack rabbit located in any direction four miles outside the facilities electrically charged chain linked barbed wire fences. The system also had a night vision capability so any animal with a body temperature signature warmer than a Gila monster popped up immediately on the detection system. The night vision system automatically directed the video system to that same signature. For the last 10 minutes the van has been on the monitor controlled by Hoppe, the Palo Verde Director of Security. Hoppe had mandated the covert entry into the facility as the only real way of keeping the team's presence under secretive wraps, despite the difficulty using the construction access.

As usual Sean pulled up to the gate not having to come to a complete halt as the remote control locking system disengaged the lock and the gate swung open. It was as if some unknown force was clearing the way for the Cal-Tech team. As the van entered the facility, the gate swung closed with a loud clang behind them.

"Well as usual someone inside must be okay with our entrance to their site. I guess I can put away my $150,000." Nodded Sara watching the locking mechanism secure itself again. "Sean does Kathryn know how often we have enter into the facility?"

"Yeah Doc, nuclear power plants are suppose to effect your fertility. Is she okay with your being here and career with nuclear materials?" Jake loved teasing to Sean too knowing full well that he enjoyed it.

Sean retorted half laughing, "Enough about that, I don't want you to be concerned about my fertility when radioactive materials are effecting all the males on the team. We'll know when your urine glows in the dark." Then Sean added "What you don't know is that Kathryn's Aunt is Dr. Grace Gibson the Director of National Nuclear Security for our entire project. Not only is Kathryn okay with this trip, her guardian aunt is an expert on the varied effects of radiation on fertility. She knows more than anyone else on the planet." Sean quickly reflected back on *Kathryn's spontaneous and weird reaction to seeing the facility...realizing that the reaction really threw him off a bit.*

Another fifteen minutes on slightly better security dirt road brought the Cal-Tech van to the remote building a quarter mile west of reactor #3. This was the location where they would be verifying the effectiveness of the redundancy system design during the *force-on-force* exercise for all three reactors. Sean knew that they needed to be ready to verify all aspects of the system for all three reactors during the force-on-force exercise. That meant getting their monitors and communications system up and going in the dark. The desert location was usually like a furnace. The cooler 47-degree night temperature would make it more comfortable for the team while testing his system. "I just hope the systems components just don't malfunction in the wide variance of desert heat and coolness."

Opening the van's sliding side-door, "Lets get the monitors and communications equipment up and running and complete a quick check with both the guys on campus and the NSA satellite link with NNS as fast as possible. I want to verify the presence of assigned NSA drones and their video feeds. We can take turns sitting in the heated van if anyone gets cold. Craig and DeJesus, you'll be monitoring reactor #1, Craig and Sara take #2, and Sam and I'll monitor #3. The earliest the exercise can start is after 10:15 p.m., so we should be fine for time."

Just then Hoppe pulled up in a desert tan Humvee with the plant logo on the doors. He walked over to the van, tapped on the dust covered driver side window. "Welcome back Dr. McMurray. I hope that using the back way into the facility wasn't too much of a problem on this trip. That road can be fairly tricky especially after an occasional rain creates washes and wipes out parts of the road. I had one of my captain's inspect the road yesterday to ensure it was okay for your last entry. At this point only seven of our personnel are aware of your work and secret entry into our facility. We did not want a majority of the personnel to know that you were here during our force-on-force exercise."

Sean responded, "The trip in wasn't a problem just wished we had better shock absorbers on the van. Does your staff ever do any maintenance on that cattle path you called the back road?"

"In fact there has not been much maintenance at all since the construction back in the 1980s. By the way our audio monitoring system was working great. I could hear your van conversations for the last hundred feet before you reached the fence.
It was a good thing one of your team didn't urinate on the fence or gate. The 1,000 volts would have knocked him on his ass."

Hoppe chuckled to himself, "I've got to get back to the security command post. Dr. Grant, my executive staff, control-room managers and I are the only personnel that know that you have been working on site. We'd like a full report on how your system worked after the exercise. When do you expect to schedule a debriefing?"

"I will have a complete report ready in less than a week. I'll make an appointment to go over every aspect of the system and how each reactor functioned during the exercise. If everything checks out as expected we can have a meeting of your key personnel to explain the numerous aspects of the system to make the facility safer."

"That will be great. Please call Dr. Grant's assistant Mary Tagger to set up an appointment when your report is complete." Hoppe hopped back in his vehicle.

"How will we get off site in the morning after packing up all our equipment?" Sean posed to Hoppe.

"The cloak of secrecy on the facility will end with the exercise. We'll let you and your team exit out the front gate for the first time. That is unless you would prefer the longer route the way you came." Hoppe laughed, "Good Luck during the exercise. I have to run. Grant and I will be awaiting the code to begin the force-on-force exercise. The force-on-force is incredibly important in keeping our security staff and operations personnel updated and sharp on repelling an external threat." With that Hoppe was gone as the Hummer left a trail of dust twenty feet in the air.

"Lets get moving team." Sean immediately refocused the team. "The sooner we are set up the sooner we are in the air conditioning. It is not going to get much cooler until after 9 p.m."

Chapter 50: Transitioning to Attack Mode
Sunday November 24, 10:00 a.m. PDT (UTC/GMT+8)
Imperial Valley, California

After months of preparation, Nassar Bin Hassan, Yassar's son in-law, the leader of *Tolem Series*, a second level terrorist cell, gathered members of his cell. The cell was scattered in migrant worker camps throughout the Imperial Valley of Southeastern California. Nassar and his cell were tired of eating dust and living in the dirty squatter poverty living conditions of the camps. His month of living in the luxury of the *Shura* headquarters had spoiled him and made him soft. As unprepared as he was for his critical new role, Nassar was fully dedicated to the success of his cell's mission of revenge.

Nearly two years earlier the cell underwent eleven months of extensively military training in a remote mining facility in the northern portion of Iran near Ashgabat prior to their individual departures for the United States. Their training included extensive lessons in both English and Spanish.

It had taken the cell seven additional months to enter the U.S. from Canada, Mexico, and still others flew directly into Los Angeles (LAX) on student visas. Months and millions had been spent on providing each member with expertly forged documents, social security cards, and drivers license. The cell members slowly moved individually to Southern California, where they were hired as migrant agricultural workers. Each was given two extensive cultural backgrounds to use as they assimilated into the Latino migrant subculture. They found that their skin color and command of Spanish was more than sufficient to blend into the picker camps. They were far better versed in English than their companion day laborers and acted as translators at times to gain the trust of their fellow workers. When not doing military training they hardened their calloused hands in the cotton and grain fields.

Nassar and the cell members of his *Tolem Series* had been working in thirty-seven different migrant labor camps throughout the Imperial Valley of California for over nineteen weeks. Migrant workers can easily get lost in the vast fields and poverty stricken camps located around the Salton Sea. Nassar's cell was spread across small rural communities including Brawley, Calexico, Calpatria, El Centro, Holtville, Imperial and Westmorland.

The massive farms were forever etched in Nassar's memory because the hot dessert was brought to life by the amazing irrigation projects. The mighty Colorado River was being drained to the point that not even a drop ever reached the delta area and the Sea of Cortez. But this too was being threatened by the extraordinary drought conditions and the use of water to cool the Palo Verdes nuclear plant. The area reminded him of the Arabian Peninsula without the massive sand dunes, wild camels and Bedouin nomads. The immigrant laborers in the camps came from Central and South America, and Philippines. It was relatively easy for his team from Indonesia, Malaysia, and Iran to blend in with the mixture of workers. The utter poverty and over-crowded living conditions were a common experience for his cell hiding in plain sight.

Each cell member had access by cell phone to the *Tolem Series*, Pinterest page to receive updates on their operation. The only thing that brought happiness to the cell members was their phone access to *Al Zagaheer* broadcasts and being able to monitor the success of other cell attacks. They knew that other cells would be attacking the enemy and that their time would come.

Nassar knew that the next few days were going to test his courage and leadership. His life was much more complicated since the cruise missile killed his family. He knew that his wife, Khadiija, and his four sons would have been proud of his leadership role in avenging their deaths regardless of the outcome. He hoped that with Allah's guiding hand the mission's success would make his cell heroes in the eyes of Muslims worldwide.

Nassar worked hard at keeping his men informed and motivated by roaming the vast fields of vegetables, carrot, melons and cotton and having short individual conversations. He used his cover as a visiting agricultural student from the University of California at Davis. This allowed him to roam freely from farm to farm. He had spent months studying the UC Davis campus map, faculty, courses, and web site. Posing as a student was relatively easy with his forged graduate student identification. He quickly found that asking questions about irrigation techniques, soil moisture levels, GMO seeds, pesticides and seed production consolidated his credibility among farm management staffs and owners.

At 10:00 a.m. *Tolem Series* met in a church parking lot in El Centro to boarded two busses for Arizona. Phoenix was barely four hours away, but their target was much closer. The busses loaded and departed from the parking lot without a problem. A church parking lot with an assortment of abandoned cars from all over the Imperial Valley would not raise any suspicions on Sunday after regular services. The dirty old, slightly damaged 1980s style buses at his command were typical of those used to transport migrant workers from farm to farm in the area and to other states. As planned the cell moved into Arizona under the cover of being a huge crew of migrant workers scheduled to work the massive cotton fields outside Buckeye, Arizona.

The busses traveled along the I-10 interstate into Arizona crossing at the Blythe border. The normal agricultural and INS inspection stations located near the border were closed from 12 – 1pm on Sundays. Weeks of observation of the inspection stations revealed that on Sundays the smaller staff closed the stations for lunch. As planned the busses flew through during the one-hour border closure window. At the Flying J Travel Plaza outside Ehrenberg, AZ the busses met Amir Hassam, Kaji Hassam's nephew. Hassam parked his massive semitrailer truck full of weapons behind *Tolem Series*'s busses.

Nassar greeted Amir his old friend. Jumping up on the running board of the truck cab, he smiled, "Amir, you are a sight for sore eyes. Allah must be blessing you. How have you been?"

'"Nassar it has been over nine years since we last had mint tea together. I am sorry to hear of the missile attack on the **al-Kindi** wedding and deaths of your beautiful wife and sons?"

"I'm still in mourning, after Khadiija and my sons were killed by the U.S. cruise. I miss them so much. My life will never be the same. My sons were my pride and joy." Tears filled his eyes as he wiping his eyes with his hand.

"I am so sorry. You must have a heavy heart filled with sorrow and anger. I heard of their deaths and knew your life would change."

"I will get an opportunity to avenge their deaths. Amir, I see you have started a new career as a truck driver. You are moving up in the world." Laughing as he spoke, "You look good behind the 18 wheeler. Have you brought us gifts from Allah?"

———

454

Amir paused a moment, "As planned you have everything that was on your shopping list and a few extra presents. Kaji worked hard at acquiring the weapons throughout the country. My truck is a fully equipped arsenal. You can see for yourself. Allah has been good to you, Nassar." Amir opens the rear of the semi trailer.

"Praise Allah, what do we have here?"

"Kaji was able to obtain three experimental Tomahawk cruise missiles and the necessary "green screen" launch system and three high intensity lasers from the U.S. Navy China Lake research facility to ensure your mission is successful."

"This is an amazing gift. I will be sure to mention it to my father in-law."

As most of the *Tolem Series* members used the restrooms and ate in the picnic area, the leadership backed the semi up to the rear doors and moved the automatic weapons into the busses. The group looked like the usual group of migrant laborers being moved into Arizona to help with the cotton harvest. Few travelers at the rest stop even noticed the group, in fact others deliberately avoided the shaded area that the cell occupied. During lunch Nassar and the four members of the *Tolem Series* leadership reviewed the updated detailed intelligence of the security at the Goodyear Airport and Palo Verde facility. After a long leisurely lunch the busses departed with the 2016 Peterbilt 389 truck duel-trailer arsenal less than a quarter mile behind. The small three vehicle caravan stopped for three hours at the Burnt Well Interstate 10 rest area 45 miles from their target to have the five teams run through their final preparations and to provide some rest time as there was a long night ahead and possibly days without sleep.

Their timing thus far had been perfect. They had to be at the Goodyear Arizona airport hangar slightly before 8:30 p.m. They would be in place well before the planned time. The Goodyear Airport was located 23 miles west of Phoenix. It was a Phoenix Municipal airport used for training commercial pilots from numerous international airlines and general aviation. Occasionally the Arizona Air National Guard used the facility for touch and go landings to maintain their military flight status. Numerous corporate jets occupied over half of the 17 hangers. Smaller general aircraft were parked on the tarmac and aircraft maintenance occupied two large hangers. The largest hanger #2 was the commercial pilot training center for Lufthansa Airlines.

Kaji Hassan and Amir had spent the past three years gathering important logistics and incredible intelligence critical for the *Tolem Series* mission. Amir observed the important details of the airport operations for months, and had served as a maintenance worker on the two Lufthansa A380 and Dreamliner aircrafts stored in their hanger. The Hassan's gathered details on the Palo Verde *force-on-force* annual security exercise from socializing with Palo Verde personnel and hacking into the security office computer. Amir provided all the intelligence to Yassar and Shura members via a "Go-To-Meeting" conference nearly a year earlier. Amir handed Nassar a detailed update on the intelligence for both the airport and the security exercise.

On Sunday evenings the Goodyear Airport facilities were relatively deserted after the general aviation terminal shutdown at 8:00 p.m. The facility had 24-hour air traffic control tower and flight operations for general aviation and corporate jets, but rarely were there any vehicles on the facility or aircraft flying on Sunday evenings.
After 9:00 p.m. there were normally two unarmed guards in separate white Ford 150 pickup trucks roving the huge 800 acres fenced aviation facility.

———

The trucks were clearly marked AIRPORT SECURITY with the Phoenix City seal on the doors and a pair of rotating yellow light beacons on the cab roof. This made the security vehicles easy to spot. The usual weekend security guards were two retired Phoenix police officers in their late 60s.

Sunday, November 24, 8:30 pm MST (GMT-7)
Goodyear Airport Hanger/Facility, Avondale, Arizona
As in the past ten years, Palo Verde security had rented the Lufthansa hangar #2 and had informed the airport management of the use of the hanger, arrival of numerous vehicles and busses on Sunday evening. As in the past Palo Verde paid overtime to two security team officers to provide additional security for the airport. One additional guard was in another roving pick-up truck and the other stationed at the electronic gate adjacent to the Lufthansa hanger #2.

At 8:00 p.m. the cell's busses were within ¼ of a mile of the airport, they pulled over into a side road. Nassar had the eight-man Alpha team do visual reconnaissance on the airport facility. They quickly located the three white security pickup trucks by their rotating yellow beacons and the sole security guard at the electronic gate. The three security pickups were well spaced around the airport facility, so it was easy for the Alpha team to use a silenced *Longsword Whisperhead **SERSR*** riffle to eliminate the guard posted at the electronic gate. Amir had provided the four-digit code for the electronic main gate outside hanger #2. Alpha team, dressed in the uniforms of the security guards, entered the gate, hid the security guard body in a dumpster, and one took up the guard's position at the gate.

Amir provided the five-digit security code for the keypad for the Lufthansa hanger side entrance and the Airbus A380 aircraft security codes permitting the terrorists to open the hanger and open the two locked aircraft within the hangers.

The busses entered the gate to the secure area near hanger #2. The Alpha team opened the hanger for Nassar and the rest of the cell. Within five minutes the entire cell and their equipment were within the hanger and their buses left the facility. Using Amir's intelligence, Nassar had the buses transport two Bravo team members to awaiting cars in Avondale, Arizona. The busses were abandoned at the Pilot Flying J truck stop. Bravo team picked up the bus drivers and left for their special mission.

Alpha team members waited for each security pickup truck to reach the corner adjacent to the hanger #2. When a truck approached they quickly stepped out of the shadows and shot the guard. Removing the dead guard, placing the body in the dumpster, and a terrorist replacement guard continued his route around the airport in his pickup truck. The second and third roving security guards were dispatched in the same manner. The tower and other people on the airport facility were none the wiser as the security trucks continued making their security check routes.

The terrorist plan was to neutralize the Palo Verdes Security off-duty staff when they arrived at the hanger and replace them with terrorists prior to their scheduled *Force-on-Force* exercise at the Palo Verde nuclear facility. The exercise scheduled once per year required all off-duty security personnel to participate in an organized attack on the facility while the on-duty security force repelled the staged attack. The normal objective of the exercise was to make the exercise attack as real as possible using sophisticated paint guns. The drill permitted the administration and NNS to evaluate the security system, on-duty security staff response, detection systems, counter attack strategy and ability to repel a real attack. The exercise used a dumbed up computer facility that simulated an actual control room to make the attack as real as possible.

Amir's intelligence indicated that in all the past exercises Palo Verde had arranged the use of the large Lufthansa hanger as a mustering place for their security exercise. The Palo Verde off-duty security officers had always reported to the Goodyear Airport hanger #2 for a briefing on the exercise, including tactics and their role as simulated terrorists attempting to make the drill as real as possible. The off-duty security force met to distribute their paintball equipment and organize their teams for the simulated attack. Depending on the scope of the exercise the drill normally was finished by 1:00 am. The off-duty security force members were given an incentive of being paid time and a half for participating in the exercise.

The *Tolem Series* cell was fully aware that the Goodyear Airport was one of the Phoenix area facilities where two of the *al-Qaeda* terrorists received flight-training lessons in preparing for the 9/11 attacks on the Twin Towers and the Pentagon. Once inside the hanger Nassar and the Tolem cell conducted a brief ceremony to honor and thank the two 9/11 *al-Qaeda* terrorists that trained at the Goodyear flight school facility and ultimately gave up their lives for their Muslim cause.

Nassar ordered Charlie team of four cell members to remain inside the A380 aircraft. The other A380 aircraft would play a part in the terrorists escape plan. Once opened, the large aircraft would be used to keep the off-duty security force out of sight from those entering the hanger.

The next step was pretty simple, the cell waited for the arrival of the leaders of the off-duty security force. At exactly 9:00 p.m. the leadership members of the off-duty security force team leaders began showing up for their planning session for the scheduled force-on-force exercise. The very first to arrive was Captain Jeff Wilson, second in command of security at Palo Verde. He was responsible for organizing the entire force-on-force exercise and maintaining the readiness of the security force. Wilson was followed shortly by Ralph Jefferson, the materials officer bringing a 17 foot U-Haul rental truck full of paintball weapons, equipment, helmets and flight suits. Five minutes later three lieutenants and six sergeants followed Jefferson, entering the side door to the hanger.

As each of the leaders entered the hanger four armed terrorists quickly bound them with plastic restraining zip ties around their wrist, removed their cell phones, car keys and took them to the A380 where they were seated and quickly executed. Wilson and Jefferson were taken to the Lufthansa office. Two heavily armed terrorists of Delta team held Jeff Wilson and Jefferson out of sight in the flight office. Nassar had a critical role for Wilson to play that was crucial in the success of the cell's mission. The same process was used as each of the security force entered the hanger.

Once a Palo Verde security guard was securely seated in the Airbus, cell members used silenced Glocks to efficiently slaughter them in their seat. The terrorists worked efficiently as teams ensured that each of the 125-man off-duty security team faced the same horrible death. At 10:20 p.m. after the final off-duty security team member had been eliminated, the terrorist retrieved the Palo Verde exercise materials from the U-Haul truck. Amid Rabanni, third in command of the cell, ordered the teams to don Kevlar NIJ Level IIIa vests, paintball flight suits and paintball helmets.

The cell looked exactly like the simulated off-duty security force as they waited until 10:30 p.m. for the arrival of the three Palo Verde busses scheduled to transport the off-duty security team to the *force-on-force* drill. The *Tolem Series* plan was simply to replicate the exercise attack mirroring those of previous *force-on-force* exercises, but using real silenced automatic weapons. The real attack under the guise of the exercise would give the cell the edge of time necessary in taking over the largest nuclear facility in the United States.

Chapter 51: *Tolem Series* Attack Palo Verde
Sunday, November 24, 10:30 p.m. MST (UTC/GMT-7)
Goodyear Airport, Litchfield Rd, Goodyear, AZ

Shortly before 10:30 p.m., three busses assigned to transport a large portion of the off-duty security force to their force-on-force exercise arrived at the fence outside the Lufthansa hanger. A member of Alpha team playing the role of security guard gave the bus access through the gate. Another Alpha team member dressed in the paintball suit and helmet entered each bus and asked the driver to come into the hanger for a quick briefing. The drivers needed to review the *force-on-force* exercise plan for the bus approaches to the Palo Verde facility. Four members of Echo team of the *Tolem Series* cell quickly captured and immediately executed the three bus drivers just inside the side door of the hanger. The short burst of silenced Glock bullets ripped through the drivers slaughtering the last element of the exercise to arrive.

As planned the stage was set marking the final piece for *Tolem Series's* assault. Nassar carefully followed the exact timetable established for the mission. He waited patiently in the flight office for a cell phone call from Bravo team. The cell phone came to life with a FaceTime alert. He answered the call and spoke softly into his phone.

I assume أفـترض أن كل شـيء عـلى ما يرام. ", Nassar, that everything is as planned."

A Bravo team voice responded outside of the frame of the camera's range, The ".مم ها ، يرام ما عـلى شـيء كل" camera focused on a woman and three emotionally upset and crying young children gagged and tied. The forty-one year old mother attempted to console them while her eyes betrayed her own incredible fear as two silenced Glock weapons were in the picture pointed at her head and at the oldest child..

Nassar hands his phone to Jeff Wilson. Within a split second Jeff recognized the familiar setting of his heavily soundproof insulated game and media room, but more importantly the horror his family faced at the hands of the terrorists. It was one thing to be in the hands of the terrorists, but seeing his family facing the same horror was far worse. A wave of panic crept into his very being and he began to physically tremble.

"Your family is extremely frightened for their lives. They are anxious about their survival and panicked at being held at gunpoint by strangers. Look at the eyes of your loved ones." Jeff saw the mask of fear in the face of each child and his wife. "Jeff their fate is in your hands." Nassar seemed to enjoy controlling this situation. "All you have to do is call Dr. Grant and give the code to set the force-on-force exercise in motion. If you comply I can guarantee that your family will not be harmed and will be set free within the hour. I would hate to have them tortured and slaughtered before your very eyes, if you decide not to cooperate. Their lives are totally in your hands."

Nasser's eyes focused on Jefferson the Materials Supply officer seated back on his knees adjacent to the desk. "I would hate to have you see them tortured and executed like this." Nassar pointed his silenced weapon at Jefferson and fired a shot into each of his knees. The soft muffled spit like sounds were less than a whisper, but the result was blood and tissue splattered against the floor and Jefferson's body collapsing on the floor as he screamed in excruciating pain. A few seconds later Nassar coolly pointed the Glock at Jefferson's head, the weapon spit twice putting him out of his misery. Death came instantly. Jeff Wilson knew that his family faced the same ugly fate. The terrorists had no qualms about torturing and killing his innocent family in cold blood.

Jeff knew that he had no options, if he wanted to see his family alive. He was under incredible duress as he thought about life threatening extortion. His body continued to tremble uncontrollably. He knew regrettably that he probably wouldn't survive nor his family, but he had no options if he hoped his family would be spared. He decided to force Nassar's hand. "I will initiate the required *force-on-force* code call, but only after my children are permitted to leave immediately. They can be sent to a neighbor's house. I want to watch Christine released immediately after the call." Wilson suggested this, knowing that they may never arrive at the neighbors, but he had to try something.

"Ah that seems reasonable Jeff. Place the call and your family will be safe. Now call Grant." Nassar smiled to himself, "A wise decision." Taking a moment, he added, "Set the children free and have the wife tell the kids to go to a neighbor's house." The team went through the motions of releasing the children and instructing the mother to send them to a neighbor's house. Christine cried as she hugged and kissed each child before instructing the kids to leave and go to the Sullivan house two doors down. The children ran crying as they disappeared out the game room door.

"Now make your call, or Christine will be forced to watch as I shoot each of your arms and legs and blow out your brains before ordering that she be tortured and executed."

Reassessing the few options, and despite knowing that he and his families lives were in danger, Jeff reluctantly placed the call on his company cell phone to Dr. Lawrence Grant's direct line.
As part of the exercise process he coded in the eight character alphanumeric secret code to activate the scheduled *Force-on-Force* drill as a text message.

The drill was initiated on the facility security office computers within seconds. This was the final step indicating that the off-duty security force was ready to commence the scheduled exercise and all was A-OK.

As part of Yassar's plan, he anticipated that the threat to Wilson's family would be successful in pressuring the use of the code to start the exercise. Two of the team had waited outside the family game room to quickly recaptured the children, took them into a powder room well away from the game room stairs and used plastic restraining cuffs and gags to ensure that they did not make a sound.

"You made the right decision for your family." As promised Nassar, spoke into the phone. "I want you to release the wife." Jeff watched relieved at seeing his wife hands freed. She blew Jeff a kiss and began walking out of the game room. Jeff called out, "Christine tell the kids that I will always love them. I love you." As planned Christine was recaptured, bound and heavily sedated in the powder room as Bravo team raced to their vehicle and headed off to Palo Verde.

"You may join the rest of your security force in the A380." As Wilson turned to leave the office, Nassar quickly pointed his silenced Glock and placed a bullet through the back of Wilson's head. Wilson's body fell in a bloody heap next to Jefferson as Nassar walked around the blood splatter. Nassar spoke out loud without anyone in hearing distance, "I should have killed his family in revenge, but knowing that they will suffer without their husband and father is the start of my personal revenge for the loss of my family."

Sunday, November 24, 11:00 p.m. MST (UTC/GMT-7)
Palo Verde Nuclear Facility, Tonopah, Arizona
Dr. Lawrence Grant, General Plant Manager of the Palo
Verde facility operations, and Daniel Hoppe, Security
Director were seated in the Security Command Center.
Three other security Captains were strategically located in
each of the three distinct reactor areas prepared to evaluate
the effectiveness of the counter terrorist measures employed
by the on-duty security staff. They did not know the basic
plan for the exercise's feigned attack, only that it would
occur sometime after 10:30 p.m. during this shift. Just prior
to 10:30 p.m. all the on duty security personnel were
inspected to ensure that they were equipped with paintball
weapons and headgear. The normal weapons were stored to
ensure that no one was accidently killed during the exercise.
At 10:31 p.m. Jeff Wilson's alphanumeric code was entered
remotely. Grant, Hoppe and the Captains were aware that the
drill was on as the Exercise Commencing flashed across their
computer and cell phone screens.

Tolem Series's cell spent nearly 15 minutes in the parking lot
using the car keys of the off-duty security teams to locate,
open the cars and organize into teams for the final assault.
The 20-mile trip from the Goodyear Airport to the Palo
Verde plant took nearly 29 minutes. The three buses split up
on Baseline Road to enter the nuclear facility from three
directions. The largest group of 15 vehicles followed Nassar
in bus #1 down Baseline Road to the 1 Entrance Gate and
reactor Unit 1.

The second bus with nuclear expert Rowel Nashbi turned on
West Southern Avenue to #4 Entrance Road and Gate and
reactor Unit 2, followed by ten vehicles. The third bus led by
Amid Rabanni followed the second bus, but turned to #5
Entrance Road and Gate to reactor Unit 3.

A convoy of ten vehicles followed the third bus. The massive semi two-trailer truck containing three Tomahawk cruise missiles, jury-rigged electronic launch system, and lasers followed the third bus closely. It had the critical assignment to deliver the missiles and a laser to each reactor area after the plant had been secured. The launch system capable of launching all three Tomahawks simultaneously would be located just outside Reactor #2.

The convoy was spotted on the plant security video system, "Here they come!" Hoppe yelled to the exercise evaluators over his secure walkie-talkie, after spotting one bus heading towards the #1 Entrance gate and another bus heading to #4 Entrance gate. Moments later the video system picked up the third bus heading to #5 Entrance gate. As in the past each bus led a convoy of between ten and fifteen cars that Hoppe instantly recognized from the security force parking lot. He actually enjoyed the annual exercise, but wished that it would end before 1 a.m.

The *force-on-force* exercise was always a highlight for the security force members. The exercise was a real break from the dull monotonous tedium and drudgery of day after day guarding a facility while baking in the hot Sonoran desert or cold desert nights. A short night of security games was one way of breaking the monotony keeping the force fresh and prepared for their duties. The on-duty staff had actually created a pool as to which reactor would be defended best and the maximum number of paintball hits on one of the off-duty staff. The fresh 11 p.m. shift of the on-duty security-force had detected the attackers well before a half-mile from reaching each of the gates.

The sensors and video systems worked perfectly. The various perimeter security gates and outpost reported to Daniel Hoppe that unauthorized personnel vehicles were approaching the facility, indicated the precise number, location and estimated speed of the vehicles.

Guards that were roaming the facility were ordered to their assigned post on the perimeter. The entry spikes and heavy reinforced steel barriers were deployed at each of the three gates. Automatically each control rooms and reactors doors were closed and locked down electronically as part of the normal security procedure once the *force-on-force* exercise was initiated from the security office and guardhouses. The facility went into complete lockdown. This was like playing a game just as it was in their past exercises.

Sean and the Cal-Tech team were excited to see the security exercise move into action on the facility video system. It was like watching an action movie on multiple screens. The NSA drones for the Beta testing, the NNS-Cal-Tech team monitoring systems, and the Palo Verde internal video systems gave a dynamic view of the exercise. It looked like it would be a paintball battle of epic proportions.

The facility was in a complete lockdown mode, but Nassar laughed to himself knowing that he could circumvent the seemingly elaborate security measures. The facilities security design for the door lock-down system had been purchased by Kaji from a disgruntled security company employee for a mere $3,000, and a method to circumvent the system cost an additional $2,000. The obvious greed of the disadvantaged would ultimately be the key to the success of the Tolem's mission.

Nassar was in the lead bus as it hit 65 miles per hour. He knew that the convoy was spotted on the facilities long-range sensors and video system a half-mile before they reached the gates. The inert tire spike system and reinforced steel barriers would be activated by the time the bus was within a quarter mile of the gate.

Each of the security procedures had been fully anticipated in Yassar's original plan of attack, thanks to the intelligence work of Kaji. The buses in the exercise would have stopped before hitting the imbedded tire spikes to deploy paintball fighters. At the last minute each bus swerved, crossed a small ditches hitting the electrified fence at full speed. All the terrorists inside the bus were careful not to be touching any metal as the electrical sparks flew outside the bus. The perimeter fences tore way as if made of tin foil. The forced entry about thirty feet past the guardhouse gates allowed the bus and other vehicles to enter the fenced perimeter avoiding the initial perimeter defenses. The spikes and steel barriers were useless in this new exercise approach. The buses slowed slightly maneuvering around to get back on their entry roads before it continued on their way. All three security gates were circumvented and breached in the same manner.

"Here is where the attack becomes very real", Nassar shouted to the bus driver.

Several Palo Verde uniformed security guards appeared with paint guns blazing opening fire at the busses and following vehicles. The security guards were using paintball weapons and the *Tolem* terrorist teams using special silenced weapons that were similar to the most sophisticated *US Army 50 Cal Stormer* paintball weapon. The real silenced weapons sounded like those fired from paintball guns on the video systems. The invading terrorists wore paintball helmets and the usual paintball gear over Kevlar vest to further convince the on-duty security staff that it was just an exercise. Everyone knew that in a real attack the guards would open fire with real weapons and using RPG (rocket propelled grenades) to stop the busses and vehicles. It looked like a short battle from the view provided by the drones above.

Hoppe and Grant applauded Wilson's innovative approach adding reality to test the facility security. Hoppe turned to Grant, "I know, I know the cost of repairing the damages to the fence and electrical system comes out of my security budget."

Behind that bus were nine privately owned vehicles and the semi-trailer truck carrying the cruise missiles and laser units. The other vehicles stopped less than 15 feet from the barriers. The vehicles within the facility split up and moved to assigned buildings and locations on the massive facility. One car stopped at each gate as some of the passengers emerged with their real weapons drawn. In a burst of real silenced automatic weapon fire, they dropped the uniformed on-duty security guard's lifeless bodies onto the pavement. *Tolem Series* Echo team members quickly took positions within the three perimeter guardhouses keeping the engaged spike and steel barriers. Thus creating a new security perimeter for the terrorists. The terrorists continued along the three roads to support the speeding busses and initial wave of vehicles.

Each vehicle contained a team with a specific target building within the huge complex. The roads to each of the reactors had three security checkpoints with guards normally armed with automatic weapons, RPG weapons and grenades. The paintball gun armed guards were no match for the wave of armed terrorists. The sheer number of terrorists and their expert snipers quickly nullified the checkpoints. The reactor towers and control rooms loomed in the distance more than a quarter-mile ahead. Each twenty story high tower emitting white steam was a majestic sight in the relatively flat desert landscape lit by moonlight. Observing the exercise using the facility video monitor system, it took slightly less than three minutes to finally fully recognize the real terrorist attack, Daniel Hoppe declared a "*Code Red*", but that short delay before the on-duty security were allowed to retrieve their real weapons caused the real battle to be over before it started.

Over the facility loudspeaker system came the chilling announcement, "This is Hoppe, those are not our exercise force involved in the *force-on-force* exercise!" Hoppe shouted into the walkie-talkie and facility microphone. "Abort the *force-on-force* exercise. This is a real attack. Lock and load live ammo. I repeat this is not our *force-on-force* exercise. It is real. Lock and load live ammo!"

The three busses continued on to assigned control rooms for reactor Units #1, #2 and #3. Frouk Gahi, the *Tolem Series*'s electronics expert used the system plans to quickly reach a secured control panel, and short out the entire lockdown system. His time had improved since dry runs during training in Iran. Ten minutes later Frouk remotely opened all of the reactor control room security doors. *Tolem Series*'s cell donned gas masks as they began their sweep of each building. They entered each building fully anticipating the next level of security measures, the deployment of massive tear gas canisters. Clearly the advanced intelligence information and immense training in Iran had the team well prepared for each phase of their attack and anticipated defensive responses and counter measures. Three terrorist teams headed to specific security locations anticipating the deployment of the three armored vehicles from their security garages. As the automatic doors of the garages opened, each armor vehicle was hit with multiple rocket propelled RPG rounds. Once the vehicles were disabled team members opened the vehicles to ensure that the security guards within were dead. Within twenty minutes the terrorists had breached the perimeter and were well in command of the facility. They began a systematic search of each building, captured and restrained with plastic tie cuffs the personnel and moved them to three large locations.

Grant and Hoppe sat wide-eyed in the security center office watching the well-organized synchronized attack through the internal security video system. In utter horror they watched as checkpoint by checkpoint was neutralized by the terrorist teams as they over ran the on-duty security force positions. Sporadic gunfire could be heard on the video system as guards opened fire on terrorists.

Hoppe couldn't help it when he turned to look directly at the general manager, "Grant you asshole, your recent security cuts to add to corporate profitability may cost hundreds of employee lives and give the nuclear facility control to these terrorist assholes." Grant did not respond, recognizing that indeed his frugality may have contributed heavily to the success of the ongoing terrorist attack.

Grabbing his secure alert red phone, Hoppe called the National Nuclear Security Division of Homeland Security. Dreading the nature of placing the call, Hoppe knew he had no alternative, but to declare a security breach emergency and hope help could arrive within the next few hours. "This is not a *force-on force* exercise Palo Verde 1-2-3 is under a Code Red attack. Code Red. This is Security Director Hoppe we have terrorists in control of portions of our nuclear facility."

Immediately there was a response, "This is Al Dalton, at NNS. Hub Nolan of NSA and I have been monitoring your situation as part of the redundancy system Beta testing here and at NSA. We have received and verified your voiceprint Mr. Hoppe. Please remain on the line as we verify your location within the facility. We are aware of the attack and have been estimating the force size, weapons and tactics of the terrorist attack force. Have you had any contact with their leader?"

Grant got on the line, "We need immediate military intervention or my staff will be slaughtered and the entire U.S. will more than likely be under a radioactive cloud unlike anything the world has ever seen. Think Chernobyl and multiply it eight times. We are in the Security Office within the administrative building with four of our security force securing the building. Terrorist teams have overrun a vast majority of our security force. Who knows how long we will be able to communicate with you as the terrorists are sweeping through our buildings."

"Dr. Grant, this is Hub Nolan of the NSA, we understand the dire situation for you and your staff, as well as the potential for a nuclear disaster. The President and the National Security Team have been alerted and will act prudently and decisively to resolve the situation."

The largest U.S. nuclear facility was falling into terrorist's control. *Tolem Series*'s team members would be doing their mop-up operation to clear up the last of the remaining isolated armed security forces for the next half-hour. Gradually each of the field leaders of *Tolem Series* reported in that they had secured assigned portions of the Reactor Unit #1, Unit #2, and Unit #3. The last *Tolem* objective was the security command center and facility's administrative offices that was located on the farthest northern portion of the huge plant complex. They knew that the U.S. FBI. NSA, military and other agencies would have been alerted of the attack and that chaos was underway in numerous federal agencies and military bases.

Within forty minutes the Palo Verde nuclear facility was 95% in terrorist hands and the 11:00-7:00 a.m. late shift personnel were detained in the auditorium and two large cafeteria facilities.

The facility personnel were bound with plastic zip restraining tie cuffs and had their cell phones and keys taken away. Thirteen personnel were able to contact their families or friends by cell phone about the facility take-over before being captured. The friends and family contacted the nearest law enforcement agencies. Both the Maricopa County Sherriff's Office (MCSO) and Arizona Sate Department of Public Safety (DPS) dispatched several units to the facilities outer perimeter. Law enforcement took positions about a half-mile from the facility perimeter to prevent any additional terrorist from entering the facility. Responding to the takeover was well beyond local and state law enforcement capabilities.

Unarmed Sean and the Cal-Tech team began to assess their personal position in the electrical transmission building at the far western part of the nuclear facility. Sean and the six on site members of the Cal-Tech team were shocked as they witness the helpless Palo Verde security force initially armed with paint guns being gunned down by real terrorists using automatic weapons. They watched helplessly as terrorist rounded up the remainder of the staff.

The team used the video feeds from 70% of the critical interior buildings to monitor the terrorist takeover and movement. As a happenstance, as part of the exercise, they had a visual of the exterior of the facilities from two NSA drones on station above the facility flying at 2,500 feet and their systems satellite hook-up with NSA Fort Meade, NNS facilities in Washington DC, and Cal-Tech team members in Pasadena, CA. It was critical that they fully understand the location of roving terrorists sweeping various buildings to ensure that they had all the Palo Verde personnel. Sean had DeJesus disabled the Palo Verde internal security video monitoring system to protect the team by putting the terrorists at a disadvantage.

Sean called Hub Nolan at NSA about two minutes before NSA was connected with Hoppe and NNS. Sean and the Cal-Tech team communicated within the facility using their encoded walkie-talkies. They understood the nuclear complex far better than the teams of terrorists and had the advantage of secretly being within the facility, certain that the terrorists and most of the facility personnel were unaware of their presence. They moved carefully using their video feeds to their advantage in remote areas of the facility after the terrorist had swept the building.

The short battle ended with the terrorists killing the last four security guards in the administrative building. Within seconds four terrorists shot the locks and burst into the security office capturing Dr. Grant and Hoppe. Minutes later Nassar made his entrance and sat with the two restrained facility leaders in the security office.

"I am going to put this in very simple terms." he explained, "The facility is an important pawn in a much larger game to get the U.S. and her allies to release Muslim detainees from Guantanamo Bay and other covert interrogation facilities throughout the world. If our demands are met within 24 hours and there are no military counter attacks, my team will leave the facility in tack. However to convince the President of our threat and serious demands we have strategically placed several devices capable of destroying each reactors five-foot thick containment system and causing the largest nuclear disaster in world history. As a sign that we will follow through with our threat we will televise the execution of four of your management personnel each hour until our demands are met. Do you understand?"

"My God, There is no need to execute any of my staff." Dr. Lawrence Grant was trying his best to remain calm and act professional. "I am sure President Reynolds and the National Security Team decision makers in Washington will meet your demands. Please reconsider resorting to any further unnecessary violence."

"I do not care about your infidel god, Dr. Grant get off you pompous ass and put me in touch with the President. We live in a violent world. It is just a reality that you and your people will need to accept. For years your drones and aircraft have rained hell upon millions of Muslins in varied parts of the world. It is your turn to experience the feeling of horror and watch as people you know and care about are slaughtered. In the meantime I want the facilities internal and external video systems restored immediately." Nassar had been listening to the nuances of Grants vocal tone, watching his facial expression, and body language. The signs were there that he valued his own life and would be easy to manipulate as part of negotiations.

Grant got on the phone and called the NNS number. "This is Dr. Lawrence Grant. Terrorists are in control of the Palo Verde nuclear facility. Their leader has requested to speak directly with President Reynolds. Please patch me through to the White House." The NNS Security Night Officer-In-Charge technologically confirmed Grant's voice, and said he would get the White House as requested for a direct line to the President.

In the meantime, Hoppe addressed the leader about the facility internal video system "I will need a few of our tech guys to trouble shoot the security video monitoring system. Can you have your guards bring Fred Gannon and Rich Facio to this office?" Hoppe appeared to have more self-control and seemed less intimidated by the armed terrorist within the office.

Three terrorists stood guard over Fred Gannon and Rich Fasio as they spent the next thirty-seven minutes unsuccessfully trouble shooting the internal security video system because as they fixed one thing the Cal-Tech team immediately caused another problem. Nassar was upset with their poor attempt to fix the system. He believed that it was a ploy on the part of Hoppe to waste time until some military units attempted to retake the facility.

"Hoppe, come with me." Nassar leads the way to the large auditorium. "Ladies and gentlemen, I have given Dr. Grant our demands and promised that I would execute four of your facility managers per hour until the demands are met." Five Alpha team members had already pulled four managers and ushered them to Nassar. "I do not make idol threats. As per my demands I deliver as stated. Drop to your knees." The four managers are forced to their knees and Hoppe was shoved to join them. Standing in front of the gathered personnel, Nassar grabbed an AR-15 from the nearest Alpha team member and shot the five managers without the slightest hesitation. The execution was video recorded and immediately posted to Facebook, and sent to CNN, BBC and *Al Zagaheer* from a confiscated cell phone. Next a recording was made of Nassar clearly stating his demands for the release of all Muslim captives and the threat that four Palo Verde personnel would be executed per hour until the demands were met was sent to the same worldwide media groups. If the demands were not met a series of explosions would destroy the containment systems on all three reactors and cause a nuclear disaster

Finally Nassar took a minute to make an entry on the *Tolem Series* book board on Pinterest. He entered "This is a very successful children's series."

The first moves of the second level attacks only proved the resolve of the terrorists and their ability to punish the infidels and destroyers of Muslim countries.

At the same time in Dubai......

Yassar's eyes beamed as he read and reread the posting on the *Tolem Series* board. "This is a very successful children's series." He knew that each individual act by each pawn cell and team created a constant element of uncertainty and fear within their enemy. They were stretching the enemy's manpower and resources. A relatively small force of well-trained pawns would ultimately weaken the American giant and their allies despite its' military strength, advanced technology resources and economic power. As a student of guerilla tactics, Yasser saw that quick tactical strikes, creating confusion, and striking low-level targets where they were unexpected, led to opportunities to attack much higher priority targets. Palo Verde was the first of such priority targets. *Tolem Series* was his first knight attacking swiftly and decisively.

"Well done Nassar. You have struck at the very heart of our enemy and avenged the slaughter of my daughter and grandchildren. I and your family honor you."

Back at Palo Verde.....

Nassar retreated to the Security Office phone and began the process of verifying the attempt to contact President Reynolds. Despite having practiced every aspect of the mission for months, the real call to the U.S. President was Nassar's most difficult task by far. President Reynolds and the Presidents before him were powerful men that had ordered drone and air attacks that murdered thousands over the years. Placing the call to a President was no easy task.

Chapter 52: The Horrified News and Reaction
Monday, November 25, 1:25 a.m. EDT (UTC/GMT-4)
NSA Headquarters, National Security Operations Center (NSOC), Fort Meade, Maryland, National Nuclear Security Offices, and White House Situation Room Washington, DC

Hub Nolan was trembling as the critical nature of the Palo Verde facility takeover struck home. Rarely does the flow of intelligence data from either the United States SIGINET System (USSS) or National SIGINT Watch Center (NSWC) shake an experienced NSA leader to the core. Hub was visibly shaken. Knowing that every minute was critical given the nature of the terrorist takeover, he reaches for the Red Alert Phone to contact the NSA Administrator serving as Night Duty Officer.

Hub, "Herb, this is beyond huge. We have confirmed from three sources that a well-armed terrorist force have taken control of the Palo Verde nuclear power plant west of Phoenix. The takeover was confirmed in a call from Dr. Lawrence Grant, Director and Daniel Hoppe, the Director of Palo Verde Security, skirmish images from our drone passing over the facility less than ten minutes ago, and confirmation from a Cal-Tech Team working on the new redundancy system within the facility. We need to enact our National Security protocols with the White House."

Herb Anderson couldn't believe his ears. In his twenty-seven years of executive level service in NSA, he had never felt shaken as his brain processed the critical nature of the terrorist potential nuclear threat. His throat was bone dry, and his mind raced as he replied, "Shit Hub, this is going to be a disaster of mega proportions, testing our patience and response protocols to the limit. I will contact the White House and Director Ford." The phone went silent as Herb hung up.

———

Hub decided to get as much information from the on site Cal-Tech team while they were still able to communicate in preparation for the onslaught of questions that were likely to come their way. He focused the NSA analysts on scanning their footage from the drone video hookups on site to provide oversight of the Cal-Tech Redundancy System Project in an attempt to estimate the size and locations of the terrorist force, estimates of types of weapons, deployed explosive devices, location of hostages and primary location of leaders.

Sean called NSA on his cell phone. Speaking quietly as not to be heard by any passing terrorists, he confirming with Hub that a large force of over sixty-armed terrorists had taken the facility during the force-on-force exercise. Some terrorists may have been eliminated in their skirmish with security, but the vast majority of the terrorists force remains, and are roaming the facility to ensure that they have captured all the personnel. His team was trying to get a more precise actual number of terrorists and documenting the locations and concentrations of terrorists.

A minute later Herb spoke with White House Security office. They had the staff wake-up President Reynolds and activated the National Counterterrorism Threat Center (NCTC), National Security Council (NSC), inform the Joint Chiefs, and inform the State Department Bureau of Counterterrorism of the nuclear plant take-over. All were headed to the White House Situation Room. Herb Anderson's call initiated the highly classified emergency assistance response protocols setting in motion a sequence of well-planned alerts to thirty-two federal agencies. The intelligence failures prior to 9/11 and poor responses had dictated newly developed new protocols, which had been altered and fine-tuned. The sophisticated protocols were specifically designed to improve communication between all intelligence, increase security and coordinate responses by agencies. Within six minutes all thirty-two agencies were online and utilizing a communication protocol, sharing information and developing various response resources. The nuclear situation would test the communications process and response effectiveness.

Dr. Gibson received a NNS alert call making her fully aware of the Palo Verde situation in her Omni Providence RI Hotel suite. Within minutes she was in direct communication with Sean's cell phone and the entire Cal-Tech team via her computer. Her primary questions were regarding the Cal-Tech team's safety, and the state of readiness of the redundancy system for each of the three reactors.

"Dr. Gibson, I have been in contact with Hub Nolan at NSA attempting to provide intelligence to assist in the planning of any response. My Cal-Tech team is safe at the moment, but armed terrorists forced all the facility personnel to assemble into three large locations making it easier for them to control.

We have the Beta form of the redundancy system fully deployed in each of the three reactor areas. That should give some valuable time to attempt to retake control of the facility as these fluid circumstances evolve. We have full access to our own video system, the feeds from drone above, and control the facilities interior and exterior video systems, which give us the advantage of knowing where terrorist team members are as they patrol the facility. We disabled the internal video system so the terrorists cannot use it to monitor any response. We may need to change our current location from time to time. I will call to inform you if and when we are repositioned."

At precisely 1:57 a.m. EST the White House operator received a call from Dr. Grant requesting to have the President speak with the terrorist leader within the Palo Verde nuclear facility. The operator stated that the President was aware of the situation and would be ready for the call within ten minutes.

Nassar was excited and energized by the early success of his cell's mission. At 11:30 a.m. MDT Nassar sat at the security office phone, "Operator, this is an urgent call from the Palo Verde nuclear power facility. I am the leader of the armed group that has taken over full control of the largest nuclear facility in the United States. I demand to speak directly with President Reynolds or the U.S. will face the largest nuclear disaster in history."

The operator had already spoken to Dr. Grant and was expecting the call. She had worked for fourteen years without facing any call that shook her nerves as much as Nassar's threatening statement. She attempted to mask her reaction, "I understand sir. I will pass your call on to Mr. O'Toole the President's Chief of Staff, please remain on the line."

Having knowledge of the attack on Palo Verde, Jerry O'Toole was prepared to give the appearance of remaining calm as he answered the terrorist call. A second later the call was picked up, "This is Jerry O'Toole, Chief of Staff, what is the nature of your call?" Jerry was trying hard to remain calm and make his voice sound as professional as possible despite a throbbing sensation in his heart and sweat covering his brow.

"I assume that the operator explained that my men hold control of the Palo Verde nuclear facility. I demand to speak directly to President Reynolds, or your country will live with the devastation and fallout of three nuclear reactors. I have just executed the Chief of Security and four others of the management team and will do so every hour until my demands are met. Now get the President on this line!" Nassar was trying to be calm and assertive.

"I understand the urgency of your call. President Reynolds is on his way to the situation room office. I need to have our White House security confirm that your call is originating from within the Palo Verde facility to validate the location of your call. Please remain online until the call is confirmed and President Reynolds takes the call."

Seven minutes earlier, President Reynolds had been sequestered in the White House Situation Room adjacent and part of the Command Bunker over 300 meters under the White House. Hub had discussed the high probability of the terrorist call with President Reynolds and key security advisors. They decided that it was in the best interest of the U.S. to take the call to fully understand what the terrorist demanded and get a sense of the terrorist leader. In fact the National Security Team, two members of the Joint Chiefs and President Reynolds were listening the Jerry O'Toole's call.

——

484

"This is President Reynolds, to whom am I speaking?"

Nassar was pleased that his demand was granted. "You may call me Abu Talib. I am the leader of a militia force that has taken over the Palo Verde nuclear facility. As such I am talking on my own behalf. I am going to make this very simple for you and your staff. After having already executed the first five facility managers, we will systematically execute four or more of the facility management personnel per hour, slaughter all 1000 plus facility personnel, and detonate multiple explosive devices in each of the three reactors releasing a nuclear cloud disaster on the United States unless our demands are met. Do you understand the serious nature of what may happen on my command?"

Reynolds had weathered a great deal in the past two years, but nothing that threatened the country at this level. His throat tightened just as he responded, "I can assure you that I am taking this situation extremely seriously. I do not want a nuclear disaster on my watch, and do not want to harm you or your force. I assure you that you have my full attention. Let's hear the details of your demands. But understand that as a policy, the United States does not negotiate with terrorists."

"Well you are going to make an exception or face a nuclear nightmare."

"I am listening."

"Good! We are off to a good start. Here are our demands: first, all 61 detainees in the Guantanamo Bay Delta Detention Center who are awaiting trial or in the interrogation process in other areas in the U.S. and abroad will be released by the U.S. and your allies within 24 hours. You need to arrange for a news team from *Al Zagaheer* to cover the Guantanamo Bay release on their TV network. We need to see the actual release. Second, but far more importantly we will trigger the nuclear disaster if there is any military response against the facility or any of my force. Finally, you will make secure arrangements for our departure from the facility after the first two demands are fully met and confirmed. The powerful lasers and multiple explosive devices capable of destroying the containment system within each reactor have two detonators. One I have in my hand and a second remote detonator that we will use if our escape is compromised. Is that understood?"

Reynolds was seated at the head of the massive Situation Room conference table in front of a huge screen showing the live drone view of the Palo Verde facility and the varied video systems feeds. As the terrorist leader spoke his voice was immediately recorded and analyzed by FBI voice recognition technology. The entire NST in the Command Bunker listened to the demands without taking a breath, fearing the worse a massive nuclear disaster, and working on scenarios of the most likely results of the nuclear event.

"You have made your demands extremely clear, Abu Talibi. I will arrange for the *Al Zagaheer* TV coverage of the detainees release. You and your leaders need to know that ultimately all acts of terrorism will be dealt with by all the resources of the United States and our allies. Ultimately members of your force, leaders and anyone supporting this attack will pay for this act of terrorism and any potential nuclear disaster."

———

486

"So be it, it may be the will of Allah. We will continue executions of four managers per hour beginning in ten minutes as a sign of the seriousness of our intention to follow-up on all of our demands or cause a nuclear disaster. We will be monitoring *Al Zagaheer* coverage. The clock is ticking. You have 24 hours from now." Nassar hung up on the President as an indication that he was in control and could dictate terms to the leader of the most powerful nation on earth. A slight smile crossed his face as he ordered two of his team to pull out four managers to execute with a live video feed to *Al Zagaheer,* and western media.

Chills ran up and down Reynolds spine and through his veins as the phone line abruptly went dead. By then each of the White House and Executive building staff were in position and fully aware of the terrorist take-over and ready to assist with putting potential plans into action. Additional members of the Joint Chiefs joined the NSC in the Command Bunker awaiting the President from the Situation Room.

FBI specialists were attempting to identify the leader and his nationality through voice recognition software, while a team used video images and facial recognition software, others determined that Abu Talib was the name of the uncle that raised and nurtured the prophet Mohammed and probably was not the real name of the terrorist leader. The best images of the leader came from the internal video system. The analysis of the drone footage of the terrorist leader entering the Security Office building was difficult given the angle the drone was recording and the night-vision camera. There were several still photographs from the footage that were being processed through image enhancement and identification programs. Ten minutes later the clear image of Nassar was on the large Situation Room screen. Face recognition software was searching through millions of images per minute.

As Reynolds exited the Situation Room and entered the smaller Command Bunker he immediately took the seat between Josephine Oliver, Vice President and Gary Dessile, Director of CIA. Around the conference table were: Dexter Ford, the National Security Agency Director, Abe Greenfeld, National Security Advisor; Gayle Swartz, Secretary of Homeland Security; Dr. Ernest Moniz , Secretary of Energy; General Ralph Shoemaker, Director of National Security; and Paul Harmon, Secretary of Defense. There were several NST members missing: Margret Dillon, U.S. Secretary of State was in Geneva, Switzerland; General Jack Marks, USMC, Chairman of the Joint Chiefs of Staff was in Brussels, Belgium at a NATO Meeting; and Frank Thomas, FBI Director dealing with the California attacks was in San Francisco. Admiral Alex Hector Hernandez, USN, Vice Chairman of the Joint Chiefs of Staff was in the Command Bunker until Gen. Marks arrived. Both Dillon and Marks were incoming and expected within three hours.

Hub at NSA requested that Dr. Gibson and the NNS Redundancy Project Task Force team led by Dr. Powers make accurate predictions as to the impact of a nuclear event in both combination and separately of each Palo Verde reactors for President Reynolds. Within twelve minutes NNS and the Director of the Nuclear Regulating Commission used the original design of the facility to create the updated detailed assessment of the potential nuclear fallout of the Palo Verde facility. That assessment used the original pre installation data, pending weather conditions for the next four days, and three different simulated explosive devices to destroy the containment system was transmitted to the White House Bunker. Jerry O'Toole, picked up the original 156-page document and highlighted the essential projected fallout data information from pages 147-148. He had the pages copied for the NST and ready to be projected on the Command Bunker screen.

Jerry knew that any nuclear incident would be a major disaster for the administration and the nation. Quickly thinking, *Fuck, fuck! The President is going to go ballistic when he sees these projections. How could the Reagan administration approve the plant construction knowing full well the projected data and potential for a disaster near a huge and growing metropolitan area?*

Entering the Command Center bunker, Jerry pulled Mark Reynolds aside as he handed him the Palo Verde report. "You are not going to believe that we knew the fallout projections prior to the approval of the Palo Verde facility project by the NRC and NNS back in 1986. The NNS Task force quickly updated the possible scenarios including weather and effectiveness of different devices destroying the containment system."

Reynolds frowned as he took the report, "How bad is it?"

O'Toole pointed to the opened pages, "I don't think it could be any worse if we detonated three of our Minuteman III W78/Mk12A nuclear missiles by mistake and far worse than any dirty bomb."

Reynolds quickly perused the two important pages of the NNS report, "Well the asshole terrorists have us over a damn barrel. We are going to have to play along until we come up with a viable alternative plan. I do not want to negotiate or appear to give in to these bastards. I have no choice but to share the whole report with the NST. I hope we have other viable options we can put on the table."

Just before joining the NSC, O'Toole hands Reynolds his cell. Hub Nolan was on the line. He informs President Reynolds of the presence of the Cal-Tech team and the advantages of having them secretly on the Palo Verde site, as well as having the internal and external video feeds, and more importantly that the Cal-Tech team had installed a state of the art Redundancy System that could help with handling the situation if the terrorist action warrants.

"Thanks Hub, I need something that moves the balance in our favor and may help contain this disastrous situation. Did NNS initiate the Redundancy System project?"

"Dr. Gibson is in charge and has been in communication with the Cal-Tech team since the takeover. Our NSA team has confidence in the on site assets as the Beta form of the system was being installed and tested tonight. I have been in communication with Dr. Sean McMurray leading the Cal-Tech team and insuring that the team has access to our satellite and drone video feeds. I know that they are gathering important information on the terrorist force that will be critical over the next few hours. I will have the direct feed from the Cal-Tech team into your Command Bunker shortly."

"A single ray of hope, Hub I want you and Dr. Gibson to join us in the Command Bunker as soon as possible with your communications link with the Cal-Tech team. O'Toole will confirm the arrangements." Reynolds stopped before entering the Command Bunker when O'Toole's phone beeped indicating a text message.

"Mr. President, We have just confirmed that both Maricopa County Sherriff and Arizona Department of Public Safety Units have responded to cell phone calls from within the Palo Verde facility. We need to contact Governor Ann Hargrove to intervene with law enforcement and attempt to hold the media at bay."

"I was wondering how long we could hold a lid on this situation." Reynolds knew that this added a huge complexity to the situation. "I was hoping for at least an hour or two. Damn! Get me Governor Hargrove."

O'Toole finds Hargrove in his contacts and places the call. Two seconds later he heard the feminine voice, "This is Governor Hargrove".

"Governor Hargrove, this is Jerry O'Toole, President Reynolds' Chief of Staff. Please excuse the hour. The President would like to speak to you on an urgent national matter."

"Good morning Jerry. I was expecting your call, this situation is bigger than my Arizona folks can handle. Please put the President on when he is available." Jerry hands his cell to President Reynolds.

"Good morning Ann," Reynolds spoke with confidence and a calm demeanor. "I understand that you are fully aware of the situation at Palo Verde. You need to know that I spoke with the leader. We are dealing with very specific terrorist demands and formulating our NST response. I need to have your law enforcement stand down to provide security at a safe distance from the facility perimeter. At the same time I need them to ensure that nobody else enters the facility and that the news media are not within a mile. I will keep you apprised of the negotiation process and any further response developments. In the meantime please keep a media lid on the situation for now. You can refer all media inquires to my Press Secretary."

"I understand that the situation is well beyond our state resources. I have already ordered the MCSO and DPS to create a secure perimeter well outside the facility. The takeover happened after the night shift reported so the media will be on this shortly. Our Arizona resources are here to lend assistance. I am really worried about the public response as the takeover breaks in the media. I saw the original fallout assessment when I took office, and know that we are facing a huge disaster. What do you and the NSC suggest that we should be doing in preparation in the event that there is a meltdown and major fallout without causing panic and a news frenzy?"

"I will have the NNS Task Force give you suggestions. However we will need to move with extreme caution to avoid panicking the public. I would suggest that you mobilize your Office of Emergency Readiness to review and prepare plans for potential mass evacuations of the Phoenix metro area as far north as Flagstaff and well south of Tucson or Nogales. We need to ensure that we keep it under wraps as long as possible. I have 23.5 hours to meet the terrorist's demands, giving us a little wiggle room. I really need to meet with the NSC. Good luck, Ann. "

"Thanks Mr. President, we will do the best that we can." The phone line indicated that the President had abruptly ended the call.

At the same time........

As Dr. Grace Gibson deplaned a Homeland Security jet at Andrews Air Base and got in the waiting Presidential helicopter, she called Kathryn. "Hi Kathryn, sorry to be waking you up." Grace was screaming into her cell to ensure that she could be heard over the chopper turbine engine.

"Hi Grace, this must be important at this ungodly hour."

"Listen, I do not have much time. I just flew into Andrew's to deal with a terrorist takeover of the Palo Verde plant. Sean and his team were safe when I talked with him, but the situation is not looking very good. There is an extraordinarily high potential for a nuclear disaster that would be over ten times worse than the level 7 disaster at the Chernobyl. It is not a good time to contact Sean due to the terrorists in all areas of the facility. He is extremely bright and capable. You need to trust that he will figure out a way to deal with the situation. Your best bet is to watch our news outlets for updates. I will try to call later if time permits.

"Grace this has to be unnerving given your role in protecting our nuclear facilities. God you must be going crazy. I left you a long e-mail that you might find interesting about Sean's Cal-Tech teams theory on the recent terrorism. It could help. Good luck, I love you.

"Thanks, I saw it in my e-mail folder. I've got to go the chopper is landing at the White House." Goodbye." The call was terminated. Kathryn wide
awake turned on CNN.

As she left the chopper Grace receives a call from Jerry O'Toole confirming that the media were aware of the crisis and a projection that she would be at the Command Bunker in 4 minutes.

Chapter 53: Unconfirmed Nuclear Plant Attack Reported

Monday, November 25, 10:00 a.m. AST (UTC /GMT +2)
Al Zagaheer Television Studio 1, Doha, Qatar

Good Morning, This is Nuru Monaga with a special news bulletin from the *Al Zagaheer* studios in Doha. *Al Zagaheer* received a video manifesto from an undisclosed terrorist organization that claimed they had complete control of the Palo Verde nuclear power facility outside Phoenix, Arizona. The facility housing three large reactors is the largest nuclear plant within the United States. The manifesto clearly indicated that the organization planned to use numerous explosive devices to cause a nuclear meltdown and destroy the containment system in all three of the huge reactors unless President Reynolds released all the Muslim detainees worldwide including Guantanamo Bay, Cuba, awaiting trial or interrogation in the United States and their allies, within 24 hours. Please use caution as the following graphic segment will contain violence." A video began, "We received a video of five Palo Verde plant managers being executed by the terrorists to reinforce their willingness to follow through with their nuclear threats if President Reynolds does not meet their demands."

The broadcast showed a file video clip of the massive nuclear plant in the middle of the Sonoran desert while Nuru continued.

"At this point White House sources in Washington have not confirmed or denied the takeover of the Palo Verde nuclear plant. Our independent nuclear sources report that any meltdown of one of the three reactors would cause panic in a huge portion of the United States. There are over 35 major cities from Chicago to Miami that would be affected by the disbursed radioactive fallout given the explosive force used to destroy the facility containment system and prevailing weather and wind patterns. Economically the potential fallout would effect the agricultural production of the U.S. Midwest "bread basket" and have huge implications for Southern California dependent on the energy produced at the 3.3-gigawatt facility. We expect an official White House statement within the next hour. This is Al Zaga the number one news source in the Middle East."

The televised commercial following the report showed school age boys dressed in school uniform reading in a garden setting under a date palm tree with a school in the background.

To be continued in ....The Master's Ultimatum (book 2 of the 5 part series)

About the author:

The Master of Deception is George C. Baker's first international thriller based on years of world travel, massive research on the operations of terrorist organizations, international government protocols and the evolution of worldwide counter-terrorism and intelligence communities since the attacks on the New York World Trade Center Twin Towers on September 11th.

Visit: **https://www.georgecbaker.com/**

Master of Deception character list is posted on the web site.